DOOM

OF THE

DRAGON

DOOM
OF THE
DRAGON

MARGARET WEIS
AND
TRACY HICKMAN

TOR

A TOM DOHERTY ASSOCIATES BOOK

NEW YORK

This is a work of fiction. All of the characters, organizations, and events portrayed in this novel are either products of the authors' imaginations or are used fictitiously.

DOOM OF THE DRAGON

Edited by James Frenkel

A Tor Book
Published by Tom Doherty Associates, LLC
175 Fifth Avenue
New York, NY 10010

www.tor-forge.com

Tor® is a registered trademark of Tom Doherty Associates, LLC.

Library of Congress Cataloging-in-Publication Data

Weis, Margaret.
   Doom of the dragon / Margaret Weis and Tracy Hickman.—First Edition.
      p. cm.
   "A Tom Doherty Associates Book"
   ISBN 978-0-7653-1976-0 (hardcover)
   ISBN 978-1-4668-8122-8 (e-book)
 I. Hickman, Tracy.   II. Title.
   PS3573.E3978D65 2016
   813'.54—dc23

                                        2015031486

Our books may be purchased in bulk for promotional, educational, or business use. Please contact your local bookseller or the Macmillan Corporate and Premium Sales Department at (800) 221-7945, extension 5442, or by e-mail at MacmillanSpecialMarkets@macmillan.com.

First Edition: January 2016

Printed in the United States of America

0 9 8 7 6 5 4 3 2 1

To my daughter, Lizz "Blizzkrieg" Baldwin,
who never fails to astonish and delight me!
—M.W.

To Jon Seyster and Miracle Pelayo. You are my heroes.
—T.H.

VOYAGE

KAIRNHOLM
MOUNTAIN

THE STEPPE CLANS

THE COMMONWEALTH

HESVO
SEA

OCEAN AYLITHIA

THE DJANSETO WESTREACH

URDA'AN

FAERIE TRIBES (UNCHARTED)

THE FORGED KINGDOMS OF THUR

EASTERN EXPANS

KHARAJIS

THE ORAN EMPIRE OF LIGHT

THE DESOLATION

KHILAT MOUNTAINS

THE STORMLORDS

SPIRIT COAST

CHIMERIAN DOWNFALL

SEA OF

ISLE OF REVELS

Miles

100 300 500 700 900

THE LANDS OF KHARAJIS

OF THE VENEJEKAR

OCEAN ESTARTHIA

ISLAND VEKTIA

APENSIA

BAY OF
LYRIC

PALE
BAY

OYRIK
BAY

WINDISH
STRAIT

SAGOSD
STRAIT

BAY OF
MAVOLIA

FAARUN
BAY

BAY OF
YANSHU

THE WARLORD STATES COAST

TEARS

CALDRIC PENINSULA

FORBIDDEN EMPIRE

RHAJAKIS

AND RHAJAKIS

A T C R

DOOM
OF THE
DRAGON

PROLOGUE

Farinn settled himself in the chair his son had placed near the roaring blaze that filled the Great Hall of the Torgun with light and warmth. Outside the hall, snow was thick on the ground. The winter wind growled and muttered and sometimes struck the hall with a gusty fist that caused the beams to creak. Gray, foam-whitened waves crashed on the shore, spraying froth that froze instantly on anything it touched, covering the fir trees and rocks with a crust of white.

A storm is coming, Farinn thought. The sun will not rise tomorrow.

He no longer had to worry about such things. He had seen eighty-five winters come and go, and tomorrow he would lie snug in his bed beneath fur blankets, drifting and dozing.

This winter would be his last. He could feel it in his bones. He would not live to see another. He was content. He was the only Vindrasi to have ever lived so long and he was weary and ready to go his rest.

First, though, he would tell the tale one last time, so that it would never be forgotten.

"I am Farinn the Talgogroth, the Voice of Gogroth, God of the World Tree. Attend me! For now I will tell the tale of Skylan Ivorson, Chief of Chiefs of the Vindrasi, the greatest of the chiefs of the mighty dragonships." Farinn paused, then said gently, "The greatest and the last."

Women quickly filled the mugs with ale, then picked up small children and held them in their laps, prepared to quiet any fretting that might interrupt the old man's story. Older children who had been running between the long tables, playing a noisy game of tag, hurried to settle themselves on the floor in front of Farinn.

Three young people, two young men and a young woman, took up a defensive posture near the door that was shut and barred against the storm and the night. They knew that no enemy was likely to burst through that door, requiring them to perform acts of bravery in defense of their people, but they could always dream.

A collective sigh rustling among the men, women, and children let Farinn know that all gathered in the hall this winter night were ready to hear his tale.

Farinn drew in a breath and began. His voice was strong this night, unusually strong. He was the only person left alive who had made the epic journey with the great Skylan Ivorson and his warriors, and this would be the last time he told the tale. He wanted his people to remember.

"To remind you where we left off last night," Farinn began, "Skylan and his friends, sailing in the great dragonship, the *Venejekar*, with the mighty dragon Kahg, had escaped slavery in Sinaria and were setting out to sail back to their homeland. Skylan had divided his crew, sending some back in a captured ogre ship to warn the Torgun to prepare for war, while he and the woman he loved, Aylaen, now a Bone Priestess; the Legate Acronis; and the fae child Wulfe remained aboard the *Venejekar*.

"They had obtained one of the spiritbones the Goddess Vindrash had told them they would need if they were to save their people. Skylan's plan was to find and recover the other four, but the threads of their wyrds had taken them in a different direction.

The *Venejekar* was beset by enemies: Skylan's cousin, Raegar Gustafson, now Priest-General of Aelon, god of the New Dawn, had attacked them, as had the ogres, led by their powerful chief, Bear Walker.

"The most powerful enemy of all, however, lurked in the deep. A gigantic kraken rose from the sea, crushing the ogre ship in its tentacles and dragging the *Venejekar* beneath the waves."

Some of the children squatting on the floor clapped their hands and one rowdy youngster cried out, "Tell the part about the kraken again!"

Farinn glowered at the offending child, for he did not like to be interrupted. The child's father, looking grim, left his seat, retrieved the youngster, and handed him over to his mother. After this momentary interruption, Farinn was free to resume.

"As you recall, Skylan and his friends were saved by Aquins, humans who dwell in cities beneath the sea. They had many adventures, which I related last night and which I will *not* relate again." Farinn fixed a stern eye upon the children, who nudged one another and grinned.

"Skylan and Aylaen had been wed in the city of the Aquins. The Sea Queen had given them the Vektan Torque, containing one of the spiritbones, as a wedding gift, and Akaria, the Sea Goddess, had given them the third and told them where they could find the fourth—in the land of the Stormlords.

"Raegar had captured Aylaen and brought her on board his ship, demanding that she tell him and his god, Aelon, where to find the spiritbones. Skylan had sailed after them in the *Venejekar*, determined to rescue Aylaen. She fought Raegar and managed to escape. She and Skylan were reunited on the *Venejekar*.

"It was then that Raegar picked up a spear and threw it—"

Farinn was interrupted by a wail from a little girl sitting in front of him with her hands over her ears.

"Hush, Greta! What's the matter?" her big brother asked irritably.

"I don't want to hear this part!" the little girl whispered. "I don't like this part. Skylan dies!"

"But he doesn't; not really," said her brother.

"He does so, too," said the little girl, removing her hands and glaring at him. "Raegar strikes him in the back with a spear and Skylan dies in Aylaen's arms."

"And then Skylan goes to Torval's Hall, but Torval won't let him in," whispered her brother. "Wait for the rest of the story. You'll hear."

"Who's Torval?" asked the little girl.

"Some old god," her brother replied with a shrug.

"Listen, both of you, and you will find out," Farinn rasped and the children meekly quieted.

He did not really mind this interruption, for it gave him a chance to sip the honey posset that soothed his throat after many nights of storytelling. He paused and drank and remembered.

One day, someday soon, he would look out across the ocean and there would be the great dragonship, the *Venejekar*. His friends would all be on board.

Well, perhaps not all.

He would wade into the waves, and his friends would reach out their hands to him and, laughing and jesting, haul him into the dragonship. He would sail away on the voyage that had no end.

But until that day, he had a tale to tell.

Farinn moistened his lips, which tasted of honey, and began. "Skylan Ivorson strode up to Torval's Hall of Heroes, his sword in his hand . . ."

BOOK

1

Skylan Ivorson trudged through the deep snow up the mountain, keeping his head bowed against a biting wind, trying to find Torval's longhouse—the Hall of Heroes, the hall where those warriors who had died a hero's death came to spend the afterlife with the god and fight the battles of heaven. Skylan carried his sword in his hand to show the god he had died in battle, slain by his cousin, Raegar.

Aylaen had survived. Skylan had breathed his last in her arms and although leaving her had been harder than dying, he took comfort in knowing she would live and keep his memory alive.

Lost and wandering in the storm, Skylan was growing more and more angry. Freilis, the dark Goddess of the Tally, who searched the battlefield for heroes to bring to Torval, should have escorted him to the hall. He had been forced to find it on his own, and he was cold and tired and alone.

He came to a grove of tall pine trees, standing straight and tall as sentinels, and pushed his way through the snow-covered boughs. The scent of pine was sharp and crisp. The trees blocked the wind. Snowflakes fell lazily from the gray clouds. And there was the Hall, an immense longhouse with a vaulted roof, built by giants who had labored on it for many centuries. According to the songs, the giants had ripped up mountains to build the foundation and dragged enormous trees from the ground for the logs that formed the walls and the cedar shakes of the roof. A thousand shields of brave warriors decorated the outer walls.

Skylan recognized many of the shields and the warriors who had

borne them from the old stories. These valiant warriors had died with
their swords in their hands, fighting for the honor of their clans, fighting to defend their homes; all manner of heroic deaths. Skylan pictured his own shield hanging among them and he was both proud and
humbled.

The door to the Hall was made of oak and banded by iron. It stood
wide open, welcoming. He could see within the orange glow of a roaring fire and he longed for its warmth, to ease the chill of death. Riotous sounds of singing and music, jests and laughter filled the eternal
night. Warriors were carousing, dancing with their womenfolk or
fighting mock battles. He was no longer alone.

He looked for familiar faces and was pleased beyond measure to
see Chloe, the daughter of Legate Acronis, watching the dancers, clap-
ping her hands with joy. Skylan had promised the dying girl that he
would dance with her in Torval's Hall and he looked forward to
taking her by the hands, leading her in the dance.

Moving nearer the door, wading through snowdrifts, he searched
until he finally found Garn talking with a man who initially had
his back to Skylan. When the man turned slightly, Skylan recognized Norgaard, his father. The two were deep in conversation,
laughing, moving nearer to the door.

Skylan was shocked. He had no idea his father had died. Skylan had
so much to tell his father. He had so much to make right.

"Father! It is me, Skylan!" he called.

Norgaard and Garn must not have heard him, for they walked past
the open door and vanished amid the crowd in the hall.

As Skylan continued toward the Hall, he wondered irritably why
Torval wasn't here to greet him. Certainly the God of Battle must be
expecting him. Skylan started to walk over the threshold.

The door slammed shut so suddenly that Skylan walked right into
it, bumping his nose and banging his head.

Shocked, he drew back to look at the Hall. The light and warmth
had vanished, leaving him in darkness that was cold and deep. He
could still hear the noise and laughter inside and he was chilled and
resentful.

Skylan reached up to the amulet he wore around his neck, the silver hammer, symbol of Torval, to touch it, thinking perhaps he had
somehow offended the god.

The hammer was gone.

"If this is some sort of jest, it is not funny!" he cried angrily. "I am Skylan Ivorson and I have a right to enter!"

He could hear only the wind sighing among the pines.

Skylan pounded with his fist on the door and continued to shout, trying to make himself heard above the raucous noise inside. His voice sounded very small and his cries seemed to float off into eternity.

Skylan was now truly outraged. The god Torval should have been ready with a hero's welcome, not treating him like a beggar pleading for a crust of bread.

Skylan beat on the door until his fist was bloody. Finally, someone must have heard him, for the door swung open. Torval stood within.

The god was wearing his armor made of the finest steel, his breastplate embossed with a dragon's head—the symbol of the Great Dragon Ilyrion, whom he had slain to gain rulership over the world. His helm was trimmed with silver and gold, his boots were fur lined, and a fur cloak hung from his broad shoulders and brushed the floor.

His armor was splendid, yet Skylan observed that the helm was dented, the hem of his fur cloak was soaked in blood, and his breastplate was splattered with blood. Judging by his fresh wounds, some of the blood must have been his own.

"Fish Knife! What are you doing here?" Torval demanded.

Skylan felt his anger grow. The god had called him by the disparaging name of Fish Knife, an insult to a warrior who deserved to be thought of as Torval's Sword, not a puny knife used for gutting trout.

"Let me inside!" Skylan demanded. "I belong in the Hall with my comrades!"

"When you are dead, come back. We will discuss it," said Torval.

The god slammed the door in Skylan's face.

Skylan stood staring at the closed door in shock at the god's words.

When you are dead, come back . . .

"But I *am* dead, great Torval," Skylan protested. "You can see the wound in my back, pierced by Raegar's spear!"

He found himself talking only to the closed door.

Skylan was completely at a loss to know what to do. He was dead. He knew he was dead, yet Torval didn't appear to think so. Wearily, Skylan eased himself down onto the snow-covered ground and sat with his back propped against the timber walls of the Hall of Heroes, his elbows on his bent knees, and tried to make sense of what was happening to him.

He didn't want to be dead. He didn't want to leave the world of the living. He longed with all his heart to go back to his beloved wife, Aylaen, and once more sail the seas in his swift dragonship, the *Venejekar* to continue his quest to find the five spiritbones of the Vektia.

Yet, all men must die sooner or later and Skylan had died a hero, which is the way men are meant to die. If he had to be dead, he at least deserved to be honored by Torval.

But Torval had said he wasn't dead and wouldn't let him inside.

Skylan gazed out dejectedly at the enormous fir trees that surrounded Torval's Hall, shielding it from the view of his foes. The sky was gray and the wind was freshening, presaging more snow. He noticed now that the snow on the ground outside the hall was trampled and stained with blood.

Skylan decided he would make one more attempt to talk to Torval, to try to find out what was going on, when he heard the sound of footfalls crunching through the snow.

He jumped to his feet and gripped the hilt of his sword. He was in heaven, but heaven had become a dangerous place these days with the Vindrasi gods fending off attacks by their rival god, Aelon, and his demonic forces.

These footfalls didn't sound like those of a warrior, however, for they were accompanied by a slurred voice singing a bawdy song. Then came a thud, followed by muttered swearing, as if whoever was approaching had fallen in the snow. The footfalls resumed, as did the singing, and the source of both lurched out into the open.

Though Skylan had never met the songster, he recognized him, for Aylaen had walked among the gods and she had described the God of the Revel.

"Joabis," Skylan muttered.

The God of the Revel carried a wineskin slung over his shoulder and he would pause every so often to tilt it to his mouth and shoot a stream of purple liquid down his throat.

Aylaen had described the god as fat and jolly, his face ruddy and flushed with merriment. That must have been in the glory days when the gods of the Vindrasi ruled heaven and the world below. Joabis appeared vastly different now that the gods were fighting for their lives and one of them was dead and another gone mad.

His plump body had run to flab, his skin sallow and sagging. He wore festive clothes, but his soft lambskin tunic was torn and shabby and stained with wine. His fur cloak was soaking wet from where he had taken a tumble in the snow. He generally wore no armor, for he took care to be far away from the fighting, but he must have borrowed a helm. It was too big for him, however, and had slipped over one eye. He kept casting frightened glances over his shoulder, as though fearing some enemy would jump out of the shadows and stab him in the back. When Skylan called his name, Joabis leaped into the air in fright, slipped on the way down and landed in a sodden heap in the snow.

"Don't kill me!" Joabis cried, raising his hand over his head. "I am no one important! Only a servant!"

Skylan eyed him in disgust.

"You are Joabis, God of the Revel, and you stand before the Hall of Heroes bleating like a stuck pig," said Skylan angrily. "Be gone! You have no right to breathe the same air as those who have died valiantly in battle!"

"I have business with Torval," said Joabis.

The god picked himself up, straightened his clothes with an air of inebriated dignity and, having managed to hang on to the wineskin, took a restorative gulp of wine. He staggered back a step, staring at Skylan with narrowed eyes, perhaps trying to bring him into focus.

"Fish Knife! Is that you?"

Skylan scowled. Maybe Torval had the right to call him that name, but not this drunken sot.

"What are you doing here among the hero dead, you cowardly cur?" Skylan demanded.

Joabis gave a sly grin. "One might ask you the same thing, Skylan Ivorson."

"I am no coward!" Skylan returned heatedly.

"Nor are you dead," Joabis said.

Skylan was growing frustrated. "So I am told, but if I am alive, what am I doing here?"

"I didn't say you were alive," Joabis replied. "I said you weren't dead." He jabbed his thumb in the direction of the hall. "Old Graybeard didn't explain?"

"If you mean Torval, no," said Skylan shortly.

He had no intention of discussing either his life or his death with this god.

Joabis tilted the wineskin to his lips, but nothing came out. Shaking his head, he tossed the empty wineskin on the ground.

"You should go talk to the Norn," Joabis suggested. "If anyone will know, they will. I'll come with you, if you like. I know the way."

Skylan considered this. Every person had his own wyrd, as did every god. The Norn were the three sisters who lived beneath the World Tree, weaving together the wyrds of both men and gods to form the tapestry that is life, cutting the threads of those whose wyrds had come to an end. The suggestion was a good one; yet Skylan was on his guard. There had to be a reason why the drunken god had taken this sudden personal interest in him.

"I thank you for the offer," said Skylan, "but I can find the way on my own."

"Oh, I very much doubt that," Joabis said, chuckling.

Skylan frowned at him. "I thought you had business with Torval?"

"That can wait," said Joabis.

He latched on to Skylan's arm, and before Skylan could divest himself of the god, who stank of wine, the forest and the Hall vanished in a swirl of blinding snow. The wind rushed about Skylan, roared in his ears. He could see nothing for the blinding snow, not even the god who had hold of him.

And then the snow stopped. The air cleared and grew extremely warm and humid, smelling like wheat fields after a summer rain. Skylan found himself standing at the foot of an immense oak tree. He had to tilt his head back until his neck ached to look up the gigantic trunk to the strong, leafy branches spreading far above him. He could see through the leaves the sun and the moon and the stars wheeling about the universe, and he felt very small and insignificant.

"Stop gaping like a peasant," said Joabis, adding in a whisper. "Those are the Norn! Be careful not to offend them!"

He pointed to three old women seated comfortably on wooden stools at the base of the tree, laughing and talking as they worked. The three were small and shrunken with age, their white hair drawn back into neat, tight buns and their black, bright eyes barely visible through webs of wrinkles.

One held the distaff of life under her arm, spinning wyrds on a wheel until they formed a fine, shining thread. This sister would cut the thread, beginning life, and hand it to the second Norn, who wove the wyrds of gods and men into the vast tapestry. The third Norn wielded a pair of golden shears, snipping the wyrds, ending life. Some of the threads were long, spanning many years. Others were quite short—a life cut off almost before it had begun. The Norn worked busily, their movements quick and deft, paying no attention to their visitors. The sisters were far too interested in their own conversation, as they gossiped about all those lives that passed through their bony hands and cackled with glee when they cut one short.

Skylan shuddered and even Joabis appeared daunted, for he was sweating profusely, mopping his brow with the sleeve of his tunic. Skylan wanted nothing to do with these terrible old women, but he stood his ground.

"Talk to them," said Skylan, turning to Joabis, only to find the god trying to slink behind the trunk of the World Tree.

Skylan seized Joabis and dragged him back.

"This was your idea," Skylan reminded him. "You're a god. Speak to them. Ask them what happened to me."

Hearing his voice, the three Norn stopped their chatter and turned their bright eyes on them.

"Well, well, if it isn't Joabis," said one.

"He looks a bit sickly to me," said another.

"That he does, Sister," said the third.

Picking up the god's wyrd in her hand, she waved her sharp golden shears perilously close to the fragile thread.

"No, no, no!" Joabis gabbled, clasping his hands and falling to his knees. "I beg you! Let me live!"

"I think he pissed himself," said one.

The Norn laughed uproariously. The sister holding the shears thrust them into the pocket of her apron dress.

"What do you want, you old sot?" said the one with the distaff. "Make haste. We are busy."

Joabis clambered to his feet.

"I've come about him," said the god and jerked his thumb at Skylan.

"What about him?" asked one in disdainful tones.

"Who is he?" asked another.

"And why should we care?" asked the third.

As the three laughed again and started to go back to work, Skylan saw the sisters steal sly, amused glances at each other. He strode forward to confront them.

"My name is Skylan Ivorson and you know who I am. I died in battle this day, yet Torval and this god both claim I am not dead. I want to know what is going on."

"Should we tell him?" asked one.

"Might prove entertaining," said another.

The three sisters again stopped their work to turn to him.

"I was doing the spinning," said the second, "when I saw my sister preparing to cut another thread. I asked her whose life she was ending."

" 'The life of Skylan Ivorson,' I answered," said the third.

" 'Past time for that rascal,' I said," remarked the first.

"I held the sharp blades over the thread and began to cut," the third resumed. "The wyrd was thick and stubborn and the shears were dull from much use. I hacked at the thread and cut apart strand after strand and finally there remained only a single thread. I tried to cut it, but my hand jerked and I dropped my shears to the ground."

"We stopped spinning," said the first.

"We stopped weaving," said the second. "We stared in shock at the shears, lying on the roots of the World Tree, and wondered what to do."

"What did you do?" Skylan asked.

"Nothing," said all three together.

"Why not?" Skylan demanded.

The Norn pointed to a wyrd—a single strand finer than a spider's silk.

"The thread of your wyrd is strong," said the first. "You alone can break it."

Skylan stared in shock. He had heard those very words before, the time when Sinarians had taken him and his people into slavery. He had been near despair, blaming himself, knowing that his arrogance and his lies and his failures had led his people to this sad fate. His friend, Garn, had come back from the dead to speak to him.

The thread of your wyrd is strong, Garn had said to him. *You alone can break it.*

"I don't know what that means," said Skylan.

"The gods have given you a gift, Skylan Ivorson," said the second.

"Or a curse," the third cackled.

Skylan looked from one to the other.

"Which is it?" he demanded. "A gift or a curse?"

The sisters nudged each other with their elbows, smirking.

"It is what you make of it," they said in unison.

They turned their backs on him. One took up the distaff. The other sat down at her spinning. The third resumed her weaving and cutting. Skylan watched her gleaming shears snap, slicing a thread.

"Then, if I may choose, I choose to return to life," Skylan said to the Norn.

The three old women frowned and shook their heads at him.

"We take life. We don't give it. Be gone, Skylan Ivorson," scolded one.

"And take that wine-soaked sot with you," added the second.

The third pointed her bony finger at Joabis and menacingly waved her shears.

"We should go," said Joabis, tugging at Skylan.

"I won't go without a straight answer!" Skylan said in frustration. Digging in his heels, he easily shook loose of the god's grip. "What do they mean, I may choose, and then they do not give me a choice?"

Joabis leaned near to whisper.

"Bah! Who knows? They're crazy, these old hags! We should leave. I don't like the way the one is waving around those scissors. I have an idea! Come with me to my island," Joabis said in wheedling tones, once more taking hold of Skylan's arm. "I have a wager for you."

"I'm not interested in gambling, especially with you," said Skylan, glowering.

"Here's my wager," said Joabis, pretending he hadn't heard. "I'm passionately fond of a game of dragonbone and I hear you consider yourself a champion. If you win, I will return you to life. If I win, you must remain with me on my island."

"If you can return me to life, then do so now," said Skylan.

"Ah, but you must make it worth my time and trouble," said Joabis. He heaved a deep sigh. "To tell the truth, I am bored. The other gods think only of their precious war. No one will drink with me or throw the dice. Come entertain me. Cheer me up. It's only a game. What have you got to lose?"

Skylan considered. He did not trust this god, but, as Joabis said, what did he have to lose? Skylan did consider himself to be an excellent dragonbone player and this was not, after all, the first time he had played the game against a god.

He grimly recalled those dreadful matches aboard the ghost ship, forced to play dragonbone night after night with what he believed to be the draugr of his dead wife. He had later discovered the fearful ghost was in truth the Dragon Goddess, Vindrash, who had used the game to teach him about the five dragonbones and their importance in the battle against Aelon.

"I will take your wager," said Skylan. "But we will not play the game on your island. We must go somewhere neutral—Torval's Hall."

"Torval is not neutral," Joabis complained. "He despises me. And he will not let you inside."

"You must convince him. That is my offer," said Skylan. "Take it or leave it."

"You drive a hard bargain," Joabis grumbled.

He waved his hand and the World Tree and the three old women vanished. Skylan found himself standing once more in the trampled, bloodstained snow outside Torval's Hall of Heroes.

Joabis knocked at the door and was admitted.

"Wait here," he told Skylan.

The door shut.

A s Skylan paced back and forth in the snow, slapping himself with his arms to keep himself warm, he pondered the words of the Norn. Unlike Joabis, Skylan did not think the old women were crazy. He had seen for himself his single thread shining in the sun.

A man's wyrd was his fate, his destiny, rolling out in front of him toward some unknown end. As for choosing his own wyrd, all men are free to make choices. That is the gift—and the curse—of the gods, for while men are free to choose, they must choose blindly, unable to foresee the outcome.

"Why am I different?" Skylan wondered. "Or am I different at all? Perhaps the Norn are toying with me."

And yet, there was that single thread.

Growing impatient, Skylan went to the door that had been left open a crack to look for Joabis and saw him talking to Torval. They must be discussing him, for Joabis gestured toward the door and Torval turned his head to look in Skylan's direction. Torval looked very grim, but he gave an abrupt gesture. The door flew open.

Joabis met him, smacking his lips over a mug of foaming ale.

"Torval has agreed to let you into the Hall, but only for the sake of the wager. Once the game is ended, you must leave."

Removing his helm in respect, Skylan crossed the threshold, pausing a moment in the doorway to gaze in awe at this holy place. He had known since he was a child and first fashioned a sword from a stick that he would die a hero and be proud and content to spend his afterlife here.

A roaring fire blazed in a great stone fireplace. The heroes of the Vindrasi, men and women, filled the Hall. Some sat laughing and talking over mugs of ale at rows of long, rough-hewn tables made of planks of wood laid across trestles. Others were on their feet, wrestling or practicing their techniques with sword or spear or axe, bashing at each other, while their fellows watched and freely criticized. Still others were gathered around a harper, listening to his tale.

Torval sat sprawled at his ease in a huge chair at the front of the Hall. He was holding a mug of ale in one hand and beating time to the music on his knee with the other. He gazed at his assembled warriors with pride and smiled with pleasure. But his smile seemed wistful to Skylan, touched by the shadow of sorrow that darkened his eyes.

Skylan searched for his father and saw Norgaard sitting with a group of his friends in the warmest corner of the Hall, near the fireplace. Most of his father's friends had died before Skylan was born, for Norgaard had died an old man of forty-five, outliving all the warriors of his generation. Norgaard appeared to be telling the tale of some battle, for he was on his feet, jabbing at an imaginary foe with his sword.

Skylan was pleased to see that his father, who had always walked with a limp, was hale and whole once more.

Feeling a heavy hand on his shoulder, Skylan looked to see Torval standing alongside, his gaze also on Norgaard.

"How did my father die?" Skylan asked.

"Bandits attacked the village," Torval replied. "With you and most of the warriors gone, Norgaard and a few other old men, the Torgun women, and their children were the only ones left to fight. Norgaard died defending his people."

"A good death," said Skylan.

Torval nodded. "I will tell him you are here."

"No, don't," said Skylan.

"Why not?" Torval asked, frowning.

"Because I have no right to be here," said Skylan, his face flushing in shame. "Because I have been ungrateful, full of my own importance, proud and arrogant. I lied to my father and mocked him. I thwarted your will and took the chiefdom of our people from him. How can I face him now, especially in company with Joabis? He will think I have chosen to spend my afterlife in drunken revelry."

He knew Torval would understand. When Torval had slain the Great Dragon Ilyrion and taken the world as his prize, he had invited his friends to join him: Aylis, the Sun Goddess; Skoval, God of Night; Sund, God of Stone; Vindrash, the Dragon Goddess; Akaria, the Goddess of the Sea; Freilis, Goddess of the Tally. Each of the gods had given the people of the world a gift and chosen a part of the world to rule.

Joabis had given mankind the gift of ale and wine and chosen to rule the Isle of Revels, taking those souls who had spent their lives in riotous living. While the Vindrasi appreciated Joabis's gifts, particularly the ale, they had small use for drunkenness and debauchery.

"When I come back to this Hall a hero, I will embrace my father and ask his forgiveness," Skylan continued. "Until then, do not let him know I am here. I would not add to his disappointment in me."

"You are learning, Fish Knife," said Torval, regarding him with approval. "Though I must say it's taken you long enough. I will send your father and his friends out on patrol."

He summoned one of the warriors, who went to carry his orders to Norgaard. Skylan watched his father arm himself with shield and sword, put on his helm and walk proudly from the Hall. He was no longer in constant pain from the broken ankle that had never properly healed. He no longer walked with the aid of a stick. Skylan could grieve his loss, but, as he said, his father had died a good death.

Torval motioned to a small table and two chairs that had been placed in front of the fire. "For better or ill, Fish Knife, you agreed to this wager with Joabis. Set up the dragonbones, play your game, and then be gone."

Skylan looked around for Joabis and found him circulating among the crowd of warriors, trying to interest them in making side bets. Skylan sat down at the table and began to set up the game, which took some time.

The game board was made of oak, and painted with pictures of the sun and the moon and the stars, dragons and dragonships, swords and shields, trees and mountains and seas. Paths marked with runes wound among them.

Skylan began to divvy up the "bones," giving half to himself and half to Joabis. The bones were made of antler carved into different shapes, painted different colors, all of them marked with runes. Players cast the bones on the table and then moved the pieces according to the runes inscribed on them. He was counting out the bones when he heard a bench scrape and he looked up to see Garn taking a seat across from him.

"My friend! I am glad to see you!" said Skylan.

"I am glad to see you, but not in such poor company," said Garn with a frowning glance at Joabis, who was shouting loudly for more ale. "What is going on?"

"You remember how you told me my wyrd was strong and that only I could sever it?" Skylan said.

"I do, yes," Garn replied.

"Well, it seems you were right. According to the Norn I died and yet I didn't," said Skylan and explained what the Norn had told him.

"I am trapped betwixt life and death and I have no idea how to get back," Skylan concluded despondently. "Joabis offered me this wager. What else could I do?"

"The question is—how did you come to be here?" said Garn, regarding Skylan intently. "You are not dead. You could not have found Torval's Hall on your own. Freilis brought me and the others. Some god must have led you here."

"That's true," said Skylan, struck by the notion. "I hadn't considered that. Do you have any ideas?"

"As far as I know, Torval and the other gods were with us, doing battle with Aelon's demonic hordes."

"All the gods?"

"All except Joabis," said Garn.

He and Skylan both turned to look at the god and Skylan thought back to their meeting in front of the Hall. "When I first met him, he said he was here to talk to Torval. He seemed deathly afraid. When I spoke to him, he nearly jumped out of his skin."

"Be on your guard," Garn warned. "He is plotting something."

They were both silent, arranging the pieces on the board.

"You spoke of the battle. How does the war go?" Skylan asked, glad to change the subject.

Garn glanced sidelong at Torval, who was once more sitting in his great chair. The god stared pensively into the fire, seeming oblivious to the laughter and music.

"We are losing," said Garn.

Skylan looked up, shocked. "That cannot be true! When I was outside, I heard our warriors boasting of victory."

"An empty victory. Meaningless," said Garn. "Aelon fights a war of attrition. Our numbers dwindle with every battle."

"How is that possible? How can the dead die?" Skylan demanded.

"They don't die. Aelon claims their souls," said Garn. "We fight hellkites—men who lived lives of such cruelty and depravity that when they died, no other god would take them. Aelon forces them to fight for him and if you fall by the accursed sword of a hellkite, you become one of them."

"Torval would not permit such an outrage," said Skylan.

Garn sighed. Looking around, he leaned nearer and said quietly, "Torval can do nothing to save his own warriors. Some say he has grown too weak."

"I don't believe it," said Skylan stoutly. "When we have recovered the Five and the power of creation, Torval will be restored to glory and might. He will drive out the other gods and the world will go on as before."

He spoke with a confidence he did not feel. He and Aylaen had recovered three of the five spiritbones of the Vektia, that was true. But two more remained hidden. The Sea Goddess had told them they would find one in the land of the Stormlords. The whereabouts of the fifth was unknown. And unless he could find some way to return to Aylaen, she was going to have to complete this dangerous quest alone.

"What will happen if I fail, Garn?" Skylan asked abruptly. "What will become of you and Torval and the others?"

"You won't fail," said Garn, smiling. "You are Skylan, Chief of Chiefs."

Skylan sighed. Not so long ago, he had believed in himself. He had been invincible. Only to find one day that he wasn't.

"What will happen?" he persisted.

"Our gods will be cast out of this world. Torval and the others will wander the universe as vagabonds. Those of us who survive will go with them."

Garn leaned across the table to add softly, "Here comes Joabis. Tread carefully, Skylan. I do not know what he wants from you, but he wants something."

"Watch my back," said Skylan.

"Always," said Garn. Rising to his feet, he dragged over a bench and sat down beside Skylan.

Joabis took his place at the table, placing the game board between him and Skylan with a mug and a pitcher of ale off to one side. Joabis lifted his mug in a toast, grinned, winked, and belched.

Skylan grimaced in disgust. He hoped the other warriors didn't think this drunken god was his friend. He was starting to wonder if coming to the Hall had been such a good idea. There was no help for it now, however. He had to go through with this wager, and he had to win.

Before the draugr had taught him the strategy to the game, Skylan had played dragonbone as he had lived his life: reckless, impulsive, haphazard, doing what he pleased with no thought to the consequences. After playing all those dreadful games with the Dragon Goddess on board the ghost ship, he had learned that in the game as in life, one needed to be patient, to think several moves ahead, to consider carefully each move before he made it.

He began the game by taking up five bones, arranging them in front of him, and then placing five in front of Joabis. He did this without thinking. In the myriad games he had played with the Dragon Goddess, Vindrash had taught him to play with what he had come to call the Five Bone Variant. She had started every game by placing five dragonbones in front of him and making him roll all five.

He had come to think everyone played this way and he was surprised, therefore, to see Joabis staring at the five dragonbones in horror.

"Why five of them?" he asked in strangled tones. "What does this mean?"

"No reason," said Skylan, puzzled at the god's reaction. "It is the way I was taught to play. Why? What is wrong?"

Joabis drank a mug of ale, refilled it from the pitcher and drank some more.

"I don't like it," he mumbled through the foam. "I never play that way." He looked to Torval. "You are the judge. What is your ruling? Must I play with five bones?"

"I always do," Torval said in stern tones. "And thus so must you."

Joabis cast the god an annoyed glance, then gulped a third mug of ale and wiped his mouth with the sleeve of his tunic. He seemed nervous, sweating and mopping his forehead with his sleeve. He picked up the five bones and tossed them on the board quickly, as though they burned him.

Skylan wondered at Joabis's strange reaction, then put it out of his mind. Sometimes players tried all sorts of tricks to throw an opponent off his game. Some talked incessantly, fiddled with the pieces, tapped their feet, or drummed their fingers on the table. He had no idea what Joabis thought he was doing, but it wasn't going to work.

Skylan cast his bones and made his first move. Joabis, after another drink of ale, responded. As they played, the music ended. The dancing and the fighting stopped. Mugs in hand, the warriors gathered around the table to watch and comment and place wagers, some betting on the god, others on Skylan.

As Skylan and Joabis continued advancing their pieces, losing some, winning others, Skylan looked at Garn to see what he thought of his strategy.

Garn smiled and nodded his head in approval. Since Garn was an excellent dragonbone player, Skylan was pleased. He played on and was soon confident of winning. Joabis, continually refilling his mug with ale, was making mistakes—picking up the wrong piece, miscounting the number of moves he could make, forgetting he must roll five bones.

Skylan moved his war chief and was just thinking that four more moves would bring him victory when he heard people in the crowd start to murmur, pointing at his side of the board, shaking their heads.

Skylan didn't understand. One would think he had just lost. He looked back at the board and saw his peril.

With a gleeful chuckle, Joabis picked up his dragon and knocked Skylan's war chief off the board.

"I win!" Joabis announced. "Skylan Ivorson, your soul is mine."

Y ou cheated!" Skylan cried.

The warriors standing around the table either vigorously nodded their heads in agreement with Skylan or denounced him as a poor loser, depending on which side they'd placed their own wagers. Torval sat back at his ease in his chair, rubbing his bearded chin. He seemed to find this amusing.

"He lost the wager, Torval," Joabis whined. "His soul is mine. Make him pay."

Skylan rose to his feet, his hand on the hilt of his sword.

"Garn, you were watching the game," said Skylan, keeping his gaze fixed on Joabis. "What did you see?"

"Skylan is right, Torval," Garn said, rising from his bench to stand beside his friend. "Joabis used some sort of trickery to switch the dragon with his eagle. In the previous turn, his dragon was on the other side of the board."

Some of the warriors added their testimony to Garn's, while others were equally loud in favor of Joabis.

"I did not cheat. He lost and now he is trying to weasel out of his wager, Torval," Joabis said nervously, careful to keep the table between himself and Skylan.

"You claim he is a liar." Torval gathered his fur cape around him. "Fish Knife claims you cheated. There is one way warriors settle such a disagreement—with their swords."

"I would, but I have no sword," Joabis said with a sly smile.

"I need no sword to deal with you!" Skylan cried.

Skylan handed his sword to Garn, knocked aside the table, and lunged. Stumbling backward, Joabis grabbed the pitcher of ale and flung the foaming brew into Skylan's face. The ale stung his eyes and flew down his throat. Half blinded, coughing, and choking, he heard Garn shout a warning and saw Joabis was about to smash a wooden bench over his head. Skylan lashed out with his foot, kicking Joabis in the groin. The god groaned and slumped to the floor.

Another warrior tried to hurl a mug into Skylan's face. Garn punched him in the stomach. His friend joined in and then everyone was fighting. A group of warriors upended a table, heaved it off its trestles, and used it to shove another group back against the wall, while others grabbed the empty trestles and started bashing heads. The floor was soon awash in spilled ale, causing some of the warriors to slip and fall, as others laughed until they, too, found themselves on their backsides.

"Joabis," said Torval, laughing heartily. "Here! Use my sword."

Skylan stood back, waiting for Joabis to haul himself up off the floor and take Torval's sword. Instead, Joabis seized Skylan around the ankles and pulled his legs out from under him. Skylan crashed to the floor, narrowly avoiding hitting his head on the table. Joabis launched himself through the air and landed heavily on top of Skylan, knocking the wind out of him and belching beery breath in his face.

Skylan floundered beneath the god's weight, lashing out at him with his fists and trying to knee him. Suddenly Joabis flew up into the air with a startled wuff. Garn had grabbed him from behind and flung him off to one side.

Garn then pulled Skylan to his feet. "Are you all right?"

"I feel as though a tree fell on me," Skylan said, grimacing and rubbing his ribs. "Where is the bastard?"

"Complaining about you to Torval," Garn said.

Joabis was jabbing his finger in Skylan's direction and shouting loudly that Skylan was trying to get out of his bet. Torval appeared more interested in the brawl than in listening to the god, however, for he kept interrupting Joabis to yell encouragement, applaud a good blow, and roar with laughter at a warrior who landed face-first in a puddle of beer.

Skylan and Garn went to argue their case to Torval, first stopping to deal with a huge warrior swinging a battle axe. Skylan tripped him and Garn clouted him on the head. Joabis, seeing them coming, ducked behind Torval.

"Make him pay, great Torval!" Joabis cried.

Torval turned to face Skylan.

"Wherever you go, Fish Knife, trouble follows." The god spoke severely, but Skylan saw a gleam in his eyes and took heart.

"Joabis cheated and therefore has to forfeit the wager," Skylan said. "Garn is my witness. Joabis must keep his promise to me, give me back my life."

Torval reached around, seized the god by his tunic and dragged him forward.

"You cheated," said Torval. "And don't deny it, for I saw you. As for you, Fish Knife, you were a fool to wager with him. All know he is dishonest."

"Perhaps I was a fool, Torval, but I am desperate!" said Skylan. "You say I am not dead. The Norn say I am not alive. Joabis promised to return my life and he must keep his promise!"

"He will keep it," said Torval grimly. "The honor of the gods is at stake."

He gripped Joabis's tunic and gave it a twist, hauling the rotund god off the floor so that his feet dangled.

"You have heard my ruling!" Torval growled.

"I did! I will!" Joabis whined. "Put me down."

Torval let go of him, and Joabis dropped to the floor. He straightened his tunic and tugged it back into place.

"Although, Skylan Ivorson," Joabis added, "I can think of four reasons you will want to come to my isle."

"I do not know of one reason I would have for coming to the Isle of Revels, let alone four," Skylan returned.

Joabis held up four fingers and counted them down. "Their names are Sigurd, Grimuir, Bjorn, and Erdmun."

Skylan and Garn exchanged startled glances.

"You name my friends, members of my clan," Skylan said. "What business do you have with them?"

"Not business," said Joabis. "Purely pleasure. They are with me on my isle, enjoying themselves in their afterlife."

"I don't believe it!" Skylan said angrily. "These are brave men,

Torgun warriors! If they were dead, their souls would be with Torval, not with you!"

"You may be surprised to hear this, but some people actually prefer an afterlife of merry living to whacking at each other with swords," said Joabis.

The god cast a disparaging glance around the Hall, where the warriors were wiping off blood, mopping up ale, and good-naturedly shaking hands and working together to right the overturned tables. Skylan looked to Torval, who was glaring at Joabis.

"We fight your battles while you sit with your head in an ale barrel," Torval said. "Explain what you mean, you sodden swine! Why do you have the souls of my warriors?"

Joabis opened his mouth, seeming about to bluster, then he caught Torval's angry eye and his courage failed him. He sank down onto a bench with a groan.

"I don't know why I have them and the gods know I don't want them!" Joabis cried, wringing his hands. "The souls of these four arrived on my island along with a host of other warrior souls and since then they have been fighting and brawling and wrecking the place! I came here to beg you to deal with them, great Torval, and then I met Skylan and it occurred to me that he could do it just as well. I wouldn't have to bother you."

"Who brought them to you?" Torval demanded. "Was it Freilis of the Tally? Why would she bring them to you?"

Joabis hesitated just long enough for Skylan to think, He's lying! and then said, "I thought you sent them, great Torval. Perhaps your Hall had become too crowded. I realize now I was wrong . . ."

Torval grunted and gave a snort of disgust.

Garn drew Skylan aside. "What were Sigurd and the others doing?"

"They were sailing back to Vindraholm to warn our people that Aelon is planning to attack our homeland," said Skylan with a worried frown. "I need to find out what happened to them."

"This could be a trap," Garn warned. "I do not trust Joabis any more than I can stand the stink of him."

"I do not trust him," said Skylan. "But I cannot abandon my men."

Skylan's thoughts went to Aylaen. He could picture her alone and grieving for him, thinking she would never see him again. Skylan longed to return to her, to put his arms around her and tell her how much he loved her. He had only to tell Joabis to send him back to her and the god would have to obey.

Then he thought of having to tell Aylaen he had abandoned their friends.

"I will go with you," Skylan told Joabis.

Torval raised a questioning eyebrow. "Are you certain, Fish Knife?"

"These men are my friends, great Torval," Skylan explained. "I am their chief. If they are on Joabis's isle, I need to know what happened to them, and to discover if they were able to take the warning to our people."

Torval said nothing, but Skylan had the impression he was surprised by his decision.

"No doubt he thought I would selfishly leave my men to their fate," Skylan commented to Garn as they walked toward the door. "I suppose I have only myself to thank for his bad opinion of me."

"You are too hard on yourself," said Garn, smiling.

"And you are too good a friend," said Skylan.

Joabis was by the door, motioning him to hurry.

Outside the sky was darkening with the coming of night, a gray gloom settling over the world. A blast of cold air hit him and he looked wistfully back over his shoulder at the fire's bright glow, the warriors returning to their drinking and singing. Torval called for ale and motioned his bard to begin to play the harp and sing.

"Someday I will return a hero," said Skylan.

"Just not too soon, my friend," said Garn. "We need you among the living. Give my love to Aylaen."

As the two embraced, Garn whispered in Skylan's ear. "Keep your eye on Joabis!"

"I would keep three eyes on him, if I had them," Skylan returned. "Farewell, my friend."

As he was leaving, Skylan heard the bard singing a song of the glory of the Vindrasi and he saw Torval sitting in his chair, listening with an expression of sorrow and melancholy that made Skylan's heart ache.

He put his hand to the amulet, only to remember that it was lost.

"Make haste!" Joabis said, shoving Skylan over the threshold.

The door slammed shut behind them, leaving Skylan and the God of the Revel out in the snow and cold.

Acronis, former Legate of the Oran Empire, woke in the night to the creaking of timbers and the feel of the dragonship gently gliding over the calm sea. He had made his bed on a pallet on deck and from where he was lying he could see the square sail black against the glittering stars and, beyond, the graceful curve of the neck of the dragon's head prow.

At first glance, the casual observer would take the figurehead for an ornate and beautiful carving of a dragon. Upon close examination, the observer would see that the eyes of the dragon glowed red with a fiery intelligence. The observer would also note that no one was rowing the ship or steering it, yet it sped across the waves, sending up foam in its wake. The Dragon Kahg had imbued his spirit into the dragonship and was sailing the vessel.

The feel, the sight, the sounds of a ship at sea were familiar to Acronis. As a Legate, he had spent most of his forty-some years at sea, commanding a Sinarian war galley, a trireme. He had been a powerful man in the capital city of Sinaria, a very wealthy man, until he had run afoul of a new god, Aelon, and her new Priest-General, Raegar.

When his beloved daughter, Chloe, had died, Acronis had lost the will to live and tried to end his life. But he was stopped by Skylan Ivorson, who had once vowed to kill him and instead had turned out to be his salvation.

Acronis had left Sinaria and his old life behind to set sail with Skylan in the dragonship, *Venejekar*, for reasons Acronis did not yet quite understand. He had been lost, adrift, desolate; Skylan had hit him like a tidal wave, crashing into his life, sweeping him up and carrying him along with him on an unusual quest to save strange gods.

Acronis was too old to have any illusions about Skylan's reasons. Skylan had not saved his former master out of friendship nor—to give Skylan credit—for revenge. His reasons were practical. Acronis knew how to read a map and chart a course. He had sailed these waters for years and was familiar with the customs and cultures of many of the world's people, including the ogres.

He and Skylan had started out as enemies, only to find friendship during the time they had spent together on board the dragonship. Acronis had come to admire and even love the courageous young man who strode through life boldly, fighting impossible odds to save his gods and his people, only to have his quest ended by a spear in the back.

When Skylan had died in the arms of his beloved wife, Aylaen, Acronis had mourned him as a son. Now the young man's body, clad in his armor and chain mail and helm, lay on the deck, only a few feet from Acronis.

He propped himself up on an elbow and looked at the corpse. Acronis had been a soldier for years and he had seen death in many gruesome forms. He had walked the bloody battlefield and watched vultures pluck out the eyes of the dead and rats swarm over the bodies. He had once, on a moonlit night, witnessed the ghouls, horrible fae creatures who feast on corpses, slinking among the dead.

But he had never seen, in all his years, a corpse that didn't decay.

The body was cold to the touch, the flesh smooth and cool as marble. The beating heart was still. No breath passed through the blue lips. Acronis knew this for a fact, for he had held a bracer to the lips to see if some faint moisture might form on the metal and had found no signs of life.

Yet, day after day, the body lay in the heat of the sun and there was no change. It was a mystery that Acronis, as a man of science, could not explain.

But then, he reflected, watching the stars as the ship sailed slowly beneath them, he had seen many mysteries during his time with Skylan and his people. He supposed one more should not surprise him.

Now thoroughly awake, Acronis sat up on the deck, moving slowly to ease out the kinks and stiffness of age. A tiny sliver of red light in the eastern sky meant that morning was not far away. He rose to his feet and went to perform his ablutions, wondering if this day would be different, if Aylaen would listen to reason.

Returning from his ablutions, Acronis heard singing coming from the direction of the stern and paused to listen. The song did not last long, and ended in a sigh.

As the morning light stole across the waves, Acronis could see young Farinn standing with his back against the bulkhead, his arms folded, gazing out across the ocean. He sang the phrase again, then shook his head in obvious frustration.

The sun glinted off the armor on Skylan's body, which lay in the center of the dragonship, beneath the mast. The fae boy, Wulfe, was still asleep, curled up beside the corpse like a dog that will not leave its dead master. Aylaen, who made her bed in the hold below, had not yet come on deck.

Acronis walked back to the stern.

"May I speak to you, Farinn?" he asked. "I do not like to interrupt your singing, but I need to talk to you before Aylaen rises."

"I am grateful for the interruption, sir," Farinn said, adding with a sigh. "The song does not go well."

"What song are you composing?" Acronis asked.

He leaned over the rail, watching the waves slide by beneath the keel. Farinn joined him, gazing down morosely at the blue water dappled with sea foam.

"I am trying to compose Skylan's death song to do him honor," said Farinn. "The words will not come or, when they do come, they are not the right words."

"Perhaps you are too filled with grief now to give the song proper thought," Acronis suggested kindly, recalling that the young bard was only sixteen.

Farinn shook his head. "I have never had this trouble with any of my songs before. The words always flow from me as naturally as breath, yet now my tongue stammers and the words stick in my throat."

He sighed again, then looked up at Acronis. "But enough of my trouble. What did you want to talk to me about, Legate?"

"I want to talk to you about Aylaen," said Acronis, lowering his voice. "You know that she is determined to pursue this mad idea of traveling to the land of the Stormlords to find the fourth bone of the dragon, the . . . what do you call it?"

"Spiritbone. I have heard the two of you discussing the voyage," said Farinn. "It sounds very perilous."

"It is," said Acronis, his voice grim. "That is why I want you to talk to her, try to dissuade her. She refuses to listen to me and, frankly"—Acronis shrugged—"there is no reason she should. I am a relative stranger. But she might listen to you."

"I know Aylaen respects you, Legate, as a wise and learned man," said Farinn. "If she would heed the advice of anyone, it would be you. But she is determined to finish the quest given to Skylan by the Dragon Goddess, Vindrash. The quest is even more sacred to Aylaen now that Skylan gave his life for it."

Acronis gazed out at the horizon. The sky was brilliant with streaks of red and orange and gold. The sun, called Aylis by the Vindrasi, was a fiery ball rising out of the sea. They believed she bore a bright torch and that she was chased by Skoval, God of Night, who hated her for spurning his love.

"There is one other matter, Farinn," Acronis said. "We must both try to persuade Aylaen to give Skylan a proper burial. She walks away when I bring it up. Admittedly I cannot explain what is happening to the corpse. Why it is not decomposing—"

"I think I might know, sir," said Farinn.

He looked pointedly over his shoulder and Acronis followed his gaze. Wulfe was awake, yawning and sitting up and scratching himself. He was dressed in the rags of a cast-off shirt, and his hair uncombed and unwashed. He was scrawny and lanky. According to Skylan, the druids who had found the child running wild with a wolf pack had thought he was about eleven.

"You think Wulfe has something to do with it?" Acronis asked, frowning.

"He claims to be the son of a faery princess," said Farinn, sinking his voice to a whisper. "Whether that is true or not, he knows fae magic. I've seen him change himself into a fearsome beast. He talks with the beautiful women he calls 'oceanids' who live beneath the waves. The boy adored Skylan. He does not want to let him go. Perhaps he is using his magic to . . . um . . . preserve the body."

Acronis would once have scoffed in disbelief, but in the past few weeks he had watched a powerful dragon level his city, breathed water as if it were air, and witnessed a dragon sailing a ship. He had learned to keep his mind open to all possibilities.

"We must convince Wulfe to let Skylan go," Acronis said.

"Aylaen would be the only one to do that. He might pay heed to her."

"But that means one of us needs to convince Aylaen," said Acronis, sighing.

"You should speak to her, sir," Farinn urged. "She will listen to you."

"She has not thus far," said Acronis.

Aylaen came up on deck to see Farinn and Acronis leaning over the rail, their heads together, conferring in low voices. When they noticed her watching them, Farinn flushed red in embarrassment and Acronis looked very grave. She knew they had been talking about her.

The Legate crossed the deck, coming to speak to her. Judging by his carefully formed expression of sympathy and understanding, he was going to talk to her again about Skylan, about burying his body at sea.

Aylaen had come to love Acronis as a father, though the transition from hatred to love had not been easy. He had taken her and her people prisoner, made them slaves. He had treated them well, however, and by a series of strange circumstances, Skylan had saved his life and brought him with them when the Torgun warriors escaped Sinaria. Aylaen knew the wise man's reasoning was sound, but she didn't want to hear his arguments, perhaps because she had no way to refute them.

Pretending not to see him, she turned her back and hurried off in the opposite direction, going to stand beside the figurehead, the Dragon Kahg, that graced the prow of the sleek, fast dragonship.

Aylaen put her hand on the dragon's neck and felt the life quiver beneath the carved wooden scales. The glowing red eyes gazed fiercely ahead into what was, for her, the unknown. She was the first of the Vindrasi people to ever sail these waters, the first to travel so far from their home.

"Acronis and Farinn must think I have gone mad," said Aylaen softly. "They don't understand, and I can't explain."

She spoke to the Dragon Kahg as if he agreed with her, although in truth she had no way of knowing what the dragon was thinking or feeling. Despite the fact that she was a Bone Priestess, with the power to summon the dragon, Kahg had refused to communicate with her.

She knew only that Kahg was following her orders to take them to the land of the Stormlords, and she knew this only because Acronis, using his mysterious navigational instruments, determined that was the dragon's destination. Acronis marked their progress daily on the map he kept with his instruments in a wooden chest in the hold.

He had taught Aylaen how to make sense of the squiggles and lines that represented the world on the map. He had shown her the place on the map that represented the land of the Stormlords and every day he showed her the dot on the map that represented the *Venejekar*. The ship was drawing closer and closer.

She stole a glance at Acronis and saw him standing near the corpse, regarding her with sympathetic understanding. He was so kind. He had a right to an explanation, if nothing else.

"Kahg, please tell me the truth," Aylaen said to the dragon. "Is Skylan truly dead, as Acronis and Farinn believe, or is he alive, as I feel in my heart?"

She saw the dragon's eyes swivel in her direction, bathing her for a moment in a fiery red glow. But it was not the dragon who answered.

"Skylan isn't dead!" Wulfe said angrily. "I keep telling you."

Aylaen looked around, startled, to see the boy crouched on the deck behind her, keeping a wary eye on the dragon. Wulfe maintained that the Dragon Kahg did not like him. For all Aylaen knew, that might well be true.

"I should give you a bath," said Aylaen, knowing from past experience this threat would frighten Wulfe off.

He did not run away, though he did back up a step, ready to flee at the first sign she might try to grab him.

"The two Uglies want to dump Skylan in the sea. You won't let them, will you?" Wulfe asked. "The oceanids say that if you try, they'll stop you."

Aylaen turned to face him, crossing her arms over her chest, huddling beneath her cloak.

"Are you using your magic to keep Skylan . . ." Aylaen paused. She could not bear to say "from rotting." She bit her lip and said, after a moment, "To keep Skylan with us?"

"I don't know how to work magic!" Wulfe cried. "Leave him alone! He's not dead! You'll see!"

The boy dashed away, his bare feet slapping across the deck that was wet from sea spray. He fled to the ship's stern where, leaning over the rail, he began to talk to the waves, sharing his grievances with his oceanids.

"The Uglies are going to dump him in the sea!" he called to them. "You must go find Skylan and bring him back!"

Aylaen saw Acronis walking toward her and she sighed and went back to staring out at the sea. The sun goddess had returned from her nightly wandering to share her warmth and light with the world. Aylaen watched the light spread across the waves.

"Aylaen," said Acronis gently, coming to stand beside her, "I know the pain you are suffering. I felt the same when my Chloe died, a pain so terrible and wrenching I tried to kill myself to end it. For your sake and the sake of the rest of us, you must face the truth. Skylan is dead. You need to let him go."

Aylaen stood with her arms folded across her chest, holding herself together, digging her nails into her flesh to keep from giving way to her grief and fear. If once she lost control and fell apart, she might never be able to pick up the pieces.

"If he were dead, I would know it," Aylaen said. "I would feel it, here."

She clenched her fist over her heart. Acronis cast a meaningful glance at Skylan's body, pale and cold and still. Aylaen knew what he was thinking, for she was thinking the same. He was dead. Dead. Dead. She would live all the rest of her life without him.

"Aylaen, you don't have to do anything. Farinn and I can—" Acronis began.

Aylaen cut him off. "Are we are on course for the land of the Stormlords?"

Acronis regarded her with such caring and understanding that she wanted to run to his arms as a child to her father, and sob until the burning pain was gone.

Instead she repeated harshly, "Are we are on course?"

"I presume we are," said Acronis. "We were yesterday. I have not taken my readings today."

"Then do so and let me know," Aylaen said.

She turned away, back to the sea.

Acronis stood still a moment, then walked over to a sea chest that he kept on deck. Taking out his instruments, he performed whatever mysteries he performed with them to determine the location of the *Venejekar* in this vast ocean with no land anywhere in view.

Aylaen closed her eyes and leaned against the dragon's neck.

"I don't know what to do, Kahg," she said. "Acronis is right. Skylan is dead. He died in my arms. I felt him draw his final breath. Yet I know my husband so well, he is so much a part of me, that sometimes I think Wulfe is also right and that Skylan is *not* dead. But if so, what has happened to him? Where can he be?"

Aylaen put her hand on the bone that hung from the nail on the prow. As Bone Priestess, she used the bone, given to them by the Dragon Kahg, to summon him.

"I have prayed to Vindrash, begged her to answer me," Aylaen continued. "All is silence. I don't understand. The goddess has always come to me before in my time of need. Why does she avoid me now?"

"Because Aelon is searching for you," said Kahg.

Aylaen looked at him, startled by this sudden and unexpected response. "Aelon is looking for me?"

"Vindrash fears if she speaks to you," Kahg explained, "Aelon will hear her words and know where to find you."

"Has Aelon grown so powerful?" Aylaen asked, doubtful.

"Aelon has grown powerful," Kahg replied in grating tones. "Vindrash speaks through me. The Dragon Goddess bids you to remember the time you cast the rune stones in the house of the old woman you know as Owl Mother."

"That gives me no comfort," said Aylaen. "When I was with Owl Mother the mad god, Sund, threatened me, ordering me to destroy the Five dragonbones of the Vektia. 'Know this, then, Daughter,' he said to me. 'If you bring the power of creation into the world, you yourself will lack it. Your womb will be barren. No children will be born to you! This I have foreseen.'

"He said my sister, Treia, is carrying Raegar's child. Sund claimed their son will become Emperor of the Oran nation and he will grind his boot into the necks of our people. He said he had foreseen this future and that it would come to pass if I did not destroy the spirit-bones in my possession."

"Apparently his threat did not work, for you have three of the Five and you have not destroyed them," said Kahg.

"I didn't believe him," Aylaen said. "He claims to see this future, but the wyrds of men are twined with the wyrds of gods to form a tapestry made up of myriad futures. Sund sees but one among the many."

"And yet, you cast the rune stones to see your future. Why did you do that?"

"I know it was foolish, but I wanted to know if Sund's prediction would come true, if I would be barren."

"What did the stones tell you?" Kahg asked.

"Owl Mother read them. 'Five of the stones are blank,' she said to me. This means that only one choice brings victory. She pointed to the sixth that was marked with a single rune. Death. A short time after that, Skylan died."

"But the runes told your future, not his," Kahg observed.

"Our wyrds are so tightly bound together that if he is dead, then I am dead," Aylaen replied. "I need Vindrash—"

"Look to the north," Kahg said urgently, interrupting. "Just above the horizon."

Aylis, the Sun Goddess, lit the sinuous coils of three winged serpents that had sprung from the sea. The serpents twisted in the air, darting here and there, as though searching for something.

"Aelon's serpents. They are looking for you," said Kahg. "Now you know why Vindrash was afraid to speak."

The serpents dipped down over the waves, whipping back and forth across the ocean, then dove into the water, sending up a great spray. Aylaen waited tensely for them to reappear, but the sea stretched on, empty and endless.

"Ask Vindrash," Aylaen pleaded. "Ask her what I am supposed to do."

"Vindrash herself does not know what to do," the dragon returned caustically. "How can she tell you?"

Raegar stood in front of the window of his grand palace, gazing out at the city of Sinaria far below, basking in the light of Aelon that flooded his bedchamber. He was in an excellent mood. He was Emperor of Oran, the most powerful nation in the world. He lived in a magnificent palace, he dined on sumptuous food, he had all the gold he could spend. His people loved him. His enemies feared him. His wife, Treia, was pregnant with his son.

True, there were some dregs in his cup of sweet honey wine. He had lost his grand dragonship, *Aelon's Triumph*, in a battle with the Dragon Kahg, who had set the ship on fire and then sunk it.

Still, Raegar was pleased to reflect, even that disaster had worked to his advantage. He had been the sole survivor, and with none left alive to contradict him, he told the story of a desperate battle against overwhelming odds from which he had emerged the victor. Only two knew the truth: the Dragon Fala, who had rescued him from the ocean, and Aelon.

His god had not spoken to him since, though Raegar had given her temple a valuable, beautiful jeweled chalice in thanksgiving and he been assiduous in his visits to her altar. He was not particularly concerned. Aelon might be angry with him, but she needed him. She would come around.

He poured himself a glass of wine and summoned a slave to dress him in robes of purple trimmed in gold. This done, he ordered the man to bring his breakfast. Raegar was once more gazing out the

window, sipping his wine, when he heard the girl who had enter-
tained him last night stirring beneath the sheets.

He walked over, smiling, and was about to yank off the silken cover-
let when the girl rolled over. The god Aelon regarded him from the
pillow, cool and unsmiling.

Raegar staggered back, shocked and stammering.

Aelon threw aside the sheets, sat up, and stepped out of bed. She
was fully clothed in robes of white lamb's wool. Her hair was braided
and fastened with jeweled pins. She wore two gold serpent bracelets
and a heavy gold necklace formed of seven serpents, each with a glittering ruby eye. Walking up to Raegar, she took the cup of wine from
his hand and drank.

Raegar began to sweat.

"Were . . . were you here all night? Were you . . . the girl . . ."

Aelon spat a mouthful of wine into his face. "Are you saying you
cannot tell the difference between making love to some human whore
and your god?"

Raegar blinked wine from his burning eyes.

"No, no, I . . . I . . . I . . ."

"Shut up," said Aelon. "Clean your face."

She turned away, saying over her shoulder. "You swore to me you
would be faithful to your wife."

Raegar mopped his face, cleansing it of wine and perspiration.
"Treia is pregnant, as you know, Revered Aelon, and she fears something is wrong with the child. She won't let me touch her. She told
me to leave her bed. The midwives think it would be best for her and
the child if I don't upset her. A man has needs . . ."

His voice trailed off.

Aelon stood in silence, drinking the wine. Raegar began to grow
frightened.

"All is well with your wife's pregnancy," said Aelon at last. "I will
reassure her."

Still she did not look at him.

"I know I have displeased you, Revered Aelon," said Raegar hum-
bly. "If this is about the loss of the ship, I can explain—"

"Ship!" Aelon snorted. "What do I care about ships? Your cousin,
Skylan, is not dead."

"Not dead? Impossible!" Raegar said, amazed. "I threw the spear that killed him. I saw his blood flow! I saw him fall! I *watched* him die!"

"Nonetheless, he is not dead," Aelon said. "He is not alive, but he is not dead."

"I don't understand," said Raegar, frowning. "How can he be both?"

"Some god loves him," Aelon muttered. She held out her goblet. "More wine."

Raegar poured the wine. He longed to pour a drink for himself, but he knew he needed to remain sober, keep his wits about him.

"Where is Skylan?" Raegar asked. "Tell me where to find him and this time, I swear, I will finish him!"

"Your cousin has gone where you cannot follow. He is now my concern," said Aelon. "I will deal with him, his wife, *and* the spiritbones. She has acquired the third, the spiritbone in the possession of the Sea Goddess. The one you promised to bring to me."

"I can explain—"

"Please do so." Aelon arched an eyebrow and said mockingly, "From the stories I hear, you were the hero of that battle. Tell me, Raegar, how many men did you kill single-handed?"

Raegar considered the god's taunt unjust. "I had to tell the people something to explain my absence and the loss of the ship, Revered Aelon. I am their emperor. You would not have them lose faith in me."

Aelon regarded him in silence, then grudgingly conceded. "I suppose not."

She poured herself more wine. Walking over to a map of the world spread out on a large table, she placed her finger at a southern point on the map and tapped her finger on a spot in the ocean.

"This is the current location of your cousin's dragonship, the *Venejekar*. His wife, that Kai Priestess of Vindrash. Your wife's sister. The one you lust after. What is her name?"

"Aylaen, Revered Aelon," Raegar mumbled, flushing.

While it was true he had once lusted after Aylaen, he found the thought of her sickened him. Whenever he thought of her now, he heard her accusations against Treia.

Treia made a bargain with Hevis, God of Lies and Deceit, Aylaen had told him. *She promised to sacrifice someone she loved and in return*

he gave her the ability to summon the Vektia dragon. She failed to keep
her bargain. Hevis will not forget. I would watch what she puts in my
soup if I were you.

Her accusations were one of the reasons he had been avoiding
Treia. He could have explained to Aelon, but he feared Aelon might
think he and Treia had conspired with Hevis together. Once his son
was born, he would see to it that Treia would never pray to a heathen
god again.

Aelon irritably snapped her fingers under his nose. "Are you listening to me?"

Raegar came back to reality with a guilty start. "Yes, Revered
Aelon!"

"I asked you a question. Where do you think Aylaen and the *Vene-*
jekar are bound?"

"I don't know, Revered Aelon," said Raegar. "Back to Vindraholm?"

"Far from it. Vindrash tried to conceal Aylaen from me, but at last
I found her. She is sailing on this course. See where it leads."

Raegar frowned, puzzled. "That route would take her to the realm
of the Stormlords. Why would she go there, to a land of foul wizards?"

"Why indeed?"

Aelon lifted her gaze to meet his, apparently expecting him to know
the answer. Raegar was in no mood to play games. He shook his head.

"Forgive me, Revered Aelon, I was up late last night, preparing for
a meeting today with these very Stormlords."

"You were up late, but not for that reason," Aelon said, her lip curling. "I know where to find the fourth spiritbone and now Aylaen has
given me the location of the fifth."

She tapped her finger on the map.

"The realm of the Stormlords!"

Raegar was astonished at first. The more he considered the matter,
the more it made sense. The wizards had been hiding in their secret
kingdom for centuries. If one believed the bards, they traced their history back to the time of the fall of the Great Dragon Ilyrion.

"I think you are right, Revered Aelon," said Raegar. "She would
not risk traveling to that dangerous region for any other reason. But
she wastes her time. Their city is said to be hidden by powerful magicks.
No one can find it."

"Yet that is what you must do, Raegar," said Aelon. "Locate the hidden city and find a way to enter it."

"The Stormlords pay us tribute yearly to be left in peace," Raegar said doubtfully. "A large quantity of gold and jewels. The treasury would suffer—"

"Let it suffer, then. I do not want their gold and jewels!" Aelon said in scathing tones. "I want the Stormlords to open the gates of their hidden city to me. I want them to worship me, to bow before me and call me their lord. I want them to give *me* the spiritbone!"

She was silent, drumming her fingers on her bare arms, stalking her prey. Raegar felt a pulse of excitement, the thrill of the hunt.

"I want you to send my priests to that land," Aelon said at last. "Their mission will be to carry the message of my love and care to these benighted people. And, if, in their proselytizing, they happen to stumble upon this hidden city or discover the spiritbone, so much the better."

"I understand, Revered Aelon," said Raegar, grinning.

Aelon smiled. "You have a way to communicate with them?"

"I will order them to report to the Watchers, who will bring their reports to me."

"Send with the priests some of the gold and jewels the Stormlords pay you," said Aelon. "One can always find a man willing to betray his country for a price. You would know, wouldn't you, Raegar?"

She cocked her eye at him. Raegar flushed in anger, but he managed to control himself.

"To betray one's country, one must have a country," he said. "My people left me wounded on the field of battle to be taken prisoner and made a slave. It was then I found you, Revered Aelon. I sought you as a man who thirsts seeks cool water . . ."

He averted his head, ashamed of his emotions.

"Forgive me, Raegar," Aelon said remorsefully, putting her hand to his cheek. "I spoke thoughtlessly. You know I value you. I would not have made you my emperor otherwise."

Aelon drank the last of the wine. Drawing close to him, she rested her hands on his broad chest. The serpents on the golden necklace jingled, her bracelets clicked.

"This mission is vitally important, Raegar. I will soon have four of the spiritbones in my possession. Aylaen has three. I now know the location of the fourth and I believe the Stormlords have the fifth. Once I have all five, the power of creation will be mine. The world will be mine."

"And you will be mine," said Raegar. "We will rule this world together as you promised me."

"I will keep my promise, if you will keep yours," Aelon said, giving him a playful slap. "Remember what I said about your wife. You vowed to be faithful to Treia. I expect you to keep that vow. Thus you will prove you can be faithful to me."

She brushed her lips against his cheek. "You will be well rewarded, Raegar."

"Once I have you, I will need no other," said Raegar.

He tried to return her kiss, but Aelon eluded his grasp and vanished. He breathed deeply, his body quivering.

Treia watched the sun stream through the window of the beautiful palace in which she lived, and wearily closed her eyes. She had been awake most of the night, shifting in her bed, trying in vain to sleep. She could not get comfortable. Her belly was huge and the baby kicked almost constantly, as though trying to kick his way out.

Rolling and pushing herself off the bed, she waddled over to look at herself in the mirror. The baby had stopped kicking for the moment. Having been awake all night, he must need rest.

She was alone in the enormous room, surrounded by every luxury. All she had to do was ring a bell and she could have anything her heart desired, from candied peacock tongues to a cask of rubies. She passed her hand over her swollen belly and shivered in fear.

She was intimately familiar with pregnancies. As a former priestess of Vindrash, she had been present at the births of countless children. She knew hers was not right and yet no one would believe her. She was only a few weeks pregnant and she looked as though she would give birth any moment.

The midwives told her she had miscalculated the date. Treia knew quite well she had not. She remembered vividly the night the child had been conceived. The god Hevis had visited her, reminding her that she had agreed to sacrifice someone she loved in return for his help with the spiritbone. She had tried to murder Aylaen, but that had failed. The only other people she loved were Raegar . . . and the baby growing inside her.

Hevis had promised to return in nine months to hear her choice for sacrifice—her husband or her child. But he would not have to wait nine months. The child was growing abnormally fast, as though her pregnancy was being speeded up, rushing, she feared, to some disastrous end.

Treia made her slow way over to a couch and ponderously and awkwardly lowered herself among the silken cushions. The baby had not yet dropped and was squeezing her lungs, making breathing difficult. She bowed her head, covered her face with her hands, and began to sob. She knew she shouldn't weep. The midwives had told her to be happy and cheerful. Dark thoughts could harm the unborn babe.

Treia was too frightened to be cheerful. She had lost control of her own body. The child had seized it and while she loved her unborn baby more than life itself, she couldn't help but be scared.

She wept hysterically, unable to stop. A hand rested gently on her shoulder and a sweet voice spoke soothingly.

"Hush, child. You will make yourself ill."

Treia was astonished to see a plump motherly looking woman sitting beside her on the couch. She might have thought this was some servant, but the woman was beautifully dressed in white robes of soft lamb's wool and wore two golden bracelets and a golden necklace of serpents. Treia did not know the woman, though there was something familiar about her.

"Who are you?" Treia gasped, drawing away from the woman's touch. "How did you get into my chambers?"

"I am Aelon, my child," said the woman. She stroked Treia's hair with a soft hand. "You prayed to me for help and I am here in answer."

Treia had not prayed to Aelon or any god, but she knew better than to argue. Weak and afraid, she needed help and she would take it from any source.

"Aelon, I am so frightened!" Treia said, choking. "My pregnancy numbers in weeks. I know it! And yet look at me! Something is wrong!"

"My dear daughter, nothing is wrong," said Aelon soothingly. "I

have hurried things along, that is all. Momentous events are happening in the world. We cannot wait nine months for the emperor's son
to be born."

Treia gaped at her. "I don't understand . . ."

"I know and I have much to tell you. But first, I will make us a
nice cup of tea and bring you something to eat. Your boy needs nour-
ishment."

Treia watched in astonishment as the god waited on her. Aelon
brewed a tea that was the most delicious Treia had ever tasted and
calmed her spirits. Then the god flicked her hand and all Treia's
favorite foods appeared. She found she was famished, and ate with
good appetite. After the meal, Aelon arranged the cushions around
Treia, fussed over her, making sure she was comfortable, and then sat
down beside her.

"Now for a nice cozy, womanly chat. May I be candid with you,
my dear?" Aelon asked.

"Yes, certainly," said Treia.

"Your husband, Raegar, is a strong ruler and a great warrior, but,
let us face it, Treia, he is a man and as such he has his limits. He knows
nothing about summoning dragons and he will need the Dragon Fala,
to fight for him should we go to war. Fala is most upset with your
husband's bungling and has threatened to leave my service. The dragon
likes you and has agreed to serve you. Knowing this, I have arranged
for your son to be born ahead of time, so that you will be ready to
help in the event we go to war."

Treia gazed at the god in wonder.

"All this time, I have felt so useless . . . so alone. . . ." Treia began
to sob again.

Aelon put her arms around her and held her close, rocking her and
soothing her.

"Never alone, Treia," Aelon murmured. "You are dear to me. I have
seen your son's future. He will be the most powerful ruler in the
world, lord of all the people of all the nations. He will make his mother
proud."

Treia sank to her knees on the floor. "Aelon, forgive me! I have been
jealous of you and my husband. The two of you seem so close. I feared
you were trying to take him from me."

"What a silly goose you are, my child," said Aelon in loving tones.

"You know better now, don't you? You are Empress of Sinaria. All will know it, for I give you this gift."

Aelon removed the heavy gold necklace made of serpents and fastened it around Treia's neck. "A mark of my love and esteem."

Treia drew in a deep breath and placed her hand reverently upon the necklace. The gold was still warm from the touch of the god.

"Thank you, Aelon! I am yours to command!"

"I know, Daughter," said Aelon, smiling. "I know."

6

Torval's Hall was high in the mountains, overlooking a vast sea where Joabis said his dragonship was waiting for him. Skylan expected the god to whisk them through the ether, as he had taken him to visit the Norn, but Joabis insisted that they had to walk.

The path that led from the hall to the shore was rocky, steep, and difficult to traverse, especially in the snow and ice. Skylan slid and slipped down the side of the mountain, and by the time they reached the shore, he was scraped and bruised and in an ill humor.

"Now you know why I rarely visit Torval," Joabis grumbled, plucking pine needles from his hair. "He won't set a toe on my island, however, so I have no choice but to come to him."

Skylan looked back up at Torval's Hall. The top of the mountain was shrouded by storm clouds and he could not see it.

"Where is this ship of yours?" he asked Joabis.

"I beached it in a cove not far from here."

Joabis led the way, walking across the sand. The air was much warmer. The sun beat down on them, as though Aylis didn't much like Joabis, and Skylan was soon sweating and regretting wearing his heavy armor.

Joabis proceeded at a swift pace, saying he was eager to leave this place and return to his island, and Skylan lost sight of him among the thick trees and heavy vegetation. He knew where he was because he could hear the god crashing among the foliage and shouting for him to hurry. After fighting his way through a tangle of vines, Skylan came to a small, sheltered bay surrounded by trees. The seawater was blue green and clear, with barely a wavelet as it flowed over the rippling sand.

The dragonship was lying on the beach. Skylan expected to find members of the crew waiting for the god or at least someone standing guard on the ship, but no one was around. The beach was empty except for Joabis, who was scratching his head and looking perplexed.

"Where's your crew?" Skylan called, slogging through the sand.

"I don't know," Joabis replied. "I gave them a full barrel of ale to keep them company. They were just broaching it when I left. Perhaps they grew bored with waiting and wandered off. I'll go search for them."

Joabis began shouting names, calling for his missing crewmen.

Skylan shook his head in disgust and went over to inspect the ship.

"I know why no one is guarding it," he muttered. "It's not worth stealing."

The dragonship was old and dilapidated. The paint was peeling, and the sail had so many patches he could not find much of the original canvas. Barnacles covered the hull and might be all that was holding the ship together. He doubted they would make it out of the cove before it sank.

Skylan continued along across the small strip of beach, keeping his gaze on the ground. He found the ale barrel tipped over on its side; the bunghole wide open. The sand beneath was wet and smelled strongly of ale.

Skylan straightened. Keeping his hand on the hilt of his sword, he continued to investigate and soon had an idea of what must have happened.

"You can stop yelling," he told Joabis. "Your crew didn't wander off. They ran away."

"How do you know?" Joabis demanded.

"They left behind a full ale barrel, overturning it in their haste," said Skylan. "The footprints are deep, made by men running off in terror, and they all lead one direction—into the forest."

Joabis paled. "Do you know what attacked them?"

"I don't see any signs of a battle," said Skylan. "But something scared them. I'll keep searching—"

"No, no," said Joabis. "We should be leaving. Help me haul the ship into the water."

"We can't sail without a crew!" Skylan protested.

"Vindrash will send us a dragon," said Joabis, puffing and panting as he hurried toward the ship.

"Don't you want to know who attacked your men and what happened to them?" Skylan asked.

"Not particularly," said Joabis, mopping his face with his sleeve. "Lift the prow. I'll take the stern."

Skylan helped carry the dragonship, taking the prow, which was the heavy end, and between them they managed to haul the ship into the warm, crystalline water. The two hoisted themselves on board.

The dragonship rocked in the water, moving gently back and forth with the motion of the waves, not going anywhere. Skylan looked around the ship. Sea chests were upended, their contents scattered about the deck. The crew had not stowed the oars properly in the center where they belonged. They had taken the mast down, the patched sail lay in sloppy folds on top, and the hatch to the hold gaped wide open.

Judging by the mess they had left behind, Skylan decided that Joabis's crew was no great loss.

Righting a sea chest, Skylan sat down and waited for Joabis, who was holding a whispered conversation with the Dragon Goddess. Skylan heard her name, "Vindrash!" and, "This is all your fault!" and, "You owe me!"

"Now what does all that mean?" Skylan asked himself.

He didn't like to think about the answer.

Within moments, a green and gold dragon appeared in the sky, flying down from the top of the mountain. The dragon hovered for an instant above the ship, then vanished, infusing the ship with his spirit. The eyes of the dragon on the prow began to glow with life. The dragonship glided out of the smooth waters of the cove and sailed out into the open sea.

Joabis was restless. He sat down on a sea chest, but after a few moments, he jumped up and began pacing the deck. Then he sat back down and looked at Skylan.

"What's going on?" Skylan demanded. "Why does Vindrash 'owe you'?"

"I'm too thirsty to talk," said Joabis, fanning himself with his hand. "Fetch me some ale. There's a barrel in the hold."

Skylan scowled. "I am not one of your souls you can order about. Answer my questions and I'll think about it."

Joabis drew a greasy leather pouch from his tunic, opened it, and shook out some dice. "We will roll for it. You win and I'll answer your questions."

"How about this?" said Skylan grimly. "You answer my questions and I *won't* kick a hole in the hull and sink your damn boat."

Joabis cast him a baleful glance, gathered up his dice and dropped them back into the pouch. "What do you want to know?"

"Even though I am not dead, I am in the realm of the dead, right?" Skylan asked.

"Yes," said Joabis, eyeing him warily.

"Your crew were all souls who come to dwell with you on your isle."

"That is true," said Joabis.

"So what frightens dead men so badly that they run off and leave a barrel full of ale behind?" Skylan demanded. "More to the point, what's frightening you?"

Joabis stood up and headed for the hatch. "I'll fetch my own ale."

"I'm coming with you," said Skylan.

"Suit yourself," said Joabis, shrugging.

Skylan headed for the hatch, noticing a strong smell of ale wafting up from the hold. Joabis descended the ladder that led down in to the hatch and Skylan followed, backing down the ladder.

The hold was dark, especially after the glare of the sunlight, and Skylan couldn't see. He could smell, however, and the stench of ale was overwhelming. He could also hear a sloshing sound, as if the hold were filled with water.

"Does this damn boat of yours leak?" Skylan asked.

Joabis's answer was a shriek of dismay.

"What's wrong?" Skylan demanded, peering into the darkness, his hand on the hilt of his sword. "What is it?"

When his eyes adjusted, he could see for himself. Every single barrel had been chopped up like kindling. The hold was awash in ale, with broken barrel staves and other debris floating on top, sloshing back and forth with the movement of the ship.

Skylan relaxed. "This must have been a merry party—"

"Party? Are you mad?" Joabis wailed. "I didn't do this! I wouldn't destroy my own ale! I've been attacked by pirates! They've stolen everything!"

He was standing at the bottom of the ladder, wringing his hands with ale lapping around his ankles, clearly agitated. Skylan waded into the mess, examining empty wineskins and picking up sodden sacks.

"This wasn't pirates. They didn't steal, they destroyed. Whoever did this came in search of something."

Joabis's knees sagged and he nearly fell, saving himself by catching hold of the ladder for support.

"What do you mean?" he asked in a quavering voice. "How can you know that?"

"Pirates would have stolen your supplies and run off with them. Whoever was here took an axe to the ale barrels, slit open the wineskins with a knife, and slashed the sacking."

"You're right," said Joabis, gnawing his lip. He had gone quite pale. "You must be right."

Skylan eyed him. "First your crew runs off in fear and then your ship is searched. Why?"

Joabis scowled. "Ask Hevis."

"Hevis?" Skylan was surprised at this suggestion. "What does he have to do with this? Why would he be searching your ship and scaring your crew?"

"He claims I lost to him at dice. I refused to pay and he must have come here to collect," Joabis replied. "I need to determine if my possessions are safe, but not with you breathing down my neck. Wait for me on deck."

"With pleasure," said Skylan. "I'll be glad to get away from the stench."

He didn't just mean the ale. Joabis sickened him. While Torval and his brave warriors were fighting for their lives, he and Hevis the Trickster—another sorry excuse for a god—were squabbling over gambling debts.

"And close the hatch!" Joabis shouted.

Skylan dropped the hatch with a bang and went to stand by the prow, looking out to sea. Foam frothed around the keel. Spray flew over the deck, spattering Skylan, who enjoyed the coolness. The sun poured her molten gold on the blue water and he wondered where they were and how long this hateful voyage must last. The sea stretched on endlessly with no land in sight.

Skylan still had more questions for Joabis and he grew impatient for the god's return. Walking back to the hatch, he stomped on it with his foot.

"Are you all right?" Skylan yelled. "You didn't drown in your own ale, did you?"

After a moment, the hatch opened and Joabis appeared, looking much more cheerful, holding something behind his back.

"Hevis didn't find it!" he announced.

"Didn't find what?" Skylan asked.

"My treasure." Joabis brought forth a small box made of wood decorated with silver on the edges and a silver lock in front. "He didn't find it this time, but I'm afraid he might come back. I'm no warrior, but you are. I want you to guard it for me."

He held out the box to Skylan, who folded his arms across his chest.

"I need to know what I'm guarding."

"Do you?" Joabis asked, adding slyly, "I don't see why the contents should matter to a warrior such as yourself. All you care about is dying gloriously in battle."

Skylan made no move to take the box.

Joabis dithered, then said crossly, "Very well, I'll show you! You must promise to tell no one."

He cast a suspicious eye on the dragon sailing their ship and then motioned Skylan to walk with him to the stern. Holding the box close to his chest, Joabis hunched his shoulders over it, fit a small silver key into the lock, then lifted the lid.

The little box seemed to blaze with dazzling fire. Sapphires and rubies, emeralds and diamonds sparkled in the sunshine.

"Beautiful, aren't they? I have traveled the world over in search of them," Joabis said proudly. "I keep the best for myself, of course, but I give some to the dragons who sail my ship. Hevis knows this and he knows I carry the jewels with me for that reason."

Skylan understood. The Vindrasi had always given jewels to the dragons in payment for sailing their ships and protecting them, a bargain the dragons and the Vindrasi people had struck centuries ago. The dragons sorted through the jewels, kept the gems they wanted, and returned the rest as a reward to the warriors.

The Vindrasi had no idea why the dragons wanted the jewels. Most believed the dragons coveted the wealth. Legend told of vast dragon hoards hidden in the mountains, though no one had ever found them or, if they had, lived to tell the tale. Skylan had come to wonder if there might be a reason that had nothing to do with the value of the gems. He had seen the Dragon Kahg select a small emerald, badly set and crudely cut, over a large ruby with a heart of fire.

"Give me the jewels," said Skylan, holding out his hand. "I will find a new hiding place for them and I'll keep them safe. On my honor as a Vindrasi."

"I'm not sure I can trust you," said Joabis, shutting the box.

"Then don't give them to me," said Skylan, exasperated. "This was your idea."

He turned to walk away.

"No, stop!" Joabis cried and reluctantly handed Skylan the box, giving it a loving pat as he let it go.

"I'll need that leather pouch," Skylan said, pointing.

"It holds my dice," Joabis protested.

"I want those, as well."

Joabis muttered under his breath, but he handed over the pouch. Skylan emptied the dice onto the deck and poured the jewels into the pouch. He then scooped up the dice and placed those in the box, which he handed back to Joabis.

"Lock it and put it back in its hiding place," he said.

"A good idea," said Joabis with an attempt at a pleased smile. "Hevis will find it filled with dice, not jewels. I can't believe I never thought of that. Where will you hide my treasure?"

Skylan went over to the mast, knelt down at the foot and stuffed the pouch containing the jewels into the hole where the mast fit into the wooden planking.

Joabis watched with approval, then announced his intention of taking a nap. "I've had a fatiguing day. You can tidy up while I rest."

Draping the sail over the hull to form a crude awning against the sun, Joabis crawled beneath it, laced his fingers over his chest, and closed his eyes.

Skylan dragged one of the sea chests into the shadow cast by the dragon-head prow and slumped down, telling himself he'd be damned if he would clean up Joabis's mess. The sea was flat, the sun blazing, and there was no breath of wind. Skylan sat and sweated, listened to Joabis's whistling snore and wondered what the god was plotting.

His claim that Hevis had chopped up barrels and sent dead men running off in a panic, all to steal a handful of jewels, stank like yesterday's fish.

"He goes to a great deal of trouble to hide his gems and the next moment, he's eager to show them to me," Skylan muttered. "He's half mad with fear. Even though we're alone on this ship on an empty sea, he can't take three steps without looking over his shoulder. And why are my men on his isle? How did they get there? If he isn't lying about that, as well."

Skylan stood up and set to work. He could no longer stand to look at the disorder. He stacked the oars in their proper place, straightened the tangled wad of fishnet, and began repacking and righting the overturned sea chests. He was still working at this when Joabis sat bolt upright.

"Voices!" he gasped, peering about. "I heard voices! Did you hear them?"

Skylan shook his head. "You must have been dreaming. There's nothing between us and the horizon. Not so much as bird."

"I tell you I heard someone talking!" Joabis said nervously. Rolling over, he managed to haul himself to his feet and went to stare into the sea.

A wave rose up and slapped him in the face. Joabis gasped and sputtered, wiping water from his eyes and swearing. From somewhere below the keel came the sound of merry laughter.

Sklyan grinned.

"Relax," he told Joabis. "The voices you're hearing belong to oceanids, the fae folk who live in the sea. They're annoying, but not dangerous."

"What do they want?" Joabis asked, still trembling. "Talk to them. Tell them to go away!"

"You tell them," said Skylan. "You're a god. I don't know them."

"They know you," said Joabis. "They're calling your name!"

"Impossible. You're hearing things," Skylan retorted.

But now he was curious, and began listening more closely. At first all he heard was the waves splashing against the hull; then it seemed the waves spoke words: "Skylan Ivorson," repeated over and over.

Telling himself he was only hearing his name because Joabis had put the thought into his head, Skylan went to the stern and leaned over. The moment the oceanids caught sight of him, the beautiful women with their silvery, sleek bodies and long, sea foam–colored hair swam to the side of the ship. Swirling about the keel like a school of fish, some even excitedly began leaping from the water like dolphins.

The oceanids reached out their hands to him, as though they would pull him into the sea. Startled, Skylan drew back. Although the oceanids had come to his aid in the undersea world of the Aquins, he still viewed all fae folk as chaotic and unreliable, not to be trusted.

"What do they want with you?" Joabis asked, coming to stand near Skylan, but not so near that the oceanids would splash him again.

"I have no idea," said Skylan.

"You had better find out and shut them up," said Joabis nervously. "All that noise and commotion they're making, they're sure to draw attention to us."

Skylan wondered whose attention the oceanids were likely to draw, but he went back to the stern to talk to them.

"What do you want of me?" Skylan asked dourly, feeling foolish.

The oceanids were greatly excited and all of them answered at once. He couldn't make out what they were saying until he caught a word he recognized.

"Wulfe?" Skylan repeated. "What about Wulfe? Not all of you together. Only one of you talk. You, there!"

He pointed to the oceanid who was closest to him, swimming in the water directly beneath him.

"Our prince is searching for you!" the oceanid called, bobbing up and down with the motion of the sea. The other women around nodded their heads. "He sent word out to all the fae folk in the world to look for you."

"Prince? What prince?" Joabis asked.

"They mean Wulfe, a foundling I took aboard my ship," said Skylan. "He says he is the son of a faery princess."

"You believe him?" Joabis was disdainful.

"No," said Skylan. "But he's my friend." He turned back to the oceanid. "Why is Wulfe looking for me?"

"Because your soul is lost, silly!" said the oceanid with rippling

laughter. "Our prince misses you and so does your wife. They want you to come back. We will take you to them."

"I miss them," said Skylan. "I want to go back to my wife and my friends, but I can't. Not yet."

"He is coming with me!" Joabis explained. "To the Isle of Revels."

The oceanid clapped her hands in delight. "We know the isle. The dragonship on which our prince sails is very near there! We will take you to him. We do not want to disappoint him."

"No, we must go to my isle!" Joabis protested. "The matter is urgent!"

The oceanids ignored him. Diving beneath the sea, they swam back with long ropes of seaweed festooned around their bodies. They wrapped the seaweed around the neck of the dragon-head prow, apparently offending the dragon, for the red glow faded from the eyes. A green-and-gold dragon materialized above the ship, spread his wings, and flew off in the direction of Torval's mountain.

The dragonship slowed to a halt, drifting in the water.

"Now look what you've done!" Joabis cried, rounding on Skylan. "We're becalmed! Sure to be caught!"

Skylan was barely listening. "They're not going to leave us here. They're going to take me to Aylaen."

Some of the oceanids grabbed hold of the seaweed ropes wrapped around the prow, twined them about their bodies, and began to swim, pulling the ship, while other oceanids pushed the ship from the stern.

The dragonship began moving through the water, slowly at first and then picking up speed until it was bounding over the waves. Foam boiled beneath the keel and seawater splashed over the prow. Joabis gave a hollow cry, lurched across the deck, and tumbled down into the hold.

Skylan stood by the prow, his hands gripping the rail, his legs braced. The seawater broke over him, cooling him. He tasted the salt on his lips.

"Torval," Skylan prayed, "all I ask is the chance to let Aylaen know I will come back to her. Wherever she is, I will find her."

Wulfe crouched protectively beside Skylan's body, crowding as close to the corpse as he could without touching the armor, for it was made of iron. He and all the other fae folk hated iron; the metal burned their flesh. Wulfe couldn't even stand the smell, which was like that of fresh blood, but for Skylan's sake he endured it.

Wulfe kept a distrustful eye on his fellow passengers, especially the old Ugly, Acronis, and the young Ugly, Farinn. Wulfe had overheard the two talking when they thought he was sleeping. They said Skylan was dead and they were going to try to convince Aylaen to dump him into the sea.

Wulfe had feared Skylan was dead, too, right after the spear had hit him and he'd collapsed onto the deck in a pool of blood. The pain of his loss had been horrible for Wulfe, seeming to set his insides on fire and searing his soul as the iron seared his skin.

After finding Skylan dying on the ghost ship and nursing him back to health, Wulfe had come to believe that Skylan belonged to him. Wulfe's duty was watch over his friend and he had failed and Skylan had died and gone to live with some stupid god in a hall filled with iron. Wulfe couldn't bear to be without him. He'd already lost his mother, who long ago had visited him every night to sing lullabies to him, and now he'd lost Skylan.

"I'm going someplace where we don't kill each other," Wulfe had told the oceanids, who had clustered beneath the ship, expressing their sorrow and sympathy for their grieving prince.

He had planned to leave that night, jump into the sea and swim away with his friends, as soon as he was certain the Uglies were asleep, for he knew they would try to stop him. But while he was waiting, hiding in the darkness, he had seen and heard some things that made him realize Skylan wasn't dead. He might not be alive, but he wasn't dead.

Wulfe didn't tell the Uglies what he had seen. He was afraid to tell them, because he knew he shouldn't have seen what he saw. And besides, he reasoned, the Uglies wouldn't believe him anyway. All he would tell them was that Skylan wasn't dead.

"You don't have to be sad anymore," Wulfe had assured the three Uglies. "We just have to wait for him to come back to us."

Acronis had looked grave. Farinn had walked away very fast. Aylaen had only stared at him with dull, empty eyes and gone over to stand beside the dragon.

"Why don't you believe me?" Wulfe yelled at them, but none of them answered.

And the very next day, Acronis had started to talk in sad and solemn tones about throwing Skylan into the sea.

"You have to find Skylan," Wulfe had told the oceanids. "You have to find him and bring him back!"

The fae loved gossip, especially if it had to do with the Uglies, and the exciting news that the oceanids were looking for a dead Ugly who wasn't dead would flash among them with lightning speed. Wulfe took comfort in the fact that every oceanid, naiad, dryad and satyr, nymph, faun, and centaur, and maybe even such evil fae as ghouls and giants would be looking for Skylan. When they found him, he had ordered them to bring him back to where he belonged—with Wulfe.

While the fae were searching, Wulfe kept watch over Skylan during the day and slept near the body at night. If any of the Uglies came near, Wulfe bared his teeth and snarled at them, and the Uglies retreated.

The Uglies were all afraid of Wulfe, including Aylaen, even though she was fond of him. The Uglies had witnessed Wulfe's inner daemons escape his control and turn him into a beast who ripped out throats and tore off limbs. Their fear made Wulfe unhappy, but he understood. He scared himself sometimes.

Aylaen was standing with Kahg this day, her back turned on the rest of them. She'd been standing beside the dragon all morning, not speaking, not moving, just staring out at nothing. She did not pay any attention to Wulfe or the other two Uglies. Wulfe kept a wary eye on all of them.

The young one, Farinn, was sitting with his back against a bulkhead, singing to himself. He'd been doing that all morning and it was starting to grate on Wulfe's nerves.

"Quit that caterwauling!" he said to Farinn at last. "You keep singing the same notes over and over and they never go anywhere."

Farinn blinked in astonishment. "I'm sorry. It's just . . . I'm trying to compose Skylan's death song and I can't seem to find the words."

"That's because he's not dead, fool," Wulfe shouted at him. "I keep telling you—"

"Stop it, Wulfe!" Aylaen cried angrily.

Before he could react, she ran up behind him, dragged him to his feet, and slapped him across the face.

"He *is* dead!" Aylaen screamed, shaking him. "He is dead! He is dead!"

Wulfe stared at her in shock and she suddenly sank to her knees and held him close.

"I'm sorry, Wulfe!" she said. "The fault is not yours. It is mine. I have let our suffering go on far too long. Tonight, at sunset, we will give Skylan's body to the Sea Goddess."

She kissed him on the cheek where she had hit him, then slowly rose to her feet and walked back to stand with the dragon. Resting her head against the dragon's neck, she gazed out over the waves.

Wulfe turned to growl at Farinn. "It's all your fault! I hate you! I hate all of you! Do you know why we call you Uglies? It's not your faces! It's your hearts!"

Wulfe ran to the stern to talk to the oceanids. "Have you found him yet?"

The women shook their heads sadly, but promised to keep trying.

Until they found Skylan, Wulfe couldn't let Aylaen throw him into the sea, for then he really would be dead. He knew he couldn't stop her and Acronis, and Farinn *wouldn't* stop her. That left only one other.

The Dragon Kahg.

Wulfe had been trying to summon the courage to talk to the dragon ever since that night when he'd seen what he'd seen. He was certain the dragon had seen it, too, because Kahg saw everything. Wulfe needed to talk to the dragon in private, however, and that meant getting rid of the Uglies.

The old Ugly had picked up his strange iron tools and was pointing them at the sky, while Farinn began making marks on a large piece of animal skin covered with dots and lines. Acronis had told Wulfe his iron tools could tell him where the ship was located on the animal skin.

This made no sense to Wulfe, who once had pointed out to Skylan that the ship was on the water, not on the animal skin. Skylan had laughed and said that Wulfe was the smartest person aboard the ship.

Remembering Skylan's laughter made Wulfe feel the pain again. He scratched his head, trying to think of a way to get all the Uglies off the deck. A plan formed in his mind. The plan was drastic and might turn out to be a bad plan, but he didn't have time to think of anything else. He glanced back at Acronis and Farinn, who were bent over the animal skin, and he looked at Aylaen, who was standing so still she might have turned into another figurehead.

Softly creeping on his bare feet, Wulfe slipped over to the hold, raised the hatch, and crawled partway down the ladder. He quietly lowered the hatch, then crept down the rest of the way. The hold was dark after being out in the bright sun and Wulfe kept still until he could see.

They had taken on food and fresh water before leaving the Aquin realm and the hold smelled strongly of fish. Wulfe didn't like being down here. He didn't like being anywhere that had walls. When his eyes adjusted, he padded softly among the jumble of barrels and stone jars, a large tangle of fishing net, a spare sail, the armor and weapons they'd brought with them from Sinaria, and sea chests where the Uglies kept their clothes and blankets so they wouldn't get wet.

Giving Skylan's sea chest a pat as he walked past it, Wulfe ventured deeper into the hold, searching for what Aylaen called the "rag bag." Nothing ever went to waste among the Vindrasi. She cut shirts and stockings worn past mending into strips to be used for bandages and cloths for cleaning, stuffing them into a gunnysack she kept near her healing supplies.

Wulfe pulled out a handful of rags, piled them in a corner, and sprinkled them with water. He cast a furtive glance back at the hatch to make certain no one was spying on him, then, bending over the damp rags, he worked his magic, chanting a rhyme his mother had taught him, saying it would be useful in case he ever needed to rid himself of a foe.

Hide me!
Hide me!
Blind their eyes.
Make them sneeze.
Make them wheeze.
Hide me!
Hide me!
Blind their eyes.

A multitude of sparks jumped from his fingertips and landed on the rags. Wherever the sparks hit, tendrils of gray smoke started to curl into the air. The blinding smoke would grow thicker and soon fill the hold. Wulfe had to hustle to return to deck before he got caught by his own magic.

He scrambled up the ladder, holding his breath to keep from coughing, jumped out on deck, and shut the hatch.

Seeing that no one was paying any attention to him, Wulfe sauntered across the deck, coming to stand close to the dragon, and waited, fidgeting, until he saw gray puffs start to float out of the hatch.

Leaning against the rail, Wulfe sniffed the air and said, "I smell smoke. Do you?"

Aylaen jumped as though he'd stabbed her in the ribs. Fire was the most feared danger on board ship. Whipping around, she saw the smoke that was now pouring out from beneath the closed hatch.

"Blessed Vindrash!" she gasped. "Fire!"

She ran toward the hatch. Farinn joined her. Acronis grabbed the water bucket and hurried after them. Aylaen lifted the hatch. Smoke billowed out, causing her to jump back. Acronis peered down.

"I don't see any flames. I'm going down there."

"I'm coming with you," said Aylaen.

"Tie this over your nose and mouth," said Farinn, handing them each some strips of sheepskin on which he'd been writing his song. They did as he suggested and the three of them plunged into the hold.

Wulfe heard them banging about below, coughing and bumping into things. He stood in front of the Dragon Kahg.

"You know Skylan's not dead," Wulfe said.

The dragon's fiery red eyes swiveled around, catching Wulfe in their lurid glare.

"That night, after he died," Wulfe continued, "I saw a woman take his soul. I recognized her. She was *your* goddess!" He pointed an accusing finger at the dragon.

Kahg's red eyes narrowed. Wulfe could hear more bumping and thumping coming from the hold and the sound of muffled voices. Smoke continued to pour from the hatch.

"I heard you and the goddess talking," Wulfe went on. "You talked about the spiritbones and the Great Dragon Ilyrion and how the spiritbones would cause the dragon to return to the world. I know about the great dragon. My mother told me stories. She said the great dragon ruled here before the gods of the Uglies came to kill her and steal the world from her. My mother said the great dragon liked us and was glad we came to live here."

Kahg rolled his eyes and muttered something Wulfe couldn't understand. He could see the smoke starting to diminish and he didn't have much time.

"I have two questions, mighty Kahg. First, if the dragon comes back to kill all the Uglies, what will she do to my people?"

"How should I know?" Kahg demanded irritably.

Wulfe considered this a fair point.

"Next question. You know Skylan isn't dead, don't you?"

The Dragon Kahg did not respond.

"Why did your goddess take him?" Wulfe asked, growing desperate. "Where did they go? Is she going to send him back?"

The dragon's eyes flared alarmingly.

"I don't like little boys," Kahg growled. "I especially don't like fae little boys who set fire to my ship!"

"I didn't set fire to your stupid old ship," Wulfe retorted. "If you won't answer my questions, at least promise that you won't let Aylaen throw Skylan into the sea."

The dragon's red eyes closed and stayed closed for so long Wulfe thought he'd fallen asleep. The smoke was gone now. He could hear the Uglies coming up the ladder. Between coughs, they sounded angry. The Dragon Kahg suddenly opened his eyes.

"I promise," he said.

Aylaen and the others emerged from the hatch, covered in soot, and took big gulps of fresh air.

Aylaen coughed again and fixed Wulfe with a irate gaze. "Wulfe, I want to talk—"

"You need a bath!" he cried, wrinkling his nose and he ran to the stern to keep as far as he could out of her reach.

Late that afternoon, a gray fog crept over the water and wrapped around the *Venejekar*. The wind died. The sea went flat. The fog shrouded the ship so that Wulfe, sitting beside Skylan's body, lost sight of Aylaen, Farinn, and Acronis. All he could see were the red eyes of the Dragon Kahg and they looked strange and eerie.

Acronis was saying something to Aylaen and Farinn about the fog not being scientific or something like that when Wulfe heard the oceanids excitedly calling his name.

He twisted to his feet and went to the rail and leaned over very far to be able to see. The fog twined and twisted over the water. The oceanids were jumping from the waves crying out, "Your Highness, we found him!"

A dragonship festooned in seaweed glided close. Wulfe peered through the fog, straining his eyes, and after a moment he could make out the figure of an Ugly standing at the rail beside a god, who was short and fat and greasy looking.

"Skylan!" Wulfe cried joyfully. "Aylaen, come quick! Skylan's here! I told you he wasn't dead!"

He couldn't see her, but he could hear Acronis remonstrating with her. "Aylaen, you have to do something about Wulfe. I am fond of the boy, but he did try to set fire to the ship—"

"I'll go talk to him," said Aylaen.

She seemed wrapped in fog. She was wearing a shawl over her head to protect her from the damp. She was pale, as though all the blood had been sucked out of her.

"Wulfe, you have to stop lying," she said wearily.

"But it's Skylan! On a dragonship," said Wulfe, jabbing his finger in the direction of the boat. "Can't you see him? He's right there in front of you."

Aylaen looked into the gray mist, sighed and said in a harsh tone, "We are burying Skylan tonight."

She turned on her heel and started to walk away.

"Aylaen, don't go! Skylan, say something to her!" Wulfe cried. "She thinks you are dead!"

"Aylaen," Skylan called to her. "My beloved wife."

Aylaen stopped walking. She looked back, over her shoulder. Acronis and Farinn came running.

"I heard the boy cry out. What is wrong?" Acronis asked.

"Wulfe says Skylan is out there in a boat," said Aylaen.

"Aylaen . . . ," Acronis began in gentle tones.

"No, I didn't believe him either, Legate, but then I heard his voice. Skylan's voice. He spoke my name. I think Wulfe is right. Can you see anything? I can't. The fog is too thick."

Acronis stared into the mist. Farinn leaned out over the rail to try to see.

"He's in a dragonship right in front of you!" Wulfe said crossly.

Acronis shook his head and frowned. Farinn drew back with a sigh.

"Their eyes are mortal, child of the fae," said the fat god. "They can't see us."

Wulfe didn't know this god. The Uglies had so many gods he couldn't keep track, and he didn't really care.

"Skylan, come back to us," said Wulfe. "Your body is here waiting for you. I've missed you horribly. Nothing has gone right since you left."

"I want to come back, Wulfe, more than anything," said Skylan. "But I made a promise to Joabis that I would go with him to the Isle of Revels. My friends are there and I must talk to them."

"He speaks the truth, Your Highness!" the oceanids said, splashing about beneath the keel. "We are taking him there. Tell her! Tell his wife! She must follow."

Wulfe turned to Aylaen. "Skylan is with a god named Joabis. They're sailing to this god's island to look for some of Skylan's friends."

"Aylaen, come away. You don't have listen to this," said Acronis.

"No, wait," said Aylaen.

She stared into the mist, her eyes wide, intense, and unblinking.

"What friends?" she asked Wulfe.

"Tell her Sigurd and Grimuir, Bjorn and Erdmun," said Skylan. "She will remember. I sent them back to our homeland to warn them about Raegar, but somehow their souls are with Joabis. I have to find out what happened to them and help them if I can."

"I don't know why you have to find them," said Wulfe, scowling. He didn't like Sigurd. "Good riddance."

"Tell her what I said," said Skylan, his voice grating.

"He says Sigurd and Grimuir and Bjorn and Erdmun," said Wulfe. "Joabis has their souls."

"Their souls?" Aylaen repeated, dazed. Shivering, she clasped the shawl around her tightly. "I think *I* must be going mad. I seem to hear his voice. . . ."

"Let me go to her!" Skylan begged Joabis.

"If you want to, I can't stop you," said Joabis. "But it won't do any good."

"Sail closer," Skylan told the oceanids.

They pulled Joabis's ship nearer to the *Venejekar*, so close that the hulls rubbed together. Skylan climbed over the rail into the *Venejekar* and walked up to Aylaen.

"My love, my wife, my own," he said.

He kissed her.

At his touch, Aylaen gasped and put her hand to her cheek.

"Skylan!" she cried and reached out her hands, grasping the fog, letting the shawl slip to the deck.

"You promised to come with me, Skylan Ivorson!" Joabis shouted. "You cannot stay."

"The Dragon Kahg knows the way, Aylaen," said Skylan, returning to Joabis's dragonship. "I will be waiting for you!"

"I'll come, Skylan!" Aylaen promised. "I will find you!"

The oceanids pulled the dragonship away. Skylan stood on the deck, watching Aylaen until his ship vanished in the mist.

"He is gone, isn't he," Aylaen murmured. "And I must follow."

She turned and ran across the deck, calling to the dragon. "Kahg, the ship bearing Skylan. Joabis's ship. Go after them!"

The Dragon Kahg was already sailing in pursuit. His red eyes, blazing in the fog, swiveled around and aimed their lurid glow at the boy.

"Told you so," said Wulfe.

Kahg gave an irate snort that caused the ship to rock alarmingly. Wulfe had to grab hold of the bulkhead to keep from falling overboard.

8

The Isle of Revels was beautiful as a summer's day in Skylan's homeland. From the deck of the dragonship, he gazed at an immense island with rolling hills of green forests and lush golden fields. The clear blue water reflected a clear blue sky.

Leaving the ship in the shallow water, he waded ashore, walking out of the surf onto grass-covered dunes. In the distance he could see a village that looked much like his village, including a tall and imposing longhouse that must be the Chief's Hall.

Skylan paused and looked back, to see if he could catch sight of the *Venejekar*. That brief glimpse of Aylaen, pale and grieving, and the sight of his body that she had so lovingly tended filled Skylan with sorrow. He could still feel the touch of her skin warm on his lips and see the joy in her eyes when she realized he had not died.

Skylan did not know how he had ever found the courage to leave her. He could not explain it, except that as his love for her made it hard for him to leave, her love gave him the strength to go.

"She's coming. Don't be so impatient," said Joabis, splashing through the water. "That dragon of yours knows where to find me."

"When she arrives, you will send me back to join her," Skylan confirmed. "That is our bargain."

Joabis kept walking and did not answer. He was headed toward the village and now Skylan could hear music and singing, shouting and uproarious laughter. Eager to join the merriment, the god could move fast when he chose and Skylan had to run to catch up with him. He took hold of Joabis by the shoulder and spun him around.

"I said—that is our bargain!"

"Of course it is, my dear friend," said Joabis with an ingratiating smile. "You have my word."

He patted Skylan on the shoulder and then hurried off toward the village, leaving Skylan to grimly stare after him.

"The bastard has no intention of keeping our bargain," Skylan muttered. Aloud he called after the god, "Where are my warriors?"

Getting no response, Skylan could do nothing except trudge after the god, thinking that perhaps his men were in the village, joining the celebration. As they drew nearer, he could see men and women dancing in the streets.

"Is today a feast day?" he asked.

"Every day is a feast day!" Joabis said. "We always find a reason to make merry."

Spreading his arms wide, he shouted, "My friends! I am back!"

The dancing stopped as the villagers ran to greet Joabis. The women kissed him and teased him. Someone handed him a mug of ale, as a group of men hoisted the god to their shoulders and, singing uproariously, started to carry him away.

"Joabis, wait!" Skylan cried, running after him. "Where are my men?"

Joabis looked back over his shoulder and made a vague gesture.

"The Chief's Hall!" he bawled, waving his mug. "You'll be able to hear them. Like I said, they're wrecking the place!"

The riotous crowd bore Joabis away. A few women invited Skylan to come with them, but he scornfully refused. Shrugging and laughing, they ran off. Once again Skylan thought of the valiant souls of the warriors in Torval's Hall, fighting against Aelon's fiends, while these fools danced and drank. He grew angry and began to wonder about his friends.

Perhaps they were here because they wanted to be here.

The longhouse stood some distance from the village, across a green field filled with wildflowers. The building appeared to have been hastily constructed and was in a deplorable condition of disrepair. He could see holes in the thatched roof and timbers sagging and starting to rot.

Reaching the door, he did not immediately go inside. He had no idea what he might be facing when he entered that building and he stood with his ear pressed against the door, listening.

Joabis had said his men were wrecking the place, but Skylan could not hear anything and that was alarming. He thought wrathfully that if Joabis had deceived him, he would shove a wineskin down his throat.

Skylan gave the door a tentative push, expecting it to be barred. To his surprise, the door swung open on creaking, rusty hinges. He put his hand on the hilt of his sword and cautiously walked in.

The hall had no windows and was lit only by a few rays of sunlight straggling through the holes in the roof. The cavernous chamber was hazy with smoke from a poorly vented fireplace. The shields hanging from the walls were covered with dust and cobwebs. Plank tables had been overturned. Trestles and benches were scattered about the floor.

Skylan stared in bleak dismay, thinking he had come too late to save his friends. Bodies of Vindrasi and ogre warriors lay sprawled on the floor, draped over the tables or the long wooden benches. The hall was covered in blood and the smell of death was overwhelming.

And then one of the corpses belched.

Skylan bent down to examine the bodies more closely and realized to his chagrin that the horrible stench in the air was not the smell of death. It was the smell of piss and vomit.

The warriors were not dead.

They were dead drunk.

Filled with shame for his people, Skylan stalked into the hall and began kicking at those on the floor, trying to rouse them and searching for his friends.

"Where is Sigurd?" he demanded, going from one to another. "I'm looking for a man called Sigurd? Have you seen him?"

Men mouthed curses and passed out again.

"Sigurd! Erdmun! Bjorn!" Skylan yelled until he finally heard what he thought was a mumbled response.

He stepped over bodies until he came to a man with black hair and a black beard slumped on a table. Skylan grabbed the man by the hair and lifted his head.

"Sigurd!" Skylan eyed him in disgust. "Sober up! We need to talk!"

Sigurd had seen forty winters, and he had never thought the much younger Skylan should be chief over him. Dour and hot tempered, he had few friends. For all that, Sigurd was a fierce warrior. He looked at Skylan with bloodshot, bleary eyes.

"Piss off," he said thickly.

Skylan slammed Sigurd's forehead against the table.

Howling in pain, Sigurd clenched his fist, took a swing at Skylan, missed, and fell off the bench.

Skylan grabbed a mug of stale ale and tossed it into his face. Sigurd sputtered, wiped his eyes, and gave a bitter laugh.

"If it isn't the great Skylan Ivorson. So Joabis caught you, too."

"Caught me?" Skylan repeated. "What do mean 'caught me'? I came here of my own free will searching for you and the others. I feared something dire had happened to you. Instead I find you swilling ale."

"Ale. A good idea," Sigurd said.

He picked up a mug and tried to drink, only to find it was empty.

"You spilled it," he said to Skylan. "Fetch me more."

"I'll be damned if I—" Skylan began.

Sigurd scowled. "*You'll* be damned! We're all damned! We're dead and it's all your fault! You sent us off in that rat-infested, leaky whoreson of an ogre ship."

He propped his elbows on the table and let his head sag into his hands. Skylan sat down across from him.

"How did you die?"

"We were caught in a storm." Sigurd's face paled beneath the thick growth of beard. "I have sailed the seas all my life and I have never seen a storm like it. The sun fled. The day grew black as night. Clouds of black and green whirled above us, turning into a waterspout that sped across the sea, sucking up the seawater and roaring like a thousand fiends. The whipping winds shredded the sail and broke off the mast. I knew we were doomed and I drew my sword so that I would die a warrior and then wind tore the ship apart. The raging seas dragged me under. I held my breath as long as I could, but the pain was too great and I gave up."

Sigurd sat in morose silence, recalling his death. Skylan was quiet a moment out of respect, then said, "What happened next?"

Sigurd shrugged. "I woke up here. Grimuir and Erdmun and Bjorn were with me. They're somewhere." He cast a vague glance around.

"So Joabis brought you here," said Skylan.

Sigurd snorted. "As if he dared! I would have slit him from gizzard to gullet. Vindrash brought us and all the Vindrasi warriors."

"But why would Vindrash bring warriors to the Isle of Revels?" Skylan asked, frowning.

"How should I know? It was dark and the winds were howling. The next I knew, we were here."

He motioned Skylan near. "And there are others!" he said, breathing beery breath into Skylan's face. "Ogres and outlandish folk! In the back of the hall."

Skylan stared into the back, but the room was so dark and smoke filled he couldn't see what "outlandish folk" Sigurd meant. He did see many more Vindrasi, some of whom he recognized, for they had been in attendance at his Vutmana, the ritual battle where he had defeated Horg and been named Chief of Chiefs.

These men are also warriors, he realized. By the looks of their wounds, they died in battle. They, too, should be with Torval. He needs all the warrior souls he can get.

Skylan glowered back at Sigurd. "Why do you men sit here all day swilling ale in company with that sodden wretch, Joabis? Why don't you leave? Go to Torval, explain to him what happened."

"Because we can't," said Sigurd flatly.

"Can't what?"

"We can't leave."

"Nonsense," said Skylan angrily. "Walk out the door."

"What door?" Sigurd frowned. "There is no door. Nothing but solid timber."

"Are you blind? I see a door!" Skylan exclaimed.

"Maybe you do," said Sigurd. "Some god loves you . . . The great Skylan . . ." He gave a drunken grin. "Yet here you are, dead, just like the rest of us."

"I'm not dead," said Skylan. "I'm not alive, either. I'm caught in between."

"You're not dead?" Sigurd seized hold of his wrist, gripping him painfully. "Then help us! Get us out of here!"

"That's why I'm here. Find the others. Something is not right. I'll go talk to Torval—"

"Skylan," said a voice behind him, a voice Skylan recognized. "Is that you?"

Skylan turned to see the bald head, guileless face, and hulking body of an ogre standing behind him. The ogre's head was painted white with a black stripe running from the neck to the chin and another black stripe crossing the nose and cheeks. Skylan knew only one ogre who painted his face like this.

"Keeper, my friend!" Skylan cried, flinging his arms around as much of the ogre as he could reach. "I am glad to see you!"

"I am *not* glad to see you," said Keeper. "For if you are here, this means you are dead."

Skylan suddenly remembered that Keeper had died and the fault was his. The ogre had been murdered by Treia, who had given him a potion to ease his pain. Her potion had eased him out of this life.

Skylan drew back, ashamed. "I am sorry, Keeper. I failed you. I should have never left Treia alone with you."

"You had no way of knowing that evil woman would poison me," said Keeper. "I knew she was a traitor. I was a fool to drink what she gave me."

He embraced Skylan in a hug that nearly broke his ribs. "We will speak of this no more."

Skylan hesitated, still not ready to forgive himself. Keeper smiled and Skylan took the ogre's hand in his own. "I will make it up to you."

He looked at Keeper and a sudden astonishing thought came to him. "How do you come to be *here*, my friend? In the afterlife of the Vindrasi? Don't you ogres have your own afterlife?"

Keeper scratched his head. "I always thought so. Yet here I am. And many others of my race. And there are others of another race, as well. Cyclopes!"

"Cyclopes!" Skylan repeated, amazed. "How do Cyclopes come to be in our afterlife?"

"Outlandish folk," Sigurd muttered. "Wait until you see them. They have three eyes and skin the color of night."

"I spoke to one of their warriors," said Keeper. "She said that after she died, the Gods of Raj carried her here to this hall, then left her."

"The Gods of Raj!" Skylan grew more and more perplexed. Was Joabis conspiring with the Gods of Raj?

"Whoever brought us," Keeper added, "Sigurd is right. We cannot leave. We have tried."

Hefting an axe, he pointed to great gouges in the log wall.

"We even tried to crawl out through the roof, but it is too far above us," Keeper added, glancing up at the ceiling that seemed as high as heaven.

"We are prisoners of Joabis," Sigurd said bitterly.

"But why did he bring you here? What does he want with you and all the other Vindrasi warriors? And what do Vindrash and the Gods of Raj have to do with this?"

"What does it matter? There's nothing we can do." Sigurd gloomily shook his head.

Skylan pondered. "Are all those here warriors?"

"All warriors," Keeper confirmed.

"Joabis said you were wrecking the place," said Skylan, looking at the overturned tables, upended benches, broken crockery, and pools of spilled ale. "I see he was right about that."

"All those here are enemies. The ogres hate the Cyclopes and the Vindrasi hate us. We exchanged insults, then fell to fighting," Keeper admitted. "Battle is thirsty work, however. Joabis brought in barrels of ale and we declared a truce and started drinking."

"And kept drinking," said Sigurd. "At least, for a time, we forget we are prisoners."

Skylan thought this over.

"Find the others and see to it they're sober," he told Sigurd.

"Where are you going?" Sigurd demanded.

Skylan looked grim. "To have a talk with Joabis."

R eaching the door, Skylan eyed it warily, fearing that it might suddenly vanish, trapping him here with the others. The door stayed where it was, however, and he was vastly relieved to be able to push it open and walk out into the sunshine.

He was accosted by a group of revelers the moment he stepped outside. Men draped their arms around his shoulders, hailing him as if they were brothers. Women offered him ale and wine and kisses.

"Where is Joabis, friends?" Skylan asked in good-natured tones, thinking it best if he played along. "I need to speak with him."

No one seemed to know. Some said he was here. Others said he was there. One woman said she thought she had seen him enter the shrine to pray.

"Pray?" Skylan said, interested. "To what god?"

"Why, Joabis, of course," the woman returned, laughing.

Only Joabis would pray to himself, Skylan thought.

The revelers offered to take him to the shrine, which they said was on a remote part of the island. As they shoved their way through streets thronged with merrymaking souls, Skylan wondered that such constant reveling didn't grow wearing after a time.

Leaving the village behind, they walked past fields of barley and wheat. Skylan was surprised to see people working among the plants.

"So people actually work on this isle?" he asked.

"I wouldn't call it work," said one of the women, who had been trying to persuade Skylan to forget about Joabis. "Everyone here does what they love to do best."

By this time most of the revelers had abandoned him for more pleasurable pursuits. Those few who remained took him to a grove of immense spruce trees.

"The shrine is in a garden and the garden is in the grove," the revelers told him.

Skylan thanked them and the revelers laughingly bid him farewell and went back to the party.

Skylan could find no path, and had to thrust his way through the spreading tree branches. He tried to move silently, but that proved impossible. Dead needles crunched underfoot, sticks snapped, and limbs rustled. Clad in his heavy armor, he was hot and sweating. Branches hit him in the face, needles stuck his flesh. He had begun to think he might be trapped forever in this forest when it came to an end.

Parting the branches, he saw a garden of such beauty that he stopped to stare, enthralled. He had not known so many different types of flowers existed in the world. Bees droned among the fragrant blossoms, birds sang in the trees. Paths of crushed marble wound among the flower beds, sparkling in the sunlight.

Joabis stood in the midst of the flowers, holding a sword in his shaking hand.

"Stop right there, whoever you are!" he cried, his voice quivering. "Don't come any closer."

"It's me. Skylan Ivorson."

Raising his hands, Skylan emerged from the shadow of the pine trees.

"Who were you expecting, Joabis?" Skylan asked. "Aelon?"

At the sound of the name, the god began to tremble. Throwing the sword to the ground, he sank onto a marble bench and groaned.

"What do you know?"

"Nothing for certain," said Skylan. "I know enough to know that you've been lying to me, however, so I suggest you tell me the truth."

"What about?" Joabis asked, mopping his head with the sleeve of his shirt.

"The warriors," said Skylan, drawing steadily nearer. "The Vindrasi, the ogres, and the Cyclopes. All those you are keeping prisoner in the Chief's Hall."

"They're not prisoners," Joabis said, trying to look Skylan in the eye and failing. "They can leave whenever they want."

"There's no door!" Skylan said through gritted teeth.

"You got out," Joabis mumbled.

"Because I am not dead. Because I am not in thrall to you or Vindrash or the Gods of Raj!"

Joabis flinched. "Keep your voice down."

Skylan stood over Joabis, glaring at him. "Tell me what is going on. Tell me what has you so frightened you're about to piss your pants. Tell me why these warriors are here. Tell me why you brought *me* here or I will shout to Torval that you are a traitor, that you are conspiring with our enemies!"

"No, no, no, no!" Joabis gabbled. "It's not what you think!"

"Then tell me."

"I'll be breaking a promise to Vindrash," Joabis quavered, backing up a step. "A sacred vow."

"You can break a vow or I can break your head," said Skylan. "If it is any comfort, I think I know the truth already."

Joabis heaved a doleful sigh. "Come with me."

He set out along one of the paths, indicating that Skylan should accompany him.

"This better not be a trick," Skylan warned.

"No trick," said Joabis wearily. "I'm through with tricks."

The path led to the center of the garden, to a small longhouse made of timber that reminded Skylan of the Hall of the Gods in his own village. The longhouse was well kept, lovingly tended. Joabis opened the door. The interior was in shadow and smelled of cedar and roses. Joabis paused, waiting for Skylan to enter.

"You first," said Skylan, resting his hand on the hilt of his sword.

Joabis inclined his head and walked inside. Skylan followed more slowly, remaining near the door, keeping it open to let in the sunlight.

A statue of Joabis, carved out of marble and looking very sleek and regal in festive garments, stood in the back of the hall. The marble god was holding a marble mug in one hand and a sheaf of marble barley in another and was wearing a marble sword hanging from a marble baldric. Joabis regarded his own image with affection.

"I commissioned the statue from a renowned artist in Sinaria. Royal sculptor to the Emperor. Before the arrival of Aelon, of course," Joabis added hurriedly. "This was done during the classical period when—"

Skylan interrupted. "Why bring me here?"

Joabis fetched a deep sigh. "Look at the brooch I am wearing."

The god was apparently referring to a large brooch carved out of marble that adorned his festive raiment. Skylan propped open the door with a rock and drew closer to the statue.

"Don't you see it?" Joabis pressed.

"I see a brooch such as a young girl might wear," said Skylan, adding drily, "It would look well on a young girl."

Joabis hesitated, then, seeming to steel himself to bold action, he reached out his hand and touched the brooch.

The marble vanished. Skylan could see now that the brooch was made of rubies set in gold flowers surrounded by golden leaves. In the center, a golden dragon wrapped its tail around what appeared to be a sliver of bone.

"The fourth Vektan spiritbone," said Skylan.

"You don't seem surprised," said Joabis, disappointed.

"I'm not," said Skylan. "Your dragonship wasn't raided by Hevis looking for jewels. Your crew wouldn't have been afraid of Hevis or any other god of the Vindrasi. The souls would be afraid of Aelon. That was the god who searched your ship and there could be only one object in your possession the god sought. What I don't understand is why would Vindrash give the spiritbone to a drunken sot?"

"Vindrash thought the spiritbone would be safe with me. After all, who would ever think to look for something this valuable here on the Isle of Revels?"

"Aelon apparently," said Skylan in grim tones. "And the god is coming to claim it."

He watched the sunlight glimmer in the heart of the rubies, warm as blood, and suddenly everything made sense.

"*This* is the reason you are keeping my men and the other warriors here," he said. "*This* is why you wanted *me* here. You are afraid Aelon will attack and you have surrounded yourself with warriors. Why not just take the spiritbone to Torval for safekeeping?"

"No one except Vindrash is supposed to know I have it. After Hevis betrayed his trust and summoned the Vektan dragon and killed all those people, Vindrash made all of us who have the spiritbones in our possession swear an oath of secrecy. As for taking it to Torval, I don't dare risk moving it for fear Aelon would catch me," Joabis added in plaintive tones. "The god would kill to get it."

"What you say makes sense," said Skylan. "I knew about the oath."

"I brought all these dead warriors here," Joabis continued dolefully. "I hoped they would help me, but all they do is drink my ale and fight."

Skylan snorted. "You throw humans, ogres, and Cyclopes together, of course they will fight. But you didn't do this alone. The ogres say their gods brought them. What have the Gods of Raj got to do with this?" He frowned at Joabis. "Are you such a coward that you conspire with our enemies?"

"The Gods of Raj hate Aelon as much as we do," said Joabis. "At first they thought they could coexist with Aelon. The god promised to let them have their own followers, but he broke his promise. Priests of Aelon are in ogre and Cyclopes lands, trying to convert people and demanding that they pay tribute to Sinaria."

"What did you promise the Gods of Raj in return for their help? Do they know about the spiritbones?"

"No, no, of course not," said Joabis hastily. "I didn't promise them anything. And I have kept the location of the spiritbone a secret."

"How did Aelon find out about it, then?"

"I don't know!" Joabis cried. "Does it matter now? You have to help me stop Aelon!"

"Me? What do you expect me to do?" Skylan demanded. "I cannot fight a god!"

"Let me explain. I was going to talk to Torval about the warriors," said Joabis. "I knew he would rant and rave and make me grovel, as he always does, so imagine my joy when I saw you standing in front of his Hall. 'I don't need Torval,' I said to myself. 'Skylan Ivorson is a mighty warrior, a Chief of Chiefs! He will be perfect!'"

"Perfect for what?" Skylan asked suspiciously.

"To lead my army," said Joabis.

"Army!" Skylan repeated, gaping at him. "You don't have an army! What you have is a bunch of humans, ogres, and Cyclopes who have been fighting ever since they arrived. The only reason they stopped was because they were bored with cracking heads and decided to get drunk. Once they sober up, they'll be back at each other's throats. I can't help you. Go back to Torval. Throw yourself on his mercy."

Joabis groaned and sank down at the foot of the statue. Putting his head in his hands, he groaned again.

"You are right. I am lost. I will keep my bargain. When your wife arrives, you may leave with her."

Joabis lifted his head slightly, peeped out between his fingers. "I only hope your beautiful wife doesn't meet with Aelon and his warriors. I would not want Aelon to find her or the other three spiritbones . . ."

Skylan glared at the god, so angry that he couldn't speak or even breathe for a moment. He clenched his hands into fists. Joabis jumped to his feet and began backing away from him.

"You can't blame me! *You* told your wife to follow us here," Joabis protested, adding slyly, "Now I guess you'll *have* to fight . . ."

Skylan drew in a seething breath, trying to keep from throttling the god and choking the immortal life from his fat body.

"Very well. I will fight your battle for you, but I have conditions."

"Name them," said Joabis.

"First, you must give Aylaen the spiritbone."

"She can take it!" Joabis cried. "Torval knows I don't want it. I will be glad to be rid of the damn thing."

"Second, you must give me my life back."

"Done!" Joabis said immediately. "Provided Aelon doesn't kill you."

Skylan ignored that last remark. "Third, you must return the lives of my warriors and the ogres and the Cyclopes who agree to fight for you."

"Certainly, certainly. Do you think I want these brutes on my isle slitting throats and bashing heads? They're ruining my afterlife! Wait," Joabis added as Skylan started to leave. "I want you to have this."

Joabis indicated the marble sword on the statue with his fingers.

"Take it," said Joabis.

"A sword made of stone," said Skylan.

"Just . . . take it."

Skylan, extremely doubtful, grasped the cold marble hilt only to find, to his astonishment, that he was holding a sword made of steel, one of the finest he had ever seen. The blade had been forged with a pattern in the steel as of running water and was sharp and unblemished. The grip was of leather bound with gold wire. The pommel served as a counterweight. Skylan tested it. The balance was perfect.

"I have never seen a sword as fine as this," said Skylan, marveling.

"Beautiful, isn't it? It is very old," said Joabis. He regarded the sword with a wistful pride. "The sword comes from a different time, a different world. It was mine once, long ago."

Skylan regarded the god in astonishment.

"I was not always what I am now," said Joabis. "I was a valiant warrior who fought at Torval's side many eons ago when we were young. For we gods were young, once. We were going to do great things. Our world was going to be fruitful, blooming, prosperous, shine as a jewel in the heavens. Our people would thrive and prosper, live forever in peace . . ."

"What happened?" Skylan asked.

Joabis shrugged. "Torval wearied of peace and fostered a race of warriors. Vindrash enjoyed being worshipped by dragons. I had my drink and my gaming, Hevis had his scheming and conniving. Skoval and Aylis quarreled. Sund went mad . . ."

Joabis sighed. "I know you despise me, perhaps with good reason. I hope this will help change your opinion of me."

Skylan wasn't sure how to react. He tried to picture Joabis as a gallant warrior and failed utterly. He watched the sunlight gild the blade gold.

"Thank you, Joabis," Skylan said at last. "I cannot think well of you, but maybe I will not think so ill. I will name the blade 'Godrage' in your honor."

Joabis gave him a fine fur-lined leather sheath and a belt for the sword. Skylan thought the tooled leather belt seemed familiar. Looking back at the statue, he saw the marble sword it had once worn was gone. The ruby and gold brooch was once again cold, white marble.

"You had best make haste," Joabis added. "I have it on good authority that Aelon will attack tomorrow at dawn."

Skylan gaped at the god. "Dawn! I can't—"

"Good luck," said Joabis, patting Skylan on the arm.

The next moment Skylan was standing in the hall, in the midst of a pitched battle, watching the warriors of his new army slaughter each other.

Raegar rode his chariot in a grand procession from his palace to
Aelon's Temple to attend the much heralded audience with the
Stormlords. As part of his preparations for declaring war upon these
people, he had sent his spies to live among them and spread lies and
rumors about them to his own people, portraying them as godless
unbelievers who planned to use their fouls magicks to destroy the
empire.

Priests of Aelon harangued against the Stormlords in the daily ser-
vices. Oran's princes and kings sent ships, soldiers, and gold to their
emperor. Few had ever heard of the Stormlords until a few weeks ago,
but now they were ready to expunge them from the face of the world.

Raegar made the day of the Stormlords' payment of their tribute a
holiday, asking all to witness his dealings with the dreaded foe. The
people filled the streets and cheered him and his soldiers, occasionally breaking through the lines formed by armed guards along the
route to try to touch him for luck, or to beg him for his blessing. No
Sinarian ruler had ever been so popular—among the people.

Raegar noticed a few sour faces and caught dark looks from some
in the priesthood. He had heard their complaints that he was acting as though he were a god, encouraging the people to worship him
and not Aelon. Raegar ignored them. Let the priests whine. He was
certain of Aelon's love. The reports he had received from his spies
about the Stormlords had been of immense value.

Raegar was in an exultant mood when he reached the Temple of

Aelon. He had purposely arrived late, intending to keep the Storm-lords' delegation waiting on his pleasure and giving them a chance to see how much his people loved him.

The audience chamber was crowded. He had invited delegates from courts throughout Oran as well as all the wealthy and influential people of Sinaria. Raegar noted with pleasure how members of the no-bility crowded around him, fawned over him, laughed at his jests. He remembered a time not so long ago when these same rich and powerful people had mocked him, insulted him, terming him slave, barbarian.

He was gracious to them, but he let them know with a cool glance in the midst of some hilarity that he had not forgotten. He liked to see them grow pale, hear their nervous laughter, keep them guessing, on edge. They would be all the more eager to please him.

He walked at a leisurely pace through the crowd, making his way to the golden throne, which had been hauled out of the palace and placed on a hastily built dais inside the temple, a move that infuriated the priests. They fully expected Aelon to punish such blasphemy, but thus far the throne had neither gone up in flames nor sunk into the floor. In fact, the rays of light coming from the skylight in the ceiling known as Aelon's Eye seemed to cause the throne to shine with a holy radiance.

He had been searching the crowd for the delegation of Storm-lords and not paying much attention to anything else, when he hap-pened to glance at the dais and saw something amiss: two thrones stood there, when he had specifically asked for only his own. The second throne was for his wife, the empress, a throne that had stood empty for many weeks. He had made the excuse that Treia was feel-ing too unwell to attend court functions. The truth was, he had not told her about them.

He turned to speak to his aide-de-camp, a soldier named Eolus, who had once been a slave himself, until he had escaped his master and run off to join the army. Finding that they had this in common, Raegar had promoted the man to commander and placed him in charge of his guard, as well as making him his confidential assistant.

"What is the throne for the empress doing here?" Raegar demanded. "I gave orders for them to bring only mine. The empress's condition is far too delicate for her to attend."

"I do not know, sir," Eolus replied. "But I will find out."

He disappeared into the crowd, returning in a few moments with information.

"It seems the empress herself gave orders to bring the throne."

Raegar had to swallow his anger and force a smile, as though this news pleased him beyond measure. "I hope my beloved wife does not overtax herself," was all he said.

He was taking his seat on his throne when there came a murmur of admiration and the heads of the crowd turned to witness the arrival of the empress.

Accompanied by her own bodyguards, Treia walked slowly, her hand on her belly, mindful of her dignity. As Raegar had done, Treia paused to greet those she knew. Women cooed and asked to feel the baby kick. Treia responded with pride and delight.

Raegar descended from the dais to assist her, knowing the crowd would like it. He took her hand, turning away from her, scarcely glancing at her. Ever since he had heard about her promise of a sacrifice to Hevis, he was disgusted by the sight of her.

"My dear, you look radiant!" he said loudly, for the benefit of the crowd. "How is our child?"

"Your son thrives, my husband," said Treia.

Together they walked up the three steps toward the thrones.

"Why have you come?" Raegar asked in a low voice.

"I was asked to attend this important audience," Treia replied.

"I did not—" Raegar began.

"No, you did not," Treia interrupted him. "But another did."

She put her hand to a necklace she wore. The gesture drew Raegar's eye. She was wearing a necklace made of golden serpents twined together, distinctive, easily recognizable. Raegar knew very well who had worn that necklace last, and whatever words he had been about to say rattled in his throat.

He assisted Treia to her throne, then sat down himself. He searched the crowd, frowned, and summoned Laurentius, the new Priest-General, the head of the Warrior Priests, a rank Raegar had once held prior to becoming emperor.

The priests chose their own leader and they had selected a man guaranteed to displease Raegar. Laurentius had been furious when

Raegar, starting to distrust the priests, had removed them from positions of power in the military.

"Where are the Stormlords?" Raegar asked, searching the crowd and not finding them. "They are late."

"I cannot say, Your Imperial Highness," Laurentius replied, smiling slightly. "Perhaps they have decided not to attend."

Raegar saw the smile and was angered. If, after all his elaborate plans, the Stormlords did not show up, he would look like a fool. Having planned on forcing them to await his pleasure, he was left to wait for them.

He had no idea what he was going to do. The Stormlords had been paying tribute to Oran for as long as anyone could remember. The idea that they might not come had never occurred to him. Raegar was starting to sweat when Treia touched his hand and nodded toward the temple entrance.

Raegar had never before met with the Stormlords. The last time they had come with their tribute, they had presented it to the late empress. He had been present, observing them from a distance, and he immediately recognized the two elderly men who had last brought the tribute.

Reputed to be extraordinarily rich and powerful, the wizards were tall, nearly Raegar's height, and wore long cloaks of black velvet trimmed in gold braid. Golden braided tassels hung from the tips of the black cowls that covered their heads. Beneath their cloaks, their robes were spun of some sort of golden thread that glistened in the sunlight.

Coming to stand before Raegar, the wizards removed the cowls. The men were clean shaven. They wore their gray hair in two thick braids bound with leather. Their faces, seamed with age, were grim, resolute.

When Raegar had last seen these two, coming before the empress, they had brought with them a large wooden chest filled with gold and jewels. They now stood before Raegar empty-handed.

Raegar was pleased. After a bad start, this meeting was going well. They were playing into his hands.

Glowering at them, he said angrily, "You arrive late. Our time is valuable and we have been kept waiting and for what? I see no tribute, no chest full of gold and jewels."

The Stormlords regarded him with the expressions of men who have found dung on their shoes, then they both clapped their hands. In response, an enormous chest made of polished wood, decorated with gold and jewels, appeared on the floor in front of them, seeming to drop out of the air.

The watching crowd gasped and murmured.

Treia cast a startled glance at Raegar, who glowered at them. He was being upstaged. He began to applaud, loudly and mockingly.

"Well done, gentlemen. All of us enjoy a good show. Priest-General, open the chest."

Laurentius hurried over to the chest, motioning one of the other priests to help him. Folding their arms, the Stormlords waited in silence. The box was large and so elaborately decorated that it took Laurentius a moment to find the clasps. Raegar could only imagine the vast amount of gold and silver it must contain. And however much it was, he was going to ask them for more.

He leaned forward, eager to see the wealth, as did Treia, her eyes sparkling. The crowd pressed near to view such a wondrous sight. The two Stormlords stood unmoving.

Laurentius and his fellow priest together lifted the heavy lid, looked eagerly into the chest, and stiffened in shock. Treia gasped and put her hand to her mouth and averted her eyes. Raegar gazed into the box and his stomach turned. Instead of seeing shining mounds of gold and silver, he looked on the mummified remains of two men, both of them wearing the robes of priests of Aelon.

The skin was stretched tight over the skulls, but there was enough left of the two men that Raegar recognized the priests he had sent to spy on the Stormlords. The faces of the corpses were frozen in terror, contorted in agony.

Word spread rapidly through the crowd. People began to cry out in shock and dismay and anger, and started shoving and jostling, trying to get a closer look.

"Silence!" Raegar thundered.

The crowd quieted, though there were angry mutterings. Rising to his feet, Raegar glared down at the Stormlords. "These men were holy priests of Aelon, to be treated with respect!"

"These men were spies masquerading as priests," said one of the Stormlords.

"By the terms of the treaty we pay tribute to live our lives in peace," said the other. "By sending your spies among us, you have broken the treaty."

"You murdered these men!" Raegar said harshly.

"We did not touch them," said the first Stormlord. "They brought their fate on themselves. They were warned to keep out of certain areas that are guarded by magical defenses. They did not heed our warnings, and death was the result."

"You lie!" Raegar roared. "The priests discovered your secret. We have their reports. You found out and you killed them. We know how to enter your hidden city and, by the might of Aelon, we will tear it down stone by stone and see the blood of your people running in the gutters!"

Raegar detected a flicker of uncertainty, unease in one of them. The flicker was gone in an instant.

"We return their bodies as a courtesy," said one of the Stormlords. "We will no longer pay tribute to Oran."

The Stormlords drew their cowls over their heads, then turned their backs on Raegar to face the crowd that was now blocking their way out of the temple. The two men said no word, but stood calmly, their hands folded in their sleeves, their eyes dark and shadowed. They began to walk toward the temple doors and the crowd, as though spellbound, parted to make way for them.

Raegar knew he should do something to stop the murdering wizards, but he was shaking with fury, so choked by rage he could not speak. Treia saw his red mottled face and the foam flecking his lips and leaned near to whisper.

"You cannot let them insult you like this! Order the guards to seize them! Send *their* heads back to *their* people!"

"Guards!" Raegar shouted. "Bar the doors! Arrest those men!"

His shout broke the spell. Guards shut the doors and stood before them, spears leveled. Raegar's bodyguards and the Warrior Priests drew their swords and ran after the Stormlords while bystanders closed in around the two wizards, brandishing their fists. The Stormlords fell beneath the onslaught. Raegar watched with satisfaction.

"Don't kill them! I want to see them hang!" he called.

Commander Eolus and his soldiers charged into the mob, striking with the flat of their blades to drive them off their prey and came upon a tangled, bloody heap of men pummeling each other. The guards dragged the combatants apart.

Underneath, Eolus found two black cloaks trimmed in gold, trampled and torn, lying on the temple floor. He jabbed his sword into one of the cloaks and lifted it up for Raegar to see. An awed and frightened hush fell over the crowd.

Raegar looked at the empty floor and then back at Eolus.

"Where are they?" Raegar demanded, feeling his skin crawl.

No one had an answer. Eolus hastily shook the cloak off his sword and left it lying beside the other one. The crowd backed away.

Raegar looked at the doors, but they remained closed with soldiers standing guard. There was nowhere to hide. The two thrones, the dais, and the chest containing the bodies of the priests were the only objects on the temple floor. The wizards were taller than most of those present, and with their pale skin, long gray braids, and shining golden robes, they could not very well lose themselves in the crowd of short, swarthy Sinarians.

"They must be here!" Raegar cried. "Find them!"

Some of the Warrior Priests, led by Laurentius, searched the temple, including his own office, the chamber of the Watchers, and even the treasure room, while others ordered people to exit one at a time and took a good look at each as they walked out the doors.

Raegar sent Eolus to call out the city guard, ordering them to blockade the harbor and search every ship. Guardsmen combed the city, going from house to house, without result. No one had seen the Stormlords arrive, apparently, for no ship had brought them. No one had seen them depart.

The Stormlords had vanished without a trace.

Raegar ordered Treia's guards to accompany her back to the palace, then he went to the Watchers to ask for the final written account of the reports the spies had sent back. After that, he retired to his office in the temple to read them.

He went over them several times; he had learned to read only late in life and he wanted to make certain he understood. Throwing them back on the desk, he began pacing the room, muttering to himself.

"The priests claim they found a traitor, one of the Stormlords. This man told them the secret, how to enter the hidden city. He provided

directions on how to remove the magical traps. Why would the priests lie?"

"The priests told the truth," said Aelon.

Raegar turned to find her seated at his desk, reading the reports.

"So it was the Stormlords who lied," he said. "They did murder them."

Aelon looked up from her reading. "The Stormlords are a peace-loving people who believe that no mortal has the right to take the life of another. Their defensive magicks are not lethal."

"I beg your pardon, revered Aelon, if I seem obtuse, but if the Stormlords did not kill the priests and neither did the magic, who did? Was it the traitor?"

Aelon dropped the report and languidly rose to her feet. "If you must know, Raegar, I killed them."

Raegar gaped at her. "Your own priests?"

She shrugged. "They grew careless. The Stormlords began to suspect them and searched their quarters where they found these same documents and drawings. They arrested the priests. I feared they would talk, and we couldn't take that chance."

Raegar tried to conceal his shock, but apparently he failed.

"Oh, don't look so horrified, Raegar!" Aelon said in scathing tones. "How many men have *you* killed in my name?"

Raegar licked dry lips. What she said was true. Still, the men he had killed had been enemies. They hadn't worshipped him, trusted in him . . .

"Revered Aelon, I didn't mean—"

She silenced him with an irate glance. "And what possessed you to tell the Stormlords about the priests' report?"

"I am sorry, revered Aelon," said Raegar. "I was angry. I saw the bodies . . . I knew these men . . ."

His voice trailed off.

Aelon glared at him, then she sighed. "Perhaps, after all, your indiscretion was for the best. The Stormlords are afraid, and frightened people make mistakes. As for the traitor, he will be in contact with you. His name is Baldev. He is a powerful man; one of their governors—those they call 'Lords of the Storm.' Unlike his fellows, he is not a pacifist. He believes the Stormlords should exert their power in this world. He could prove to very useful to us."

Raegar could hear mournful chanting outside the office, and a shuffling sound. He opened the door a crack to watch a procession of priests walking slowly and solemnly past the office, bearing caskets containing the two corpses. He waited in silence until the priests and their sorrowful burden had proceeded down the hallway. Shaken, Raegar hurriedly closed the door.

"The people will be clamoring for war," he said.

"Then by all means, give it to them," said Aelon. "That was our goal all along."

"Yes," said Raegar.

He kept his back to her, so that she would not see his face. He had been eager for war. Reading the reports of the priests, he had been exultant. He knew the secret of the hidden cities, he knew how to defeat the Stormlords. He no longer felt the same thrill, however.

Aelon walked over to him, put her arms around him.

"Don't sulk, Raegar. I did what I had to do. Look at me."

Trembling at her touch, Raegar slowly turned to face her.

"Our people are enraged. They will give you anything! And so will I, my love," said Aelon softly. "You will march at the head of an army that numbers in the tens of thousands."

Her beauty, her words, her touch rekindled the fire within him. He saw thousands of soldiers clashing their swords against their shields, calling out his name. He saw walls falling as the stones from his war machines crashed into them.

"Assembling such an army will take time," he said. "We have the ships, but I did not expect to sail until spring. I don't see how we can be ready."

Aelon gazed into his eyes, pierced him to the soul.

"Have you so little faith in me?" she asked him. "The world will stand in awe of your might. And so will I."

Raegar seized hold of her and kissed her and, to his astonishment, she let him. He would have kept on kissing her, but she slid out of his grasp.

"You must be faithful to your wife," said Aelon.

"So you keep telling me," Raegar growled.

"Our time will come. Be patient. For now, I must leave you," she said. "I have located your cousin, Skylan, and the fourth spiritbone,

and I have found his wife, the Kai Priestess, who has the other three. You will bring me the fifth. And now . . . your wife is looking for you."

Aelon left him. Raegar stood quite still after she had gone, lost in his thoughts. He was roused by a knock at the door. Opening it, he found Treia.

"I thought I would find you here. Who were you talking to?" she asked suspiciously. "I heard a woman's voice."

Raegar glared at her. Treia looked particularly unlovely at this moment.

"You are not supposed to be in this part of the temple, woman," he told her coldly. Turning away, he strode over to the desk, pretended to be searching through some papers. "Go back to your chambers."

Instead of obeying, Treia followed him into the room and shut the door.

"I will summon the guards—" he began, then he saw the golden serpents on her necklace fix him with their sparkling eyes.

"What do you want?" he asked.

"What are you doing hiding out in this office?" she countered. "People are looking for you! Important people!"

"I am busy," he said curtly. "If you must know, we are going to war."

"Good," said Treia approvingly. "Aelon will be pleased. You have all winter to prepare—"

"Now!" said Raegar, his voice grating. "This instant."

He didn't really mean that. He needed a few weeks, despite Aelon's promise of a miracle. Still, his words sounded well and they certainly left Treia speechless.

"Aelon has been insulted," said Raegar, his voice harsh. "Her priests murdered. The murderers will be punished."

"My love, you can't sail now!" Treia protested. "The storms of autumn are coming. The seas will be rough."

"Aelon has promised us a smooth voyage," said Raegar.

Treia drew in a deep breath. "Then I am coming with you. I can summon the Dragon Fala. You need me."

Raegar had to admit that was true. Fala was a wayward beast who did not respect him and paid little heed to him.

He shook his head. "I cannot permit you to come. The voyage would be too dangerous for both you and our son."

Treia came close to him and clasped her hand over his. She looked up into his eyes and said softly, just for the two of them to hear, "Our son is Vindrasi! He will be born at sea, born to flame and blood and battle! What better or more fitting birthright?"

Raegar gazed at Treia. Her belly pressed against him, and he could feel his son kicking lustily. He remembered now why he had once loved her. He kissed her.

"Start packing."

Night fell on the Isle of Revels. Aylis, the Sun Goddess, had fled, leaving Skylan to think she was as disgusted by the sight inside the hall as he was. Torches, mounted in iron sconces on the walls, burned in a desultory manner, creating more smoke than light and leaving the cavernous interior of the building in darkness.

The fighting had devolved into a drunken brawl. Warriors staggered about, swinging their weapons wildly, spilling more ale than blood. Eventually, when it grew too dark to see, the fighting petered out. All Skylan could hear were moans, retching, and cursing.

Taking a torch from the wall, he made his way among the upended tables and broken benches, stepping over drunks, heading for the corner where he had left Sigurd and Keeper with orders to find the rest of his friends.

He located Sigurd, who had been sleeping with his head on the table. Wakened by the torchlight, he squinted, trying to see.

"Who the devil is that?" he mumbled.

"It's me. Skylan."

Sigurd grunted. "You came back." He sounded surprised.

"I told you I would," said Skylan, annoyed. "Where are the others?"

"They're here," said Sigurd. He jerked a thumb toward his fellows.

Skylan placed the torch in a rusty sconce on the wall near the table and grimly regarded the warriors who were supposed to go up against the army of a god.

Grimuir had passed out and was sprawled on the floor beneath a bench. He was Sigurd's best friend and supporter; the two even looked much alike, with black hair and beards. Erdmun was green around the nose and mouth, but at least he was upright. His older brother, Bjorn, sitting beside him, was the most sober of the lot. He smiled when he saw Skylan, who was pleased to see him. They were the same age, and Bjorn had been his friend in days when everyone else had seemed to desert him. Both brothers had fair hair and both looked defeated and dejected.

Keeper rose from another table where he had been talking to some of his fellow ogres and came to greet Skylan. Between them, they managed to lift Grimuir up off the floor and heave him onto a bench, propping him up with his back against the wall.

"What did Joabis say?" Keeper asked. "Will he free us?"

Grimuir raised his head to fix his bleary eyes on Skylan. Erdmun swallowed hard to try to keep from retching. Bjorn patted his brother's shoulder. Sigurd belched.

"He has promised to return our lives on one condition," said Skylan.

The others exchanged grim glances.

"What is that condition?" Sigurd growled.

"Joabis is in peril, like the other Vindrasi gods. He fears his island will come under attack, which is why he brought all these warriors here. He wants us to fight for him."

"Fight? For Joabis?" Sigurd grunted. "Who are we fighting? A fearsome host of baby chicks?"

Grimuir made cheeping sounds and flapped his arms like wings and Sigurd roared with laughter.

Skylan waited until their mirth had subsided, then said, "We will be facing the army of Aelon."

The others stared at him, frowning, uncomprehending.

"Aelon?" Keeper repeated. "Fight a god?"

"And a god's army," Bjorn said. "What sort of army?"

"Winged serpents as big as rivers. If you cut off the head, two sprout in its place. And hellkites. According to Garn, these are the souls of men who were so cruel and depraved no god except Aelon would take them."

Erdmun got up the from the table and staggered off, clutching his stomach. They could hear him heaving. When he returned, he was quite pale and looked very miserable.

"Serpents and hellkites." Grimuir repeated, then shrugged. "Still, I could use a good fight. I grow bored slaying ogres."

He winked at Keeper, who said calmly, "As for us ogres, we never tire of killing humans."

The others laughed. Skylan did not.

"What's wrong, Skylan?" Bjorn asked. "Why the dark look?"

"There is more you must know. If anyone dies by the sword of a hellkite, Aelon will claim his soul," said Skylan. "Garn told me when I saw him in the Hall of Heroes."

"Torval would not allow another god to take souls that belong to him," said Bjorn.

"Torval and the other gods and heroes are fighting their own battles in heaven," said Skylan. "They can do nothing to help us."

The others stared at him, then glanced at one another.

"From way you talk, it seems they are losing," Erdmun said gloomily.

Skylan flushed in anger. "I did not say that."

"But it's true," said Grimuir.

Skylan was silent.

"Then Joabis be damned," Sigurd said in grim tones. "Let him fight his own battles."

"I agree, Skylan," said Keeper. "This god of yours brought us here against our will and now wants us to fight Aelon. I don't like it."

"Joabis was not the only god involved in this," said Skylan. "You said yourself Gods of Raj brought you here. They have joined forces with him. I told you. Joabis promises to give us back our lives—"

"And we all know what a promise from the God of Liars is worth—goat piss!" said Grimuir, sneering.

"This is one promise he will keep. I will see to that," said Skylan, resting his hand on the hilt of his sword. "And Torval will back us."

"If Torval still lives," Sigurd muttered.

They sat in silence, all except Bjorn, who had been mulling things over. "I have a question. Why is Aelon attacking Joabis? What threat to Aelon is a god who spends eternity swilling ale?"

Skylan had known this question would come up and he had wondered how to answer. He trusted his own men and he trusted Keeper, but he worried about those who might be out there in the smoke-filled darkness, eavesdropping. He was going to ask his friends to wager their very souls on this battle, and they deserved to know the truth. Seating himself at the table, he motioned for them to draw near.

Keeping his voice low, he spoke: "Vindrash gave Joabis one of the spiritbones. It is hidden on this isle. Aelon discovered the secret and now he is searching for it. Aylaen has three of the other spiritbones. Joabis has promised to give us this one in return for our protection and we know where to find the fifth. Once we have all five, we can use them to drive out Aelon and restore our gods to power."

"What if someone asks us why Aelon is attacking this wretched god?" Erdmun wondered. "What do we say?"

"The truth. Joabis may be a drunk and a liar, but he is Vindrasi," said Skylan proudly. "He is one of us. Of course, Aelon fears him."

The others grinned and nodded.

"I will put it to you plainly," Skylan continued. "Joabis says Aelon will attack at dawn. We can spend the remainder of eternity here, drinking and heaving up our guts, or we can fight for our gods."

"A worthy wager," said Grimuir. "I'll take it. What about you, Sigurd?"

"I can fight a hundred of these hellkites single-handed," Sigurd replied. "But I'll need help to destroy an army."

"I'll fight," said Bjorn. "And so will my brother."

Erdmun jumped up and ran from the table again.

"Keeper, will the ogres fight?" Skylan asked. "Tell them Joabis and the Gods of Raj have promised to restore their lives."

"I will answer for them," said Keeper. "They will fight."

"Good. What about the Cyclopes? I have never met a Cyclopes. What are they like? According to legend, they are humans with three eyes. Is that true?"

"We have no idea," said Bjorn. "We have never seen one ourselves. They fight the ogres in a different part of the hall. We know they are here only because Keeper told us about them."

Skylan looked dubious. "They are in this hall and you've never seen them?"

"It's a big hall," said Sigurd defensively.

"Big as eternity," Keeper affirmed.

Skylan sighed. "Very well. Go talk to them, Keeper. Tell them that I need to confer with their war chief—"

"They will be a problem," said Keeper. "The Cyclopes have no war chiefs. They are fiercely independent. No Cyclopes tells another what to do. In battle, each warriors acts as he sees the need to act."

At first Skylan thought the ogre was jesting, and he was annoyed. They had no time for jests. Then he realized with shock that Keeper was serious.

"No war chief?" said Skylan. "Without a chief, every fight would end in chaos. How do these Cyclopes form a shield wall?"

"They do not fight in a shield wall," said Keeper. "You must understand. Cyclopes consider warfare wasteful. They can fight, if they are forced to do so, but they have no love for battle. Their tactics are simple. Each knows what to do without being told. Their archers fire from a distance, felling the enemy with arrows, then, once the majority of their foes are dead or wounded, the foot soldiers finish them off with clubs and spears."

Sigurd made a crude derisive noise. Skylan agreed with him.

"These Cyclopes are obviously cowards who fight without honor."

"We might not have honor, Vindrasi, but we Cyclopes have what is more valuable," said a woman, speaking from the darkness. "Common sense."

Sigurd and Bjorn both stood to face the stranger. Grimuir had to shove himself up from the bench, but he managed to get upright, though he swayed on his feet. Skylan rose, his hand on his sword and turned to the speaker.

"Step into the light where I can see you," he said. "What are you doing here? I was told your people stay in the back of the hall."

As the woman came to stand beneath the flaring torch, Skylan and the others stared at her in silence, struck speechless. Perhaps there had been a time far back in Vindrasi history when his people had encountered the race of humans known as Cyclopes. If so, that time was long forgotten.

The woman's skin was black as jet. She had long black hair that she wore in a myriad of small, tightly bound braids. She was slender, long-legged, dressed in a long leather tunic and leather boots. And she had three eyes: two large and lustrous brown eyes, one on either side of her nose where eyes should be, and a third eye, round and white-rimmed with a red iris, in the center of her forehead.

She gazed at them with all three eyes; all three appeared disdainful.

"I heard from the ogres that there was a Vindrasi here who was not dead. I came to see for myself."

"This woman is Dela Eden," said Keeper. "My people would call her a shaman of the Gods of Raj."

He leaned close to whisper in Skylan's ear. "Dela Eden is not a war chief, but as near to the mark as you will come. Her people have chosen her as spokesman. While you talk to her, I will go fetch the ogre godlord and shaman."

As Keeper started to leave, Skylan grabbed hold of him.

"What does she see with that third eye of hers?" Skylan asked uneasily.

Keeper looked at him, astonished, then burst out laughing. "The third eye is not a real eyeball. It is painted on the forehead of every Cyclopes when they reach the age of majority at sixteen."

"We call this eye, 'the world eye,' Vindrasi," said Dela Eden, overhearing. "It gives us the ability to see into hearts and minds."

"Is that true?" Skylan asked Keeper. "Can she see what I am thinking?"

The ogre shrugged. "I do not know from personal experience. Many of our people believe that to be true. You must find out for yourself."

Keeper departed, leaving Skylan and the others with Dela Eden. The torchlight gleamed on round rings of gold that hung from her ears. Her movements were graceful and sinuous. When she walked, she seemed to flow like a wave on the ocean.

He could now see for himself that the third eye was painted in white with a red iris and black pupil on her shining black skin. The technique was remarkable. The eye looked disconcertingly real and Skylan could almost feel it piercing his skull.

"If you want me and my people to join you in battle against the Faceless God, you would do well not to insult us," said Dela Eden. "True, we do not like fighting. No *civilized* race does, but we are not cowards."

She spoke with a slight curl of her lip. Her scornful gaze swept over Sigurd and Grimuir and the others who had ranged themselves around Skylan.

"Our tactics are highly effective, as the ogres know from sad experience," Dela Eden boasted. "You need us in your battle against the Faceless God—"

"Why do you call Aelon by that name?" Skylan asked, interrupting.

"The god wears a thousand faces, appearing to mortals in whatever guise Aelon believes will enable him to control them. The god can be male or female, old or young, man or beast. Aelon came among us as a dragon."

"A dragon?" Skylan was amazed.

"Our people have long revered dragons," Dela Eden explained. "The dragons use the portal in our mountains to travel back to their world, the Realm of Fire. The Faceless God did not fool us, however. We knew the truth at once."

"How?" Skylan asked, skeptical, thinking she was bragging.

Dela Eden grinned and tapped her forehead. "The world eye, Vindrasi. We see the truth about a lot of things."

Skylan had noted that even when Dela Eden turned to look with two eyes at something else, her third eye seemed to be always looking at him. He quickly changed the subject back to a more comfortable topic: war.

"Your tactics may be all that you claim, Dela Eden, but what good are your warriors to me if they will not obey my commands?" Skylan asked.

Dela Eden gave a rippling laugh. "We Cyclopes are not sheep to be driven by the snapping of the dog at our heels. We know what needs to be done in a battle and we do it. For example, our arrows will be particularly effective against the serpents, since these creatures can be killed only by piercing the heart. We also know the secret of making flaming arrows that rain fire down on the heads of our foes."

"You have fought these serpents of Aelon before," said Skylan.

"Never," said Dela Eden. Her third eye seemed to shimmer. "But *you* have fought them."

"You are trying to impress me, no doubt, by pretending you can read my thoughts," said Skylan dismissively, "but you are only repeating what you heard me tell my men about the serpents while you were eavesdropping on us."

Bjorn nudged him in the ribs. "You didn't tell us anything about piercing their hearts. She is reading your thoughts."

"Let her read *my* thoughts," Sigurd growled. "I'm thinking I'm not going anywhere near these three-eyed freaks."

Before Skylan could argue, Keeper arrived with an ogre godlord and his shaman. Skylan was glad to see them. Although they had long been enemies of the Vindrasi, at least they could not see inside his brain. He turned to greet the godlord and the shaman, then stopped to stare.

"I know you!" Skylan exclaimed. "Bear Walker and Raven's-foot!"

The ogre godlord was hard to forget. He was the tallest ogre Skylan had ever seen, standing over eight feet in height, and he wore a distinctive bearskin cloak with the paws as clasps. The shaman was likewise memorable, a skinny ogre with legs like a heron's, who wore a black feather cape and carried a gourd he used to work magic. He had once worked his foul magic on Skylan, stealing the Vektan Torque from him.

The godlord appeared equally amazed to see Skylan. "I remember. You kept the body of our friend, Keeper, on board your ship. You tried to keep our ship from sinking."

"And then the kraken attacked us," said Skylan. "But what are you two doing here in the afterlife? I saved you both from the Aquin prison. The Aquins promised to take you safely to land."

Bear Walker shook his head. "I don't know anything about an Aquin prison. All aboard our ship either drowned or were killed by the kraken. Our bodies lie at the bottom of the ocean."

The shaman squinted at Skylan then turned to the godlord to mutter something Skylan couldn't hear.

"What did he say?" Skylan demanded.

"Raven's-foot says you must have encountered the Gods of Raj. They were testing you. He says you must have passed the gods' test, because when you died they brought you here with the rest of us," said Bear Walker. "Raven's-foot doesn't like you, but since our gods accept you, so will he."

Skylan didn't believe such nonsense. Why would the Gods of Raj test him? He concluded that the ogres were lying. Undoubtedly they didn't want to be beholden to him for saving their lives.

"How did *you* die, Vindrasi?" Bear Walker asked.

Skylan didn't want to take time to explain that he was both dead and not dead. "Never mind. We have more immediate worries. The god Aelon is going to attack this island at dawn. I need all your warriors to help defeat him. Joabis promises that if we defend his island against Aelon, he will give us back our lives."

Raven's-foot drew Bear Walker aside and the two were soon deep in conversation.

Skylan waited impatiently. All he could think about was that Aelon was planning to attack at dawn and Aylaen and the *Venejekar* were sailing ever closer.

"Bear Walker?" he called. "Do you and your ogres stand with us?"

Raven's-foot scowled, but Bear Walker ignored him. "The ogres will stand with you, Vindrasi."

Skylan looked at Dela Eden. "What about the Cyclopes?"

"We will fight *with* you, Skylan Ivorson," Dela Eden answered with a grin and a shake of her head that made her earrings flash. "Just not *for* you."

Skylan turned to Bear Walker and Raven's-foot.

"Tell your people I am grateful to them—" he began.

He was interrupted by the astonishing sight of the hall evaporating around them. Walls disappeared. Tables and mugs and benches vanished, and he was standing on a sandy beach beneath the stars and a black dome of a sky. Keeper and Bear Walker and an army of ogres stood with him, along with his men and Dela Eden with her Cyclopes.

The sky was clear and cloudless. No moon shone this night. Waves lapped on the shore. Men and women were streaming toward them, their voices shrill with panic.

"Aelon is coming!" they cried.

"Where?" Skylan demanded.

They pointed to the east. Skylan could see a fiery glow light the sky. The revelers did not stop, but kept running, racing past Skylan to disappear into a grove of trees that seemed to spring up out of the sand to conceal them.

Skylan watched them flee in disgust. "The glow is only Aylis, the Sun Goddess . . ."

His words trailed off.

"Your goddess is gone," said Dela Eden in grim tones. "She has fled the heavens. The light you see is the New Dawn. Aelon's New Dawn."

A ball of fire, bright and glaring, rose from the sea, heralding the arrival of the Faceless God. Aelon rode in a chariot of burnished gold drawn by four winged serpents. Four more serpents flanked the chariot, their long, sinuous bodies rippling in the air, their silver scales red in the light of the fiery new sun.

He held a shining sword in one hand and a fistful of spears in the other. He flung a spear to the ground, then another and another, splitting the earth, opening huge cracks in the ground. What seemed at first to be hordes of vermin swarmed out of the cracks, then Skylan saw that these were hellkites.

He could not count their numbers.

Skylan watched their ranks grow, then turned his back. "They crawl out of the ground like worms," he said to Bear Walker and Dela Eden. "I have a plan of battle—"

"Good for you, Vindrasi," said Dela Eden, walking off. "I'll be with my people."

"You haven't heard the plan yet!" Skylan said.

"I don't need to," Dela Eden called over her shoulder. "Whatever it is, we know what to do."

Skylan made a mental note to keep well clear of the Cyclopes.

12

Aelon soared above his army in his chariot, bellowing commands to the hellkites below. Their shiny obsidian armor, forged in the bowels of hell, glistened in his light. Armed with spears in their right hands and shields marked with serpents in their left, the hellkites obeyed the god's commands and formed into ranks.

"I was right," said Skylan, watching. "Aelon is not using the shield wall against us."

"The hellkites are forming into phalanxes," said Keeper. "That does not bode well for us."

The hellkites stood shoulder to shoulder, with those in the front row holding a solid wall of shields that protected the men in the rows behind them who were armed with spears and short swords. The ranks of the hellkites increased, forming row after row, bristling with spears. The sheer weight of numbers would break through his defenses.

"The phalanx has a weakness," said Skylan. "Acronis described it to me."

Observing the swelling ranks of the hellkites, Keeper shook his head. "We face an army of the damned led by a god. And you talk of weaknesses. Do you never despair, Skylan?"

"To despair is to lose hope," said Skylan. "So long as I breathe—and even when I don't—I will always have hope."

Skylan formed the Vindrasi warriors into the traditional shield wall comprising warriors standing shoulder to shoulder in long rows. Those in the first row were armed with battle axes, war hammers, swords. Each warrior carried his shield to protect his neighbor, standing with shields overlapping.

The warriors in the back rows were armed with spears, as many as each man could hold, in addition to battle axe, war hammer, or sword. Their spears were used against the enemy and to bolster the courage of any in the front row who might think of running.

According to Skylan's plan, the ogres under the command of Bear Walker formed into a shield wall on the left flank of the Vindrasi. Skylan had fought against ogres before and held them in high regard, for the ogres were fierce, brutal warriors. They painted their heads and faces when going into battle to look more fearsome and each ogre carried a shield as big as Skylan and spears by the fistful in their huge hands.

Keeping one eye on the foe, who were still forming ranks, Skylan took the opportunity to see what the Cyclopes were doing. Hundreds of Cyclopes were taking refuge far behind the shield wall, all of them milling about in seeming confusion. Some of the Cyclopes were armed with small bows made of wood and horn and sinew. Other Cyclopes carried lead-tipped wooden clubs and spears.

"What are you doing back here far behind the shield wall?" Skylan asked Dela Eden. "The battle will be up there."

She gave him a soothing pat on the shoulder. "Go to your shield wall, Vindrasi. When it falls apart, you will be glad we are here."

Skylan glared at her, about to argue, when a shout from Bear Walker caused him to hurry back to take his place in the front row of the shield wall, with Bjorn on his right and Sigurd on his left. Erdmun fidgeted nervously beside his brother and Grimuir stood on the other side of Sigurd. Skylan had removed one of the dust-covered shields from the wall, cleaned it up as best he could, and carried that, along with his sword, God-rage. The other Vindrasi had their favored weapons: battle axes or war hammers or sometimes both. Many, like Sigurd, also carried spears. They would throw the spears first, then use their weapons.

Other Vindrasi warriors stood behind the first row, armed with spears and war hammers and battle axes. Their task was to assist the warriors in the first row, keep pushing those in the first row forward, and attack any of the enemy who broke through.

In forming his strategy, Skylan had borrowed the tactics the ogres had used to attack his people last spring. He could still vividly remember the jarring impact when the ogre shield wall had crashed into his own, smashing through the line, causing it to disintegrate. He had freely admitted that if were not for the Dragon Kahg, who had come to their aid, his people would have lost the battle.

Thinking of Kahg made him think of Aylaen and his friends on the *Venejekar*. He had been keeping watch for the dragonship, worried that Aylaen would reach the isle in the midst of the battle. His hopes and his fears vied with each other. On one hand, he hoped she would be able to find the isle; on the other, he feared she would be in danger if Aelon found her.

"Here they come," said Sigurd, gripping his sword.

Skylan looked up and down the line of warriors. Back when they had been alive, warriors in the shield wall boasted of how many foes they would kill, making grim jests about death to ease fear. The dead did not jest about death. The warriors stood in silence, vastly outnumbered, waiting to face an army of the damned.

Aelon flew above his army. At his command, the hellkites began their advance, moving at a walk to keep in formation. The closer they came to the wall of waiting dead men, the more their speed would increase.

Skylan exchanged glances with Bear Walker, standing to his left. The ogre shield wall was close, but not touching the shield wall of the Vindrasi, all part of Skylan's plan. He and his forces had to survive long enough to put his plan into action. As he watched the advancing forces, he began to think that surviving might be more difficult than he had anticipated.

Skylan did not fear any living foe. He had fought giants; he had once killed an ogre godlord in single-handed combat. But now, as he watched the hellkites draw nearer, he could not repress a shudder. They wore black helms over their skull-like heads. All one could see were the eye sockets and they were empty, their lives, their souls gone. They lived their unholy lives to kill.

"You should leave while you still have the chance, Skylan," Bjorn told him.

"Do you take me for a coward?" Skylan asked angrily. "Why would you say such a thing?"

"Because you are still alive," said Bjorn. "You should quit the field of battle. Let us deal with these fiends."

Skylan smiled at his friend. "I know you mean well and I thank you. But we are Vindrasi. We stand—or we fall—together."

Skylan looked at his men and he was proud. For the most part, they were holding firm and steady. Only a few, such as Erdmun, were shuffling their feet or gripping their shields in hands that shook.

He looked to the ranks of the ogres. With their heads that seemed too small for their massive bodies, and their small eyes and chubby cheeks, ogres looked very childlike and, as such, did not tend to inspire fear in a foe. To compensate, ogre warriors painted their faces with stripes of blue or red and brown, both to mark their rank and to appear more intimidating.

Bear Walker had painted his face red with a black stripe running over his head and down his nose and he was holding a spear that looked as big as an oak tree. In the rear, behind the shield wall, Raven's-foot in his black feather cape was dancing about, waving the gourd and howling something.

"What sort of magic is your shaman working?" Skylan shouted at Bear Walker. "He's not going to rain down frogs on us, is he?"

Bear Walker gave an explosive laugh.

"Raven's-foot is calling on our gods to bless our weapons and join us in battle."

Hearing them talk, Raven's-foot ran up to Skylan and poked him with the gourd that worked his magic.

Skylan started as though he'd been burned.

"For luck," Raven's-foot grunted and then he dashed off with feathers fluttering to continue his dance.

Skylan glanced over his shoulder at the Cyclopes. Dela Eden and her archers had each chosen a patch of ground and were nocking their arrows and raising their bows, some of them calling on the Gods of Raj to guide their aim.

The ground began to shake beneath their feet. Bjorn nudged Skylan, who turned to see the front ranks of hellkites had broken into a run, pounding over the beach, hoping to smash into the shield wall and cause it to collapse. Aelon's chariot circled in the sky above. The god was laughing, confident of victory.

Seeing the vast numbers of the hideous foe, Skylan couldn't blame him.

"Stand firm!" Skylan shouted.

"Can we even kill these fiends?" Erdmun asked, his voice quavering. He looked as if he was going to be sick again. "Will they die or just keep coming?"

"A good question," Skylan admitted. "I guess we'll soon find out."

Braced for the shock of the collision of two armies, Skylan heard a strange whistling sound and saw Cyclopes' arrows arcing over the shield wall to rain down on the foe. The arrows pierced the obsidian armor, decimating the ranks of the hellkites, creating confusion and slowing the advance, as those still on their feet tripped over the bodies or tried to avoid them.

Skylan started to cheer, but his cheer died abruptly as he watched some of the fallen hellkites rise to their feet, pluck the arrows from their chests, pick up their swords or their spears and keep moving. He noticed that other hellkites struck by arrows lay still and unmoving.

Some lived. Some died. He could not see what made the difference and he didn't have time to puzzle it out, for the hellkites in the front ranks had leveled their spears and were rushing straight at his line.

As Skylan had anticipated, the majority of the hellkites were choosing to hit his side of the shield wall, doubtless figuring that the weaker humans would be easier to kill than the ogres.

"Spear throwers! Now!" Skylan bellowed.

The Vindrasi in the lines behind him hurled their spears. Most hit the hellkites' shields and either bounced off or stuck there. Others found their targets, striking the hellkites in the head or chest. Some of the hellkites fell to the ground and did not rise. Skylan was frustrated to see others, struck down by the spears, climb to their feet.

The hellkites did not throw their spears, but attempted to drive them into the bodies of their foes. Since the spear had a longer reach than war hammer or axe, the hellkites could inflict damage on Skylan's warriors before his men could return the favor. The disadvantage was that once they had made use of their spears, the hellkites would have to waste precious time drawing their swords. Not much time, perhaps, but in battle, every second counted.

Another flight of Cyclopes arrows flew overhead, striking the middle ranks of the hellkites and throwing them into disorder. Skylan was baffled to see a dead hellkite with an arrow piercing his skull stand up and keep marching, while another hellkite with an arrow stuck in his chest turned into a rotting corpse.

Skylan gripped his sword, God-rage, and picked out his man—one of the hellkites running slightly ahead of the others. Like all the hellkites, he was armed with a spear in his right hand, a shield in his left, and wore a short sword at his side.

The hellkite jabbed at Skylan with the spear. Skylan raised his shield, blocking the blow and knocking the spear aside. He thrust his sword, trying to hit the hellkite's midriff, only to strike the hellkite's shield. The two combatants pushed and shoved with their shields and slashed at each other's legs with their swords, each hoping to strike a blow or at least throw the other off balance.

The hellkites were unbelievably strong and this one struck Skylan a horrific blow that knocked him off his feet and sent his sword flying. A Vindrasi warrior standing behind him straddled Skylan as he lay on the ground and drove his spear into the hellkite's breast. The hellkite dropped.

Skylan picked himself up and reached for his sword, only to see the hellkite grab the spear sticking out of his breast and use it against the Vindrasi who, thinking his foe was dead, had turned to fight another. Skylan shouted a warning and leaped at hellkite, only to watch him thrust his spear between the warrior's shoulder blades. The Vindrasi fell without a cry, disintegrated into a pile of dust that was trampled into the dirt, and his soul was gone.

"Die, damn you!' Skylan cried and thrust God-rage into the hellkite's throat. The fiend fell to the ground. Skylan watched it, ready to strike again, but the hellkite stayed dead.

The fighting went on around him, the noise and confusion of battle: shouts, curses, the thud of spears slamming into shields, the ring of metal striking armor. Something was missing and at first he could not think why this fight was different. Then he understood. No one cried out in pain. No one bled. The dying died without a sound, simply disappearing.

He glanced swiftly at the ogres and was pleased to see them putting his plan into action.

Having thrown the main body of his force against the humans, hoping to finish them off quickly, Aelon had left his right flank exposed to the ogres. The right flank of a phalanx was, according to Acronis, the weakest side, because the soldiers carried their shields with their right arms. Bear Walker and his ogres were on the move, rushing forward to hit the hellkites on the unprotected flank, hurling their spears, sending them plowing into the enemy. Every hellkite struck by an ogre spear fell to the ground and did not get back up. That moment, Skylan heard a shout and turned to see a hellkite Sigurd had killed seize him by the ankle and drag him off his feet. Skylan drove his sword into the hellkite's gut. This time, it stayed dead.

"I killed the damn thing!" Sigurd shouted angrily, bounding to his feet.

"I know. I saw you," said Skylan.

Three hellkites jumped them. Their spears were gone and two had lost their shields, but they had their swords and they were vicious fighters. Sigurd swung his war hammer and Skylan slashed with his sword and the three hellkites went down.

Sigurd kept bashing the foe, screaming, "Stay dead or I swear by Torval—"

The hellkite disintegrated.

"That's the difference!" Skylan cried.

He looked at the ogre shaman, running behind the advancing shield wall, waving his gourd and howling a prayer to the gods. He recalled seeing some of the Cyclopes archers praying to the gods as they fired.

"What are you raving about?" Sigurd asked, breathing heavily.

"The gods! You called upon Torval!" Skylan exclaimed. "My sword is a gift from a god."

He filled his lungs and shouted with his battlefield voice, "Strike in the name of the gods!"

Bear Walker and his ogres smashed into the right flank of the hellkites, throwing them into disarray. The Cyclopes warriors had stopped shooting arrows for fear of hitting their own allies. Armed with clubs and spears, they waded into the fray, bashing and stabbing. But, still, the hellkites seemed to flow over Skylan and his warriors in waves, endless as the ocean. Guarded by his serpents, Aelon rode his chariot over the field of battle, exhorting the hellkites to keep fighting.

Skylan destroyed another hellkite, slicing through the neck, severing the head from the body. The hellkite dwindled into dust and Skylan braced himself to fight again, only to find himself without a foe. The tide of battle had swept past him.

He stood alone on the shoreline and wondered if he had been fighting for minutes or if days had passed. He was not tired; nor was he wounded. He could fight on endlessly and the idea filled him with dread. The enemy never stopped coming and it occurred to him that perhaps this was his doom, to spend eternity battling hellish fiends, killing them over and over.

He shuddered and then remembered his boastful words to Keeper about never succumbing to despair. He gave a rueful smile and supposed he had better live up to them. He gripped his sword and was about to wade back into the fray when he heard his name, like a sigh carried by the wind.

He turned to see the *Venejekar* sailing toward the shore. Aylaen stood at the prow, wearing shining silver armor and carrying the sword blessed by the goddess, Vindrash. She seemed to be searching for him. His name was on her lips and in her heart.

Skylan was about to shout to her, when he stopped himself. Aelon continued to fly above the field of battle, hurling spears, bringing forth more hellkites. Absorbed in directing his army, the god had not yet caught sight of her.

Skylan gave a shout that echoed to the skies and, gripping Godrage, ran back toward the fighting. The only way to return to Aylaen was to win this battle, if he had to kill every fiend in hell to do it.

Watch over her, Torval, Skylan prayed and reached to touch the amulet, forgetting that it was gone, only to feel his hand close over the small hammer on its leather thong.

Skylan smiled. He had no idea where his amulet had been or how or why it had come back to him, but he took its return for a hopeful sign.

Plunging into the midst of the fray, he wielded God-rage and fought, so he might return to Aylaen.

13

The Dragon Kahg carried the *Venejekar* swiftly over the sea to the Isle of Revels. Aylaen stood at the prow, her hand on the dragon's neck, as she had done for so many days after Skylan's death. Only now, she was filled with hope. Skylan was alive. They had three of the five spiritbones in their possession, and needed only the other two in order to gain the power of creation and stop Aelon, perhaps even drive the god from the world.

Recovering the five spiritbones had been Skylan's quest, assigned to him by the goddess Vindrash, and when he had fallen, Aylaen had done what Vindrasi women had done for centuries. She had picked up her dead husband's sword and fought on.

"When Skylan returns, we will continue the quest for the Five," she told the Dragon Kahg.

"What will you do with the sacred spiritbones once you have them?" the dragon asked.

Aylaen was startled. The dragon rarely spoke to her and never about the spiritbones. Wondering if she had heard correctly, she looked up at the proud head of the dragon to see one of the red eyes glaring down at her.

"I will use the spiritbones as Vindrash intended, to summon the Five Vektia dragons—"

"No, you won't," said Kahg. "Vindrash lied."

"Lied!" Aylaen gasped. "I don't believe you. What about?"

"The five spiritbones," said the Dragon Kahg. "Your mate—the warrior who is dead and not dead—knows the truth. You know the truth yourself, or you would if you would think about it. You are the Kai Priestess. The responsibility is yours."

"I have been thinking of the Five," Aylaen returned. "At night, when I could not sleep. During the day, when I could find no respite from the pain of Skylan's death. The mad god, Sund, looked into the future and warned me that if I did not destroy the Five, the destruction of the gods would follow."

"Yet you have three in your possession and you do not destroy them," said Kahg. "Why is that?"

"I have told you. Sund saw one future among many," said Aylaen dismissively. She was silent a moment, remembering, then said softly, "The spiritbones are very beautiful. And I have felt their power."

"The power of creation," said Kahg. "I will tell you a story. The story of creation."

Aylaen started to say she knew the story, but Kahg continued and she did not want to interrupt.

"The Great Dragon Ilyrion was the guardian of this world, which she loved. The god Torval was a young god then, searching for a world of his own to rule, when he came upon this one. He demanded that Ilyrion give it him. She refused to let him, and he attacked her. The blood and smoke from the fighting grew so dense that it blotted out the sun. The world turned dark and cold. All life began to die.

"Realizing in sorrow that their battle was going to destroy the world she loved, Ilyrion sacrificed herself. She let Torval's sword pierce her heart. The five spiritbones sprang from her crest as her blood rained down from the heavens. Each drop of her blood became a gemstone that holds a baby dragon. Thus are our young born of Ilyrion. Her crest holds the power of creation."

"That is not the story of creation," said Aylaen.

"Not to you humans." The Dragon Kahg scowled. "In your version, Torval is the hero. Not in ours."

Aylaen pondered the tale. "You said Vindrash lied. What does the lie have to do with your story?"

"Vindrash told your people and ours that the five spiritbones embodied the power of creation. She promised that in time of need, a Priestess could summon five dragons who would return to fight for the Vindrasi. *You* battled the evil being that attacked Sinaria. You fought it. You know it was not a dragon."

Aylaen was troubled, for Kahg was right. Her sister, Treia, with the help of the god Hevis, had used one of the spiritbones to summon a Vektia dragon, or so Treia believed, in order to help save her city from the ogres. Instead, the evil creature had escaped her control, laid waste to the city, and killed. Years ago, another Kai Priestess had tried to use one of the spiritbones to summon a dragon with equally disastrous results. The Five presumably held the power of creation. Yet up to now, they had brought only death and destruction.

"If it was not a dragon, what was it?" Aylaen asked.

"The embodiment of fear," said Kahg. "The gods' fear. Fear cannot create. Fear can only destroy."

"What did the gods fear?" Aylaen asked.

She put her hand on the spiritbone of the Dragon Kahg that still hung on a leather thong from a nail driven into the prow. Plain and unadorned, the dragon's spiritbone was quite different from the beautifully adorned spiritbones of the Vektia.

"Themselves," said the Dragon Kahg.

Aylaen watched the shadows of the clouds glide across the water. She was thinking she knew the truth. The idea was awful, terrifying, but she needed to know for certain. As Kahg had said, the decision to use the Five would be up to her.

"Kahg, why do you stay with us? You never used to. You have no care for humans. You can't even remember our names."

The dragon was silent; in his silence was the answer. He stayed to guard the spiritbones.

She glanced about the deck. Acronis was taking his afternoon nap in the sunshine. He had ceased trying to persuade Aylaen to bury Skylan at sea.

"I have no rational explanation for why the body is not decaying," Acronis had told her. "The idea that he is dead and not dead will do as well as any."

Farinn was gazing into the sky, humming to himself. He was composing a new song. He did not have to sing Skylan's death song yet. Wulfe was back at the stern, gossiping with his oceanids.

Leaving the deck, Aylaen descended into the hold, closing the hatch behind her. She had hidden the spiritbones down here in a large stone jar used for storing dried beans—not a very safe hiding place.

She knew of a place that was more secure, and she had been meaning to transfer them. After Skylan's death, however, she had not been able to find the will to do anything. To keep them safe, she had placed the sword of Vindrash across the lid of the jar.

The sword remained where she had put it, undisturbed. She touched the hilt, thinking of the goddess who had given it to her. Aylaen had walked among the gods since she was a little girl. She had not thought much about it, believing that walking with gods was a thing done by all mortals. Only later would she realize that she had been given a gift. Perhaps even then the gods had foreseen that the thread of her wyrd would be bound with theirs.

"Why me?" Aylaen asked softly, aloud. "Was I chosen? Or did I choose?"

She smiled wistfully to think that Skylan would never ask such a question. He knew he was the chosen of the gods and whether he was right or wrong, he lived his life in that belief, putting his faith in Torval, knowing the god had faith in him.

She remembered clearly the night she had found the blessed sword. She had gone to the Hall of the Gods, a grand name for a small shrine built to honor Vindrash.

"I knelt before the goddess to confess that I had lied," Aylaen murmured. "I had told everyone I was going on the voyage with Skylan and Garn and the other warriors as a man-woman, to honor the gods. I had told a lie. In truth, I was running away from home, running off to be with my lover. But the lie was the truth—as Vindrash knew.

"You did not doubt me, Vindrash. To prove your faith, you gave me this sword, forged long ago in your honor and then left, covered in dust and forgotten, in a corner. *You* gave me the sword," said Aylaen. Her hand closed over the hilt. "But *I* chose to pick it up."

She set aside the sword, took the stone lid from the jar, and plunged her hand in among the beans, feeling about until she had found all three of the spiritbones. One by one, she drew them out. The hold was dimly lit, cool, and shadowy. What light there was seemed to coalesce in the gold and jewels that adorned the three spiritbones.

The Vektan Torque was her favorite, for it belonged to her people. As a mark of her favor, Vindrash had given the spiritbone to them.

Horg's failure to protect the spiritbone, bartering it away to save his own craven skin, had been the beginning that led to this end.

So many wyrds, bound into one.

The Torque was made of heavy gold formed in the shape of two dragons, their tails intertwined, their heads facing each other, holding the spiritbone in their front claws. The bone was adorned with a beautiful sapphire that glowed with the light of the stars.

She set the Torque aside and picked up another.

Vindrash had given this spiritbone to the god Sund to protect. Of all the gods, Sund was the only one who could see into the future. Foreseeing what he believed was the destruction of the gods, he had given the spiritbone to Aelon to try to bribe the god, persuade him to leave them in peace. It hadn't worked.

The spiritbone formed the body of the dragon. Golden bands twined about the bone, becoming the dragon's tail. Golden wings spread from the bone. A golden head reared up from the body. Emeralds adorned the spiritbone, set above the head. Two smaller emeralds were embedded in the wings. A long golden chain extended from the two wingtips.

Sacred, Kahg had called the spiritbone. Aylaen laid this one beside the first.

Vindrash had given the third spiritbone to the Sea Goddess for safekeeping. The Sea Queen had given the bone to Aylaen as a wedding gift. The spiritbone was set in a bracer made of twelve brass rings attached to a bar in the center and studded with emeralds and sapphires and pearls. The bracer was meant to fit over the lower part of the arm, extending from the wrist to the elbow. Every ring was decorated with various sea creatures: dolphins and whales and all manner of fish.

The bone was mounted on the bar in the center. A dragon made of brass twined around the bone, holding it firmly to the bracer with wings and tail. Blue sapphires and green emeralds reminded her of the colors of the shafts of sunlight slanting down through seawater. Pearls shone with a lustrous radiance.

Aylaen had come to love and admire the Sea Queen and grieved her death in a war Aelon had brought to her people. This spiritbone was doubly precious in her eyes.

She arrayed the three on the floor in front of her, touching each of the bones with the tips of her fingers. As Kahg had said, she felt their sacred power.

Lies. Fear. The truth.

Above all, she must keep them safe from Aelon.

The Sea Queen had given Aylaen a pouch made of fabric spun of bamboo in which to carry the spiritbones. She placed all three together in the pouch, thrust the pouch down the front of her dress, then reached out with her hand and knocked over the stone jar, sending a torrent of beans onto the deck.

She lifted the hatch and called out, "Farinn, Acronis! One of the jars has tipped over and there are beans everywhere!"

"I will clean it up," Farinn offered, jumping to his feet.

Acronis followed more slowly. Observing the large quantity of beans scattered across the deck, he remarked, "How do you suppose a jar came to fall over in a calm sea?"

"The time may come, Legate, when the seas are no longer calm," Aylaen said. "The less you and Farinn know, the better."

"And when that time comes, what will happen to you, my dear?" Acronis asked, his smile gone.

"I suppose we will have to wait to hear the end of the song," Aylaen replied, with an affectionate glance at Farinn, who was on his hands and knees scooping up beans and putting them back in the jar.

"In the meanwhile, I'm picking up beans," Acronis said wryly.

He joined Farinn, grunting as he bent to the work, and Aylaen hurried up onto the deck. Wulfe had quit talking to his oceanids and was hovering near Skylan's body, convinced Aylaen was going to throw him into the sea.

Seeing her approach him, he watched her warily. "What do you want?"

"I need you to do something for me."

"You're not going to take Skylan," Wulfe said.

"We've talked about this. I promise," said Aylaen.

"You Uglies always say one thing and do another."

"It's not about Skylan. I need you to—"

Wulfe started backing away. "Then it's about a bath. I don't need a bath."

"You do, but that's not what I want," said Aylaen. She held up the pouch. "I need your magical hidey-hole. You hid something in there once for me. I need you to hide this."

When Wulfe had first come aboard the *Venejekar*, he had worked his magic to hollow out a hole in the bulkhead, using it as a place to stash his most valuable possessions.

Wulfe crept toward her, watching her suspiciously from beneath his shaggy thatch of hair, undoubtedly still expecting to be scrubbed within an inch of his life with foul-smelling soap.

She held out the pouch to him. "These are the spiritbones. I want you to take them and—"

Wulfe shrank away from her, putting his hands behind his back. He cast a nervous glance at the dragon. "Those are god bones. Kahg doesn't want me to touch them. If I do, he'll hurt me."

"God bones!" Aylaen repeated. "Why would you say that? These are the bones of dragons, like Kahg's."

Wulfe opened his mouth, then looked up at the dragon and shut it again. He shook his head. "Go away. You'll get me in trouble."

"Wulfe, I need to know. You said these were god bones—"

"Dog bones. You heard me wrong," Wulfe said. "Clean out your ears."

The bones of dragons. Spiritbones. Sacred bones. God bones. The reason Vindrash had lied to the dragons, the reason Owl Mother's five rune stones had come up blank; the reason the Dragon Kahg stayed with the *Venejekar*.

"I know the truth," Aylaen said to herself. "But what am I meant to do with it?"

"Why are you staring at me?" Wulfe asked, scowling. "I didn't do anything."

"I wasn't staring at you," Aylaen said.

She had been staring at the vision of an immense and beautiful dragon coming to life, her wings spanning the heavens, sweeping the stars from the sky and the gods from this world.

Aylaen sighed and went over to sit down near Skylan's body. She patted the deck beside her, inviting Wulfe to sit with her.

"I didn't meant to upset you, Wulfe," she said. "I have a problem and I was trying to think what to do. You don't have to touch the . . . bones. All you have to do for me is use your magic to unseal the hole."

Wulfe looked up at the dragon. Aylaen knew what he was think-ing. Wulfe's hidey-hole was in the bulkhead directly beneath the nail on which hung the dragon's own spiritbone.

"Kahg won't mind," said Aylaen. "He will use his own magic to guard it."

"Is it all right?" Wulfe asked, talking to the dragon. "Kahg says it's all right."

Wulfe apparently didn't altogether trust the dragon, because he crept toward the bulkhead like a thief, all the while keeping an eye on Kahg, who was gazing out to sea in seeming unconcern. Aylaen knew better. The dragon was conscious of their every move.

Squatting down on the deck, Wulfe touched one of the wooden planks. Since it looked like all the other wooden planks—faded and rough and worn—Aylaen had no idea how he could tell one from an-other. Wulfe began to sing.

> *Open to my waiting hand.*
> *Open to my knowing eye.*
> *Open to my little song.*
> *Open it and don't take long.*

The plank disappeared, revealing a hole filled with the boy's trea-sures. Last time Aylaen had looked inside, she had seen an assortment of odds and ends, a lock of her own hair and a silver thimble. This time a flash of light caught her eye and she recognized the amulet Sky-lan had always worn around his neck: a small silver hammer.

"Don't look!" Wulfe cried, putting his grimy hand over her eyes.

"Wulfe, I didn't mean to, but I saw—"

"I didn't steal it. Skylan wanted me to have it. To remember him."

He took away his hand and glowered at her.

"I know he did, Wulfe," said Aylaen gently. "But when Skylan comes back, you're going to have to give it back. That is not just a piece of silver. It is his amulet, given to him to honor Torval."

Wulfe gasped, horrified. "And I took it away from him! I didn't know! Now he'll be in danger."

He grabbed hold of the worn leather thong, snatched it from the hole, and sprang to his feet.

"Wait! Where are you going with that?" Aylaen askcd, noting that even in his haste, Wulfe took care not to touch the silver hammer. Despite the boy's fear of all things metal, he had risked harm to take this token of Skylan.

"To give it back," Wulfe cried. "He needs it to protect him!"

Crouching beside Skylan's body, Wulfe gently tied the leather thong around his neck, then returned to Aylaen, who was kneeling on the deck in front of the hidey-hole.

"Skylan looks angry," said Wulfe, sniffling and wiping his nose with his hand. "I told him I was sorry, but I don't think he believes me."

"I'll explain it to him," said Aylaen.

She eyed the secret place that was packed with Wulfe's treasures.

"It won't fit," she said, disappointed. "There isn't room."

"Yes, there is," said Wulfe. "It's magic. Don't you know anything? Put them inside."

One by one, Aylaen drew the spiritbones out of the pouch and tucked them into the hole. To her surprise, they fit as snugly as if all the strange objects the boy had collected had moved aside to make room for them. Aylaen let her fingers rest on the spiritbones, feeling the sharp edges of the wingtips and snouts, crests and tails.

"The responsibility for the Five is mine, Vindrash," said Aylaen. "All my life, you have favored me, given me insight into the lives of the gods. Am I right about the spiritbones?"

Aylaen waited, but there was no response.

Wulfe began to fidget. "Are you done?"

"Yes, I guess I am," Aylaen said, rising to her feet. She clasped her hand over the empty pouch.

Wulfe sang the second part of his "hiding" song.

> *Keep safe from thieving hands.*
> *Keep safe from spying eyes.*
> *Let them meet a swift demise.*

The planks returned to worn, weathered rough-hewn wood.

"If someone tried to steal what was inside, would the person die? Would your magic kill him?"

Wulfe cast a glance up at the dragon and then looked back at her. "If my magic didn't, Kahg would."

"Thank you, Wulfe," said Aylaen. She reached out to brush back the ragged hair. "You know, you really do need a bath—"

Wulfe dashed off, racing across the deck toward the stern to get as far from her as possible. Aylaen walked over to the prow, to talk to the dragon.

"The Five do not belong to five dragons," she said softly, for only Kahg to hear. "They belong to one—the Great Dragon Ilyrion."

The dragon's red eyes gleamed with pleasure. "Your name, human, is Aylaen."

Aylaen smiled, but then she sighed. Now that she knew the truth, what was she meant to do with it?

T he Isle of Revels lies up ahead," said the Dragon Kahg. "I can
see it on the horizon."

The sky was clear, the sun bright. A light breeze ruffled the water.
Aylaen eagerly searched the horizon, but could not sight any sign of
land. She called Acronis to bring his magic glass and he used it to
scan the ocean. Farinn came to look, as well, for he had the best eye-
sight of all of them on board.

"All I see is a patch of mist," Acronis reported. "Though I must
admit that is strange, considering the day is fine and the sun bright."

"Farinn?"

"I see the mist," he said. "But nothing else."

The dragon snorted. "You look with mortal eyes. I see an island
and now I hear the clash of arms. What you see as mist are ghosts.
The dead fight the dead." He sounded awed.

"Told you," Wulfe muttered. "Dead Uglies."

"But why would the dead be fighting?" Aylaen demanded. "Especially on an island devoted to pleasure."

"I see the winged serpents of Aelon," Kahg reported. "The god is
leading the attack."

"Skylan is on that isle . . . Aelon has long pursued him!" Aylaen
stared at the horizon until her eyes ached.

The dragon's eyes flickered red. "Aelon has raised an army of hellkites, dragging them from the bowels of hell. The god would not go
to all this trouble to capture one mortal, no matter how valiant. Aelon
seeks bigger fish."

The dragonship bounded across the waves. Sea spray broke over the bow.

"On the Isle of Revels?" Aylaen was perplexed. "What treasure could Joabis possibly have . . ."

Her voice trailed off, for she knew the answer.

"Make haste, Kahg! Increase our speed." She turned to run down into the hold, intending to arm herself, when Acronis and Farinn both stopped her.

"You forget, my dear, that we hear only one side of your conversation with the dragon," said Acronis. "You look dismayed. Wulfe says that we are sailing to an island belonging to a god, and that Skylan is on that island. You speak of treasure and Aelon. What is going on?"

"Vindrash gave spiritbones to the Sea Goddess and to the god Sund," said Aylaen. "Those two are in my possession, as well as the one she gave to the Vindrasi people. I believe she gave the fourth to Joabis. Aelon is desperate to find it and now the god is attacking the island. The dead fight the dead."

"Then we living must arm ourselves," said Acronis. He smiled at Aylaen. "For I assume you plan to sail into the midst of the battle?"

Aylaen flushed. "Thank you, sir, for not telling me to flee to safety."

"I would if I thought it would do any good," said Acronis.

Aylaen hurried off. As she was leaving, she heard Wulfe say, "You're going to be fighting hellkites. If they kill you they'll eat your soul."

"Having my soul eaten?" Acronis laughed. "Just another day's work on board the *Venejekar*."

Aylaen had packed in her sea chest the armor she had worn when she had disguised herself as one of the Legate's soldiers. Lifting the lid, she looked inside, drew in a soft breath, and sat back on her heels to marvel at a miracle.

A shaft of sunlight from the open hatch gleamed on a shirt that she thought at first was made of chain mail, only to discover, on taking it out to admire it, that the shirt was not made of chain. It was far lighter in weight, smooth to the touch, and glistened with rainbow opalescence that reminded her of the Dragon Kahg.

"Armor made of dragon scales," said Aylaen.

She had heard tales of such armor in legend and song. The Vindrasi hero Hagbard, who was said to have fought the fearsome monsters that roamed the land when the world was new, had worn armor made of dragon scales.

She found, as well, a white tunic of softest leather to wear beneath the armor, white leather breeches, and matching boots. A wonderful gift and there could be only one giver.

"Thank you, Vindrash," Aylaen said reverently. "I take this as a sign—"

She was startled by a loud thud, as of something falling, and then sounds of a scuffle and then silence. The sounds had come from the back of the hold.

"Farinn? Is that you?" Aylaen called.

She had left the young man on deck with Acronis, but perhaps he had come down into the hold in search of something.

No answer.

"Wulfe, after you started that fire, I warned you not to come down here," Aylaen said in stern tones.

She waited to see Wulfe bolt out of the back, making a mad scramble for the ladder before she could catch him.

Nothing happened. Wulfe did not appear.

Aylaen took hold of her sword, slowly rose to her feet and began to pad softly toward the stern, where they stored empty barrels, coils of rope, and the nets they used for fishing.

She heard the sounds again and she was thinking some of the cargo must have shifted when a pile of tangled fishnet gave a heave and started to stand. She could see feet poking out from underneath the net and arms flailing about, trying to cast it off.

Aylaen pointed her sword at the netting.

"I am armed," she said. "Show yourself!"

A rotund figure emerged, finally managing to fight his way out of the fishnet. He was dressed in fine clothes, such as one might wear to a wedding, but they were filthy and disheveled and smelled of fish. He looked very forlorn and very frightened.

"Joabis!" Aylaen said, amazed and not particularly pleased. "What are you doing hiding on my ship?"

"My island is under attack," Joabis said, wiping his brow with the sleeve of his tunic. "We must leave at once. Tell your dragon to sail away as fast as he can and take me with you. Oh, and by the way," he added, regarding her with a hurt expression, "*I* was the one who gave you that fine dragon-scale armor. Not Vindrash."

"You! Why?" Aylaen gasped.

"To thank you for saving me—"

"I'm not saving you!" said Aylaen. "Where is Skylan?"

"Off somewhere fighting," said Joabis. "He was the one who sent me. He said to tell you it isn't safe and you must flee—"

"Do you have the spiritbone?" Aylaen asked, lowering her sword. "Is that why Skylan sent you?"

"The what?" Joabis asked uneasily.

"The spiritbone of the Vektia," Aylaen repeated. "I know Vindrash gave it to you. Have you saved it from Aelon? Do you have it with you?"

"No," said Joabis. "But I left it somewhere safe."

"For Aelon to find," Aylaen said, glowering in anger.

"Aelon doesn't have time to look for it," Joabis assured her. "The god is busy fighting—"

"Fighting Skylan!" Aylaen exclaimed. She pressed the point of her sword against Joabis's belly. "That is why you brought him to this island. You flee and leave him to fight your battle!"

"We made a bargain," said Joabis, gulping. "If he and the other dead warriors drive away Aelon, I will restore their lives. If you could just . . . remove that sword . . ."

Aylaen glared at him and then let the sword fall.

"Skylan is fighting the army of a god," she said. "Can he win?"

"He seemed to think so," said Joabis.

Aylaen shook her head with a smile. "Skylan has never met the foe he did not believe he could defeat."

She thought a moment. "If you are right and Aelon is preoccupied with battle, then this would be a good time to recover the spiritbone. Where is the hiding place?"

Joabis recoiled, staring at her in horror. "You're not serious! Aelon is looking for me!"

"He won't be looking for me," Aylaen said. "Tell me where to find it."

"Are you sure you wouldn't rather just sail away?" Joabis asked plaintively.

"Positive," said Aylaen. "You did give me that fine armor. This will be my chance to wear it."

Joabis heaved a deep sigh. "So long as you don't expect me to come with you."

The god gave her directions to the shrine and instructed her on how to remove the spiritbone from the statue. Aylaen listened carefully, making certain she understood.

"How goes the battle?" she asked when he was finished.

"Skylan and his forces are outnumbered," Joabis answered, adding in reassuring tones, "But the last I saw, they were holding their own. Your Skylan is a bold rascal. Torval thinks well of him. Still, you should hurry if you're going to find the spiritbone before Aelon does. Oh, and don't tell anyone I'm here. Aelon has spies everywhere."

Joabis dropped to his hands and knees on the deck and crawled back under the fishnet.

She went back to change into the leather breeches and tunic, and thrust her arms into the dragon-scale shirt, pulling it over her head and shoulders. The shirt was long, extending to her knees, and fit her well. She buckled on her sword, cast an exasperated glance in the direction of the pile of net, and started up the ladder.

"If you must know," said a sepulchral voice from out of the fishnet. "I lied. Vindrash was the one who sent the armor."

Aylaen smiled and went up on deck, trying to think what she was going to tell Acronis and Farinn. Acronis was wearing his breastplate and his sword and was assisting Farinn to put on his leather armor. The two stopped what they were doing to stare at her.

"What marvelous armor!" said Acronis in admiring tones. "I've never seen chain mail like that."

"It is made of dragon scales," said Aylaen, flushing with pleasure. "I need to talk with all of you and the dragon. Where is Wulfe?"

"At the sight of our weapons, he ran off to the stern," Farinn replied, adding by way of explanation, "The iron."

Aylaen might not have believed Wulfe's claim that iron burned his flesh, but she had seen for herself the bloody wounds on the boy's hands when he had tried to clean Skylan's sword.

She raised her voice. "Wulfe, I need to talk to you."

"Take off your swords," said Wulfe.

"No iron will hurt you," she promised.

Wulfe refused to budge and at last Aylaen and Acronis laid down their weapons. Farinn drew his sword from its sheath and nervously dropped it; the blade nearly sliced through the bard's boot. Wulfe made a hooting noise, Farinn blushed, and Acronis cast a resigned glance at Aylaen. He had been trying to teach Farinn to wield a sword, but thus far the young man hadn't made much progress.

Aylaen walked over to speak to the Dragon Kahg. His eyes were narrowed and hooded, but she could see a slit of angry fire.

"You know Joabis is on board," she said.

"I know," Kahg growled. "The wretch begs me to protect him."

"The task is onerous, but I think you must," said Aylaen. "Aelon is searching for him and if he finds him, Joabis will reveal all he knows."

The Dragon Kahg snorted. His gaze shifted, and Aylaen's new armor shone red in the glow of the dragon's eyes.

"A gift from Vindrash," said Kahg.

"I believe so, yes," said Aylaen. "I think the armor is very old and valuable. Only the ancient heroes wore such armor."

"It is very old," said Kahg. "The scales are Ilyrion's."

Aylaen caught her breath, not sure what to make of this. By this time, Farinn and Acronis had joined her at the prow. Wulfe sidled closer to inspect her armor, taking care not to touch it.

"Those are dragon scales," he said in tones of respect. "Is it magic? Dragon magic?"

"I don't know," said Aylaen. "I hope not. Listen, I have to tell you something important and I don't have much time. I know the reason Aelon sent soldiers to this island. The fourth spiritbone is here. He is searching for it and I believe I know where it is. I must find it before he does. I am going ashore—"

"We will go with you," said Acronis.

Aylaen shook her head. "I need you to stay on board, guard the *Venejekar.*"

"What about the god in the hold?" Wulfe asked. "Are we supposed to guard him, too?"

"There is no god. I don't have time for such nonsense," Aylaen said, fixing Wulfe with a grim look.

"It's not nonsense," Wulfe said, aggrieved. "You talked to him."

"*Is* there a god in the hold?" Acronis asked.

Aylaen sighed. "Yes, but I'm not supposed to tell anyone. Joabis fled his island and came seeking the dragon's protection. He told me where to find the spiritbone."

Acronis and Farinn both looked amazed and obviously were eager to ask more questions. Aylaen turned back to the dragon. She didn't have the answers.

"We must sail east along the isle until we come to an inlet protected by mangroves," she told the dragon. "You can hide the ship there."

"I can see the fighting," said Acronis suddenly.

They lined the rail to watch.

"A strange and terrible sight," said Farinn, awed. "The dead fight the dead."

The battle was eerily, utterly quiet. Warriors were ghostly, insubstantial images, reflections floating on the sea of death. Swords struck shields and hammers battered helms without making a sound. The dead died silently.

Aylaen looked for Skylan. She knew where he would be: where the fighting was fiercest, the battle blazed hottest. She could not see him and, as the ship sailed east, the battle receded into the distance and then vanished like mist in the bright sunshine.

The *Venejekar* rounded a point and they kept a lookout for the inlet Joabis had mentioned. He had said it was sheltered among the mangroves, but that was not much help, for this part of the isle was thick with mangroves, perching like herons on their prop roots that thrust up out of the water.

They had almost sailed past the inlet before anyone saw it. Farinn caught a glimpse of an opening among the leaves and called to the dragon. Kahg sailed the *Venejekar* into the inlet, gliding between banks lined with mangroves. Aylaen knew they were in the right place when they came across Joabis's own dragonship tied to a tree root.

The sun blazed in the sky, shining on the water. The air was hot and humid and so still she could hear the waves gently lapping among the mangrove roots. She was already sweating in the leather tunic, pants, and armor.

Joabis had told her that a narrow trail led inland. Kahg edged the *Venejekar*'s prow in among the roots near the trail. The ship bumped on the roots and came to halt.

"Do you insist on going alone?" Acronis asked.

"I will be in no danger," said Aylaen. "This part of the island is deserted. I need you to stay with Farinn and Wulfe and . . . Skylan."

She looked over at Skylan's body lying on the deck. His face was ashen, showing no sign of life. She felt a jab of fear. What if Wulfe was wrong? What if Joabis lied? What if Skylan's kiss had been nothing more than a breath of wind on her face?

She shivered, despite the heat.

Acronis felt her shudder and guessed her fears. "What does your heart tell you, Aylaen?"

"That Skylan is alive," she replied. "But he looks so pale and cold and still."

"The eyes of reason can sometimes be blind, whereas the eyes of love see clearly," said Acronis. "A lesson you and Skylan have taught me. I will keep strict watch for any enemies. After all, we have a god in the hold."

The *Venejekar* floated among the prop roots of the mangroves, nudging the bushlike trees as it rocked gently back and forth in the shallows. Acronis secured the ship with ropes around the roots, holding it steady while Farinn helped Aylaen climb onto the thick tangle of roots and from there to the swampy shore.

When she finally reached solid ground, her hands and arms were scratched and she was parched and sweating. She was wearing the dragon-scale armor over the leather tunic, her sword, and a drawstring bag that she had tied to her sword belt. She paused to drink from a freshwater stream that flowed into the swamp, then followed the trail into the village of the dead.

The place was deserted. Longhouses were empty and silent. No one walked the streets. Looking inside a dwelling, she could see half-eaten food on the tables, overturned benches, spilled wine. The revelers had fled in haste.

Even the gods and dead men feared Aelon.

The trail led past the village into a forest, where it became more difficult to follow, sometimes disappearing altogether in the thick growth. After a hot and weary hike, Aylaen pushed through trees that formed a green wall of vegetation and entered the garden. She paused a moment to catch her breath and marvel at the beauty.

Flowers of every hue and shape that could possibly exist spilled their fragrance into the air. Butterflies of many types fluttered among the blossoms. Sunlight flashed on ponds filled with darting golden fish.

The only sound was the droning of the bees and the occasional rustle of leaves. Aylaen found it hard to imagine that a battle raged not far from this peaceful, idyllic place.

The Hall of the Gods was identical to the Hall in her village. Cool air washed over her in the shadows as she went inside. She had to wait for her eyes to adjust to locate the marble statue of Joabis. He had described it as magnificent. She would have said it was grandiose, more suited to one of the marble temples of Sinaria than to a simple wooden longhouse. Aylaen drew near the statue to examine the marble brooch pinned to the statue's marble chest.

She could see at once that the brooch was one of the spiritbones and she wondered how Joabis thought it would fool anyone. She touched the cold marble and spoke what Joabis had taught her to say, which was, of course, a prayer in homage to Joabis.

"God of Revels, you who ease sorrow with ale that lifts the spirit and banishes the cares of the day and wine that celebrates all the epochs in our lives, bring joy to my heart now and ever after."

The marble seemed to melt beneath her fingers like frost and the brooch came to life. The rubies sparkled with fire, the gold petals burned with a bright sheen. The dragon holding the spiritbone gazed at her with unblinking red ruby eyes. She quickly took the brooch from the statue, tucked it inside the drawstring bag and was starting to leave when she heard, outside the shrine, the sounds of children laughing.

Aylaen was astonished. Freilis, the Goddess of the Tally, cared for the souls of dead children, keeping them safe until their parents could come for them. She went to the door to look out into the garden, thinking that such laughter came from the living, not the dead.

A girl of about eight was hiding behind a tall flowering rosebush. The girl had greenish blue eyes, a face covered with freckles, and fair hair with a tinge of red that she wore in two braids down her back. She was wearing boy's clothes—leather tunic and trousers—and she crouched behind her bush, clutching a wooden sword in her hand, as a boy of about the same age ran into the garden.

He was tall with the same fair, red-tinged hair, except that his was cut short, and the same freckles. He was also armed with a wooden sword and he slowed as he entered the garden, searching warily, holding his sword in front of him.

"I know you are here, Holma," he called. "You might as well give yourself up."

Aylaen gave a little gasp. Holma was her mother's name and she had always thought that if she ever had a daughter, she would name her Holma. Aylaen retreated into the shadows of the shrine so that the children would not see her, and watched their play.

The girl kept quiet as the boy continued to search, sometimes lunging at a bush and once leaping behind a tree, shouting that he had caught her. At this, the girl began to laugh and had to cover her mouth with her hand so he would not hear her.

Picking up a rock, the girl tossed it so that it landed behind the boy and when he swiftly turned toward the sound, the girl jumped out with her sword and smacked him on the backside.

The boy rounded on her and swiped at her with his sword. She laughed and struck back and a good-natured battle ensued between the two.

There can be no doubt, thought Aylaen, seeing them so close together, that these two are brother and sister.

"You should be home sewing with the other girls," said the boy.

Ducking her swing, he chopped at her ankles and caused her to fall. Aylaen winced, for the fall was a hard one. The girl scrambled to her feet and lunged at him.

"Father says girls should know how to fight," she retorted. "Like this!"

A swipe with her blade forced the boy to retreat, coming perilously close to tumbling into the stream. He recovered and was once more on the attack.

"You'll never catch a husband with a sword."

"I don't want a husband," she said. "Boys are stupid. I'm going to be a warrior."

Absorbed in watching the battle, Aylaen crept closer to the entrance for a closer view. A ray of sunlight, slanting through the entrance, caused her dragon-scale armor to blaze with shimmering light.

The boy suddenly stopped fighting. Raising his hand in warning to his sister, he turned his head toward the Hall of Gods and cried out boldly, "Who is there?"

The girl ran to her brother's side, watching his back, each protecting the other. Both seemed more curious than afraid.

"You are very beautiful, lady. Are you a goddess?" the girl asked.

"Our father tells us stories of the old gods," the boy added. "Perhaps you are one of them."

Aylaen smiled and shook her head. "I am not a god. But my armor and my swords are gifts from a god."

"See there!" the girl whispered loudly. "She wears a sword!"

"Your father is right," said Aylaen, overhearing. "Girls should learn how to fight. What are your names?"

"I am Skylanson," the boy said proudly. "My father is Chief of Chiefs. Holma is my sister. We are twins, but I am the oldest. I was born first."

"You may be the oldest, but I am the smartest!" cried the girl.

Deftly snatching the sword from her brother's hand, Holma ran off with the spoils of war, brandishing both weapons in the air with a whoop.

The boy shook his head in fond exasperation.

"What I am to do with such a sister?" he demanded of Aylaen, then, laughing, he dashed off in pursuit.

The children disappeared into the forest. The sound of their laughter faded away. Dazed, Aylaen stared after them. She longed to call to them to come back, tell her more, but the boy's words had stolen her breath and she couldn't speak a word.

My name is Skylanson . . .

"They resemble their father," said a voice. "But they have their mother's eyes."

Startled out of her daze, Aylaen drew her sword and turned to confront the man, who came sauntering along one of the paths.

He was tall and powerfully built, his handsome face clean shaven. He wore the ornate breastplate and leather skirt of his soldiers. A purple cape fell from his shoulders. His helm was silver and gold, trimmed with silver serpents, and adorned by a purple crest and Aylaen knew him at once. Aelon looked as she had always imagined him.

She caught herself about to touch the drawstring pouch tied on her belt and forced herself to drop her hand, fearful of drawing his attention to the spiritbone. She felt ridiculous, holding her sword on a god, but her very soul seemed to wither in fear.

"Who are those children?" she asked, trying to sound nonchalant.

"You talk as if I should know them. What are they doing here? They are not . . . dead." Her voice caught. She couldn't help herself.

"They are not dead, Aylaen," said Aelon with a slight smile. His voice was deep and rich. He took a step closer, not threatening, but as if he wanted to have a friendly talk. "They have not yet been born. Whether they will be or not is up to you."

"So this is some trick you are playing on me," said Aylaen, not lowering the sword.

"No trick. I have shown you the future. What *can* be the future," said Aelon, placing emphasis on the word. "The choice is yours."

"Your choice is no choice," said Aylaen.

She sheathed her sword and started to walk around him, sweep past him. He blocked the way, imposing, but still not threatening. Not yet.

"Swear allegiance to me, Kai Priestess, and I will bring peace and prosperity to your people. Those beautiful children will be yours. Skylan will be Chief of Chiefs for many long years and you will rule at his side."

"And what is the price?" Aylaen asked.

She glanced surreptitiously about the garden, hoping to find a way out, although she knew she was a fool to even consider trying to flee.

"The three spiritbones I lack," Aelon replied. "The Vektan Torque. The bone given to me by the mad god, Sund. And the one the Sea Queen gave to you. They are well hidden. Even I cannot find them."

Hearing his tone of calm satisfaction, seeing the amusement in his eyes, Aylaen put her hand to her belt. The god had not moved nor come near her and yet the drawstring bag was gone.

"Don't worry," said Aelon. "You did not mislay it. I have it safe."

He held up the bag. Releasing the drawstrings, he reached inside and drew out the brooch. The rubies sparkled, the gold shone.

"Give me the three I am missing and Skylan lives."

Aylaen was shaking, more in anger at herself than with fear. If she had only left when she had the spiritbone, not stopped to watch the children, not fallen into his trap!

"Another trick," she said.

"Let us call it a bargain," Aelon replied. "My army has forced Skylan and his warriors to retreat, take refuge in the hall. Give me the spiritbones and Skylan and his children live. If you don't, Skylan dies and your children will never be born. The choice is yours, and you had best decide quickly."

"I will!" Aylaen gasped. "Don't harm Skylan."

"A wise decision. Where are they?"

Aylaen shook her head. "They are well hidden. If I told you, you couldn't find them. I will bring them to you."

Aelon regarded her intently, probing her soul. "If you don't, Skylan will die." The god added drily, "Not even dragon-scale armor and a blessed sword can save him."

Aylaen met his gaze. "I will do as you ask. I will bring you the spiritbones."

"You have until the sun sets."

Thrusting the brooch with the spiritbone into the bag, he tied the drawstrings to his sword belt and disappeared.

She stumbled along the path and blundered into the forest, trying to find the path that would take her back to the ship and not having any luck, for she was desperately trying to think of what to do. Hot and exhausted, she realized she had to calm herself. She stopped beneath a tree to take a deep breath. Hearing a rustling sound, she feared Aelon had returned, and she yanked her sword from the scabbard, terrifying Wulfe, who gave a yelp and scrambled backward.

Aylaen sighed in relief and sheathed her sword.

"What are you doing here?" she asked. "I told you to stay on board the ship."

"Skylan and the other dead Uglies are losing the battle," Wulfe said. "I came to tell you."

"How do you know?" Aylaen asked. She continued along the narrow path that wound among the trees. Wulfe trailed after her, shuffling his bare feet through the dead leaves.

"A dryad and some naiads and a couple of centaurs have been watching the fight and they told the oceanids, who told me. What are you going to do?"

"What I have to," said Aylaen shortly, not wanting to elaborate. Aelon could be anywhere, watching, listening.

"That's not an answer!" said Wulfe.

"It's the best you'll get," Aylaen replied, increasing her pace. Glancing over her shoulder, she saw Wulfe lagging behind. "You need to keep up. I don't have much time. Here, take my hand—"

Wulfe drew back, glowering at her. "You're going to let Skylan die."

Dropping to all fours, he ran back into the forest.

"Wulfe!" Aylaen called.

He did not reply and she couldn't waste time chasing after him. She broke into a run, following the path back to the deserted village and from there to the ship.

Aylaen was relieved when she found the *Venejekar* was safe, still floating among the mangroves. She had been afraid Aelon might have attacked it.

Acronis and Farinn were keeping watch for her and they sprang to help as Aylaen crawled among the mangrove roots.

"Where's Wulfe?" Farinn asked, helping her board. "He said Skylan and his warriors were losing. He was going to tell you—"

"I saw him," said Aylaen. "I tried to talk to him, but he ran off. I don't know where he's gone and we can't wait for him to return."

"Aelon paid us a visit," Kahg reported. "The god didn't stay long. One of his serpents came to summon him. Despite what he claims, the battle is not going well for him."

At this point, Aylaen didn't know who to believe. She decided to see for herself.

"Cast off the ropes," she told Acronis. "Kahg, take us to the battlefield."

Kahg obeyed at once, almost before she had finished speaking, easing the *Venejekar* out of the tangle of prop roots and taking the ship out to sea. The dragon didn't ask what she was going to do, for which she was grateful. Either Kahg had confidence in her or he had made his own plans. Aylaen suspected the latter.

Having done all she could for the moment, she decided she had time for a brief rest after her exertions. Lowering herself onto the deck, she leaned back against a bulkhead and pressed her hand against her rib cage.

Acronis regarded her with concern. "Are you hurt?"

"A stitch in my side," she said, grimacing. "It will pass."

"Is what Wulfe said true? About Skylan losing?" Farinn asked anxiously.

"I don't know," said Aylaen. "Aelon told me the same, but Kahg says the god is lying."

Farinn gaped at her. "Aelon! The god! Did he harm you? Is everything all right?"

"No," Aylaen said grimly. "But we will make it right. Is Joabis still on board?"

"Wulfe said the god left suddenly," said Farinn. "Something frightened him."

The arrival of Aelon probably scared Joabis out of what wits he has left, Aylaen thought. She was thankful the god was gone. She could proceed without interference. Feeling the pain ease, she rose to her feet.

"I'll be in the hold," Aylaen told them. "I have to change my clothes."

As she climbed down the ladder, she saw Acronis and Farinn exchange startled glances.

She took off the dragon-scale armor and the leather tunic and pants. She unbuckled her sword belt and laid armor and sword aside. Opening her sea chest, she took out her wedding dress, an apron dress, the kind worn by Vindrasi women, made of green wool, embroidered with dragons, clasped at the shoulders by two gold dragon pins.

She pressed the fabric to her breast and closed her eyes, remembering her wedding day and their happiness. She seemed to feel Skylan close to her and she thought of their talk of the future and that made her think of the girl, Holma, and her brother, Skylanson.

She could see their faces and hear their laughter. She saw her children coming home, tired and hot and sweaty, cut and bruised and eager to tell their parents about the day's adventures.

With each choice we make, each road we travel, each door we open or close, we change the future of both men and the gods, for our wyrds are bound together.

Aylaen put on a plain linen shift, drew the apron dress on over that, and fastened it at the shoulders with the gold pins. This done, she rummaged clear to the bottom of the sea chest and took out what she sought, a small knife with a thin blade; the type of knife used to gut fish.

She had found this knife after she and Skylan and the others were captured by Acronis and his soldiers. Blaming herself for Garn's death, she had planned to use the knife to die, but her sister, Treia, had stopped her.

Aylaen touched the knife's sharp point and thought of the irony, for not so long after that, Treia had tried to have her killed. Raegar had said Treia was carrying his child. Aylaen regretted telling Raegar about the bargain Treia had made with Hevis. She did not wish Treia well, but neither did she wish her ill, and she feared what Raegar might do. All Treia had ever wanted was for someone to love her.

Aylaen slipped the knife beneath the skirt of the apron dress, tucking it into a belt she had tied around her shift, then went to Treia's sea chest that had remained, forgotten, in the hold of the *Venejekar* ever since her sister had left them. Aylaen searched for the robes Treia had worn when she performed her duties as a Bone Priestess and found them wadded up in a heap and stashed at the bottom.

The robes were worn and frayed. The hem was caked with dried mud and there were spots on them that might have been blood, for Treia had worn these in the battle against the ogres, the battle that had, in a way, led Aylaen to where she was now.

Marveling at the twists and turns of their wyrds, Aylaen thought about what she planned. Her decision might not be the right one. The thread might snap in her hands. But this was the only way she could think of to secure the future she had seen. If Aelon had meant to frighten her by showing her a vision of her children, he had not succeeded. He had given her strength and courage and resolve.

She returned to the deck wearing her wedding dress over the plain linen shift and, over that, the ceremonial robes. Acronis and Farinn both stared. They must be thinking she had lost her mind.

She returned to her familiar place at the prow beside the dragon. The *Venejekar* bounded over the waves. The wind of their swift passage blew in her face, cooling her. The sun was starting to slide into the sea, but she had time yet. She tugged at the folds of the robes, rearranging them.

"The knife doesn't show, if that's what you are concerned about, my dear," Acronis whispered.

He had come up behind her and Aylaen turned to him, dismayed. "How did you know I was carrying a knife, sir? If you were able to tell, then so will Aelon."

"Aelon lacks my genius," said Acronis drily, with a reassuring chuckle. "The robes are loose-fitting, ideal for concealing a small weapon, though not a sword. You would not go into battle unarmed, therefore I deduced a knife."

His expression grew grave. "For you are going into battle, aren't you, Aylaen?"

"I am, sir. I have to," she replied.

"To save Skylan?"

"To save more than him," she said softly.

"We are rounding the point," Farinn called. "You can see the battle. At least, I think that's what I'm seeing."

Aylaen tried to make out what was happening, but she was a mortal looking upon the realm of the dead. She stared into a gray mist that roiled and shifted, seeing disembodied faces and hands, skulls and eyes slide into view and then vanish. Mouths were open, shouting, screaming. Swords clashed on shields. Hammers on axes. And the only sound she could hear was the waves splashing beneath the keel.

Aylaen took Kahg's spiritbone from its place on the nail and held it into the spray breaking over the bow, dousing it with seawater. Kahg was watching her. His eyes gleamed fiercely.

"Take us ashore," Aylaen ordered the dragon.

For a moment, Skylan thought they had won.

The ogres under the leadership of Bear Walker had crashed into the right flank of the enemy phalanx with the force of an avalanche roaring down a mountainside, rolling over them and flattening them. Skylan and his forces had shouted in derision as the hellkite forces crumbled. They hoped this meant Aelon and his fiends would retreat.

Unfortunately, the ogres' success proved their undoing. They drove so far forward that the enemy was able to outflank them, attack them from the rear. The ogre shield wall disintegrated as the hellkites swarmed around them, hitting them from all sides.

Skylan was about to call on his warriors to go their aid when he felt a hand grasp his shoulder. Thinking it was Sigurd, he turned and was amazed to see Joabis.

The god was wild-eyed with fear and shaking so he could barely speak. He managed to blurt out, "Aylaen!"

Skylan grasped hold of him by the tunic. "What about her?"

"She's gone to save the spiritbone!" Joabis gasped. "Aelon mustn't see her! You need to keep him occupied!"

Skylan looked overhead to see the god in his serpent-drawn chariot flying overhead, shouting commands to his hellkites.

The thought came to him that Aelon was well occupied in planning their destruction, but he knew what Joabis meant. If he and his warriors went down to defeat, Aelon would be free to pursue Aylaen.

Joabis disappeared and at the same instant the doors of the

hall—where there had been no doors—opened wide. Joabis stood inside, waving his arms.

"In here!" the god was shouting. "You'll be safe!"

Not so long ago, Skylan would have never considered retreating. He would have fought to the death and gone proudly to Torval. Now he had more at stake than his own honor and glory. Aylaen was on this island trying to recover the spiritbone. He had to keep Aelon from finding her.

"Fall back!" Skylan roared, grimacing as he spoke, for the words tasted more bitter than wormwood. "Keep together! Fall back!"

The Vindrasi warriors looked startled. He couldn't blame them. Probably no chief in Vindrasi history had ever ordered a retreat. They obeyed, however, and began the long march to the rear, joined by Bear Walker and the surviving ogres, and by Dela Eden and her Cyclopes, picking up spent arrows as they went.

Skylan kept a close eye on his forces. If one warrior broke and ran, others would follow and the retreat would become a rout. His command held together, continuing to fight even as they inched backward step by step until they reached the hall.

Skylan and Bear Walker were the last to enter, holding off hellkites until the last warrior was inside, then they dashed through the door. Several hellkites charged after them, only to be cut down by Sigurd and Grimuir, who had been lying in wait for them.

Sigurd started to slam shut the door.

"Leave it open," Skylan ordered. "We have to see what they're doing. Drag that table across the opening."

Bear Walker and Keeper picked up one of the heavy tables that had been lying across trestles and rested it on its side in front of the door.

"What about our friends?" Skylan asked Sigurd. "Bjorn and Erdmun. Are they all right?"

"They're as alive as dead men can be," Sigurd replied, indicating Erdmun collapsed on the floor with Bjorn standing beside him. "The hellkites are rotten fighters. They're slow and clumsy and barely know one end of a sword from another."

"True," said Skylan. "The problem is, they just keep coming."

He looked about for Joabis, but, of course, he was gone. Still, Skylan had to give the god grudging credit. He'd risked his own precious skin to come tell Skylan about Aylaen.

The ogres and Cyclopes, working together, began overturning tables and setting up barricades. Skylan was figuring they could hold the hall for a considerable length of time.

And then he smelled smoke.

"They are building bonfires," said Keeper.

Stands of trees were going up in flames, orange fire and black smoke leaping to the heavens. The hellkites were carrying flaming brands.

Skylan grimly nodded. "They don't need to lay siege to the hall. They're going to burn it down."

His voice carried clearly in the silence of the hall. Ogres, Cyclopes, and humans stood together. Their numbers were reduced and Skylan found it odd to see no blood, to hear no screams. There were no wounded. The dead were simply gone, as if they had never been.

Skylan climbed up on one of the few tables still standing, so he could address them.

"We face a choice," he told them. "We can die in the flames or we can die and take some of our foe with us. I, for one, say that—"

"Skylan!" Bjorn shouted. "It's Aylaen!"

Sigurd and Grimuir and Erdmun crowded the doorway, trying to see. They moved aside for Skylan.

From this vantage point, he could see Acronis and Farinn splashing through the shallow water, their hands on the hull, guiding the *Venejekar* toward the shore. He wondered why Kahg wasn't sailing it, then realized that the eyes on the dragonhead prow were dark, nothing more than carved wood.

Aylaen had already left the ship and was walking across the beach.

"Move that barricade. I've got to go to her!" Skylan said, gripping his sword.

Bjorn and Keeper caught hold of him.

"You wouldn't get three feet from the door," said Keeper.

"He's right. Besides, Aylaen knows what she is doing. Look at how she is dressed!" said Bjorn.

Skylan looked and realized she was not dressed for battle. She was not wearing armor or carrying her sword. She was dressed in her finest clothes, wearing the rune-embroidered robes of a Bone Priestess.

"Looks like she's going to a bloody wedding," Sigurd grumbled.

Skylan remembered that dress and the last time she had worn it. She was carrying a pouch in her hand and Skylan recognized that, as well. A silken pouch made of bamboo given to her by the Sea Queen. Aylaen kept the spiritbones inside that pouch. His friends were right. She was planning something. He had to be ready to act.

The hellkites caught sight of her and surged forward menacingly. Flying overhead in his chariot, Aelon give an angry shout and the hellkites fell back.

Aylaen turned her head to look straight at Skylan, almost as if she could see him. He raised his hand and she raised hers in response, the hand carrying the pouch that held the spiritbones. The look lasted no more than a heartbeat, and then she turned from him to the god.

"Aelon! I have the spiritbones as I promised!" Aylaen called. "In return, you have promised me that my people will not be harmed."

Skylan's friends turned to stare at him.

"She's a damn traitor!" said Sigurd.

Skylan slammed his fist into Sigurd's jaw, knocking him to the floor. He turned back to watch Aylaen. The pouch she carried, the robes she was wearing. He was starting to think he understood.

"Ready your weapons," Skylan ordered. "Wait for my command. Where's Dela Eden?"

He looked around for the priestess of the Cyclopes and, catching sight of her, motioned her over. "I'll need your archers to give us cover."

"We have very few arrows," said Dela Eden.

"Then make every one of them count," Skylan returned.

Dela Eden took her place beside him and looked out the door. Aelon was ordering his serpents to take his chariot to the ground. Aylaen stood alone, surrounded by an army of the dead, waiting to confront a god.

"She is your woman?" Dela Eden asked.

"My wife," said Skylan.

"Do you know what she is plotting?"

"No," Skylan admitted.

"But you trust her?"

"Yes," Skylan answered simply.

Dela Eden's eyes—including the painted eye—looked at him and then seemed to look inside him.

"You must always remember," she said.

Skylan thought that an odd thing to say.

"What do you mean? What did you see?"

But Dela Eden had crouched down on the floor and was busily sorting through the spent arrows she had managed to retrieve, trying to find those that were still in good condition.

She did not answer him.

Aylaen had known a moment's terror when the dead had started to come for her, creeping toward her, heads without eyes, eyes without heads, hands and arms with swords, but no bodies. Her courage had almost failed her, and then she heard Skylan's voice.

She turned to look and thought she caught a glimpse of him, standing in the door of an immense hall. He would see the wedding dress and the robes she wore. He would not know what she was planning, but he would trust her, as she trusted him.

The chariot landed, wheels touching the ground.

Aelon did not descend, but gave a peremptory wave of his hand and ordered, "Come to me."

Aylaen walked toward him. As she drew near the chariot, the serpents opened their fanged mouths and hissed at her as though they would strike, while Aelon watched with a slight smile on his face.

Aylaen knew quite well the god was trying to intimidate her and she steeled herself to walk past the serpents slowly, without flinching, to the rear of the chariot that was made of bronze trimmed in silver and gold and adorned with gilded serpents biting their own tails. Aelon stood inside the chariot. Aylaen saw without seeming to see that the rucksack containing the spiritbone was still hanging from his sword belt.

"You have the three spiritbones with you?" Aelon asked.

"In this pouch," said Aylaen.

He reached for it, but she drew it back.

"I want to see Skylan," Aylaen said. "Show me that he is alive and well and then I will give these to you."

Aelon seemed amused. "What stops me from taking them? Certainly not a mere mortal."

"They are guarded by the same magic that kept you from finding them," said Aylaen. "If you try to take them by force, the magic will destroy them."

"I think you are bluffing," said Aelon. "But I will play along."
Aelon raised his voice.

"Skylan Ivorson! Come forth from the hall! Come greet your wife!"

Aylaen looked toward the hall. She had not been able to see him
when he had come to her on board the *Venejekar* for they were in the
realm of the living. But now, in the realm of the dead, she saw him
clearly, saw the difference between him and the dead. He was both sub-
stance and shadow, not dead nor yet alive.

He did not immediately come forth, and Aylaen could see that
others were arguing with him, probably warning him that this was a
trap. Knowing him as she did, she was not surprised to see him shake
off their restraining hands and walk out onto the field of battle.

"Lay down your sword," said Aelon. "You will not need it."

Skylan shook his head.

"I know you mean to kill me and I will not come before Torval
without my hand on my sword."

"I have no intention of killing you, Vindrasi. Your wife has arranged
that you will live a long life and die peacefully in your old age."

Skylan's eyes flicked over Aylaen. His face was cold and set.

"I do not thank her," he said harshly.

Aelon chuckled. "You will one day. And now, Priestess, I have done
as you asked."

"Restore him to life," said Aylaen.

"Do not push me," said Aelon coldly. "Or he may yet stand before
his god and you with him. Give me the spiritbones."

Aylaen walked slowly and with seeming reluctance toward the chariot. The god stood waiting for her, watching her warily.

Coming to stand before him, she loosened the drawstrings of the
pouch, reached inside, and drew out a spiritbone. Plain and unadorned,
no gold, no jewels, it dangled from the end of a worn leather thong.

Aelon scowled. "What is this?"

"A message from Vindrash."

Aylaen flung the spiritbone into the air.

The Dragon Kahg burst into life above Aelon's chariot. The dragon's scales were the slate gray of a stormy sea, his mane white with foam. Seawater fell from his wings and rolled off his body, dousing the bonfires. His eyes glowed with fire.

Aelon stared at the dragon, paralyzed by shock. The drawstring bag hung from his belt, forgotten.

Aylaen darted her hand beneath the robes, drew her little knife and in a swift motion, swept the blade through the strings of the drawstring bag with one hand and grabbed hold of it with the other. She could feel the brooch inside the bag; the pin pricked her finger, and she thrust the bag into her shift, cast one swift look of love and longing at Skylan, then hiked up her skirts and ran.

Skylan stepped between the god and Aylaen. Grasping his amulet, Skylan said a prayer to Torval and thrust his sword, God-rage, into Aelon's ribs.

Forged of the same stuff as the gods, the sword bit deep into Aelon's immortal flesh. Blood spewed. Bone splintered. Aelon cried out and doubled over in pain, cursing.

Skylan yanked the blade from the god's flesh and stared at the blood-covered blade in amazement.

"God-rage," he said, awed. "You are aptly named."

He would need such a blade. For Aelon was drawing his own sword.

Waiting on the beach, standing guard over the *Venejekar*, Acronis saw Aylaen running for the ship. She did not see the danger behind her—two of Aelon's serpents in pursuit.

The serpents had no wings; their silver, sinuous bodies undulated in the air. Their mouths gaped, tongues flicked, and venom dripped from their fangs.

Aylaen stumbled in the wet sand and fell to her knees. She tried to scramble to her feet, but she was tangled in her skirts. Acronis and Farinn ran to her aid, standing protectively over her, his sword in his hand, as Farinn dropped the axe he had been holding to help her to her feet.

Acronis was bracing for the serpent attack when a stream of water, shooting out of the air, struck one of the serpents with such force that it flipped head over tail and plunged into the sea.

The Dragon Kahg roared and shot another geyser of water, missing the second serpent, but forcing it to give up on its prey and whip around to face the dragon.

"Farinn, you and Aylaen run to the ship!" Acronis ordered, seeing more serpents coming.

Aylaen saw them, too, and she hesitated.

"You have the spiritbone to guard and you are not dressed for battle," Acronis told her. "Let me earn my keep."

Aylaen cast a rueful glance at her wedding dress, now covered in wet sand, and the robes that had tangled around her feet. "I will go hide the spiritbone. Then I'll be back to help. Farinn, come with me. I need you to stand guard."

Farinn cast a glance at Acronis, who mouthed the words, "Don't let her!"

Nodding in understanding, Farinn followed Aylaen into the sea, wading out to the *Venejekar*.

Acronis turned to see the serpent trying to strike Kahg from underneath, hoping to sink its fangs into his belly. The dragon twisted in the air, rolled out of the way, and seized the serpent by the head. Clamping his jaws over the snake's skull, Kahg crushed it and flung the corpse to the ground.

The serpent that Kahg had knocked into the sea had recovered from its drenching and now flew to attack the dragon. Kahg seized it, too, in his claws, trying to bite it, as the serpent twisted and tried to strike the dragon with its venomous fangs.

Acronis was watching the battle and keeping an eye out for more serpents, when he heard Farinn call his name and shout a warning. Acronis turned to see the first serpent, the one Kahg had killed, had come back to life and was slithering toward him. The crushed and mangled head dangled from the body and Acronis recalled Skylan saying that the only way to kill these creatures was to pierce the heart.

Sword in hand, he ran toward the serpent, looking at the enormous writhing body and wondering just exactly where the heart was located. Figuring he'd just start stabbing, he saw, to his dismay, two heads starting to sprout like some horrid fungus from the ruin of the first.

As the heads grew rapidly, he lunged at the monster, driving his sword deep into the body. Blood spurted, but he had apparently missed the heart, for the serpent reared up, towering over him, and attacked.

The two heads darted at him. He struck at the nearest head and cut it from the body. He couldn't recover in time and the second head was diving toward him. Acronis dropped his sword, flung himself to the sand and rolled.

He felt a stinging pain on the back of his sword hand where a tooth grazed him in passing, but that was all. The serpent hissed in anger and coiled, prepared to strike again.

Regretting his years, Acronis pushed himself stiffly to his feet and picked up his sword. Two more heads were growing out of the body to take the place of the head he had cut off and now three heads were darting at him, tongues flicking, fangs dripping.

He drove his sword into one head, jabbing it in the jaw. Yanking the sword free, he started to strike again when a wave of dizziness assailed him. He staggered and fell to the sand.

Acronis tried to stand, but his throat burned and a strange lethargy seized hold of him. He could only watch in a dreamlike haze as a wolf with yellow blazing eyes came running across the beach to attack the serpent. The wolf struck the monster from behind, jumping on its body, snarling and biting at the backs of the heads.

The serpent twisted in fury, attempting to free itself, and then reared up, throwing off the wolf, who landed on its side with a pain-filled howl. Before the serpent could strike, the sea began to boil, and outraged oceanids sent waves crashing over the serpent, half drowning it, as a bevy of shrieking dryads and satyrs attacked it. The dryads stabbed it with sharpened sticks while the satyrs trampled the serpent with their goat legs and slashing hooves.

When the serpent at last quit wriggling and lay dead, the wolf picked himself up and limped over to sniff at Acronis.

Acronis grimaced as the horrible burning spread from his throat throughout his body. He drew in a shuddering breath and saw Wulfe crouched near him, careful not to touch his armor.

"You need to get up, Ugly," said Wulfe, frowning.

"I agree," Acronis said weakly. He coughed, finding it hard to breathe. "But I can't seem . . . to feel my feet."

He paused, struggling to speak, then asked in a whisper, "Were those faeries I saw?"

"My people," said Wulfe. "I brought them with me to help Skylan. I keep telling you, but you won't believe me."

"I believe you now. I have seen such wonders. Wait until I tell Chloe . . . ," Acronis murmured.

"You don't have to wait much longer, dear Father," said Chloe.

She was standing on the beach beside him, holding out her hands to him.

"I lead the dance just as Skylan promised," Chloe told him. She knelt beside him. "You will come dance with me."

Acronis was overcome by joy. He tried to speak, to answer his beloved child, to tell her how he longed to dance with her. The pain was too great, closing his throat. He struggled to breathe.

The struggle did not last long.

On board the *Venejekar*, Aylaen left Farinn to keep watch while she ran down into the hold. Without Wulfe and his magic, she could not hide the spiritbone in the bulkhead with the others and she feared any moment Aelon might come searching for it.

She hurriedly threw off the robes of the Bone Priestess, removed the golden dragon pins and let the wedding dress fall around her ankles, leaving her in her shift. Catching up the dress, she pinned the spiritbone brooch to the bodice, folded the fabric over the pin and stowed them in her sea chest.

It was a poor hiding place, but she hoped that the strength of her love for Skylan would keep the spiritbone safe. She was about to close the lid, then caught sight of the robes lying on the deck.

The robes of the Bone Priestess were sacred to Vindrash and the goddess had served Aylaen well, keeping Aelon from discovering the knife. Treia had hated and despised these robes that symbolized a life she had hated. She had abandoned that life and Aylaen had chosen it.

Aylaen ran her hand over the runes embroidered onto the cloth. Treia's needlework had been done in haste and with an ill will, and many of the threads were frayed or broken. Aylaen rested the robes on top of her wedding dress, shut the sea chest and was commending it to Vindrash's care when she heard Farinn shouting to her.

"Aylaen! Wulfe is here and he says Acronis has fallen!"

Aylaen thrust her arms and head into her dragon-scale armor, picked up her sword, and ran back up on deck.

As the battle raged around him, Skylan waited, sword in hand, to see what Aelon would do. Thus far, the god had done nothing: Aylaen had reached the *Venejekar* safely. Acronis and Kahg were fighting the serpents. When the warriors in the hall saw the dragon join the battle, they shouted to their gods, Torval, and the Gods of Raj, and ran to the attack.

Aelon watched the battle from his chariot. The god smiled, as if amused by the entertainment. Skylan grew uneasy, wondering what the god was plotting. He had to keep him from going after Aylaen.

"Do you fear to fight me, Aelon?" Skylan taunted. "My sword bites deep, as you know."

"Fear you?" Aelon gave a grim smile. "I could kill you like a gnat, with a swat of my hand."

"Then why haven't you?" Skylan challenged.

"Because, for now, you are protected," said Aelon. He pointed with his sword to the amulet. "Once I have destroyed the sorry gods who shield you, you and your people are doomed. Raegar and his armies will slaughter them like sheep."

"My people do not slaughter easily," said Skylan proudly.

"And neither do their gods," said Joabis.

Skylan turned in astonishment to see at his side the God of Revels, wearing ancient armor, clutching a battle axe and smelling strongly of ale. Joabis swayed slightly back and forth; the hands holding the axe were far from steady. He belched defiance.

Aelon laughed and seemed to swell, expanding, soaring, towering above them, his head brushing the heavens. His sword flashed red in the light of the setting sun and hissed as it sliced through the air in a blow that would obliterate Skylan. He held Aylaen's face in his mind, the last sight he would see, and stood his ground.

An arrow streaked from the heavens, hit Aelon's sword, and knocked it from the god's hand. The blade spun in the air, twisting and turning, and plunged into the ocean, sending up a huge cloud of spray.

Torval and Vindrash and the other gods of the Vindrasi strode onto the field of battle. The Gods of Raj joined them, taking the forms of two enormous ogres, carrying war hammers the size of oak trees. A female Cyclopes walked with them, firing arrows from her bow.

Joabis belched and grinned.

"I brought help," said the god.

The Dragon Kahg gave a loud roar as Vindrash, in her dragon form, flew to join him. Torval and his heroes smashed into the ranks of the hellkites.

Garn took his place at Skylan's side.

"Some god loves you, my friend," he said.

"Not that one," said Skylan, laughing and pointing to Aelon.

The laughter caught in his throat, nearly choking him.

The most beautiful woman he had ever seen stood before him. Her black hair, unbound, fell over her shoulders. Her eyes were brown flecked with gold. She held out her hands to him to show him she was not armed, a fact that he could see plainly for himself, for her flimsy dress of some filmy fabric concealed almost nothing.

She started to touch his face with her hand. He drew back from her and she let her hand fall.

"Do not be so quick to say Aelon does not love you, Skylan Ivorson," the god said with a charming smile. "To prove it, I will give you this piece of advice: go home. You see, this attack was a diversion. While you and your gods have been battling ghosts, your cousin, Raegar, is sailing to the land of the Stormlords with the largest army ever assembled in the history of this world."

Skylan was shaken by this news, but he would remain in the realm

of the dead forever before he would let Aelon see she had unnerved
him.

He shrugged. "Let my cousin sail where he pleases. I care nothing
about these Stormlords."

Aelon cast him a glittering glance between lowered lashes. "Then
I don't suppose you care about the spiritbone they have in their possession."

Skylan gripped the hilt of his sword and looked past the god, out
to sea. "I don't know what you are talking about."

Aelon drew closer and he shivered.

"Because I love you, Skylan," she said softly, "I will do something
gods rarely do for mortals. I will tell you the truth. I would like to
have the five spiritbones and the power of creation. I could do many
wondrous things for this world if I had such power. But I don't *need*
it. I've done quite well without it."

Skylan was puzzled. Did this mean Aelon was giving up the fight?
He glanced at Garn, who looked grim.

Aelon gave Skylan a charming smile, then languidly walked back
to her chariot. She moved slowly, taking her time. Pausing, she looked
at him over her shoulder and added, "I just need to stop you from
getting it."

She stepped inside and picked up the reins. "Your wife could have
saved your people. She chose not to and now my armies march on
them. Go home. Give up the fight. No matter what you do, you cannot win. So you have four spiritbones. You need five."

"I have won this day!" Skylan shouted, goaded into speaking.

"Because I let you," said Aelon.

Her serpents carried her chariot into the sky. The Dragon Kahg
chased after them, but god, serpents, and chariot vanished in a dazzling flash of white light.

"She speaks the truth," said Skylan, downcast. "She needs only one
spiritbone and that one is with the Stormlords. How can I fight an
army?"

Joabis snorted. "As a gambler myself, I can tell you this, my friend—
Aelon is playing you for a fool."

Skylan cast Joabis a look of disgust. "When I want your opinion,
I'll ask for it."

"Much as I hate to agree with him, Skylan, Joabis is right," said

Garn. "Aelon has chased you around the world, gone beneath the sea and even entered the realm of the dead to find those spiritbones. You and Aylaen thwarted Aelon and now that he has lost, what else can he do except claim victory?"

"And make me doubt myself," said Skylan.

"Aelon doesn't need one spiritbone to stop the gods. Aelon needs one to stop two mortals: you and Aylaen."

Skylan considered Garn's words, then said, "You are right, my friend. There might be a chance—"

Someone smote him from behind, sending him staggering. Skylan whipped about, sword raised, to see Sigurd.

"You and Garn having a cozy chat?" Sigurd asked, sneering. "Sorry to interrupt, but the rest of us are fighting for our bloody lives! If you two old women are finished with your gossip, we could use your help."

"I thought you could handle this lot yourself, Sigurd," said Skylan, laughing.

Sigurd glared at him, muttering, and ran back to the battlefield. Despite the departure of their god, the hellkites were still fighting. Perhaps death was preferable to their unholy lives.

Skylan rested his hand on Garn's shoulder. "We will fight together one last time before I join you in Torval's Hall."

"May that time be long in coming," said Garn.

Wulfe took Aylaen and Farinn to where Acronis lay on the sand. Aylaen had not wanted to believe the boy when he told her Acronis was dead and, seeing no wound, no blood, she hoped he was mistaken. Falling to her knees beside him, she started to feel for a pulse.

She knew when she touched him, he was gone. His skin was already cold, his lips tinged with blue.

"I told you," said Wulfe, standing back, keeping clear of her sword. "You never believe me."

"How did he die?" Aylaen asked.

"Poison. The snake bit him." Wulfe pointed to Acronis's hand.

Aylaen brushed her hand over her eyes, which were burning with tears. "Once I would have rejoiced in his death," she admitted, remembering when he had captured them, made her and her friends his slaves. "Now I grieve his loss. Where is his sword? He should have it with him."

Farinn, after a brief search, found the Legate's sword lying the sand. Picking it up, he gently laid it on his breast and clasped the cold hands over the hilt.

"I hope you and Chloe are together, sir," said Aylaen.

Perhaps it was her fond imagination or perhaps because she was in the realm of the dead, but she looked out across the sand and saw two figures, shadowy and indistinct, and yet she knew them.

Acronis and his daughter, dancing.

The hellkites could not withstand the combined forces of the gods and the dead heroes attacking the fiends in the name of their gods. When the last hellkite had been dispatched, Skylan and Bear Walker and Dela Eden met in the middle of the battlefield.

"The day is ours," said Skylan.

"And now this god of drunks must keep his promise," said Bear Walker, with a frowning look at Joabis, who was happily celebrating their win with a foaming mug of ale.

"He will," said Skylan. "Torval will see to that. When your lives are returned, I have something important to discuss with you both."

"You need an army to go to the land of the Stormlords," said Dela Eden.

Skylan flushed, disconcerted. "Stop sneaking into my head!" he told her with a baleful look at her third eye.

"Don't worry, Vindrasi," said Dela Eden, laughing. "There's very little there worth stealing."

Before he could make a cutting retort, Dela Eden looked past his shoulder. "Here comes your woman. You have a treasure in her, Vindrasi."

"I know," said Skylan.

He had the impression that Aylaen was standing quite near him, yet she seemed as far away as if she were on the other side of the world. He reached out to her, and she to him, but their hands could not meet. The gulf that separated them was too deep and vast for them to cross.

"Joabis will keep his promise," said Skylan. "He will restore our lives and I will come to you soon."

She smiled, but there was a sadness about her smile that troubled Skylan.

"I came to tell you that the fourth spiritbone is safely hidden with the others. Wulfe and Farinn and the Dragon Kahg are guarding it."

"That is good," said Skylan, wondering what was wrong. He went back over her words and thought he knew. "You spoke of Farinn and Wulfe, but you did not mention Acronis."

"He is dead," said Aylaen gently. "He died saving Farinn and me from Aelon's serpents."

"I am sorry," said Skylan. "But do not grieve. I will ask Joabis to restore his life, as well."

"Acronis won't come back to us, Skylan," said Aylaen, adding with a faint smile. "He is with Chloe now."

"Then we will meet again in Torval's Hall," said Skylan.

"Come to me soon, Skylan," said Aylaen. "Every moment we have together is precious."

She turned and walked away, her arms clasped across her chest. There seemed a shadow of sadness over her.

"She grieves for Acronis," said Skylan.

Dela Eden grunted and he turned to see her watching him. She raised an eyebrow, causing her third eye to twitch, then walked off.

Joabis invited the souls of the warriors and the gods to assemble in the hall. He was in a jovial mood, broaching a huge barrel of ale and handing out mugs, inviting them to drink to their glorious win. The warriors eyed him askance and stood in grim silence.

"Keep your ale," said Sigurd. "We want our lives."

The rest rumbled their agreement.

Joabis looked sheepish and tried to sidle behind the barrels. "There is a slight problem. I can't really do that—"

Ogres, men, and Cyclopes roared in fury.

"But I can!" said Torval, halting the angry clamor.

The god took his place at the head of the hall to address them. He stood straight, and his eyes burned with a fierce light. He was not the weary, sorrowful god Skylan had seen in the Hall of Valor. He was the god of legend, who had fought the Great Dragon Ilyrion and claimed a world.

Torval gestured to Skylan. "This strange alliance was your doing, Fish Knife. I know our people . . ."

The god's keen gaze swept over the Vindrasi warriors, who stood straight and tall, proud of their god in front of the unbelievers.

"But I do not know these others," Torval continued. "Introduce me."

Skylan described the actions of both the Cyclopes and the ogres and told of their heroism in battle. Torval complimented Bear Walker and Dela Eden, who were gracious, if reserved in the presence of a god they considered an enemy.

Torval smiled, understanding.

"I honor all of you this day, whether you are Vindrasi, ogres, or Cyclopes, and it will be my privilege to restore the lives of such brave warriors. When you leave this island, you will return to the realm of the living."

A cheer went up from everyone in the hall. Sigurd and Grimuir slapped each other on the back. Bjorn shook hands with Bear Walker and Dela Eden, and even Erdmun couldn't find anything to be gloomy about. Joabis, relieved, started passing out mugs.

Skylan stood apart, watching the warriors celebrate.

Torval eyed him. "I will restore your life, as well, Fish Knife."

"Thank you, Torval," said Skylan.

"But that is not all you want of me, is it," Torval said, rubbing his chin.

"Aelon sends an army to the land of the Stormlords," said Skylan. "The god plans to attack them and take the fifth spiritbone."

"And you intend to see to it that Aelon does not get it," said Torval.

"That is my hope, Torval, but my force consists of Sigurd and Grimuir; Bjorn and Erdmun; myself and Aylaen; young Farinn, a poet, who is skilled in singing of battles, but not so skilled in fighting them; Wulfe, a fae child who says he is the son of the faery princess; and the Dragon Kahg."

Skylan shrugged. "Sigurd would say that one Vindrasi warrior is worth one hundred of Aelon's, but that still leaves me short."

"You have an idea to even the odds," Torval said.

"If there was time to sail back to our homeland and raise an army of Vindrasi warriors, I would do so. But we are far from our home land and Raegar's fleet is already at sea. I want to ask the ogres and the Cyclopes to join me in the fight."

Torval's expression darkened. "You would not find help at home even if there were time. The Vindrasi will soon be fighting their own battle against Aelon. In fact, I was going to take the Vindrasi who fought with you back home to warn our people."

"All except Sigurd and Grimuir, Bjorn and Erdmun," said Skylan. "They are my friends."

Torval smiled. "Agreed. Your idea is a good one. I will speak to the Gods of Raj. Perhaps we can make a bargain with them."

Skylan had started to turn away, thinking they were finished, when Torval stopped him.

"I have not yet finished with you," said Torval sternly. He called for silence and when the warriors had settled down, he placed his hand on Skylan's shoulder.

"Skylan Ivorson, I forged you in fire and in blood. I struck you with my hammer and you did not break. You failed me and yourself and others, but you learned from failure. True, you have made me proud and I hereby relieve you of the name Fish Knife. You have earned the name Torval's Sword."

Walking over to Skylan, Torval handed him a leather sheath.

"Joabis has given you God-rage, a sword that I once gave him. Keep it safe in this sheath and the blade will never break."

The sheath was made of stiffened leather ornately worked in gold, with a gold chape at the tip and gold at the throat. Skylan fell to his knees before the god, his heart too full to let him speak.

He wished Aylaen could be here, but he would have the joy of telling her.

"Rise up, Torval's Sword," said a familiar voice.

Skylan looked to see his father standing before him, his eyes shining with pride.

Skylan shook his head and remained on his knees.

"Say you forgive me, Father," said Skylan. "Or I will be Fish Knife all the rest of my days."

"Between father and son, there is nothing to forgive," said Norgaard. "May you wield God-rage in honor and die with your sword in your hand."

"Thank you, Father," said Skylan. He touched the amulet around his neck. "In Torval's name."

He stood up, intending to embrace his father, thank Torval, and celebrate with his friends.

But his father was gone; Torval was gone. Garn and his other friends were gone, as was Joabis. Skylan was standing on an empty beach at sunset. He inhaled deeply and smelled the sea air. He tasted the salt spray on his lips and felt the cool water break around his ankles as the waves rolled up the shore where he stood. He heard Aylaen call his name and turned to see her splashing through the waves, running to his arms. He felt her embrace, warm and strong.

The realm of death was gone. At long last, he was back in the land of the living.

Keeping fast hold of Aylaen, Skylan walked farther up the shore to see Bear Walker standing among hundreds of ogre warriors, talking to them. The ogres listened to their chief, silent and attentive. Far different were the hundreds of Cyclopes warriors, who were making a riotous clamor. Each Cyclopes had to have a say and they were saying it all at once.

Sigurd and Grimuir, Bjorn and Erdmun stood on the shore chatting with Farinn, who had been delighted to see them and left the dragon-ship to greet them. The other Vindrasi warriors had departed, sailing with Torval back to Vindraholm to prepare for Aelon's attack.

Skylan turned to Aylaen. "We have to make a decision, my love, and we don't have much time. Aelon told me that Raegar is leading the largest army ever assembled to attack the land of the Stormlords."

Aylaen regarded him in dismay. "He seeks the spiritbone!" Then she paused, frowning in perplexity. "Why would the god tell you? Aelon knows we will try to stop him."

"The very reason why he told me," said Skylan. "If we sail to the land of the Stormlords seeking the fifth spiritbone, we bring the other four within Aelon's reach."

"And risk losing them all," said Aylaen. "Still, that is a risk we must take. Our gods have entrusted us with four of the spiritbones. We *must* find the fifth."

"We need an army," said Skylan, drawing her even closer. "I asked Torval to help me convince the Gods of Raj to fight with us. He said he would speak to them, make some sort of bargain."

"And what would that bargain be, I wonder?" Aylaen asked, her brow furrowed.

Skylan shrugged. "I don't know. They will agree upon something—gold, jewels. Whatever gods consider valuable."

"I don't think gods value gold and jewels," Aylaen said, troubled.

Before Skylan could reply, Bear Walker shouted for them.

"Vindrasi! We have made a decision!"

"We must go see if we have an army," said Skylan.

He and Aylaen were joined by Keeper, Bear Walker and Raven's-foot, and Dela Eden. Aylaen embraced Keeper and said she was glad to see Bear Walker and Raven's-foot again. Skylan introduced Dela Eden, who gazed at Aylaen intently.

Aylaen, for her part, stared at the Cyclopes warriors in shock.

"They all have three eyes!" she whispered to Skylan.

"The third eye is not real," Skylan returned with seeming nonchalance. "It is only painted."

"Your gods kept their promise, Vindrasi. We breathe again," said Dela Eden.

Bear Walker gave a solemn nod while Raven's-foot grunted and rolled his eyes as if to indicate nothing could have surprised him more.

"Our gods have been talking to your gods," Dela Eden continued. "Your god tells us that Aelon plans to attack the land of the Stormlords and that you need our help to recover the spiritbone now in the keeping of the Stormlords."

Aylaen and Skylan both stared at her, speechless. The gods of the Vindrasi had kept the spiritbones a secret. Aelon knew about them because of the betrayal of the mad god, Sund. How did the Gods of Raj find out? Skylan could not imagine Torval would have told them. He wondered if he should try to deny it.

"Don't bother," said Dela Eden. "We know about the spiritbones."

"How?" Aylaen demanded.

"When the Gods of Raj came to this world, they realized they lacked the power to create. They were not overly concerned. They had much work to do with what was already here, your gods having left the world in such a sorry state. Still, the mystery intrigued them and they set about searching for the answer."

"Who told them?" Aylaen asked.

"The dragons," said Dela Eden. "Our people and the dragons have long been on friendly terms. The portal that leads to their world, the Realm of Fire, is located on Mount Joka of our land. It seems that Vindrash swore the dragons to secrecy, but they found out that Vindrash lied to them and they were no longer bound by their oath."

"So now your gods want the spiritbones for themselves," said Skylan in grim tones.

"Not really," said Dela Eden. "When our gods came to this world, they were too busy fighting your gods to notice that they lacked the power to create. Aelon told them he had it and promised to share. The Gods of Raj discovered Aelon was lying, biding his time until he defeated your gods, then he was planning to turn on them. The Gods of Raj want the power of creation, but our gods will not destroy to get it."

Skylan blinked at this, trying to untangle her words.

Bear Walker cut through the knot and came to the point. "Your gods and our gods agree upon one thing—the power must not fall into the hands of Aelon."

"Yet you said yourself you were once his ally—" Skylan began heatedly.

Aylaen gave him a sharp jab in the ribs with her elbow and he fell silent.

"We are all agreed on this, I think," said Dela Eden.

"We are," said Bear Walker.

"We are," said Aylaen. "Aren't we, Skylan?"

"I suppose," said Skylan, still wondering if he could trust them. At this point he didn't have a choice. "Does this mean you will help us fight Aelon?"

"We talked it over," said Bear Walker, glancing back at his ogre warriors. "Aelon's soldiers killed us once. We want a chance to avenge our deaths."

Dela Eden added in agreement. "Your gods offered us a bargain. My people and I have accepted. Of course, the decision is up to each one individually, but speaking for myself, I will go with you to fight Aelon."

Skylan should have been glad to have their help. He had asked Torval and clearly Torval had made some sort of deal with the Gods of Raj. He was tempted to ask what that bargain was, but he feared that would make him look weak, as though he didn't have the confidence of his gods.

He drew Aylaen off to one side, to speak in private. "What do you think we should do?"

"What we have to do," Aylaen said. "We need their help."

"What if they try to take the spiritbones for themselves?"

"I suppose that is a risk, but I don't think they will," Aylaen answered. "The dragons trust them."

Skylan glanced up at Kahg, caught the faint red glimmer of his half-closed eyes.

"And what about this bargain Torval made?" Skylan asked. "We have no idea what it is."

"If Torval had wanted us to know, he would have told us," said Aylaen.

Skylan sighed and ran his hands through his hair. "Our song is missing a great many verses."

"Better than not being sung at all," Aylaen told him.

Skylan regarded her fondly. "What did I do to deserve such a wise wife?"

"Not a thing. Because you don't," said Aylaen with a kiss. "Now go take command of your army."

Skylan returned to Bear Walker and Dela Eden. "I will be honored to have your courageous warriors join us in battle. The only problem now is how do we sail to the land of the Stormlords? We cannot all fit in one dragonship."

"There is your answer," said Aylaen, pointing out to sea.

Four dragonships—the largest dragonships Skylan had ever seen—were sailing toward the island. The Dragon Kahg gave a roar of greeting and the other dragons roared back in return.

"Where do these come from?" Skylan asked.

"Kahg says this is a gift from the dragons," said Aylaen. "The four dragons will not fight, because they have not forgiven Vindrash for lying to them, but they will carry us across the sea."

Skylan looked up at the dragon. Kahg's eyes were shining with a fierce red glow.

The ogres and the Cyclopes boarded the dragonships. Although they were not a seafaring people, the Cyclopes were accustomed to dealing with dragons and had no qualms about sailing in a ship guided by a dragon. Skylan assigned Sigurd and Bjorn to the Cyclopes to assist them in the techniques of sailing the unfamiliar dragonship.

The ogres presented a problem. They did not trust the dragons. Many ogres had been attacked by dragons in battles with the Vindrasi and the ogres were not happy about entrusting their lives to the beasts. In addition, the ogres did not like the dragonship itself, declaring it too fragile. Ogres could not swim and they felt safe only on large, hulking ships.

Raven's-foot refused to board and Bear Walker looked grim.

Skylan explained to them that the ogres were far safer in the dragonships than in their own, reminding Bear Walker that in the fight with the kraken, the ogre ship had perished, while the *Venejekar* survived.

Bear Walker at last agreed. All the ogres tromped on board, with the exception of Raven's-foot. The shaman stubbornly refused to come anywhere near a dragon. Bear Walker solved the problem by punching his shaman in the face, knocking him out cold, then ordering his men to carry him on board.

The dragonships were stocked with food and water and even with weapons and shields for the ogres and humans, as well as new bows and arrows for the Cyclopes—gifts from Torval and the Gods of Raj. While the others were stowing their gear, Skylan boarded the *Venejekar* and looked around his ship with a heart filled with pride and eyes blurred by tears.

He looked first at the place on the deck where he had seen his body, carefully tended, loved. The body was gone.

"I need to ask your forgiveness, Skylan," Farinn said, flushing with shame.

"What for?" Skylan asked. "You have done well in my absence. Aylaen praised you for your courage and your care of her."

"I thought you were dead," Farinn confessed. "I wanted to give your body to the sea."

"*I* thought I was dead," said Skylan, grinning. "So I can understand your mistake. Do not sing my death song yet."

He walked to the prow. Kahg's spiritbone was back in its customary place, hanging from its nail. Skylan greeted the dragon and thanked him for his help. The dragon had nothing to say, but his eyes glowed with pleasure.

The only person Skylan had not yet seen was Wulfe. He had assumed he would find him talking with the oceanids, but he wasn't anywhere on deck.

"I think he's afraid you're mad at him. He was the one who took your amulet," said Aylaen.

"Why would he do that?" Skylan wondered.

"He wanted something to remember you by," said Aylaen. "I believe you'll find him hiding in the hold."

Skylan went down into the hold in search of the boy. He found Wulfe crouched on a pile of fishing net, hugging his legs, his chin on his knees.

Skylan sat down beside him.

"Wulfe, I'm not mad—"

Wulfe interrupted him. "Is it true what Aylaen says—that we are sailing to the land of the Stormlords?"

"Yes," Skylan answered.

Wulfe cringed and hugged his legs closer.

"Why? What is wrong? Are you afraid to go there?" Skylan asked.

"No, yes, maybe," Wulfe mumbled.

Skylan waited for the boy to explain. When Wulfe remained silent, Skylan stood up.

"Keep your secret then," he said good-naturedly. "I have work to do. We'll be ready to sail soon—"

"My mother lives there," Wulfe blurted out.

"With the Stormlords?" Skylan asked, startled.

"Not *with* them, silly. Close by. In the Uncharted Lands, with the rest of my people."

Skylan didn't understand what the boy meant. He'd never heard of these Uncharted Lands, and he was fairly certain he didn't believe him. If what the boy said was true, then somehow he'd managed to travel halfway around the world to the place near Vindraholm where the druids had found him and where he had found Skylan.

"You could go visit her," Skylan said, unable to think of anything else to say. He didn't want to hurt Wulfe's feelings. The boy was unhappy enough as it was.

Wulfe startled him by leaping to his feet.

"But what if she doesn't want to see *me*?" Wulfe cried. "What if she doesn't even remember me? She used to come every night to sing to me and she hasn't come to me in a long time. Not in a long, long time."

Wulfe collapsed back onto the fishnet and buried his head on his knees.

Aylaen shouted down into the hold, "Skylan, we are ready!"

"I'm needed on deck," said Skylan to Wulfe.

He paused, then awkwardly rested his hand on the boy's shoulder. "Wulfe, you don't have to go back to your people if you don't want to. You can stay with me."

"For always?" Wulfe peered up at him through his shaggy hair.

"For always," said Skylan, smiling.

"You mean until you die," said Wulfe. "Uglies are always dying."

"Not much we can do about that," said Skylan, laughing.

"It's not funny!" said Wulfe. Glaring at Skylan, the boy scrambled to his feet and ran off.

Skylan took his place at the prow, alongside Aylaen. Together, they looked around at the other dragonships. His friends raised oars into the air, indicating they were ready.

"Take us to the land of the Stormlords," said Skylan.

Kahg steered the *Venejekar* through the water. The sea was sparkling, the skies clear, the wind fair. Skylan looked back at the Isle of Revels, thinking he might see Joabis and his reveling souls celebrating the departure of the rowdy warriors.

The god and the souls must have been in their longhouse, making merry, for he saw no one.

BOOK
2

20

The news that the Stormlords had murdered two of Aelon's priests spread throughout the Oran Empire. People were outraged and demanded retribution. When Raegar announced he was going to war, kings and nobles from all over the empire sent soldiers, weapons, and gold.

Raegar's immediate problem was how to transport his vast army to the land of the Stormlords. He could have marched his army overland, for the Stormlords ruled the southern part of the same continent, Kharajis. The march would have taken months, however, and winter was closing in, which meant he would have to wait for spring. Aelon had promised her help, however, and Raegar waited for a miracle.

The miracle came one day, in the form of a decrepit old man who accosted Raegar in front of the temple as he was going to his morning meeting with the priests. Thinking the old man was a beggar, Raegar gave him a coin and bid him be off.

"Two galleys, each as big as a palace, your lordship," said the old man. "Could be of some use, I'm thinking, and I know where to find 'em."

The guards were about to hustle the old man out of the emperor's sight, but Raegar stopped them. The old man did not appear to be senile, nor did he have the slovenly look of a beggar, now that Raegar studied him.

"What are you talking about, old man?" Raegar asked.

"Come with me, your lordship, and I'll show you."

"Lead the way, then," said Raegar.

"You'll be needing torches," said the old man. "Terrible dark it is in there."

Raegar ordered Commander Eolus to fetch torches and they set out. Raegar didn't really believe this tale, but he was intrigued and also glad to have an excuse to avoid yet another boring meeting with the priests, who wanted to advise him on strategy and tactics, about which they knew less than nothing.

Raegar's relationship with the priests had worsened of late, as had his relationship with Aelon herself. Aelon's casual admission that she had killed her own priests had badly shaken Raegar. The thought lurked in his mind that if she could betray them, she could betray him, too. He wanted some proof that she was as loyal to him as he was to her. A miracle would go a long to reassuring him.

Accompanied by Commander Eolus and six members of his guard, Raegar followed the old man to the outskirts of the city. They tramped among the docks and warehouses, eliciting curious stares from the workers, and entered a part of Sinaria that had been long abandoned.

An earthquake had leveled this portion of the city some fifty years ago, causing much destruction and considerable loss of life. Since only the poor had been living here, no one wanted to spend the money to rebuild. The poor who had survived had moved out. Rats had moved in and life went on.

Raegar and his men picked their way through the ruins, dodging the rats that scurried around them in a furry, screeching torrent. Reagar could see that Commander Eolus and his men were growing increasingly uneasy, fearing an ambush. Raegar found the outing enjoyable, a welcome break from the dreary routine of church politics. He winked at Eolus and pushed on.

The old man led them to a cave in the side of one of the Sinarian hills and indicated that Raegar was to enter.

"In there?" Raegar was amused. "Two galleys as big as a palace?"

The old man gave an eager nod.

Raegar shrugged and started forward. Commander Eolus stepped in front of him. "Sir, you're not serious! You don't believe this old geezer."

"Why would he make up such a tale?" Raegar asked.

"To get you killed, sir," said Eolus grimly. "At least, let me go in first and check to see if it's crawling with assassins."

"Nonsense, Commander. We'll go in together. I haven't had a good fight in a long time," said Raegar. Drawing his sword, he gestured to the old man. "Let's go see your galleys."

His men lit their torches and Raegar entered the cavern, flanked by Eolus on one side and the old man on the other. The cavern was cool and dry and smelled of wood. He saw no assassins. What he did see, emerging from the darkness, illuminated by the torchlight, were the prows of two enormous war galleys.

Raegar was startled. He had certainly not expected to find war galleys in a cave. He was also disappointed. He had been expecting something far more miraculous.

"Bring the light, your lordship," said the old man, "and come inspect her. You must get the full effect."

"What I see are two galleys," said Raegar.

"The eye can be fooled," said the old man, grinning.

Raegar took one of the torches himself to view the first galley, accompanied by the old man, who regaled him with the galley's features.

"She is four hundred and twenty feet long, fifty-eight feet from gangway to plank, and seventy-two feet high to the prow ornament."

Raegar had to admit that the galley was solid, built by men who had obviously taken pride in their labors, unlike the work of today's slipshod laborers. The dry atmosphere and constant temperature of the cave had kept the galley preserved for what the old man claimed to have been over fifty years.

"She and her sister ship were built for the father of our late empress, based on designs that came from an ancient people who once ruled the world, so the story goes," said the old man. "I was a shipwright, one of many who worked on her. Then came the earthquake. The ships weren't harmed, but many people died in the city. The priests of the old gods—those who came before Aelon—read the omens and said the gods were offended and that work on the galleys must stop immediately or worse disasters would befall."

"And so the emperor stopped work," said Raegar.

"He didn't have much choice," said the old man drily. "Many workers and their families had been killed in the quake and the rest believed the omens and refused to come back."

He lovingly rested his hand on the hull of one of the galleys. "She's a wonder, and that's no mistake. During a trial run she took aboard

over four thousand oarsmen and four hundred other crewmen, and
on deck two thousand eight hundred marines."

Raegar snorted in disbelief. "You exaggerate, old man. No galley,
no matter how big, could carry that many."

"Ah, but *she* can, your lordship," said the old man with a glint in
his eye. "If you'll give me the loan of your torch, I'll show you how . . ."

Raegar handed over the torch and followed the old man deeper into
the cave. At about amidships, he stopped to stare, hardly crediting
what he was seeing.

"Blessed Aelon be praised!" Raegar murmured.

For here was an even greater miracle. What he had thought were
two separate war galleys were actually two galleys connected by a large
platform that extended from one galley to the other.

"Double-prowed and double-sterned," said the old man. "With
room to transport not only men, but war machines, cattle, horses,
weapons, and such."

The old man went on to describe the ingenious system the galley's
designers had developed that allowed the rowers on the inner sides of
both galleys to row without knocking oars, but Raegar was paying
scant attention.

He was making calculations. Two such double-hulled galleys each
carrying four thousand rowers, who were also soldiers, and another
two thousand marines would give him an army of twelve thousand.

"What do think, Commander?" Raegar asked.

"She is certainly impressive, sir," said Eolus. "But a ship that size—
will she float?"

"Like a leaf on a stream," the old man boasted.

"We will name her *Aelon's Miracle*," said Raegar. "And her sister
will be *Aelon's Revenge*. I'll give orders to haul them out of the caves
and start work immediately."

He rested his hand on the old man's shoulder. "You have earned
rich reward, old man. What would you like?"

"To see my beauty sail the sea will be reward enough, your lordship," said the old man with tears in his eyes.

Within weeks of declaring war on the Stormlords, Raegar had assembled an army of twelve thousand and he had his miracle war gal-

leys to carry them, as well as supply ships and transports and ships to carry Aelon's priests. The day he and his army set sail, all of Sinaria came to the harbor to cheer them on. Raegar experienced one of the proudest moments of his life as he walked on board *Aelon's Miracle*, wearing the crown of the Emperor of Oran, resplendent in his new ceremonial armor that shone so brightly men said he rivaled the sun.

His wife, Treia, was with him. She was huge with child; the midwives had said the baby could come any day. Despite telling her that she could come with him, Raegar was nervous about the safety of his son and tried to encourage her to remain at home. Treia reminded him curtly that he needed her to deal with the Dragon Fala.

"I have been trained as a Bone Priestess. I know how to use the spiritbone to summon the dragon, how to determine the elemental form the dragon should take. And besides," Treia had added, "the dragon and I are friends."

Raegar gave in. After a couple of bad experiences with the dragon, he was well aware that Fala considered him a numbskull and might well refuse to come with the army unless Treia was along.

Raegar walked the deck of his galley, listening with pleasure to the beats of the drum marking time for the rowers, watching the oars rise from the water, sweep forward, splash into the water, sweep back, all in one elegant rhythmic motion.

He did not say it out loud, for the priests would have warned him of hubris, but he knew victory was assured. And the Stormlords would be only the first to fall to his might. After that, he would conquer the ogres and the Cyclopes, and then—sweetest of all—his own people, the Vindrasi. He pictured his triumphal return to Sinaria with hundreds of Vindrasi trailing behind him in chains.

The voyage south to the land of the Stormlords should have been a short one and relatively easy. Unfortunately, on just the second day, when the galleys and the flotilla of smaller support ships reached the open sea, the weather turned against Raegar, as if the sea and sky were declaring war on him.

The wind blew from every direction except the north, which would have sped them south to their destination. Storms came upon them out of clear skies, blowing them off course and scattering the fleet, so that they had to spend precious time waiting for the other ships to catch up.

Everyone on board was seasick, including the rowers. His soldiers were so sick and demoralized they could not have vanquished an army of kittens. At this rate, Raegar figured, a journey that should take the fleet a week at most could last a month and they would be in no condition to fight once they arrived.

Raegar blamed the gods of the Vindrasi. He was thinking bitterly that Aelon hadn't, after all, done much to weaken them, when the god herself arrived to disabuse of him this notion.

He descended to his cabin from the main deck, where he had been inspecting the latest damage done by the storm, to discover the god in his cabin. He was in a mood as foul as the weather and not particularly pleased to see her.

"You have not been around lately," said Raegar.

"I have been busy," said Aelon.

She was also in a foul mood, restlessly roaming about the cabin, examining the maps, tasting his wine and spitting it out, opening his sea chest and slamming it shut. Outside the sky was black, hail rattled among the rigging, and torrential rains swept the deck.

"Can't you do something about these blasted storms?" Raegar demanded at last.

Aelon rounded on him, eyes flashing in anger.

"How dare you speak to me like that?"

"I ask forgiveness, Revered Aelon," Raegar said, blanching. "I fear the ship could sink at any moment and that would be an ignominious end to all our plans. I blame the gods of the Vindrasi—"

"Not the Vindrasi," Aelon returned.

"Then who?" Raegar was mystified.

She cast him a scathing glance. "These wizards call themselves 'Stormlords.' Even you should be able to make the connection."

Raegar was uneasy. "You are saying the storms are caused by magic? Wizards are doing this?"

The thought came to him that if these wizards were this powerful, conquering them might prove more difficult and fraught with more danger than he had imagined.

"If this is the worst these wizards can do, you have very little to fear," said Aelon, reading his thoughts. "I will put an end to the storms. I would have done so sooner, but, as I said, I have been busy."

"Tell me Skylan Ivorson is dead and my world will be sunshine," said Raegar.

He had hoped to get on her good side, but his well-meaning words had the opposite effect.

"He lives," she said, adding coldly, "because I let him. He is sailing to the land of the Stormlords, bringing with him four of the spiritbones—"

"Four?" Raegar sucked in a startled breath. "The last time we spoke, he had only three. Now he has four—"

"And he is coming here to get the fifth and we will stop him and destroy him," said Aelon. "Have you talked to that traitor Stormlord? Baldev?"

Raegar realized that she was no longer disposed to talk about Skylan and that he would pursue the subject at his own risk. He had to take a moment to bring his mind around to this new topic.

"I did not hear from him before I left," said Raegar. "I expected a letter—"

"Letter!" Aelon snorted. "He will come in person. He wants to make a deal. You will agree."

"A deal for what?" Raegar was suspicious.

"Just do as I tell you!" Aelon said angrily.

A particularly violent gust of wind hit the ship. Raegar staggered. He could hear a loud cracking sound, a thud, and shouts and cries. With Aelon in a bad mood, he hadn't been going to mention this again, but he didn't have a choice.

"Revered Aelon, we need to reach the realm of the Stormlords in all possible haste. These storms—"

"And so you are back to complaining about the weather!" Aelon glared at him. "I have said I would fix it!"

Rebuffed, Raegar stood in silence.

Aelon seemed to relent, for she walked over to him, her thin silk gown rustling against her bare skin, her fragrance filling his nostrils. She ran her hand over the ceremonial breastplate, tracing with a finger the decorative serpents done in gold.

"Quit sulking," she said. "You look jowly when you pout. Today your child will be born. A strong and healthy son."

"My son! This day!" Raegar gasped. "Will all be well?"

"I promised Treia an easy delivery," said Aelon. "You will name the child Aelonis. And now I must leave." She added cuttingly, "I have to attend to the weather."

Raegar felt the sting of her sarcasm, but he was too happy to care. He would teach the boy to fight in battle as a Vindrasi, not a Sinarian. Phalanxes and spears were all very well, but to be a true warrior, a man needed to learn how to take his place in the shield wall, stand shoulder to shoulder with his comrades, test his courage in the face of death.

Going to his sea chest, Raegar opened it and took out a child-size shield and wooden sword. He was six when his father had first taught him to use a sword. He remembered those times he had spent with his father and he imagined teaching his own son.

"You hold your shield like this, Aelonis," Raegar said. "See how it guards your left arm and the sword arm of your comrade? You will stand in the front line in the place of honor—"

"Ahem!" said a voice coming from right behind him.

Raegar dropped the shield, drew his own sword, and whipped around to find a stranger in his cabin, watching him with a faintly derisive smile on his lips. Raegar glanced at the door. It remained closed. He had not heard anyone enter.

"What the devil—" Raegar raised his sword and shoved it at the stranger's face. "Who are you?"

The stranger's smile increased. He touched the sword's tip, moving it aside.

"I am Baldev," said the stranger. "Lord of the Storm. You must be Raegar. I was told you were a barbarian. I came to talk. Put down your weapon."

Baldev looked about, saw a chair, and settled himself uninvited. Raegar lowered the sword, but kept hold of it.

"How did you get on board my ship, let alone into my cabin?" Raegar asked, glowering.

"I would explain the magical technique, but I doubt a man with your mental capacity would understand," Baldev replied. "My time is limited. Shall we proceed with our business?"

Raegar regarded him grimly, longing to wipe that supercilious smile off the man's face with the back of his hand. Unfortunately, he needed this arrogant bastard, and so he swallowed his anger and sat down in the chair behind his desk. He noticed, as he did so, that the rain had stopped and the wind was dying down.

He eyed Baldev and wondered how to begin. The wizard gave him no help. He was slender, appeared to be about forty, with long, sleek dark hair, large dark eyes, and a fine-boned, elegant face. Dressed in sumptuous sky-blue robes, he sat perfectly at his ease.

Raegar came straight to the point, hoping to send his unwelcome guest on his way.

"I have information that you Stormlords have the fifth spiritbone of the Vektia in your possession," said Raegar. "Is that true?"

"I believe we have one of them," Baldev replied offhandedly. "Whether it is the fifth, the third or the first I really couldn't say. Does it matter?"

Baldev was making sport of him and Raegar had to clench his fists beneath the desk to keep from jamming one of them down the wizard's throat.

"It is a trifling thing, but I have need of it," Raegar stated. "I want you to bring it to me. That should be an easy task for one with such wondrous powers. In payment, you can name your price: gold, jewels . . ."

"I have no need for such things," said Baldev scornfully. "I have named my price to Aelon and he has agreed. I want to be king, ruler of my people."

Raegar's jaw dropped. He gaped at the man. "She agreed to what?"

"*She?*" Baldev raised an eyebrow. "Ah, of course, the Faceless God would come to you in female form. Quite the temptress, or so I would imagine. I gather Aelon failed to mention our bargain."

Raegar struggled to compose himself. "Perhaps because she never made it."

Baldev gave a disdainful smile.

"Let me reduce this to simple terms even you can understand. You cannot succeed without me. The only way for your army to enter the city is for me to provide you with access to the stormhold. I presume you know what the stormhold is? The gateway to the city?"

"I have read the reports of my priests," Raegar growled.

"You can read? Will wonders never cease," said Baldev. "Then you know you cannot enter the city without going through the stormhold. My price for this access is the kingship of Tsa Kerestra and Tsa Terestra."

"You! King! Impossible!" Raegar retorted.

"Then so is the likelihood you will enter the city or acquire this so-called spiritbone," said Baldev. "You have heard my price and your god has agreed to it."

He rose to his feet. "I will be in touch."

He vanished without a word. Raegar stared at the empty air where the wizard had been, then turned back to his desk. He found Aelon sitting in his chair.

She gave him a charming smile. "You are angry."

"You promised that bastard he would be king!" said Raegar, his voice shaking.

Aelon shrugged. "You need him. As for my promise . . ."

They were interrupted by excited voices outside his door, calling for him.

"Her Imperial Majesty is in labor!"

Raegar forgot about Aelon, forgot about the wizard. Flinging open the door, he found two priests—High Priest Benignus and his assistant, waiting there, eager to tell their news.

"Get out of my way," said Raegar. "I want to see her."

Shoving the priests aside, he strode down the narrow hall to Treia's cabin and was about to enter when a frightful scream brought him to a halt.

The door to cabin opened and one of the midwives came out carrying a bowl of bloodstained water, which she threw into one of the slop buckets. Raegar had fought in the shield wall without a qualm of fear, but that scream and the sight of the bloody water unmanned him. He broke out in a chill sweat.

"Is my wife . . . is everything . . ." Raegar swallowed.

"All is proceeding well, Your Imperial Majesty," said the midwife. "In truth, I've never seen a labor progress so fast."

She hurried back inside and shut the door. Raegar stood in the hall, not knowing what to do with himself. The smell of the blood was making him queasy. The two priests hovered near him, saying something about praying to Aelon. Then came the sound of a baby's wail.

Raegar took a breath so deep he made himself dizzy and had to brace himself against a bulkhead. The baby continued to cry. After a time, the door opened again and the midwife stepped out carrying the baby wrapped in a blanket of royal purple.

"You have a son, Your Majesty," said the midwife.

She drew aside the blanket to let Raegar see the naked infant as proof the child was male. He looked down at a wrinkled, red-faced infant with black hair.

Raegar took hold of one of the tiny clenched fists.

"My son is ready to take on the world," said Raegar proudly.

By custom, he had to take the child in his hands to acknowledge the baby as his own. Raegar did not hesitate.

"Let me hold my son!"

The midwife wrapped up the baby in the blanket and handed the child to him. Raegar cradled his son, marveling that he was so small and so perfect. He quickly handed the child back to the midwife, fearing he might break it.

"How is my wife?" Raegar remembered to ask.

"Her Imperial Majesty is quite well," replied the midwife. "She has asked to see you."

Raegar recalled the sound of that scream and he hesitated. But the priests and the midwives were both watching him and he braced himself and walked into the cabin.

Treia was sitting up in bed. She did not even look at Raegar. Her gaze fixed on her child.

"Bring my son to me," she said, holding out her arms.

Raegar remained standing near the cabin door. The midwives were cleaning up, but the odor of blood and bodily fluids was foul. He fidgeted, wanting to leave.

Treia put the baby to her breast. Raegar had hired a wet nurse, but Treia had refused to allow any other woman to touch her son. She gazed down on the child lovingly.

"I thought we could name him Vagal, which means 'bold warrior'—"

"His name is Aelonis," said Raegar.

Treia raised her head, staring at him, slightly squinting with her nearsighted eyes. High Priest Benignus expressed his approval of this honor to their god. The midwives said it was a lovely name. Raegar knew Treia wouldn't like it.

Ever since they had married, she had been jealous of Aelon, believing Raegar was more devoted to his god than his wife. Lately her jealousy seemed to have moderated. Aelon had told Raegar that she had visited Treia and that his wife was now devoted to the god. Raegar saw in a moment that Treia's devotion had limits.

But perhaps not her devotion to another god.

Treia made a bargain with Hevis, God of Lies and Deceit. She prom-ised to sacrifice someone she loved . . . Hevis will not forget. . . .

Raegar had not wanted to believe Aylaen, but her words had stayed with him. He heard them again and again, especially in the middle of a sleepless night. Now, seeing Treia's pale face and the glitter of fury in her eyes, Raegar believed.

He watched his precious son suckle at the breast of a murderer and he longed to snatch his child away. He fought the impulse. No one would believe him, not even Aelon. Treia was the Empress of Oran, his wife, the mother of the crown prince. He could get rid of her, by accusing her of worshipping heathen gods, but he needed proof.

Raegar manufactured a smile. "I see that you are tired, my love. I will leave you to rest. I am needed on deck."

He walked out, leaving the door open, and summoned one of the midwives.

"I am worried about my son," he told her. "Babies often fall ill and die after birth. Keep near him at all times. He is a prince, heir to the empire."

The midwife assured him that his son was healthy, but promised that she would. Somewhat reassured, Raegar went on deck to cheers from the crew and his men.

He drew in a deep breath of fresh air and realized that the sun was shining, the weather clear. The wind blew strongly, pushing his ship southward to glory.

And he had a son.

21

Treia lay in her bed, exhausted, but blissfully happy. She had never known such joy. The midwife had wanted to put the child in his cradle to allow Treia to rest, but she had sent the midwife away and held her son in her arms long after he had fallen asleep.

She loved him fiercely, as she had never before loved anyone, not even Raegar, and she had loved him with a passion that she had feared might kill her. Treia had been nearsighted since a young age and thus everything in the cabin she looked on was a blur—except her son. She could see him clearly, perfect in every detail.

"Vagal, my darling, my sweet," she murmured, running her fingers through the crisp black ringlets of his hair, gently, so as not to wake him. "Bold warrior. That is your name. Not Aelonis."

Her lip curled in disdain.

"On the other hand," said a voice, "with a name like Aelonis, the boy would soon learn how to use his fists."

Treia gasped and clutched her child close. "Who is there?"

She squinted, trying to see, but the room had been darkened and she could not see clearly. She was aware of a presence, someone stealthily moving about.

"Midwife? Is that you?" Treia asked, nettled. "I told you I no longer needed you. I don't care what my husband says."

An oil lamp on a table where she took her meals suddenly burst into flame. Two eyes, bright with reflected fire, gazed at her from the darkness. Treia recognized those eyes.

"Hevis!" Treia whispered, choked by terror.

God of Lies and Deceit. His hallmark was fire.

The god gave a soft laugh. "And here I was trying to be so quiet; not wake the baby."

He seemed to linger over the word *baby*.

Treia clutched her son close and said desperately, "I know I have not yet fulfilled my part of our bargain—"

"Too true, dear lady," said Hevis. "You offered to sacrifice someone you loved in return for the magic you needed to summon the Vektia dragon. I did my part. I gave you the magic. But the people you love are still breathing—your sister, your husband. And now your son . . ."

Treia had to gasp for breath enough to speak. "I know I have been remiss, but I have not yet had a chance to act. Look, I will show you what I have done in preparation! Please, please"—her voice broke—"do not harm my child!"

"Show me, then," said Hevis.

The flames in his eyes seemed to scorch her.

Treia placed her baby in his cradle, then climbed out of bed. Her legs trembled; she could scarcely walk. Keeping a wary eye on Hevis, she crept across the deck to her sea chest, lifted the lid and rummaged about beneath her robes and gowns until she found the casket she had hidden among her clothes. She drew it out and carried it over to the table, shoving aside plates and knives that had been laid for her meal to make room.

The casket was made of wood inlaid with mother-of-pearl and bore the name "Raegar" done in a pattern of fanciful flowers and vines and the obligatory serpents.

She sank unsteadily into a chair. Hevis's eyes, watching her, were two pinpoints of flame. Treia opened the casket with fingers that shook. The god's fiery light illuminated a massive golden ring—a man's ring by its shape and size. A square-cut ruby surrounded by small diamonds sparkled in the center.

"A bribe?" said Hevis. "Thank you, but it is far too flashy for my simple tastes."

"Wait! Let me show you!" Treia pleaded.

The baby started to whimper. She glanced at the cradle that was on the far side of the cabin and then cast a fearful glance at Hevis.

Picking up a knife, Treia deftly thrust the blade through the ring, lifted it from the box and set the ring on the table. She touched the ruby with the tip of the knife's blade and a tiny needle popped out of the ring beneath the setting.

"The needle is tipped with poison," said Treia in a smothered whisper. "My own concoction."

"And who is meant to wear this ring?" Hevis asked.

Treia had to swallow twice before the words came out. "My husband. It is to be a gift."

"When?" Hevis asked.

"I don't . . . After the battle . . ."

"Now, tonight," said Hevis.

Treia gulped. "No! It is too dangerous! Aelon would be furious! She is counting upon him to win this battle—"

Hevis drew near. The flames in his eyes flickered. "How is Aelon to know who killed him? Raegar has a great many enemies. The priests resent being ruled by a former slave and would not mourn his death. And he had a mysterious visit from a treacherous wizard this very night. One can blame anything on treacherous wizards."

"No, please, don't make me—"

"Consider it in these terms, dear lady." Hevis's voice hardened. "Your god can replace a military commander far more easily than you can replace your child."

"I'll give the ring to him," Treia gasped. "Tonight."

"Good," said Hevis. "Be assured. I will be watching."

The flame wavered and he was gone.

Treia closed her eyes. Weak and dizzy, she staggered over to the cradle, picked up her baby, and sank down in a chair. She held him so tightly he whimpered in protest and she loosened her grip.

She drifted into a horror-filled sleep.

Raegar was standing on the deck of *Aelon's Miracle*, talking with Commander Eolus about his son.

"I won't have him raised to be some namby-pamby princeling, holding an orange to his nose to ward off bad smells and dining on peacock tongues," said Raegar. "I'll raise him to be a soldier, take him with me on campaign, teach him what it means to sleep in the mud and march fifty miles in full armor carrying all his gear."

"That is how my father raised me," said Eolus.

"And mine, as well," said Raegar. He was about to continue relating his plans for his son when he saw, to his consternation, the midwife he had left with orders to keep a watchful eye on little Aelonis come up on deck.

Raegar confronted her. "I ordered you to stay with my son. Why have you disobeyed me?"

"The empress ordered me to leave, Your Majesty," replied the midwife. An older woman of vast experience, she was not in the least intimidated by one she apparently considered an overprotective parent. "I cannot very well disobey my mistress."

"I will go myself," Raegar said and was about to descend to the lower decks when one of the lookouts called his attention to a storm boiling up out of the west, creating water spouts that snaked down out of the clouds, as if in mockery of Aelon's serpents.

Cursing the Stormlords, Raegar went in search of High Priest Benignus. He found him in his cabin with his assistant eating supper.

"High Priest," said Raegar, "I need you and your fellow up on deck praying to Aelon to stop the storm that's about to hit us."

"I am surprised you did not simply ask the god yourself, sir," said the high priest. "You being one of her favorites."

"I would," said Raegar coolly, "but I must go see to the welfare of my wife and son. I am certain you can handle this, but if you need my help, you can always send someone to fetch me."

He left, smiling, and went below.

Treia woke with a start, with the feeling she had forgotten or overlooked something. She looked first to the baby, but he was asleep in her arms, so it could have nothing to do with him.

She pondered, with that vague feeling of unease and irritation that comes with forgetting something important. A flash of light caught her eye and she saw, to her horror, she had left the ruby ring on the table with the point of the tiny needle still exposed. She had meant to return the ring to the casket to be given to Raegar tonight. Exhaustion had overwhelmed her and she had fallen asleep.

Shuddering at the thought of what might have happened if someone had seen it, Treia hurriedly rose from her chair, keeping her baby in her arms. She sat down at the table and placed the baby on her lap, then, picking up the knife, she carefully nudged the needle back into its compartment, lifted the ring, and placed it into the casket.

Belowdecks, Raegar approached Treia's cabin and saw a stripe of light shining from beneath the closed door. He found that suspicious; Treia had said she was exhausted and had wanted to sleep. Instead of knocking, he thrust open the door, barged into the cabin. The door swung shut behind him, but he did not notice.

Treia was seated at the table, holding a knife over their slumbering child. At the sight of him, her face went ghastly white, her eyes widened with fear.

Raegar wanted to snatch the child to safety, but the blade was perilously close and he feared he might drive Treia to commit the terrible act.

"Treia," he said, trying keep his voice under control, "what are you doing?"

Treia licked her lips. Her mouth worked, as if she would answer, but she couldn't speak. She dropped the knife onto the table and he sighed in relief. He could see her guilt in her wavering eyes, in the stiff muscles of her face, in the quivering of her lips.

"Aylaen told me you were going to kill me," Raegar said, advancing on her, his fury growing with every step. "But she was wrong. You were going to sacrifice my son!"

He lunged at her and tore the baby from her grasp.

"No, no, I would never, never harm my child!" Treia stretched out her trembling hands. Roused by the rough treatment, the child was wailing. "Give him back to me! He cries for his mother!"

Raegar held the baby safely out of her reach. "I know about the bargain you made with Hevis. You promised to sacrifice someone you love in return for the power to summon the Vektia dragon!"

"The sacrifice should have been Aylaen," said Treia harshly. Her gaze had not left the baby. "She escaped unharmed."

"So you admit that you made an unholy bargain with your heathen god!" Raegar cried.

"I summoned the dragon for you!" Treia said, wringing her hands. "Because you wanted to be Priest-General! I did this for you!"

The baby was screaming in a frenzy now, kicking his legs and flailing his arms.

Treia rose to her feet and walked toward Raegar. "Let me have my child."

Raegar backed up, holding the baby. "You will never see him again! I will denounce you to the priests as a witch. You will be put to death!"

Keeping the baby, he turned to walk toward the door.

"I wasn't going to sacrifice my child, you fool!" Treia shrieked. "I was going to kill you!"

Grabbing the knife from the table, she rushed at him.

Raegar saw the flash of the blade out of the corner of his eye. His one thought was to protect his child and he rounded on Treia and struck her a blow with all the strength of his fury.

He felt his fist smash into bone.

Treia's head snapped back and she dropped without a cry.

Raegar stood staring down at the body.

"Treia . . ."

She didn't move and he saw a pool of blood, black in the firelight, begin to ooze onto the deck.

Still holding his screaming son, he nudged her shoulder with the toe of his boot, rolling her over. Her head lolled at an odd angle; her face was nothing but mangled bone and bloody pulp. Her eyes were fixed.

Raegar felt his gorge rise and he swallowed, trying to keep from retching. He couldn't think. He didn't know what to do. He started toward the door, planning to summon help, and found Aelon blocking his way.

"She was right," said Aelon. "You are a fool!"

He blanched beneath her furious gaze.

"It was an accident," said Raegar in a hollow voice. "I didn't mean to kill her. She came at me with the knife . . ."

"Do you think the priests will believe you?" Aelon asked him. "You are a barbarian who sleeps with anything in a skirt. This would give them the excuse they need to be rid of you. Give me the baby."

Aelon took the child and, wrapping the baby in his blanket, rocked him back and forth, hushing and soothing him.

Raegar gazed at her, stricken, helpless. "What do I do?"

"Get rid of the body, of course. You will make it appear as if she fell overboard."

Raegar groaned. "But the men on watch! They'll see me."

"Not in a raging storm," said Aelon.

The high priest and his fellows gathered on deck and prayed to Aelon to save them from the storm. The god was deaf to their pleas, however. The worst storm they had yet encountered struck, hurling rain with the force of lances, and pelting all those on deck with hail the size of eggs. Priests and sailors fled to safety belowdecks. Raegar even dismissed the watch, saying quite rightly that they could not see anything in the pitch darkness anyway.

The storm raged all night. In the dark hours before dawn, Raegar tied lead weights used to sink the fishing lines around Treia's waist, wrapped her corpse in a blanket, and tied it with rope and more lead weights. He slung the body over his shoulder and carried it onto the deck. He had some difficulty. By this time, the corpse had grown cold and was starting to stiffen.

He paused before going out on deck. Aelon had assured him that even those who remained on deck would not be able to see him due to the storm, but he wanted to make certain.

He had never known a darker night. The wind struck him a pummeling blow, rain beat on him. He could not even see his feet, much less anyone else who might have the misfortune to be on deck this terrible night.

Raegar heaved the body over the side. He could not see the corpse hit the water, but he heard the splash. Weighted down, it would sink immediately.

He stood a moment in the darkness, shaking in reaction. He was chilled to the bone and wanted only to drink himself into oblivion, but he had more work to do. The storm was starting to pass. The driving rain turned into a drizzle. The wind ceased to howl.

"Help!" Raegar bellowed. "Help me!"

His cry carried through the night, rousing the weary rowers from their slumbers. Men poured onto the deck, demanding to know what was wrong.

Eolus ran to Raegar's side.

"What is it, sir?"

Raegar was in a wretched state, weeping and pointing over the side.

"My wife!" he cried. "She was running a high fever . . . delirium . . . She wandered up here and . . . and jumped into the sea."

Raegar sobbed. "I tried to stop her . . . We have to save her."

He stripped off his clothes with the obvious intention of leaping into the black, churning waves. Eolus tried to reason with him and when that didn't work, flung his arms around Raegar and shouted for men to help him.

Raegar fought them, but they knocked him to the deck and pinned him down while they explained to him that it was hopeless, Treia was lost.

Raegar collapsed with grief and Eolus assisted him to his cabin, accompanied by the high priest, who reminded him that his beloved wife was with Aelon now and that he must pull himself together for the sake of his son.

"You are right," said Raegar, his voice harsh from weeping. "I need to see my son."

The high priest asked if he would like him to sit with him, perhaps recite some of Aelon's teachings. Raegar thanked him and said he needed to be alone with his child.

He walked into the cabin, shutting the door behind him. The oil lamp still flickered on the table. Aelon was rocking his son in the cradle, singing to him softly.

She stopped to ask, "Did everything go as planned?"

"Yes," said Raegar wearily. "I told them Treia started hemorrhaging, which will explain the blood on the floor. She began running a high fever, grew delirious, and jumped into the sea. If the midwives had been with her, they might have saved her, but she insisted on being alone."

He picked up the knife Treia had dropped and put it back onto the table.

Aelon brought over his son and handed the child to him.

Raegar held his child close. "I didn't mean to kill her." He closed his eyes and buried his head in the baby's blanket.

"I know," said Aelon in soothing tones. "Take the child back to your cabin. He is hungry. You need to summon that wet nurse."

Raegar nodded. He was about to leave when he saw the dragon's spiritbone hanging from the wall. He turned to Aelon in alarm.

"What about the Dragon Fala? She will have to be told and she will be furious. She might leave."

"I will deal with Fala," said Aelon.

Raegar had recovered from his grief the next day and brought his son up on deck, where he received the condolences of his crew and soldiers. He thanked them for their service and told them that Treia would have wanted them to continue with their plans to defeat the Stormlords. Overhearing some of the men talking with admiration of his fortitude and courage, Raegar smiled.

The sun was shining brightly. The day was fine. No sign of rain. It seemed the Stormlords had given up.

Raegar received the daily report on their location from the navigator, who pointed to distant mountains, whose peaks were hidden in the clouds, and said that they were very near the destination.

While he was on deck, one of the slaves who had been sent to clean Treia's cabin discovered a beautiful casket lying on the deck with a name on the top that was decorated with flowers and serpents.

The slave could not read, so she had no idea who the casket might belong to, but she could see it was valuable. Fearful she might be accused of stealing, she carried the casket to Commander Eolus.

He recognized the name and realized that this must be some gift Treia had meant to give her husband.

"Poor man," said Eolus. "This will only increase his grief."

Eolus took the casket to Raegar's cabin, opened his sea chest, and buried the casket at the very bottom, thinking he would tell Raegar about it later.

As it happened, the small matter slipped the commander's mind.

22

The Sea Goddess provided calm seas and a fair wind for the *Vene-jekar* and the four other dragonships and they sailed swiftly north. Farinn proved himself an apt pupil of Acronis. He took readings and charted their progress and when land came in sight, he was able to tell Skylan that they had reached the Spirit Coast, a long stretch of coastline on the eastern side of the Kharajis continent known as the Chimerian Downfall.

"To the west is the Desolation," said Farinn. "The land north of that is uncharted. No one ventures there. Legend has it the fae claim those lands as theirs."

"That's because the land *is* ours," said Wulfe.

Skylan glanced at him. This was the first time the boy had talked to him since they had left Joabis's isle. Unhappy and withdrawn, Wulfe had spent most of his time gossiping with the oceanids.

"The Chimerian Downfall. What are chimera?" Skylan asked.

"Fae creatures, according to the old songs," Farinn answered. "Part lion, part goat, and part serpent."

Wulfe was nodding his head. "Fierce. Very fierce."

"So why do they call this land Chimerian Downfall?" Skylan asked Wulfe.

"My grandmother says that in the First War, when we were fighting you Uglies, a group of chimera wanted this land and they attacked both the fae and the Uglies who lived here. The Uglies were frightened and ran away, but my people fought the chimera and drove them back into the Realm of Fire. Stupid Uglies," Wulfe added sullenly, glowering at Skylan, then running off.

Skylan shook his head, then turned his attention to the map. Although he could not read the words, he was starting to understand the concept, which Farinn had once explained.

Imagine you are a dragon flying high in the air, as high as the clouds. If you look down at the land below, everything would seem very small. A river would look like a snake, mountains would look like teeth. The mapmaker has drawn what the dragon sees.

"Where are the Stormlords?" Skylan asked, trying to imagine he was a dragon.

"If we follow the coastline north, we will reach the realm of the Stormlords, which is located here," Farinn said, putting his finger on a dot on the chart.

"What are these words beside it?" Skylan asked, pointing to some squiggles near the dot. "The name of their realm?"

Farinn shook his head. "The mapmaker wrote, 'Keep Away.' Acronis said that the Stormlords are dangerous people. They live in walled cities guarded by lethal magicks."

"Yet my emperor cousin, Raegar, does not 'keep away,'" Skylan muttered. "He has no fear of these magicks. He knows something, while I am in the dark, sailing blindfolded with my hands tied."

He ordered the dragonships to hug the coastline and keep careful watch. The next day, just as dawn lit the horizon, Dela Eden hailed the *Venejekar* from her dragonship.

"My people have a small colony near here," she shouted over the water. "They are friendly with the Stormlords and can give you the information you need."

Skylan thanked her, but instead of being grateful he turned away, scowling.

"What is wrong?" Aylaen asked.

"I do not like these Cyclopes," Skylan replied. "Dela Eden is on board another ship and yet she can still see into my head, know what I am thinking."

The coastline appeared deserted and Skylan gave the order for the dragonships to land. Dela Eden suggested that the ogres remain on board their ships.

"Although an uneasy truce exists between our two races, brokered by the Gods of Raj, the sight of a large contingent of ogres on their land would certainly cause my people alarm," said Dela Eden.

"We will ask Bear Walker to come with us," said Skylan. "So he will know we are not plotting behind his back."

Bear Walker agreed to come, and his shadow, Raven's-foot, tagged along. They were joined by Aylaen in her capacity as Kai Priestess.

She wore the robes she had worn to confront Aelon, now cleaned and mended, all traces of Treia removed. Skylan wore his armor and carried his sword, though he kept it sheathed. Bear Walker carried an axe in a harness on his back and Raven's-foot brought his gourd.

"A sensible precaution," Skylan told Dela Eden, thinking she might object to the weapons. "We are going among strangers who have no love for us."

Dela Eden grinned. "My people know you are Vindrasi. They will make allowances."

On the beach lay several boats, along with a quantity of fishing net, buckets, knives, and spears that Dela Eden said were used to spear fish, not men. Skylan saw footprints in the sand, but no one was around except a few dogs investigating the buckets, hoping to find fish that had been left behind.

"Where is the village?" he asked.

"About two miles inland." Dela Eden frowned. "Strange to find no one here. The men should be out fishing at this time of morning."

Skylan felt a prickle of alarm and rested his hand on the hilt of his sword, while Bear Walker removed his axe from the harness.

"What do you think is wrong?" Aylaen asked Dela Eden.

Dela Eden shook her head. "I do not know. I will go find out."

"I don't like the looks of this," said Skylan, going to talk to Bear Walker. "I will go with Dela Eden. You return to the ships, warn the others."

Bear Walker agreed and he and Raven's-foot went back to the dragonships. Skylan was going to send Aylaen back with the ogres, but she refused and before he could argue, she set off across the beach with Dela Eden, leaving Skylan to catch up. They headed inland over soft, white sand mixed with dirt and covered with sharp-bladed grass. Dela Eden walked rapidly and seemed to know where she was going.

"I have been here before," Dela Eden answered, though Skylan hadn't asked. "I came many years ago when I was young. My husband had family here. We lived here until he died, and then I returned home."

"This colony is far from the Cyclopes' homeland," Skylan said. "How did your people come to settle here?"

"The Stormlords invited us," said Dela Eden.

"I thought these wizards didn't like strangers," said Skylan.

"They don't. But we are not strangers. Legend has it that once we did them a great favor and they gave us this land in return."

"So your people don't live with them in their city," said Skylan.

"Oh, no," said Dela Eden with a glance at the sky. "We prefer living on the ground."

"Not on the top of a mountain," suggested Skylan.

"Not in the clouds," said Dela Eden.

Coming to a sudden halt, she raised her hand in warning.

"What is wrong?" Skylan asked.

"There is the village," said Dela Eden, pointing. "But I see no people. No one is about."

With the sun blazing in the sky the heat was oppressive. The village was almost lost to sight, hidden among a large grove of odd-looking trees. The trees were enormous, each tree formed of a great many trunks that had all grown together. The houses were little more than huts with roofs made of grass.

"Those are fire pits," said Dela Eden, indicating holes that had been dug in the ground. "The women should be preparing the midday meal. There should be children playing and going about their chores."

Skylan saw kettles for cooking and plates and bowls made of wood stacked neatly off to one side of the fire pits. Bright colored blankets lay on the ground.

"They weren't attacked," said Skylan. "There are no bodies, and the village was not ransacked. The fire pits are cold."

Dela Eden cupped her hands around her mouth and whistled, sounding so much like a bird that Skylan almost mistook her for one.

The whistle was evidently a signal of some sort, for a male Cyclopes emerged from the trees. He was practically naked, wearing nothing except a strip of cloth tied around his thighs. He carried a bow with a quiver of arrows slung over his shoulder. At the sight of the strangers, the Cyclopes moved with remarkable speed, nocking an arrow to his bow and aiming it at Skylan's heart.

"It is me, Kamau. Dela Eden," she called.

"You walk in strange company, Dela Eden," said Kamau.

"We come as friends," Dela Eden told him. "We fought a great battle together against the forces of Aelon."

Kamau lowered the bow, though he kept a wary eye on Skylan, who made certain to keep his hands well clear of his sword.

"The Gods of Raj be with you, Kamau," said Dela Eden.

The two touched their foreheads together, third eye to third eye, an exchange of greetings. She introduced Skylan and Aylaen. Kamau gave them polite, though cold, greeting.

"Many years have gone by since you were last among us," said Kamau. "Sadly you come back in troubled times."

"What has happened?" Dela Eden asked.

"A messenger from the Stormlords warned us to seek safety in the hills. A large army is sailing from Oran to attack them."

"The army of the Emperor Raegar," said Dela Eden with a glance at Skylan. "We learned of this ourselves. That is why we are here. How did the Stormlords find out?"

"The wizards discovered the bodies of two of Aelon's spies in one of the stormholds. The Stormlords returned their corpses to the emperor and warned him to stay away."

"Good for them!" said Skylan, laughing.

"You find violent death amusing?" Kamau asked in stern tones.

"He is Vindrasi," said Dela Eden.

"Ah, of course," said Kamau. "The wizards believe that the emperor's army will attempt to capture one of the stormholds and use it to enter and conquer Tsa Kerestra. Once the emperor has the Kingdom Above, he will send his armies to lay claim to the Spirit Coast. Aelon has no love for us. The emperor will enslave us or, more likely, simply destroy us."

"What will you do?" Dela Eden asked, concerned.

"We have made plans to sail back to our homeland," said Kamau.

"Aelon's reach is long," said Dela Eden gravely. "It stretches far across the sea. Nowhere is safe from him."

Kamau gave a shrug. "What else can we do?"

Skylan was about to tell him what the Cyclopes could do: they could fight. Aylaen cast him a warning glance, reminding him that this was none of their business, and he kept silent.

"Let the emperor capture a stormhold," Dela Eden was saying. "Much good it will do him. He does not know the secret of the magic."

"On the contrary, the Stormlords believe that Aelon's spies discovered the secret of the magic and how to dismantle it."

"Even if that were true, the spies did not live to tell what they found," said Dela Eden.

"The spies had ways to communicate with priests in Oran. The Stormlords found references to the magic and how it works, and evidence that the spies shared this secret with the priests in Oran before they died."

Looking grave, Dela Eden turned to Skylan and Aylaen. "This is very bad news, my friends."

"I do not understand," Skylan said. "What is a 'stormhold' and what is this secret that is so valuable?"

"The stormholds are located in the kingdom of Tsa Terestra, the Kingdom Below. They guard the keys to the gate of the kingdom of Tsa Kerestra, the Kingdom Above. If Aelon's soldiers know the secret, they can use it to open the gate, and nothing will stop the enemy from entering Tsa Kerestra."

"The army of these Stormlords will stop them," said Skylan. "And your army and our army will fight with them, join them in their shield wall."

Kamau laughed out loud.

"What is so funny?" Skylan demanded.

"The Stormlords do not have armies, Vindrasi," said Kamau. "I doubt if they have ever heard of a shield wall. They spent centuries fighting for their lives in the Realm of Fire. When they escaped that realm, they vowed that they would live in peace, which is why they refused to worship Torval after he defeated the great dragon. They wanted nothing to do with a god who finds honor in butchery and glory in slaughter."

Skylan barely heard the insulting reference to Torval. He was far more intrigued by the information that these Stormlords had come here from the Realm of Fire, the same realm where the dragons lived, and that they had been here during the time when Torval fought the Great Dragon Ilyrion. Perhaps that explained why Vindrash had given them the spiritbone.

"The Stormlords may not soil their hands with blood, but we have heard that their magic is deadly," Aylaen was saying. "They can fight with their magic."

"But they won't."

"Their magic killed the priests," said Aylaen.

"No one knows how the priests died, but the Stormlords did not kill them. The magic acts as a warning. A very powerful warning, but a warning nonetheless."

Skylan grunted. "Even if these Stormlords cannot stomach battle, they will certainly fight to save their people—"

"On the contrary," said Kamau, "the Stormlords will do everything in their power to keep from fighting."

"Are they fools?" Skylan demanded. "Do they know the terror Raegar will bring to them? His soldiers will rape their women and spit their children on their spears and burn their city to the ground."

"He is right about the soldiers of Aelon, Kamau," said Dela Eden. "They will show no mercy."

"The wizards believe the emperor will permit them to surrender peacefully," Kamau replied. "They have in their possession a relic coveted by Aelon and they plan to give this relic to the emperor and hope that he will leave them in peace."

"Raegar cares nothing about some old relic—" Skylan began.

Aylaen stopped him, digging her nails into his arm.

"He means the spiritbone, Skylan," said Aylaen. "What else would Aelon consider so valuable?"

"They cannot do this!" Skylan said angrily. "Vindrash gave these Stormlords the spiritbone in good faith, to keep it safe! Once they give Aelon the spiritbone, the god will grow in power and will not rest until he drives your gods and mine from this world!"

"The Stormlords care nothing for your gods or mine, Vindrasi," said Kamau. "They care only for the safety of their city and their people."

"And I care for *my* people. I will not allow these wizards to give Aelon the spiritbone," said Skylan, gritting his teeth. "Show me how to find this kingdom. I will talk with them and if that fails, I will take our spiritbone by force, since these Stormlords have so little care for it."

To Skylan's ire and chagrin, Kamau burst into laughter so loud it disturbed the birds and sent them flapping up out of the trees. Skylan drew his sword. Seeing this, Kamau raised his bow. Dela Eden stepped swiftly between them.

"Put your weapons down, both of you," Dela Eden said. "Let me explain. Look to the north. Do you see that massive cloud bank?"

Skylan saw towering clouds, white with the pinks and golds and oranges of the sunrise. The lower part of the clouds were tinged with gray and he could see wisps of rain.

"I see them," he said.

"You see Tsa Kerestra," said Dela Eden.

Skylan frowned. "Beneath those clouds?"

"*In* the clouds," said Dela Eden. "Tsa Terestra: Kingdom Below; Tsa Kerestra: Kingdom Above. Tsa Kerestra is a city built in the clouds."

Skylan flushed. "People cannot live on clouds! What do you take me for?"

"I do not think she is making sport of you, Skylan," said Aylaen. "She is in earnest."

"Why didn't you tell me this before we came on this journey?" Skylan demanded.

"You would not have believed me. It was hard for me to believe, at first," Dela Eden admitted. "Then I saw for myself. When you are closer, you can look into the clouds and see the silver towers of their castle."

Skylan looked back to the cloud bank and perhaps it was only his imagination, but he thought for a moment he caught a flash of silver shining in the midst of the gray. He shook his head.

"People cannot live on clouds," he repeated.

"So it would seem, yet we have seen a great many wonders, Skylan," Aylaen said in thoughtful tones. "We lived with people who dwelt beneath the sea, people who breathed water like air. We would have said *that* was not possible."

Skylan considered in silence, then, making up his mind, said to Kamau, "Suppose I concede you are right. I ask that you take me to the stormhold. I need to speak to these Stormlords. I will go in peace!" he added, seeing the man's expression darken. "I want only to reason with them."

"Dela Eden can take you to the stormhold, Vindrasi, but unless you know the secret to how to make it work, the gates to the city will not open."

"Do you Cyclopes know this secret?" said Skylan.

"We do not want to know. As I said," Dela Eden replied, "we live on the ground."

"Perhaps there is another way," Aylaen said, turning to Kamau. "How do the Stormlords in the Kingdom Above communicate with those who live in the Kingdom Below?"

"Through the seneschals," Kamau answered. "The wizards who oversee the stormholds."

"We can talk to them, Skylan," said Aylaen. "We will ask them to carry a message to the wizards in the Kingdom Above."

"How long before the emperor's army arrives?" Skylan asked Kamau.

"According to the seneschal, the Stormlords are doing what they can to delay the fleet, but the god Aelon is working against them. A few days, but not more. The nearest stormhold is up the coast. If you depart now, you can reach it before noon."

He was obviously eager to be rid of them. Bidding farewell to Dela Eden, Kamau ignored Skylan and Aylaen and departed, melting into the shadows of the trees.

"He keeps watch over the village," Dela Eden explained, as they walked back to the dragonships. "He will let our people know when it is safe to return."

She glanced at Aylaen, who was walking rapidly, her cheeks flushed, her arms folded across her chest.

"This news has upset her," said Dela Eden.

"Can you blame her? She is the Kai Priestess of our people. She has risked her life to save the spiritbones, and these wizards would barter one of them away to save their own skins!"

Skylan had rarely seen Aylaen so angry. She was shaking with outrage. He tried to calm her.

"We have four spiritbones," he said. "We traveled beneath the waves for one and to the realm of the dead for another. These wizards will see reason."

"They have to, Skylan," said Aylaen. "The lies, the fear. All that is behind us. I understand. I see so clearly! The five must come together as one, as the runes foretold."

"We will get the five spiritbones," Skylan said confidently. "And once we have them, you will summon the Great Dragon Ilyrion, and she will drive out Aelon. Our gods will be strong again, our people will be safe and all will be as it was before."

Aylaen took hold of his hands, clasped her hands around them, and looked at him as if she could see deep within him.

"You would give your life for that," said Aylaen, not asking a question, but seeking assurance.

"I would. I am Chief of Chiefs," said Skylan.

"And I am Kai Priestess," she murmured.

He saw that she was still troubled and he thought he knew why.

"The Stormlords will see reason," he repeated, but she only sighed.

The *Venejekar* and the small dragonship fleet sailed north along the Spirit Coast until they came to an enormous promontory jutting up out of the sea, which Dela Eden said was named Gray Beak, because it was shaped like the beak of an eagle. She told them to stop.

"You cannot see it, but through those trees is the mouth of the river that leads west to Tsa Terestra, the Kingdom Below," said Dela Eden. "The stormhold is on the peak above. It guards the mouth of the river and serves as a gate to Tsa Kerestra, the Kingdom Above."

Skylan had hoped to see the stormhold, but Gray Beak towered over them, dwarfing the dragonships, and he couldn't see anything. He gave the wizards grudging approval for having chosen an ideal location for their outpost. Anyone standing on that high bluff would be able to see clear to the horizon and have ample warning of the approach of an enemy.

The dragonships glided past the deep and wide river with densely forested banks. The river was named Abundance, for it flooded every spring, providing rich, fertile soil for the crops. Dela Eden told Skylan that if he followed the river to its source, they would eventually reach the Khilat Mountains, the ancient home of the Stormlords.

"No one lives there now," said Dela Eden. "But it is still sacred to the wizards."

Skylan cast a glance at the storm clouds that were now much closer, where the Stormlords were presumably now living. No storms raged at the moment, but trailing fingers of mist brushed over the land beneath.

"Where is this city of the other kingdom?" Skylan asked. He couldn't remember the strange-sounding name. "The Kingdom Below."

"There is no city. Nothing but a few villages and farms where the Stormlords of the Kingdom Below grow the crops that sustain their people in the Kingdom Above."

"Perhaps we could talk to the Stormlords living there," said Skylan.

"The villages are located far inland. And if the Stormlords warned *my people* to flee, you may be certain their own people have long since sought safety in the Kingdom Above," said Dela Eden.

The dragonships sailed past the promontory and Skylan looked on rolling hills with broad swards of grassland where sheep and cattle could graze, orchards thick with fruit, and vast stretches of golden wheat that rippled with the wind like ocean waves. He mentally compared this land to the rock-strewn ground the Vindrasi struggled to farm.

"You see why the wizards would not want to give this up," said Dela Eden.

"I see why I would fight for it," said Skylan grimly. "Where is Oran from here?"

"Oran's borders lie well to the north. The land of the fae is said to be on the other side of the Khilat Mountains."

"I trust we will stay well clear of the fae," Skylan said.

"The fae will stay clear of us," said Dela Eden, grinning. "They do not like those they call the 'Uglies,' which is why I find it odd that a fae child has chosen to be with you. He seems much attached to you. Where did you find him?"

"I didn't," said Skylan. "He found me."

"What do you mean?"

"He sneaked on board my ship, a stowaway. I had been badly hurt and he saved my life."

"And so now you belong to him." Dela Eden nodded her head, as if this made sense.

The sun vanished as the dragonships sailed into the cool shadow cast by the gray clouds. As Skylan looked back at the promontory, Dela Eden pointed.

"The stormhold," she said. "You can see it from here."

The stormhold was not nearly as formidable in appearance as its name implied, being nothing more than a solitary tower of gray stone.

"How do we reach it?" Skylan asked. "The rock walls of the cliff are smooth; they look impossible to climb."

"A trail leads up from the western side," said Dela Eden.

After conferring with Bear Walker and Dela Eden, Skylan decided to sail the dragonships partway up the mouth of the Abundance River. They could haul the dragonships onto the beach and hide them. While Skylan and his group went to investigate the stormhold, the others could make camp, hunt and fish, and replenish their water supply.

As the warriors carried the dragonships out of the water and dragged them onto the shore, the red glow left the wooden eyes.

"The dragons who sailed the ships from the Isle of Revels are leaving," Aylaen told Skylan. "I thanked them for their service and said I regretted we had no jewels to pay them."

"Did you ask Kahg to persuade them to stay?" Skylan asked, disappointed. "We could use their help."

"Kahg is angry about something," Aylaen said, troubled. "His voice grated. His eyes glinted with a fierce light. He said only that the dragons could ask for payment at a later time, depending on what happens."

"What does that mean?" Skylan asked, glumly watching the dragons fly north.

Aylaen shook her head. "I do not know. At least the Dragon Kahg remains with us."

"I have an idea," said Skylan. "We can ask the dragon to talk to the Stormlords. He could fly up to the city that's supposedly in the clouds— What? Why not?"

Aylaen was shaking her head. "I had the same idea and I spoke to Kahg. He will not even consider it. The dragons and the Stormlords are ancient foes, dating back to the time when they lived in the Realm of Fire. The wizards used powerful magicks against the dragons."

"These wizards have made enemies of everyone," Skylan said. "No wonder they live in the clouds. They fear to live anywhere else."

While the others made camp on the shores of the river, Skylan and those who volunteered to accompany him to the stormhold began the ascent up the west side of the promontory, which was heavily forested land that sloped at a steep angle from the top of the promontory to the sandy beach far below. Skylan chose Dela Eden, Sigurd, Bjorn, and Farinn, to go with him. He had been afraid that Aylaen would want to go, but she remained on the *Venejekar*, saying she wanted to clean and polish the gold and jeweled settings of the spiritbones.

Skylan was relieved. From what he had heard about the dangers of the stormhold, he didn't want her anywhere near it. He knew that if he told her that, however, she would perversely decide to go. Skylan was curious as to why she was going to all this trouble to clean the jewelry, but he was so grateful that she was staying safely in the ship that he did not ask, for fear she might change her mind.

Skylan told Wulfe that he was to stay with Aylaen. Wulfe stared at him as though he didn't understand a word Skylan was saying and followed after them the moment Skylan turned his back.

The trail leading up to the stormhold turned out to be well tended and easy to climb. The path wound among ancient trees and there were even parts of it where they found steps cut into the rock to assist them over the steeper portions. The sun had been shining brightly when they set out, but now rain clouds, blown by an offshore breeze, drifted overhead. Beneath the clouds, the air was cool and moist.

They lost Wulfe about halfway through the journey. The boy had been lagging behind, and no one saw him leave. Skylan hoped he had merely grown bored with the climb and gone to the ship.

The forest straggled to an end about forty paces from the stormhold. Skylan called a halt at the tree line. To reach the stormhold, they would have to cross a large stretch of bare rock, visible to whoever—or whatever—was keeping watch. Their only advantage was that the rain had started, little more than a drizzle, giving them some cover.

The Vindrasi wore their armor and all except Farinn carried weapons. Dela Eden had smiled at this, asking what good Skylan thought swords and axes would be against magic.

"I suppose these wizards bleed like other men," Skylan had replied, refusing to be intimidated.

Skylan and his friends walked forward. Having to move out in the open now, being watched by perhaps malevolent eyes, he heeded Dela Eden's warning and kept his hands well clear of his sword. He advised the others to do the same.

Those forty paces seemed the longest journey Skylan had ever made. He expected every moment to feel an arrow thud into his ribs or a spear to strike his chest, for he did not entirely ascribe to this notion that the wizards would not kill when threatened. Something had killed those two priests.

No arrow flew from the stormhold; no spear crashed down at their feet. No voice commanded them to halt or even shouted a warning. All Skylan could hear was the wind whistling through the crenellations on top of the tower, the rain pattering on the rock, and the crash of waves far below.

The rain had obscured their view of the stormhold, making it seem solid and formidable. But as they drew nearer, they could see it more clearly and they began to breathe easier.

"The only danger I fear is that this heap will come crashing down on our heads," Sigurd stated.

The stormhold consisted of a single round tower that seemed old beyond reckoning. The stone walls were dark and dingy gray tinged green from lichen, and starting to crumble. Cracks zigzagged up the walls and there were places where stones had either disintegrated or fallen out.

The stormhold had no windows and only one entrance—an arched doorway without a door. Skylan tried to see inside, but the interior was pitch dark in the gloom. The only sound was the incessant dripping of rain falling off the wet stones.

"Seneschal!" Dela Eden called. "I have brought visitors. We come in peace."

They waited for several moments in silence, while the mists and the rain closed in around them, making it seem as if they were in a world that consisted of only the tower and the stony ground. When no one responded, Dela Eden shook her head.

"The seneschal is always at the door to greet visitors. I fear we are too late and even he has fled. I will go inside to see. The rest of you wait."

"I'm coming with you," said Skylan.

Dela Eden shrugged. "Be careful. Do not touch the key or anything around it. Remember the two dead priests."

Skylan could think of nothing else. Dela Eden entered first and he immediately lost sight of her in the darkness. Drawing in a deep breath, he plunged in after her.

A short, narrow corridor opened into a large, circular chamber with no ceiling, open to the air. In the center of the chamber was a circular stone wall, standing about waist-high, reminding Skylan of a well, except that it was far larger.

No one was here. That much was obvious.

"Do you know where this seneschal lives?" Skylan asked.

"I have no idea," said Dela Eden. "I have never been to either kingdom."

Frustrated, Skylan walked over to the wall and peered down into the well with some thought that perhaps it led to an underground chamber where the seneschal might be hiding.

A huge globe made of smooth gray stone floated in the center of the well. Astonished by the unexpected sight, Skylan rested the palm of his hand on the top of the wall, planning to lean over get a better view.

"Don't touch!" Dela Eden cried.

Her warning came too late. The moment Skylan's fingers touched the stone, a jet of air shot out from the wall opposite him, and struck him in the chest with such force that it lifted him off his feet and slammed him into the stone wall behind him.

He collapsed onto the floor and lay there, dazed and stunned. He glowered at Dela Eden, who was grinning at him.

"I warned you not to touch anything. Are you hurt?"

"What do you think?" Skylan returned, grimacing.

He moved gingerly, rubbing his shoulders and feeling to see if any ribs were broken. None was, but he must have bruised them, for it hurt to breathe.

"What's going on in there?" Bjorn shouted. "Skylan, are you all right?"

"I'm alive," Skylan told them in no very good humor. "You can come in. Just don't touch anything!"

Sigurd and Farinn cautiously entered.

"I told Bjorn to keep watch outside," said Sigurd, eyeing Skylan, who was taking his time getting to his feet. "What happened to you?"

"I tripped some sort of magical trap that threw me against a wall. Don't go near that well."

"It is *not* a well," said Dela Eden. "It is the key that opens the gate."

Skylan was barely listening. He had noticed an iron ladder leading to the walkway at the top of the tower.

"Is that ladder safe to touch?" he asked.

"Only the key is guarded," Dela Eden replied. "When the mists part, the view from the top is splendid."

The room had been growing steadily brighter as the watery image of the sun appeared through the clouds.

"Sigurd, you and Farinn climb up there, take a look around," said Skylan. "The seneschal must live somewhere close by. See if you can find a dwelling."

Sigurd shook his head and backed away. "Not me. I'm not touching anything in here."

Dela Eden was scornful. "All my life I have heard of the courage of Vindrasi warriors. Now I see you are milksops."

She began to climb the rungs of the ladder, moving swiftly, hand over hand. Pausing halfway, she called down to Farinn. "Come join me on the walkway, young bard. I will show you sights for your song."

Farinn glanced uncertainly at Skylan, who was looking very grim. Receiving his nod, Farinn nimbly climbed the ladder after Dela Eden.

"You have shamed us," said Skylan to Sigurd in a low voice.

"Yeah, well, I don't see any foul magicks slamming *me* into a wall," Sigurd returned. He cast a nervous glance around. "I'll keep watch outside with Bjorn."

Dela Eden reached the walkway, a platform made of stone built at the top, encircling the tower. Farinn pulled himself up after her and after a moment's hesitation, walked over to the edge and looked out. He gave a little gasp.

"It's wonderful, Skylan!" he called down. "The sea is so vast. I must be seeing the world as the gods see it."

"You're not up there to see what the gods see," Skylan said sharply. "Any sign of a dwelling?"

"The forest is so thick . . . ," Farinn began. Catching Skylan's baleful glare, he added hurriedly, "I'll keep looking."

Skylan turned his attention back to the well. Being careful not to touch the wall, he looked into the well to see a globe made of the same gray stone as the tower, striated with golden and silver strands as fine as cobweb, suspended in the middle of the well. As he stared, incredulous, he saw the pale sunlight flash on striations and realized in wonder that the globe was slowly rotating on some unseen axis.

Skylan didn't believe what he was seeing. Keeping a wary eye on the wall, he drew closer to investigate. The stone globe was as big as two ogres the size of Bear Walker and must have weighed as much as a hundred ogres the size of Bear Walker and yet it floated on air, as light as thistledown. He looked about for the chains or rods, anything that might be holding it, and saw nothing.

"Dela Eden, what is this floating rock?" Skylan called.

"I told you," said Dela Eden, looking down on him from above. "That is the key to the gate of Tsa Kerestra, the Kingdom Above."

"But if this is the key, where is the gate?" Skylan asked. "And how does it open?"

"According to the seneschal, there is a matching globe in the Kingdom Above. When the wizards perform the magicks, the globes align, the gate opens and the Stormlords can travel from the Kingdom Below to the Kingdom Above. I have heard that the beauty of Tsa Terestra makes the heart ache. I would love to visit it someday, but, of course, none except Stormlords may enter."

Skylan watched the stone globe revolving on its axis. The sunlight flashed on the myriad golden and silver strands, as fine as the thread of his wyrd. He tried to fathom the powerful magicks that must be at work just to keep the globe afloat.

"These wizards must be gods," he muttered.

"Not gods," said Dela Eden, climbing down the ladder to come speak with him. "Humans with godlike powers."

"Then why do people with such power grovel on their bellies in front of Raegar when, from what I've seen, they could use their magic to destroy him and his army?" Skylan demanded, frustrated.

"You are a simple soul, Skylan Ivorson," said Dela Eden, smiling at him. "Everything with you is either bright sunshine or dead of night. You do not understand those who dwell in the twilight."

"All I know is that these wizards are cowards who lack the courage to fight to save themselves," Skylan said. "Instead they will betray a trust and give Raegar the spiritbone! And not even that will save them, for he will attack them anyway!"

"Since you cannot talk to them, what will you do?" Dela Eden asked.

"The only thing I can do," said Skylan in grim tones. "If the Stormlords will not fight Raegar, then we must."

"Skylan!" Farinn called. "Come up here! You need to see this!"

Hearing the warning tone in the young man's voice, Skylan quickly scaled the ladder, which was made of iron and looked very flimsy.

Thinking he'd had his fill of magic, he stepped from the ladder onto the walkway and looked out to sea.

The view took Skylan's breath and he understood now why Farinn had said the gods must see the world like this—ripples of sunlight on blue-gray water stretching to the horizon.

The shoreline where the dragonships had landed ran from Gray Beak north, vast stretches of gleaming white sand and sawtooth grass extending up the coast. To the west, thick forests of dark green vied with the gold of the wheat fields and the lighter green of rolling hills. Due north, an enormous mass of dark gray storm clouds hovered protectively over a large plateau with steep, sheer walls that thrust up out of the grasslands.

"Dela Eden says that Tsa Kerestra is built on top of those dark clouds over the plateau," said Farinn. "Look north of that, along the horizon."

Skylan squinted against the brilliance of the sunlight on the water and saw what seemed like small dots floating on the surface of the water.

"I see dots," said Skylan. "What do you see?"

"A fleet of ships," Farinn answered readily.

"Raegar's fleet," said Skylan.

"I cannot be certain—" Farinn hedged.

"You can be certain," said Skylan grimly.

The Stormlords were also certain, apparently. Dark clouds suddenly descended from the sky and boiled around the ships, enveloping them in rain, striking them with lightning. The squall did not last long, driven off by the sunlight. The dots sailed on.

"Sigurd, Bjorn!" Skylan shouted, climbing down the ladder with Farinn following behind.

The two entered the stormhold with caution and stopped just inside the doorway.

"Raegar's fleet is on the way," Skylan reported.

"That means a fight," said Sigurd, grinning. "Against the living this time, not ghosts. Real heads to bash."

Skylan smiled. He did not like Sigurd, but he had to give the man credit. When it came to battle, Sigurd had never yet met the skull he couldn't crack.

"The rest of you go back to camp," Skylan said. "Tell Aylaen and

Bear Walker about the fleet and assemble the chiefs. I'll talk to them when I return."

"What are you going to do?" Bjorn asked.

"I'm going to take one more look around this place. There might be something I missed," said Skylan.

"Don't let any magicks knock you on your butt again," said Sigurd.

He, Bjorn, and Farinn left the stormhold, accompanied by Dela Eden, the three continuing a running argument about the effectiveness of the Vindrasi shield wall as opposed to Cyclopes archery.

Skylan remained by himself in the stormhold. He didn't really expect to find anything. He just needed a moment alone, to think, make plans. He watched the globe, serenely floating in its dark well, and swore in vexation.

"If you are this powerful, why give up without a fight? I don't understand!"

The globe had no answer for him. Shaking his head, Skylan left, glad to walk out into the sunshine. He was following the path through the trees, deep in thought, when something sprang at him from the shadows.

Skylan drew his sword, terrifying Wulfe, who gave a yelp and scrambled backward.

"Torval's balls, Wulfe!" Skylan swore. "Don't sneak up on me like that! I could have killed you!"

He sheathed his sword and continued walking. Wulfe padded along by his side.

"I wasn't sneaking up on you," said the boy. "I came to give you something."

"Wulfe, I'm not in the mood—" said Skylan.

Wulfe dashed past him, jumped in front of him, and stood blocking the path. Skylan glared at him.

"What is it, then?" he demanded. "Be quick. I have to get back to the ship."

"You'll like this," Wulfe assured him. "If you still want to talk to the Cloud Dwellers, my mother said she would take you."

Skylan stared, amazed, not understanding. "Your mother . . ."

"Princess of the Faery," Wulfe said proudly. "You know that. I've told you. She will take us. Aren't you pleased? It's what you wanted."

Part of Skylan was pleased. The other part wanted to turn and run.

CHAPTER

24

Returning to the *Venejekar*, Skylan sent Farinn, along with Erdmun and Bjorn, back to the stormhold with the spyglass to try to get a closer look at the approaching fleet, perhaps make a guess at the numbers of troops he might be facing. He also asked Bjorn to look for a place along the coastline where Raegar was likely to land his ships and set up camp.

Skylan missed Acronis, who would have been able to tell him how many troops each ship could carry and provide him with other valuable information about Raegar's army. Skylan also missed the older man's advice and counsel, especially now that he was trying to decide what to do about Wulfe's startling offer for his mother to take him to Tsa Kerestra.

Skylan had mulled it over all the way back to the dragonship. At first he thought he would accept. He didn't have any choice. He had to either talk to the Stormlords or steal the spiritbone from them; he hadn't yet decided which. But just when he had made up his mind to go, he thought about placing his trust in Wulfe's mother, who might or might not be the daughter of the faery queen.

The fae had come to Skylan's aid more than once. He owed his life to the oceanids and he was grateful, but he couldn't put his trust in any of them. He was one of the hated "Uglies." The only reason they had helped him was because he was important to Wulfe, who obviously wasn't that important to his mother. According to Wulfe's own tale, his mother had abandoned him, leaving her child to run wild with a wolf pack.

Skylan determined he wouldn't risk it, not on the eve of battle. And yet . . .

While he was still going back and forth in his decision, Farinn returned from the stormhold with a disappointing report. The enemy fleet had been engulfed by storm squalls and he had not been able to see them. His best guess, based on his original sighting, was that the fleet consisted of two very large ships and a host of smaller ones and that they were two, maybe three days out.

Skylan and Farinn calculated that given the number of ships the bard saw, Raegar had around four thousand troops, while Skylan had maybe five hundred.

"The odds are against us, but not by that much," he said, "considering that each of my warriors is worth ten Sinarians. I have two days to make plans. Two days to talk to the Stormlords, acquire the spiritbone, and return."

At this, Skylan surprised himself. He just realized he had reached a decision.

Skylan called a meeting of the captains, including Bear Walker and Raven's-foot and Keeper, Dela Eden, Aylaen, Sigurd, and the other Vindrasi. The warriors met on the beach. Wulfe remained on board the *Venejekar*, complaining that there would be too much iron, for which Skylan was grateful. He had not yet told anyone about his decision to travel to Tsa Kerestra, and was afraid the boy would blurt it out before he had a chance to explain to the others.

Skylan described the stormhold, the floating stone globe, and the magic that had blown him across the room. When the ogres appeared skeptical, Dela Eden confirmed his words. At this, Raven's-foot scowled and softly rattled the gourd in a circle around himself, presumably meant to ward off evil. Skylan added that they had seen Raegar's fleet approaching, about two days distant.

"Which gives us two days to make preparations," he said. He paused a moment, then added as calmly as he could, "I believe I have found a way to enter Tsa Kerestra."

"Tsa Kerestra!" Aylaen gasped.

He looked at her, startled. She had gone white to the lips and pressed her hand against her chest, as though she were having trouble breathing.

"I plan to talk to the Stormlords," he said. "You knew I meant to do this."

"Just not . . . so soon . . ." she murmured.

He regarded her with concern, but she gave him a faint, pale smile and he turned to the others, who were far more vocal, demanding answers.

"How? Are you going through the stormhold? What about the magic?"

Skylan raised his hand, calling for silence. "This is a risk I take on myself. I ask no one to go with me. If I succeed, then all is well. If I fail . . ." He shrugged. "We are no worse off than we are now."

"We might be better off," Sigurd called out, laughing. "For I will then be Chief of Chiefs."

Skylan let this pass. Bear Walker and Raven's-foot were arguing. Dela Eden looked at him with all three of her eyes. Aylaen was silent, withdrawn. She stood with her arms clasped around herself, gazing out to sea. She seemed not have heard anything he had said. He gave an inward sigh. She feared for him, of course. He foresaw a difficult time persuading her that he must go.

"I have been considering what we must do!" Skylan shouted to re-capture their attention. "Aelon will warn Raegar that we are coming to stop him. He will be on the lookout for us and I do not want him to find us. Not yet. At first I thought we could sail farther upriver, but I like this location. Our dragonships are well hidden and we are close to the stormhold."

He gestured to the beach, to the myriad footprints in the sand, bundles of fishnet, dead fish, and fish guts.

"Unfortunately, Raegar has only to see this mess and he will know we are here and he will come looking for us."

"Let him find us!" Sigurd shouted.

"I want him to find us when we are ready for him to find us," said Skylan. "Not before."

"We could make it look as if we took fright at the sight of the emperor's fleet and ran away," said Dela Eden.

Sigurd and the other Vindrasi raised their voices in anger.

"Raegar is a Vindrasi himself," said Skylan. "He knows that we would never flee, no matter what the odds. I was thinking we could make it look as if we fought a great battle here, leave some broken shields and weapons scattered about. Raegar will think the wizards defeated us—"

"Bah! No one would believe that!" Sigurd scoffed. "Raegar will think we knocked their city from the clouds and drove the wizards into the sea and then sailed home, triumphant, too filled with glory to bother about him."

Skylan and Bjorn exchanged glances.

"He's only partly jesting, you know," said Bjorn.

Skylan shook his head and asked Bjorn if he had found a site where Raegar would be likely to land his army.

"The beach is too narrow here, near the stormhold," said Bjorn. "There is a wide stretch of beach located about a day's journey north of the stormhold, close to that plateau underneath the city in the clouds."

"The Stormlords call the plateau Foundation Rock," said Dela Eden. "Bjorn is right. If the emperor is going to try to attack Tsa Kerestra, that would be an excellent site to make his camp."

"I don't like all this skulking about," Sigurd grumbled. "When do we fight?"

"We must wait to see the outcome of my meeting with the Stormlords," said Skylan. "If all goes as I hope, they will join us in battle."

And if it doesn't, he thought, and I have to steal the spiritbone, we may be fighting two enemies: Raegar and the Stormlords.

He asked Dela Eden and Farinn to go back to the stormhold tomorrow morning at dawn to keep watch on the progress of Raegar's ships. Sigurd and the others were to make the beach look as if there had been a battle, and suggested that perhaps they could always fight a mock battle to churn up the sand, make it look more realistic.

Seeing Sigurd look a bit too enthusiastic, Skylan added severely, "Use deer blood, not your own."

Bear Walker demanded to know how Skylan was going to travel to a city in the clouds and the others wanted to know, as well. Skylan said he would trust to Torval to find a way. No one liked that answer, but when it became clear that was all Skylan would say, they walked off, shaking their heads.

Skylan had to tell Aylaen the truth. She had not said a word since he had said he was going to Tsa Kerestra. By unspoken agreement, they walked back to the *Venejekar* to discuss the matter. Wulfe pounced on Skylan the moment he boarded.

"Well? Will you come?" the boy asked eagerly.

"I can't talk now," Skylan said with a glance at Aylaen.

She looked at Wulfe and then back at Skylan. "The fae are part of this plan of yours?"

"My mother said she would take him," said Wulfe.

Aylaen's eyes widened. Skylan cast a grim look at the boy, then took hold of Aylaen's arm and steered her toward the hatch.

"I need to talk to you in private," he said.

They went down into the hold and Skylan closed the hatch. When the darkness closed around them they instinctively drew together.

"Wulfe says his mother can take me to Tsa Kerestra," Skylan said. "I know this sounds crazy, but according to Wulfe, his people visit the Kingdom Above on a regular basis. He says they go to admire the beautiful things. My guess is that the fae go to *steal* some of these beautiful things."

"Like the objects he has in his hidey-hole," Aylaen said thoughtfully. "But how do they travel there?"

"He won't tell me. He said the way is secret. But he promised me that they don't go through the stormhold."

"When do you plan to leave?" she asked.

"Tonight. The fae are holding some sort of feast in the forest and I am invited to attend. I will leave from there."

Aylaen was quiet. Skylan couldn't see her face in the darkness, but he thought he could guess her thoughts.

"I know you don't want me to go—"

"You must go," said Aylaen. "And I must go with you."

Skylan gave an emphatic shake of his head. "I will go alone, Aylaen. The danger is too great. We can't trust the fae, and as for the Stormlords—"

"I am going with you, Skylan," said Aylaen. "And I will give you my reasons. How will the Stormlords know you are telling the truth about the spiritbones if they do not see them?"

Skylan had not considered this. Since he could not answer, Aylaen answered for him. "You must have the other four to show them. I am Kai Priestess. The spiritbones are in my care and their care is my duty. I will take them.

"That is the first reason," she continued. "Here is another. You do not know how to negotiate. If people won't do what you want, you threaten to bash them over the head. Look what happened when you met the Queen of the Aquins. You offended her and ended up in prison. Even the peace-loving druids nearly killed you. You need me, Skylan, and I am coming with you."

"I *do* need you," said Skylan, drawing her close. "And that is why I do not want to risk losing you."

"You do not care for me, that I risk losing *you*," Aylaen returned. "Men stand in the shield wall and women are left to bury the dead. You will say that this is our way of life."

"Yes, of course," Skylan said, puzzled that there should be any argument.

"It is also our way that the wife of the Chief of Chiefs should be a Kai Priestess," said Aylaen. "As you are chief of their physical well-being, so I am chief of their souls."

Her voice quavered slightly and he felt her shiver in his arms. "Vindrash has given me her blessing, her sword and her armor, and she has entrusted me with the spiritbones. I am coming with you, Skylan. If there is danger, we will be stronger if we face it together."

At that moment, Skylan loved her so much he thought his heart might burst.

"If we have a daughter and she is as stubborn and rebellious as her mother," he said, "I will never find a husband for her."

Aylaen twined her arms around him and rested her head against his chest.

"Her name will be Holma," she said softly. "And she will have a twin brother named Skylanson. They will have red hair like their mother and blue eyes like their father."

Skylan stared at her, amazed. "How do you know this?"

"A pretty dream," she said. "Nothing more. And now I must change. We must wear our finest."

As she slipped out of his embrace, Skylan thought he felt something wet, like a tear, fall on his hand.

"Aylaen . . . ," he began, but she pushed him away.

"Go talk to Wulfe," she told him.

The boy had been waiting for Skylan, and he accosted him the moment he set foot on deck, jumping about in his excitement. "You are coming to see my mother!"

"Aylaen and I are both coming—against my better judgment," Skylan said. "How far away is this feasting site?"

"Not far," Wulfe said evasively.

"Then it's nearby," Skylan persisted.

Wulfe scratched his head. "Not near *here*."

"Then near where?" Skylan demanded. A sudden thought came to him and he frowned at the boy. "Dela Eden said your people live in a kingdom beyond the mountains. You're not taking us there, are you?"

"No, silly. My grandmother wouldn't let you in," Wulfe returned. "The place where my mother is holding the feast tonight is not far and it's not near. It just *is*."

Skylan was going to ask more questions, but stopped himself. He realized that the boy had actually taken a bath without anyone forcing him. Wulfe had also washed his face—or most of it—and had apparently even had tried to comb his hair. One of Aylaen's wooden combs was caught in the boy's shaggy mop.

"You can't go dressed like a beggar," Skylan said, eyeing the rags Wulfe was wearing. "Aylaen will find you a clean tunic."

"My mother has clothes for me. Can you get this comb out? I think it's stuck."

Skylan began trying to free the comb. "Was your mother glad to see you?"

"At first she didn't know me," Wulfe answered. "And then she kissed me and hugged me and asked me if I remembered the magic she had taught me and I said I did, most of it. Ouch! That hurts!"

"What else did she say?" Skylan asked.

"She said she'd heard from the oceanids that I was living with you and the other Uglies and I was coming here and she was hoping to see me, only when she did, I wasn't what she expected."

"What did she expect? That you'd stay a baby forever?" Skylan finally managed to untangle the boy's hair, though he ended up breaking two of the comb's teeth.

"I think she thought I'd be grown into a man by now," said Wulfe.

"Why would she think that? How old are you?"

Wulfe shrugged. "I don't know. A hundred? How many is that?"

Skylan laughed. "Too many."

He left Wulfe and went to dress for the feast. His beard had grown long and unkempt and he decided to bathe in the ocean and shave. He put on his best tunic, or rather the tunic that was the least worn, clean breeches, and his leather armor. He combed out the tangles in his long blond hair and tied two braids in the front, leaving the rest unbound in back. He added the silver arm rings that he had won in battle, to impress the wizards, and then presented himself to Aylaen for approval.

She came on deck wearing her dragon-scale armor over a white leather tunic and pants and boots. She had also bathed and washed her hair, which she wore tied in a single heavy braid down her back with curls straying around her face. Wulfe had opened his hidey-hole for her and she carried the spiritbones in a pouch tied onto her sword belt.

"You are too beautiful," said Skylan. "You will make the faeries envious."

"And you are too handsome," Aylaen said. "I fear some dryad will run away with you."

"Are you two finally ready?" Wulfe demanded impatiently.

"Not quite," said Aylaen. "I must talk to the Dragon Kahg. I need to tell him where we are going."

"I will come with you," said Skylan.

To his surprise, Aylaen refused to allow him, saying it was business between Kai Priestess and dragon. "I must speak with Kahg alone. Besides, someone else wants to talk to you."

Skylan looked around to see Farinn wearing a mended tunic, pants, and boots, with his hair combed and braided. Judging by a cut on his face, he had even shaved, though what he had to shave was open to question.

Skylan frowned. "Where do you think you are going?"

"I asked him to come with us," said Wulfe, before Farinn could answer.

"Out of the question," said Skylan curtly.

"My mother likes music," said Wulfe. "She wants to hear him sing."

"Please, Skylan, let me come," Farinn pleaded. "This meeting is an important part of your song and I should be there."

"I'm not certain I want a meeting with the fae to be in my song," Skylan muttered.

He was about to insist that Farinn remain behind, then he thought of what might happen to the young man if by some mischance Sigurd ended up taking command. Sigurd had always thought Skylan was too soft on Farinn. He'd put him in the front row of the shield wall.

"Very well, you can come," said Skylan. He began to buckle on his sword belt.

"What are you doing?" Wulfe cried, shocked. "You can't take your sword with you! My mother won't like it!"

"I'm not going to go roaming about a strange land filled with wizards without my sword," said Skylan. "Aylaen is bringing hers, as well."

"Then I can't take you," said Wulfe, blinking back tears, his lips quivering.

"I will make a bargain with you," said Skylan. "We will carry our swords . . ."

Wulfe violently shook his head.

". . . but we will take them off before we go to the feast," Skylan finished. "We'll hide them under a bush or a tree or somewhere so your mother won't see them. Will that work?"

"No," Wulfe said, scowling. "She'll smell the iron on you. But she might let you come if you bring her a present."

"A present?" Skylan repeated, amazed. "What sort of present?"

Wulfe thought this over. "You could give her Farinn."

"I am not giving her Farinn," said Skylan grimly.

Turning to see that Aylaen was still talking to the dragon, Skylan set off in search of Bjorn and found him flinging buckets of animal blood onto the sand, while Dela Eden was dropping torn scraps of leather, broken spears, and arrows that were no longer of use.

"The tide will probably wash most of this blood out to sea, but Sigurd thought this was a good idea," said Bjorn.

"Watch Sigurd," said Skylan. "Don't let him get himself and everyone else killed."

"I'll keep a club handy," said Bjorn, grinning.

"How in the name of Torval do you plan to get up into the clouds, Vindrasi?" Dela Eden asked, joining them. She glanced at the storm raging over the plateau, gray and angry, flickering with lightning.

"To be honest, I don't know," said Skylan. He touched the amulet at his neck. "Torval is with me. He will find a way."

Dela Eden eyed him. "I think this has less to do with Torval and more to do with the fae child."

"And I think your three eyes should stay out of my head," Skylan replied, annoyed.

Dela Eden smiled, and reached out and, before he knew what she was doing and could escape, she was tracing the outline of a third eye on his own forehead.

"Go with the Cyclopes' blessing as well as Torval's, Skylan Ivorson," she said. "And be careful. Some doors even the gods fear to open."

Skylan walked back to where Aylaen, Farinn, and Wulfe were waiting for him. His skin itched where she had pretended to draw the eye and he longed to rub his forehead, but he didn't dare, for fear of offending her.

Skylan, Aylaen and Farinn left the *Venejekar* at dusk, slipping away quietly while the others were celebrating a good day's work with a great feast. The Cyclopes prepared fish. The ogres roasted deer, and Sigurd and the Vindrasi contributed a keg of honey mead—a gift of gratitude from Joabis.

The warriors sat around a blazing bonfire telling tales of valor and singing the old songs of their people. Skylan watched the flames leap in the air, smelled the tantalizing aroma of roasted meat and listened to the boisterous laughter, then thought of the fae feast he was destined to attend. He would have given twenty silver arm rings to join his friends.

He pointed to Sigurd and Raven's-foot, sitting with their arms around each other, bawling out some ogre love song, and shook his head.

"Of all the strange things we have seen, none is stranger than that," he told Aylaen. "I may have nightmares."

Aylaen took hold of his hand and said with quiet pride, "You did this, Skylan. These people have been killing each other for years and you brought us together."

"Being dead changes one's outlook on life," said Skylan.

Aylaen laughed at him, which was what he intended. He loved to hear her laughter. But he was secretly pleased with her praise.

"Where is Wulfe?" Farinn asked, trudging alongside of them. "Isn't he going to guide us?"

"He went on ahead to tell his mother we were coming," said Skylan. "We are supposed to meet him on the beach at the foot of Gray Beak."

"Did he say what time?"

"When the moon rises from the sea," said Skylan. "We are supposed to dine with them."

Farinn looked alarmed. "I have heard that their food is enchanted, so that anyone who eats it is forever forced to live among them."

"Then we won't eat," said Skylan.

The night sky was clear overhead, though the ever-present storm clouds massed in the north. Skylan had brought wood-and-rawhide candle lanterns to light their way, but for now they did not need them. The lambent light of the stars made the sand gleam. Skylan sent Farinn on ahead to scout the way, then asked Aylaen about the dragon.

"How did your talk go with Kahg?"

After a moment's pause Aylaen said, "I not only spoke to him, I summoned him."

"You did?" Skylan was startled. "I didn't see him."

"He asked to be a dragon of air and I thought that was a sensible suggestion," said Aylaen. "Since he may have to attack ships."

Skylan thought this over. He would have liked to have the dragon fight as an earth dragon, ponderous and strong, with crushing fangs and a tail that could knock down walls. But an air dragon's powerful breath could blast a ship apart or sink a fleet in a gale.

"Summoning him was good idea. Sigurd and the others might need him in our absence."

"Yes," Aylaen agreed, but he had the impression she had summoned the dragon for a different reason.

He waited for her to tell him, but she said no more. He was disappointed, but then he reminded himself that Priestesses of the Kai have their sacred mysteries, not to be revealed to any others.

He looked at her as she walked beside him, her hand twined in his. Her red hair was the color of dark wine. Her dragon-scale armor glimmered with a faint luminescence in the starlight. She was more somber and serious than usual, yet serene. Her eyes were clear and bright and unafraid, and when they looked at him, filled with love.

"Are we doing the right thing?" Skylan asked. "Trusting Wulfe?"

"The boy loves you, Skylan," said Aylaen. "He wants to help."

Skylan looked to the north to the dark mass of clouds that blotted out the stars and tried to imagine a city—dwellings, shops, a Chief's Hall floating in the air—and he failed. But then, he could never have imagined a floating globe of stone.

"Wulfe loves us," said Skylan. "But to the rest of the fae we are the Uglies."

When they reached the outskirts of the forest Skylan called a halt. They were early. The moon had not yet risen. Farinn collected driftwood and they built a fire to keep them warm, for the breeze off the ocean was cool, and also to let Wulfe know where to find them.

Colorful sparks from the driftwood rose on fragrant smoke. Their talk circled around to their homeland, as they wondered what might be happening to their friends and families. They spoke of how good it would be to return.

"The first thing I will do," said Skylan, "is find Farinn a wife."

Farinn blushed and mumbled something about no woman would want him.

"Nonsense! The Talgogroth is an honored position among our people," said Aylaen. "Any woman would be proud to be married to the one who keeps the laws and history of the Vindrasi."

"Talgogroth!" Farinn's blush deepened. "I could never aspire to such an honor."

"You can and you will," said Skylan. "I will recommend you to the current Talgogroth. You will have to study with him for many years, of course, but I can think of no one better."

Farinn was so overcome with emotion that Skylan feared he might start weeping, and hurriedly changed the conversation. As they were laughing over some remembered childish adventure, the moon rose out of the sea, gilding the waves with silver, and a boy of astonishing beauty seemed to materialize in silvery light.

The boy's glistening hair fell in sleek ringlets around his face. He wore a shirt and breeches made of soft green fabric decorated with feathers and strands of pearls and other gems.

They were all startled, for none of them had heard the boy approach, and they rose hurriedly to their feet. He regarded them expectantly, as though waiting for them to do something.

"Who are you?" Skylan demanded.

"I'm me, of course," the boy said, frowning.

"Wulfe?" Aylaen gasped, amazed.

"Yes," said Wulfe and eyed her and the others suspiciously. "What's wrong? Who did you think it was? We should go now."

As Skylan lit the lanterns and Farinn threw sand on the fire to put it out, Aylaen reached out to touch Wulfe's shining ringlets.

Wulfe drew back. "What are you doing? Why are you acting so strange?"

"I had no idea you were so beau—" Aylaen stammered. "I mean . . . that you could look so . . ."

"It's the clothes," said Skylan. "You don't look like yourself."

Wulfe scratched and tugged at his shirt. "I don't like them. They itch."

Once the fire was extinguished, they started off, following Wulfe.

"My mother says that so long as you take your swords off before you enter her bower, you may still come. Did you bring her a present? I told her about Farinn. She thinks she would like to have him."

Farinn cast an alarmed glance at Skylan.

"We have a present for your mother and it's *not* Farinn," said Skylan.

"I think she will like her gift," Aylaen added. "I chose it myself."

"I don't know . . ." Skylan heard Wulfe say in a low voice. "She might still like Farinn better."

The trees closed in around them. Skylan lost sight of the moon beneath the thick cover of branches and leaves and was glad he had thought to bring the lanterns.

"Keep together," he said, taking hold of Aylaen's hand while she clasped hold of Farinn's.

Wulfe had no need of light, seemingly, for he often pattered on so far ahead that he lost them and kept having to come back, accusing them of dawdling.

Skylan judged they had walked more than a mile from the shore when Wulfe suddenly called a halt in a clearing.

"We're here," he said.

Skylan lifted the lantern to look around. Trees formed a circle around a patch of bare ground covered with dry pine needles. In the center was a ring of mushrooms. Wulfe stepped into the center of the ring.

"Well, hurry up," he said.

"Oh, Skylan!" Aylaen whispered. "A faery ring!"

She shivered and drew near. Skylan felt cold sweat trickle down his
chest. All his life, he had heard the tales of faery rings: traps set by
the fae to lure humans into slavery. Once a human stepped into the
ring, he would plunge through it to the fae kingdom below and be
forced to serve them the rest of his days. Wulfe's own father had been
caught in such a trap.

"We are staying here," said Skylan. "Tell your mother she must
come to us."

He was startled by the sounds of laughter: light, lilting laughter like
the tinkling of silver bells.

Wulfe shrugged. "If you want to meet my mother, this is the only
way. Leave your swords beneath the trees. Don't worry. No one will
touch them."

Skylan unbuckled his sword belt, wrapped the belt around the
sheath, and commending the sword to Torval's care, laid it beneath
a tree with a misshapen trunk and covered it over with pine needles.
Aylaen took off her sword belt and placed it beside Skylan's. He steeled
himself, telling himself he was going to go stand in that mushroom
ring with Wulfe, but he couldn't move a muscle.

"I'll go," said Farinn. "You stay here with Aylaen."

Before Skylan could stop him, Farinn jumped straight into the
middle of the ring of mushrooms. The soft ground gave way beneath
his feet and both he and Wulfe disappeared as the ground closed
over them.

"Damn it!" Skylan swore. "Farinn!"

There was no answer, but he could hear voices and more laughter
coming from down below. He found Aylaen's hand in the darkness,
clasped it, and together they stepped into the faery ring.

The ground gave way beneath Skylan. Air rushed past him, bright colored lights blurred around him and he had the terrifying sensation of falling a great distance. He was certain he was going to dash out his brains, only to make a tumbling landing onto some soft, cushioned surface. He lay still a moment, too shaken to move, then hurriedly climbed to his feet and looked around.

He had landed on soft green moss that covered the floor of a woodland arbor, lit by tiny twinkling lights flitting among the vines and the leaves. A canopy of trailing morning glory vines draped over the boughs of trees formed the ceiling. The trunks of the trees glowed with foxfire.

He could see eyes watching him from the shadows and sometimes faces—some lovely, some grotesque—that appeared in an instant and vanished the next. Whispering voices rustled around him.

"Aylaen?" he called softly. "Farinn?"

"I am here," Aylaen whispered, stepping out of the shadows. "But I don't see Farinn."

"I have him," said a woman's voice, adding with lilting laughter, "I would tell you that he is safe, but since he is with me, perhaps he is not."

The twinkling lights and shifting shadows confused Skylan, and he could not see who was speaking.

"Faery folk!" the woman called. "Our prince has come back to us and he has brought guests! Let the celebration begin!"

Small creatures with laughing faces, big ears and stomachs, and spindly little legs came running from the forest. Each carried a giant white lily whose fragrant blossom glowed with bright light. The brownies hung the gleaming lilies from boughs and vines or stuck the stems in the ground, then gathered around Skylan and Aylaen and stared at them, giggling and whispering.

Other fae folk ran into the arbor, dryads and satyrs, fauns and oreads, laughing and calling, while other tiny faeries flew into the arbor on wings like dragonflies. Joining together, the fae folk began to sing and clap their hands.

"All hail our radiant princess!"

A woman walked into the light—or perhaps she was the light—Skylan was so dazzled he could not tell. Silver hair cascaded over her shoulders, falling to her feet. Her eyes, gazing upon him, glittered with starlight. Iridescent wings sprouted from between her shoulder blades, fanning the air gently, wafting the perfume of the lilies through the bower.

The fae bowed down before her, while Skylan stood staring, dumbstruck, unable to move. The woman smiled at him, seemingly amused by his discomfiture.

"Fae folk," she called in a voice that was like the brushing of harp strings, "I give you our prince, my own dear son, Casimir."

Reaching into the shadows, she brought forth Wulfe.

The fae folk cheered and bowed. Wulfe wriggled, obviously embarrassed and uncomfortable. His face brightened when he saw Skylan.

"*This* is my mother," said Wulfe, presenting her proudly. "Her name is Emerenta."

Turning to the woman, he gestured to Skylan and Aylaen. "Mother, these are the Uglies I was telling you about."

Wulfe whispered something to his mother, who bent down to hear him, all the while keeping her beautiful eyes on Skylan and Aylaen.

"My son tells me you take good care of him," said the woman. "Though I do think you should make him bathe more often. What are you called?"

"I am Skylan Ivorson, Lady of the Fae," said Skylan, his voice sounding gruff as a crow's raucous caw after the woman's musical tones. "My wife, Aylaen Adalbrand."

"I am honored to meet you, Princess Emerenta," said Aylaen. "I have never seen anyone so beautiful."

"Of course you haven't," said Emerenta languidly. "Silly Uglies!"

The fae folk all laughed heartily. Skylan looked around the crowded arbor, searching for Farinn, and couldn't find him. He was starting to grow worried.

Emerenta was calling for food and drink and the fae began running everywhere, eager to obey her commands.

"Please be seated," she said.

Skylan saw no table, no chairs, and could only assume she meant the ground. He remained standing.

"Where is my friend Farinn?" he asked, trying to sound stern and severe and ignoring the fact that several of the brownies were untying his bootlaces. "What have you done with him?"

"I told you, Ugly," said Emerenta. "He is in my care."

She made a graceful gesture to a bower set amid flowering bushes. Farinn was sitting on a moss-covered log, while several lovely and scantily dressed dryads bound him with daisy chains. He cast a pleading glance at Skylan.

Emerenta regarded the young man with pleasure. "My son says he is a gift, that I may keep him."

Skylan cast an angry glare at Wulfe. "Your son is wrong, madam! Farinn is—"

"Is but a poor gift," Aylaen said, stepping in front of him. "Seeing your wondrous beauty, lady, we have a gift that we believe you will like much better."

Emerenta gave a languorous smile. "Show me this other gift. I will judge."

Aylaen removed the pouch from her belt. Opening it, she brought out a box made of seashells and decorated with jewels.

"This is a gift from the Queen of the Aquins," Aylaen said. Caressing the box, she added in a softer voice, "She is dead now, which makes her gift very dear to me. I would like you to have it because of Wulfe. Because Skylan and I have grown very fond of him."

She smiled at Wulfe, who flushed with pleasure and began digging his toe into the moss.

Emerenta seemed intrigued by the box. She gestured to an attendant. "Fetch it to me."

Several of the brownies took the box from Aylaen and carried it to Emerenta, offering it to her with many bows and giggles. She opened the box, peered inside, sniffed at it, then looked intently at Aylaen.

"This once held an artifact of powerful magic," said Emerenta.

"It did, lady," Aylaen answered in some confusion.

Emerenta handed the box to one of her attendants. "I like this gift. You may have the young man."

The dryads merrily tore off the daisy chains and Farinn, mortified, slipped over to stand behind Skylan, trying to keep out of sight of the dryads, who were waving at him and blowing him kisses.

Emerenta turned back to Aylaen. "You brought this artifact and more like it with you. I want to see them. My dear son, Casimir, told me—"

Wulfe went red in the face. "Stop calling me Casimir! I told you. My name is Wulfe!"

"But that is such an ugly name, my lovely one," said Emerenta, running her hand through his curls.

"I don't care. I like it," Wulfe muttered.

"Whatever my darling boy wants," said Emerenta with a kiss on the head.

Wulfe squirmed, embarrassed but pleased.

Emerenta turned her smile on Aylaen. "Let me see these artifacts."

Aylaen glanced at Skylan, who shook his head.

"I am sorry, Princess, but I do not think that would be wise."

"Wise or not, let me remind you, Ugly Ones, that you are in my domain," Emerenta said, adding airily, "I have only to say the word to summon a legion of imps who will torment you until you do as I require. As I was about to say, my own dear son told me that you relied on his magic to keep these artifacts safely hidden from the Faceless God."

"My mother means Aelon," Wulfe explained. "She says he has no face."

"I have heard the god called that before," said Skylan.

"It is a cruel god," said Emerenta. "A god who has killed many of our people. A god who seeks our destruction."

"Aelon wants to destroy our people, too," said Aylaen. "Wulfe was a very great help to me."

She opened the pouch again and reached inside.

"What are you doing?" Skylan whispered. "You can't show her the spiritbones! What if she steals them?"

"She won't. They are made of metal, Skylan," said Aylaen.

She took out the spiritbones. The many colored gemstones glittered in the lily lights; the silver and gold work gleamed. The fae folk crept nearer, whispering and murmuring, but keeping their distance.

Emerenta knelt down to examine them.

Skylan tensed, ready to snatch them up, not trusting her. Emerenta passed her hand over them, but she was careful not to touch the metal. She studied the spiritbones, one by one, then lifted her lilac eyes to gaze at Aylaen.

"Each of these bones is a piece of the god and they are a matching set. Did you know that?"

Aylaen paled and cast a quick glance at Skylan.

"I know," she said softly.

"You are not quite the fool I thought," Emerenta remarked after a moment.

She turned back to admire the spiritbones.

"You are missing one of the set. I have seen it. The largest and the most beautiful. A god bone set in a helm of gold adorned with diamonds fashioned like a dragon's crest."

"Where did you see it?" Aylaen asked.

"In the land of the Stormlords." Emerenta rose gracefully to her feet. "My son says you want me to take you there. You want to steal it."

"Only as a last resort, lady," said Skylan. "We have heard that the Stormlords plan to give this sacred relic to Aelon's minion, the Emperor Raegar, who leads a great army against them. The cowards refuse to fight him and they will give him our relic to save their own skins. I am first going to try to reason with them and, if they refuse, then I will do what I must."

Emerenta gazed at him a moment, and then burst into wild laughter, like the pealing of silvery bells. All the fae in the arbor joined in her merriment, hooting and roaring, some even falling down and rolling around on the ground.

"What is so funny?" Skylan asked.

"You are, Ugly One, though I don't think you mean to be," said Emerenta. "The Stormlords . . . cowards . . ."

She laughed again, wiping her eyes, then waved her hand. "Put the god bones away now so that we may enjoy our meal."

"Forgive me, lady, but shouldn't we be traveling to Tsa Kerestra, as you promised?" Skylan asked.

"We have all night," said Emerenta carelessly. "Don't worry. The way is not far. We can be there in the flash of a falling star."

"She can travel there that fast," Skylan said dourly to Aylaen. "*She* has wings."

"Hush," Aylaen whispered. "We are her guests."

She hurriedly picked up the spiritbones, tucked them back inside the pouch and once more tied it to her belt.

"What was all that about god bones?" he asked under cover of the noise in the arbor. "Why didn't you tell her she was wrong? They are the bones of the Great Dragon Ilyrion."

"We'll talk about it later," said Aylaen.

Emerenta ordered her people to serve the feast. The fae folk carried in pitchers filled with honey wine and water, platters of roasted meat, bowls of fruit and nuts, breads and puddings and sweetmeats.

Emerenta took her place on a throne made of a fallen log covered with moss and peacock feathers and made Wulfe sit beside her. He seemed glad to be with her, though he wriggled when she kissed his cheek, fussed with his hair or tried to feed him.

She invited Skylan and Aylaen to join them, indicating seats on the soft moss.

Skylan politely refused, saying they were not hungry.

"He thinks the food is enchanted," said Wulfe. "And that if he eats he'll have to stay here with us."

Emerenta laughed her bell-like laughter. "I shouldn't think the food was enchanted. After all, we steal it from you humans."

Wulfe explained that all the food, plus the utensils and crockery, came from the kitchens and larders of the Uglies. As near as Skylan could make out, the fae did no work of any kind except for thieving, which they seemed to consider more of a diverting sport than an occupation. Sitting awkwardly among a crowd of other fae folk, Skylan waited to be served, then realized that no one except Emerenta had an individual plate, and she shared this with Wulfe. The fae around him were eating from large, communal platters being handed around seemingly at random.

The wine flowed and the meal soon turned riotous. The fae folk sprawled on the moss, danced among the trees or, most disconcerting, pelted one another with fruit. Skylan drank only water, for he needed a clear head for the night's adventures. He was hungry and did justice to the meal, though he learned he had to be quick about grabbing a choice piece of meat before anyone else could snag it.

Aylaen politely tasted the wine and ate some fruit and bread, but she seemed lost in her own thoughts. Farinn was clearly too nervous to do more than nibble at his food, especially as the dryads sat next to him and took great delight in teasing him.

The meal ended, but Emerenta made no move to leave and Skylan grew nervous. Time was passing. He had hoped to question Emerenta about the Stormlords, what he might expect when he reached the city, how they were to get inside, but the noise in the arbor made conversation impossible.

The music ended and the laughter gave way to yawns. Skylan was alarmed to see the fae folk settle down to nap, lying in each other's arms, draped over tree boughs, or simply sprawling among the dishes.

Wulfe was asleep, his head in his mother's lap. Emerenta stroked his hair and softly sang a lullaby. The song must have been infectious. Farinn's eyes closed and he slumped forward. Aylaen blinked drowsily and leaned her head against his shoulder. Skylan didn't like this strange slumber.

"We should leave now, lady," he said.

Aylaen stirred and sat up. "My husband is right. Either take us to the Stormlords or tell us how to enter the city on our own."

"Do you imagine we knock on the front door and beg admittance?" Emerenta asked, amused. "We fae are like the moonbeams or motes of dust. We glide through chinks, slip through cracks, crawl into crevices."

Skylan glowered at her. "I am not likely to slip through a crack."

"How very droll you are," said Emerenta. "The Stormlords traveled to this realm, the Realm of Stone, from the land of their birth, the Realm of Fire."

"So I have heard," said Skylan, growing increasingly impatient. "Don't change the subject. How do we get inside?"

"Some say the wizards followed us," Emerenta continued as though he hadn't spoken. "Some say they followed the dragons here and some say they found this realm on their own. Whatever the truth, the Stormlords, like the dragons, must periodically return to the Realm of Fire. The dragons go back to nurture their young and to heal themselves if they suffer wounds. The wizards, being human like you and not born to magic like us, must periodically return to replenish their power. They leave a door open and we can walk through."

"A door to where?" Skylan asked, not following.

Emerenta raised a silvery eyebrow. "For a people who are always in such a hurry, you are very slow. The Realm of Fire, of course. We go from here through that realm and into the city of the Cloud Dwellers."

Skylan remembered Dela Eden's words, *Some doors, even the gods fear to open.*

"The Great Dragon Ilyrion came from that realm," Aylaen said. "Kahg says it is a terrible world, populated by fearsome monsters and cruel men."

"It is safe enough for those of us who have magic," said Emerenta with blithe unconcern.

Skylan remained silent.

Emerenta saw his dark expression and laughed her sparkling laughter. "But you do not have magic, do you, Uglies?"

"This was all a game," said Aylaen bitterly. "She never meant to take us."

Emerenta was smiling slightly, toying idly with Wulfe's hair, running one of his curls through her fingers as he slept.

"What do we do now?" Aylaen asked.

"We find another way," said Skylan. Reaching down, he touched Farinn by the shoulder. "Wake up. We're leaving."

Farinn gave a start, opened his eyes, and groggily scrambled to his feet.

"Good-bye, Wulfe," said Skylan, raising his voice.

The boy opened his eyes and stared at them in sleepy confusion. "Good-bye," he mumbled. "Where are we going?"

Emerenta smoothed back his hair and murmured soothingly, "All is well, my little love. You are staying with me. Your friends are going away."

"Going away!" Wulfe repeated, startled. He shoved aside his

mother's hand and jumped to his feet to face Skylan. "Where are you going?"

"We have to go back to the *Venejekar,* Wulfe," said Skylan.

"You can't leave!" Wulfe cried. "We are going to see the Cloud Dwellers."

Skylan shook his head. "Your mother was making sport of us."

Wulfe turned to glare at Emerenta. "You promised me."

"You and I were having some fun with the Uglies," said Emerenta, smiling charmingly and holding out her hands. "Tell them good-bye, Casimir, and come with me—"

"Don't me call me that!" the boy shouted angrily, stamping his foot. "My name is Wulfe!"

He took hold of Skylan's hand. "I know the way to the Realm of Fire. I'll show you."

"Don't go! Casi—Wulfe!" Emerenta cried out. "You can't leave me!"

"Why not?" Wulfe demanded. "You left me."

Emerenta sank back, stung by his words. The fae in the arbor began to wake up, startled by the shouting. They peeped out of the shadows, whispering in scandalized delight. Emerenta rounded on them.

"Get out!" she ordered and the fae folk fled in haste, rustling among the undergrowth, gliding through the air, crawling among the tree branches. The lights disappeared, as if blown out by a breath, leaving them in starlit darkness.

"This way," said Wulfe, tugging on Skylan's hand. "I've never been there, but I think I know—"

"Wait!" Emerenta called out in harsh tones. "I will take your Uglies to the Stormlords—*if* that is what they want."

"That is what we want," said Skylan.

"I did not lie about the danger, Ugly," Emerenta warned in sulky tones. "We will have to pass through the Realm of Fire and, as your wife says, that world is a terrible world, fraught with perils. Without magic you are defenseless."

"Wait here," Wulfe said.

Letting go of Skylan's hand, he ran off into the night. The boy quickly returned, his face twisted in pain, his body shivering so that he nearly dropped what he was holding.

"Here," Wulfe said. "You will need these."

He handed Skylan and Aylaen their swords.

At the sight of the swords, Emerenta gave a screech of anger and then burst into tears.

"Go live with your Ugly friends, my son," she wailed. "You love them better than you love me!"

Skylan buckled on his sword belt, keeping his eyes on Wulfe. Aylaen cast him a questioning glance and Skylan shook his head, not certain what the boy would do. At first Wulfe pouted, refusing to look at his mother, but the sound of her weeping unnerved him. He ran to her and flung his arms around her.

"Don't cry, Mother," he begged.

"I won't, but you must tell the Ugly Ones with the iron to go away and leave us," Emerenta said tearfully. "I will take you dancing on the moon glade like we did when you were little."

"Mother, you promised," said Wulfe. With a sly glance at Skylan, he added, "You said the Cloud Dweller city was filled with magic. Maybe I could find a gift for Grandmama so she will stop hating me."

Emerenta sniffed and then smiled and kissed him on the forehead. "I suppose, after all, the journey might be amusing," she said with a shrug and a sigh. "Follow me. The way is not far."

Skylan didn't like her sudden capitulation, but all he could do was add this to the growing list of things about this venture he didn't like. She led them from the arbor. With her wings flashing in a shimmer of silvery light, she floated over the ground, dipping down every so often to delicately touch the grass with her foot, then taking to the air again. A faint glow of faery light clung to the leaves and the branches, glittering and sparkling for a few moments after her passing, then slowly fading away.

Wulfe ran alongside her, skipping and jumping. Crying out for her to race him, he dropped down on all fours, running like a dog.

"Stop that!" his mother ordered sharply. "Your grandmama will never love you if you behave like that!"

Wulfe flushed in shame and stood up straight, and there was no more skipping.

As they traveled farther from the arbor, the trees bunched around them, the leaves forming a dense canopy overhead. The lambent light of the stars was gone and they had not thought to bring their lanterns. Emerenta moved rapidly, not inclined to wait for them, leaving them to stumble through the undergrowth and bump into tree trunks until the trees suddenly vanished and they found themselves in a clearing beneath the stars. Emerenta fluttered to a halt, lightly settling to the ground, and catching hold of Wulfe when he would have run on ahead.

"We are here," Emerenta said.

A shaft of moonlight illuminated a rickety old house made of sticks and twigs and branches stuck together seemingly at random. The house had a door, no windows, no chimney, and half a roof. The other half had fallen in. The yard was overgrown with weeds that gave off a faintly noxious odor.

"Where is here?" Skylan asked, trying to catch his breath.

"Where you wanted to come, Ugly," Emerenta said with a tinge of impatience. "The portal to the Realm of Fire."

"The portal is in a hut not fit to house goats," Skylan said, frowning.

"If you had something important to hide, where would you put it?" Emerenta asked.

Skylan stood in the shadow of the trees, studying the house and thought of the spiritbone of the Dragon Kahg hanging on a nail, plain and unadorned.

"The hut reminds me of Owl Mother's," Aylaen whispered, tightly clasping his hand.

Skylan grunted in assent, not particularly reassured. Owl Mother was strange and her house was even stranger. He recalled the first time he had met the old woman who lived in a hut in the woods outside the village.

At the time, ogres had been threatening his people. He was war chief and he'd been wounded in a boar hunt and feared he couldn't fight. Aylaen had cajoled him into going to Owl Mother and ask her to use her magic to heal him. That day he had asked Aylaen to marry him. Well, he hadn't really asked. He had commanded her. He smiled ruefully, wondering if Aylaen remembered.

She proved she did by giving a smothered laugh. "I married you anyway," she whispered.

"You and Farinn wait here while I go inside, take a look around," Skylan said.

"You are the only one in danger, Ugly," said Emerenta. "Your woman will be safe enough, so long as she carries the god bones. The magic of the great dragon will protect her. As for the young man, I will keep watch on him."

Farinn's blush was visible even in the dim starlight.

Skylan remained standing outside the hut. The glade, the hut, the foul-smelling flowers seemed to stink of magic and he would rather have faced a shield wall of ten thousand ogres, each bigger than the next, than enter that hut.

"You were the one in haste, Ugly," Emerenta pointed out. "If you insist upon going, we should go now while the Stormlords are deep in slumber."

Skylan thought it best not to mention that the first thing he planned to do on his arrival was to wake them up. "We will go together," he said.

Stringy weeds tangled around their ankles; the smell made them gag. The sticks and branches that formed the walls were daubed with mud, which was apparently all that was holding the hut together. Skylan had seen more substantial birds' nests.

A large piece of tattered deerskin hung over the entrance. Skylan reached out to gingerly pull the skin aside, half afraid the movement would bring the house down around their ears, when Wulfe shouted at him.

"Don't touch it," Wulfe warned. "It's a trap!"

Skylan cast a baleful glance at Emerenta, who was standing off to one side, watching with a faintly derisive smile.

"I was going to tell you before you tripped it," she said. "I wanted to see if my son remembered our lessons."

She gave Wulfe a fond caress in passing, then laid her hand, palm flat, in the center of the deer hide and began to sing in a soft undertone to Wulfe.

She sang the song through once, then turned. "Do you remember the words, my son?"

"'Shining portal, open wide. Let my friends and me inside,'" said Wulfe proudly, pleased with himself.

They both sang the phrase several times with different inflections, and once it seemed to Skylan they sang it backward, then Emerenta pulled the deer hide to one side. Standing in the doorway, she graciously invited them to enter.

Skylan looked at Aylaen. "You and Farinn wait for my signal. Please. Let me make certain it is safe."

Aylaen made a face at him. "I will wait. But only because I love you."

Keeping his hand on the hilt of his sword, Skylan walked through the doorway. Expecting sticks and mud and a collapsed roof, he was shocked to find himself walking into an immense chamber whose walls and floor were made of polished marble. Shafts of silver moonlight shone through arrow-slit windows into a bare, empty room. The only sound was the sighing of the wind. The floor was thick with dust, but someone had left a trail leading to a hall filled with shadows. Worn and faded tapestries hung from the walls.

The room had a desolate and mournful feel to it. Some of the tapestries appeared to have been burned; the walls were charred. Catching a glimpse of movement, he quickly turned, his hand on the hilt of his sword, only to see the fringe of one of the tapestries fluttering in the wind coming through the windows.

The tapestry depicted a battle scene with warriors in strange-looking armor mounted on horses, battling each other with what looked to be exceptionally long spears. The tapestry looked strangely familiar.

"Aylaen!" he called.

"Here," she said, her voice coming from the other side of the tapestry.

She and Farinn entered, gazing around in amazement, followed by Emerenta and Wulfe. The boy dashed past Skylan with a whoop of excitement that echoed loudly back from the walls, jarring Skylan and shocking Wulfe, who crouched in alarm.

Emerenta hissed, "You silly boy, you must keep quiet! Things are out there, listening!"

"I'm sorry," Wulfe whispered, subdued.

"Where are we?" Farinn asked, awed.

"The Realm of Fire," said Emerenta. "You must make haste. It is dangerous for you to linger."

Aylaen turned to face Skylan, then stared past him. Her eyes widened in astonishment. She gripped Skylan's arm and pointed. "The tapestry!"

"What about it?" Skylan asked, turning to stare at it.

"I've seen one like it," said Aylaen, marveling. "And so have you. In Owl Mother's house."

" 'The wyrds of both men and gods together form the tapestry that is life,' " Farinn said softly, reaching out to run his hand over the fabric. " 'A single thread is fragile. The tapestry itself is strong.' "

The tapestry stirred at his touch, almost seeming to shiver. Farinn quickly withdrew his hand and cast a shy glance at Skylan.

"Those words are part of your song," he said.

"Down the hall," said Emerenta. "Make haste!"

Skylan cast a last lingering look at the tapestry as they left.

"This song is making me nervous," he muttered.

They passed under an arched doorway and down a short corridor
that took them to the splintered remains of a massive oak door.
Skylan pushed on the door and walked into desolation, the ruins of
what must have once been a mighty city.

The sky glittered with stars. The moon looked much the same as
the moon he had just left behind, except this one seemed tinged with
a faint red glow. Cracked cobblestones were overgrown with weeds
and covered with lichen that was black in the moonlight. The streets
were filled with mounds of rubble. Not a single building remained
standing; the field of destruction stretched as far as they could see.

"What was this place?" Skylan asked, speaking softly in a tone of
respect, as one does in the presence of death.

"An old, old city of the Stormlords," Emerenta replied. She seemed
subdued, oppressed by the sense of doom. "I never knew the name."

"What happened to it?"

"Who knows? Fearsome monsters, wicked Uglies. The Stormlords
built a wall to keep out the evil." Emerenta glanced over her shoulder, adding with a careless shrug. "It didn't work. And so the Stormlords fled—those who survived."

The ruins were surrounded by a stone wall at least three times
Skylan's height. Unlike the rest of the surroundings, the wall remained relatively intact, standing mournful guard over those it had
failed to protect.

"Where is Tsa Kerestra?" Skylan asked.

"Through a portal in Starfall Tower," said Emerenta.

"How far away is that?" Skylan asked.

"Not far," said Emerenta, with a vague gesture. "Atop that hill. Keep to the shadows. Stay out of the light."

Taking hold of Wulfe's hand, she struck out along a narrow path that hugged the wall. Skylan tried to see their destination, but a curve in the wall blocked his view and he moved into the street to try to see more clearly.

A mountain peak, far in the distance, was on fire, glowing brightly, and he knew now why the moon was tinged with red. He located the tower.

"Skylan, behind you!" Aylaen cried.

Looking over his shoulder, Skylan saw a monstrous creature, a hulking beast that looked similar to a dragon, only with a misshapen head, a single flaring eye, and a ponderous body with a thick, stubby tail. The beast dove at him, jaws gaping, flying fast. Skylan barely had time to fling himself to the ground before the beast was on him.

He flattened himself on the cobblestones and gagged at the smell of the hot, fetid breath. Drops of acid dripped from the beast's jaws, burning like red-hot pokers wherever they touched his skin.

The monstrous jaws snapped, barely missing him and the beast flew past with a growl of disappointment. Skylan scrambled to his feet and ran to where the others were crouched at the foot of the wall.

"Great Torval, look!" Farinn breathed.

Six more of the one-eyed monsters wheeled in the sky overhead, their huge wings obliterating the stars.

"Fool Ugly!" said Emerenta in disgust. "I warned you to stay out of the light!"

"What was that thing? Will it be back?" Skylan gasped, drawing his sword.

"We call it a One Eye." Emerenta hissed at the sword with displeasure. "Put away your weapon! Iron is useless against such monsters and they will see the moonlight flashing off the metal."

"Why did it attack me?" Skylan asked.

"The One Eyes are always hungry," Emerenta replied. "They are distant cousins of the dragons and they will eat anything, including silly little boys who make too much noise and foolish Uglies who do not do as they are told."

Wulfe cringed, chastened. Skylan glanced again at the monsters in the sky, seeming to be searching for prey. Fearing Emerenta was right about the moonlight, he reluctantly sheathed his sword.

"You're hurt!" Aylaen said, taking hold of his hand.

Blisters were forming where the drops of the One Eye's saliva had touched his flesh. The blisters burned like fire and he shook his hand, trying to shake away the pain.

"It stings, that's all," he said.

Remembering the moment of heart-stopping terror when the jaws had snapped so close he could hear the clicking of gigantic teeth, he understood why dragons like Kahg had fled this land.

Emerenta hurried on, following the narrow path, staying close to the wall. She moved rapidly, using her wings to fly over rubble that blocked the path. Skylan noted that she was nervous and kept a close lookout, despite her claim that those with magic need not fear.

"The One Eyes have lost interest in us," Skylan remarked to Aylaen.

Emerenta snorted. "More likely they saw something that frightened them."

Skylan hoped she was jesting.

The ground rose steadily at a steep incline and the wall rose with it. Skylan could look down on the dwelling in which the portal was located and at the ruins of the city spreading out before it.

A tower at the top of the hill was silhouetted against the red moon.

Skylan was glad to see that they were close, perhaps only a half mile away. The tower was similar in shape and design to the stormhold, except that it was much taller. Long, narrow windows on each of seven levels must have once provided a magnificent view of the city. At the top, a rampart encircled a domed roof.

The tower's windows were placed so that the sinking moon shone through them. Skylan was startled to see a figure standing at one of the windows. The figure was in silhouette, black against the reddish moon, so Skylan could not make out any details. All he could see was a head and shoulders and part of the body. He had the impression that the figure was that of a man and that he was tall and wearing some type of cloak.

Skylan came to sudden halt, trying to get a better view.

"What is it?" Aylaen asked tensely.

"Someone is in that tower," said Skylan, staring intently. "I can see a man standing in one of the windows."

"Where? Which one?" Aylaen peered over his shoulder, as Farinn came up to join them.

"The middle row, third one up from the bottom," Skylan said, pointing.

But even as he spoke, the figure left, moving on past the window.

"I don't see anyone," said Aylaen.

"I did," said Farinn. "A glimpse of a figure and then it was gone."

"Do you think he saw us?" Aylaen whispered.

"We're in heavy shadow," said Farinn. "I wouldn't think so."

"We'll know soon enough," said Skylan.

The three waited tensely for a warning shout sounding the alarm. Moments passed and the night was quiet. Emerenta and Wulfe had gone on ahead. Wulfe, missing them, came scampering down the hillside to meet them.

"My mother says to hurry—" Wulfe began.

Farinn interrupted the boy. "Hush! I heard something."

"I did, too!" said Aylaen in a smothered voice.

Now Skylan could hear a strange sound—a feline growl and the clatter of hooves on stone.

Wulfe said excitedly, "Maybe it's a giant—"

"Quiet!" Skylan clamped his hand over the boy's mouth.

Aylaen drew her sword and stood near Skylan, watchful and alert. Farinn picked up a large chunk of rock. The hoofbeats continued for a moment, then pattered to a stop, as though whatever it was had stopped to investigate.

The hoofbeats started again, coming closer, moving faster.

Skylan drew his sword. "Take Wulfe and run!" he ordered Aylaen. "Keep him safe!"

"But I want to see the giant!" Wulfe wailed.

Aylaen hesitated a moment, not wanting to leave Skylan, then she grabbed hold of Wulfe by the arm and dragged him off, struggling and protesting. Hearing his cry, Emerenta stopped and turned around to see what was happening.

The feline growling grew louder and more menacing and a monstrous beast leaped onto a large pile of rubble in front of them. The beast stopped to look them over for a split second and then jumped on Farinn, striking him in the chest and dragging him to the ground.

"A chimera!" Emerenta yelled. "You cannot fight it! Leave your friend and run! He is finished!"

Skylan stared, paralyzed by shock. He had heard of chimeras all his life, but had never seen one; this was like something from a delirium dream. The chimera was a lion in the front with a leonine head and gigantic paws. A second head—that of a goat—vied with the lion head for their prey. The lion's head roared, the goat's head brayed, and its hind hooves stomped on the cobblestones.

Farinn smashed the rock he was holding into the lion's face, striking it on the nose, causing it to roar in pain and outrage. The goat's head, seeing an opening, tried to bite him.

Skylan dashed at the monster, thinking to stab it from behind and sever its spine while the two heads remained intent on Farinn. As he raised his sword, something seized his sword arm. The chimera had a snake for a tail and it had wrapped its reptilian body around his wrist.

Skylan struck at the snake with his fist, fighting to free his sword arm. The serpent loosed its hold and he staggered backward, almost falling, as the goat lowered its horned head. Skylan made a desperate jab with his sword. The curled horns and bony forehead struck him on the left shoulder and spun him around. He landed hard, splitting open his chin and reinjuring the ribs that he had bruised in the stormhold. He could scarcely breathe for the pain and he lay still a moment, gasping for breath.

Farinn shouted a warning. Grabbing his sword, Skylan pushed himself to his feet. He and Farinn had both drawn blood. The lion's head was bleeding from the nose and the goat had blood dribbling down the side of its neck. The chimera bounded up onto a pile of rubble. The lion's head snarled and the goat's head shrieked. The snake tail lashed in rage. The chimera stood poised atop the heap of broken stone, preparing to jump.

"Torval, with me," Skylan prayed.

The chimera leaped at Skylan, who stood his ground and drove his sword into the beast's chest. God-rage bit deep, and hot blood washed over Skylan. The two heads howled and bleated in pain and rage as the wounded chimera crashed down on top of him. Crushed by the weight of the beast, Skylan was being slowly smothered and he desperately tried to shift the body. His arms were pinned and he couldn't move.

The stench was horrible. He could hear Aylaen and Farinn both shouting and then Aylaen cried, "Be ready!"

The chimera reared up, causing the crushing weight to ease, and then Skylan was free. Farinn seized hold of him and dragged him clear as Aylaen drove the sword of Vindrash into the goat's neck. The chimera crashed to the ground, dead, in a cloud of dust.

Skylan staggered to his feet. Aylaen cried out in dismay and he realized he was covered in blood.

"Not mine," he gasped.

"Are you sure?" Farinn asked worriedly and pointed. "There's something wrong with your shoulder."

Skylan looked to see his left arm hanging at an odd angle. Each breath he took was both a blessing and a curse, for it came with lancing pain.

Aylaen began to examine him, running her hands over his injured shoulder. Skylan stifled a groan. Even her gentle touch was painful.

"It's dislocated," she said.

Aylaen turned to Farinn. "We're going to put it back."

Farinn paled and swallowed. "I don't know how! I've never done anything like that!"

"I'll tell you how," said Aylaen. She looked down at Skylan. "I'm sorry, my love."

Skylan nodded. He had seen this done before and he knew what was coming. Lying on his back, he extended his left arm, stifling a groan as pain shot through him.

"Sit beside him," Aylaen told Farinn. "Take his left hand, enlace your fingers with his, and hold tight. Put your left foot on the side of his torso. There, that's right. You're going to pull, slow, but firm. You can't stop. No matter what happens; no matter how loud he screams."

Farinn settled himself into position, taking hold of Skylan's hand, twining his fingers through his and putting his foot into place. Aylaen clasped Skylan's right hand in both her hands. He gripped hold of her tightly.

"Ready?" Farinn asked.

Skylan managed to nod and Farinn shifted nervously. Sweat rolled down his forehead, his hand was clammy. He was in worse condition than Skylan. Just as he was about to start, Wulfe came dashing up to them.

"What are you doing? My mother says we have to leave now!"

"In a minute." Skylan grunted.

"The fight was exciting," said Wulfe, squatting down beside Skylan. "I was going to help you with my magic, but my mother said she'd never seen a human battle a chimera before and she wanted to watch. She didn't think you would win. *I* did. I told her—"

Farinn pulled. Skylan cried out in agony as the bone popped back into place. He drew in several deep breaths, then experimentally moved his fingers and flexed his elbow.

"How is your arm?" Aylaen asked.

"Better," said Skylan. He smiled at Farinn, who looked ready to faint. "You did well."

Farinn slid his arm around Skylan and, with Aylaen's help, assisted him to his feet. Emerenta landed among them with a fluttering of wings and a shimmering of silver light.

"The One Eyes!"

Skylan looked up into the sky. The monsters had apparently heard the fight and were flying back to investigate. Emerenta seized Wulfe's hand.

"Come, my son," she said. "We are fleeing this terrible place!"

"You can't leave us here!" Aylaen said angrily.

"It's your own fault. I warned you of the danger," Emerenta returned. She added grudgingly, "If you manage to reach the tower alive, you will be safe. Wulfe, come with me!"

"Go with her, Wulfe," said Skylan.

The One Eyes were rapidly approaching. He measured the distance to the tower. They'd have to make a run for it.

Wulfe shook his head. "I'm staying with you."

"You are stubborn, just like your father!" Emerenta said. Bending down, she whispered something into his ear, then straightened. "Remember!"

"I will, Mother," said Wulfe. Throwing his arms around her, he hugged her tightly.

"My brave prince!" Emerenta kissed him on the top of the head and then, with a fearful glance at the approaching monsters, she flew away.

"I'll bring you a present!" Wulfe called after her.

Emerenta fluttered her hand in response, but did not look back.

"Good riddance," Skylan muttered, but in a low voice, so that Wulfe wouldn't hear. He cast another glance at the One Eyes, who had slowed their flight to scan the ground below, their single eyes sweeping back and forth as they searched among the ruins.

Skylan went back to look for his sword and found it buried to the hilt in the belly of chimera. He yanked it free and wiped it in the weeds to clean it, then, keeping to the shadows, they continued their climb to the tower. The One Eyes were still searching, coming ever closer, and Skylan recalled the man he'd seen in the tower. Was he in there now, watching them? Ready to help them? Lying in wait for them?

Skylan caught up with Wulfe. "I need to talk to you."

"Put the sword away," said Wulfe, hanging back.

Skylan sheathed his sword. "Do you know how to get back home?"

Wulfe nodded. "Mother told me the magic spell. I go back to that house and sing a song she taught me. Do you want to hear it?"

"Not now," Skylan said, adding in a low voice, "If something happens to me, I want you to take Aylaen and Farinn home with you."

Wulfe eyed Skylan, frowning. "What's going to happen to you?"

"Nothing, I hope," said Skylan. "Promise?"

"I'll take them," Wulfe said. "But my mother will likely keep Farinn."

Somewhat reassured, Skylan studied the lay of the land they had to cross to reach the tower. For a short distance they could continue in the shadow of the wall, but at some point they would have to leave the shadows and emerge into the open.

The moon was just setting, but the night was clear, the stars bright, and the One Eyes had not given up the search. They lifted their heads, sniffing the air.

Skylan called a halt. The tower was perhaps thirty paces away. The stone walls were luminescent; they seemed to shine as if with a memory of the moonlight. He stared at the smooth stone, faintly gleaming, lighting up the area all around the tower, and realized they had a problem. Another problem.

"Where's the entrance?" Skylan wondered, startled. "The One Eyes will spot us the moment we break cover and we'll need to take cover quickly."

"The door must be on one of the other sides," said Aylaen.

"We can't go racing about the building searching for the door," said Skylan. "You stay here. I'll go—"

"Are you blind? It's right there," said Wulfe, jabbing his finger in the direction of the tower.

"No, it isn't—" Skylan began, then stopped.

For there was a door. Standing wide open.

Wulfe fidgeted. "Hurry! Let's go! I want to see what's inside."

"I don't like this. First there's no a door, now there is," Skylan said. "Who's to say the door won't vanish the moment we get there."

"We don't have a choice, Skylan," said Aylaen.

The One Eyes had quit sniffing the air and were now flying rapidly in their direction. Wulfe dropped down on all fours and began dashing across the ground toward the tower. The moment he left the shadows, the One Eyes saw him.

Skylan touched his amulet and, taking Aylaen's hand, broke into a run.

"Go on ahead!" Skylan yelled at Farinn, who was not burdened by armor or weapons and could run faster. "Keep that damn door open!"

Farinn dashed on ahead. Skylan and Aylaen raced after him and saw Wulfe disappear into the building with Farinn right behind him. The door was still there and it was still open. Skylan glanced back at the One Eyes, who were gaining. He was thinking they just might make it when one of the monsters opened its maw and spat a huge gout of saliva at him.

The liquid struck him in the back and knocked him to the ground. The acid burned his flesh and he writhed in the grass, trying to wipe it off him.

Aylaen knelt by his side.

"Don't touch me!" he said through gritted teeth. "Keep going!"

"Not without you!" Aylaen said firmly.

She drew her sword and stood over him until he could regain his feet. Skylan pushed himself up off the ground and caught hold of Aylaen. Together they ran from the monsters, who were now so close he could hear the creaking wings and smell the putrid breath.

Farinn was running back toward them. Wulfe was jumping up and down and yelling. Skylan looked back to see a single eye glaring at him. He shoved Aylaen into Farinn's arms and then turned to face the monster.

Jaws gaped and saliva drooled. Hot breath washed over him.

The sky burst into dazzling white fire. Stars fell down all around him.

29

S kylan ran through the broken streets of the ruined city trying to reach Aylaen. He knew where she was, yet every time he came to the street that led to her, he found his way blocked by piles of rubble.

"Skylan!" she cried.

"Where are you?" he shouted.

"I am right here," said Aylaen.

Skylan opened his eyes to find her sitting next to him. He blinked and looked around. He was lying in a bed in a darkened room. A fire burned low in a grate, giving off only a faint light. The fire shimmered in Aylaen's hair as she turned her head to speak to a person who was bending over the fire, poking at the embers.

"Are you all right?" Skylan asked. "What happened?"

"I don't know," said Aylaen. "I remember you shoving me into Farinn and then the stars fell and that is all I remember until Owl Mother woke me."

"Owl Mother!" Skylan sat bolt upright and stared about in confusion. "What is she doing here?"

"Waiting for you," said Owl Mother.

She left the fire and shuffled over to stand at the end of the bed, crossing her arms and scowling at him. She was exactly the same as he remembered her. Her white hair, twisted into a single untidy braid, trailed down her back. She wore the same plain smock over a plain dress, tied at the waist with a leather belt. She had always claimed to be the oldest person in the village, saying she had the wrinkles to prove it. With her beaked nose and fierce eyes, she looked very much like her namesake.

He left the bed and realized, as he stood up, that he felt no pain. His wounds and injuries were healed. Far from reassuring him, this made him feel more unease.

"This makes no sense," he said. "How could you know we were coming? We didn't know ourselves."

"You had to come sooner or later," said Owl Mother, adding testily, "Although I *did* think you might slip in quietly, not wake the whole city. You've put me to a good deal of trouble."

She shook her finger at him. "You owe me a day's work, son of Norgaard!"

She snorted and returned to poking the fire.

Skylan glowered at her back. "But how did we get here? What happened? And where are we anyway?"

Owl Mother gestured to Aylaen. "You tell him. I'll fix something to eat. Come, young Farinn, and give me a hand."

She disappeared behind a tapestry on which the strange warriors were fighting their never-ending battle. Farinn rose from a chair by the grate where he had been sitting and hurried after her.

Skylan looked at Aylaen. "Do you know where we are?"

"We are in Tsa Kerestra," she said. "I don't know how we came to be here or what happened back at the tower. Wulfe says Owl Mother's magic made the stars fall and saved our lives. Owl Mother says the tower is called Starfall Tower for a reason and we were fools to trust Wulfe's harebrained mother."

"Where is Wulfe?" Skylan asked, realizing that he had not seen the boy.

"Owl Mother told him to go back to the tower, make it look as if the fae folk were the ones who caused all the commotion."

"Wulfe lived with Owl Mother for a time, back in the village," said Skylan. "But that doesn't explain . . ."

He shook his head.

Aylaen drew near him and clasped his hand. "It doesn't explain anything. It's all so strange. I don't know what's going on. Owl Mother won't tell me."

"Magic," said Skylan grimly. "The sooner we're away from here the better."

He walked over to the tapestry and reached out to push past it, then paused. The last time he'd been in Owl Mother's house, he had encountered a wyvern behind the tapestry. He let his hand fall and spoke to the tapestry.

"Aylaen tells me that we are in Tsa Kerestra, Owl Mother," said Skylan.

"Hold that open for me," Owl Mother said, startling him by suddenly flinging the tapestry aside.

Skylan held the tapestry. She came through carrying a large platter of roasted meat. Slamming the platter down on the table, she headed back to the kitchen.

"We are here to speak to the Stormlords," said Skylan.

"You are," Owl Mother returned.

She disappeared behind the tapestry. Farinn came out holding a trencher on which was a loaf of freshly baked bread, still warm. He was pale and shaken.

"What's wrong?" Skylan asked.

Setting the bread on the table, Farinn said in a low voice, "There's no hearth, no cook fire! No kettle. Not even a table! There's nothing in that room except a door and a window."

"Then where did this food come from?" Skylan asked.

Farinn gave him a helpless glance and shook his head. Owl Mother entered through the tapestry and fixed Farinn with a stern eye, causing him to flush guiltily and nearly drop the trencher. There were no plates, the forks were made from deer antlers, and the cups were formed out of birch bark. She put a crockery pitcher on the table and spoke a word. Three candles burst into flame.

Skylan glanced around. The small dwelling was almost exactly like her hut in the Torgun village, simple and crudely built with few furnishings. Yet he had the feeling this was not her home. The dwelling felt cold, as though no one had lit a fire in a long time. The floor was swept, but there was dust in the corners. There was no life. No squirrel chattering from the back of the chair, no wolf slumbering in front of the door.

"Eat," said Owl Mother.

She sat in one of the only two chairs and indicated Aylaen sit in the other. Farinn perched on the end of the bed. Owl Mother offered Skylan a footstool, but he remained standing, not about to be deterred from his purpose.

"I said I want to speak to the Stormlords," he repeated.

"And I said you are speaking to a Stormlord," Owl Mother returned.

Skylan was angry. "I don't believe you. This is a lie! Magic, a dream of some sort."

Owl Mother picked up a fork and jabbed him in the hand.

"Feel that?" she asked.

Skylan rubbed his hand, looking down at two spots of blood.

"Yes," he said.

"It's no dream," said Owl Mother. The old woman's piercing eyes softened. Her mouth sagged. "I wish it were, child. I wish it were."

She sank back down into her chair and waved her hand at the food. "Eat while you can, son of Norgaard. You may not have another chance for a good long while."

Skylan was about to say angrily that he wasn't hungry, especially for food that had been magicked, when he caught Aylaen's warning glance and, shutting his mouth, he sat down on the stool.

He sniffed at the meat and, since it smelled like real meat, he was about to help himself when he heard a scratching sound coming from the other room. A breath of air stirred the tapestry, making it seem as if the warriors were riding to battle.

"Don't move!" Owl Mother ordered.

She hurried off, passing through the tapestry. Ignoring her command, Skylan rose to his feet and reached for his sword, only to realize that his sword was in its sheath lying at the foot of the bed. He retrieved it, noticing that the blade had been cleaned. Creeping softly over to the tapestry, he drew it slightly aside.

The small room was empty, as Farinn had described. Owl Mother walked to a door at the far end.

"Who's there?" she asked.

"Me," said a voice. "Let me in."

Owl Mother open the door a crack, peered out and then opened it wide. Wulfe darted inside and Owl Mother shut the door after him.

"Were you followed?" she asked.

Wulfe shook his head. The sleek curls were all awry, once more a tangled mess. He was missing one sleeve of his fine silk shirt and the other was ripped at the elbow. He sniffed the air.

"Food! Good. I'm hungry."

Skylan put down his sword and hurried back to the stool and was seated there when Owl Mother and Wulfe returned. Wulfe saw the meat and, grabbing pieces in both hands, began to eat ravenously. Owl Mother gave Skylan a baleful look and he had the feeling she knew he had been spying on her.

"What happened?" Owl Mother asked Wulfe.

"I went back to the tower and let the wizard find me. Then I let him chase me around for a little while, then I let him catch me," he mumbled between mouthfuls. "I told him that a chimera had attacked me and my mother and that we'd been separated and then the One Eyes started chasing me and I ran into the tower for safety. He was annoyed. He told me to tell my people to stay out of the Realm of Fire because it was too dangerous, even for fae folk. He was going to take me somewhere, but I broke loose. That's how I tore my shirt. It itches anyway."

Wulfe grabbed some bread and stuffed it in his mouth.

"What did this wizard look like?" Owl Mother asked.

Wulfe chewed bread, swallowed, then said, "He was skinny and tall—taller than Skylan. And he had a face like a frog."

Wulfe scrunched up his lips. Owl Mother looked grim.

"Baldev," she said.

Skylan waited for her to continue, wondering who she meant, but she sat hunched in her chair in silence, staring at the dying embers of the fire. He looked at the two marks the fork had made on his hand, still visible, still stinging. He shoved away his plate, as did Farinn and Aylaen. Wulfe ate until Owl Mother stood up, marched over to the table, and whisked away the food while he was still chewing.

Wulfe yelped in protest. A look from Owl Mother silenced him. Going over to the bed, he pulled off a blanket, dragged it to the grate, turned around on it three times, and went to sleep.

"I can help wash up," Aylaen offered, reaching for the pitcher.

"No need," said Owl Mother, and with a wave of her hand, the food, the platter, the forks, and the pitcher vanished.

Aylaen gave a start and edged closer to Skylan. He put his arm around her.

"You came here for the fifth spiritbone," Owl Mother said.

Skylan was startled by her statement, but he saw no reason to deny it.

"The Cyclopes told us the Stormlords plan to give it to Raegar," he said. "I came to reason with them."

"Cyclopes," Owl Mother muttered. "A notion's not safe inside your own skull when they're around."

"Please tell us what is wrong, Owl Mother," Aylaen said.

Owl Mother glanced at the boy asleep on the floor. He growled in his sleep, his feet paddling the air.

"The threads of our wyrds have led us to this point. Gods and men, the threads wrap around us, bind us tight."

Owl Mother pressed her lips together. "We Stormlords did *not* plan to give the spiritbone to Raegar. Not all of us."

She gazed, frowning, into the fire.

"Just one—the traitor."

Owl Mother walked over to the bed. "My old bones need rest. Dawn will come too soon this day. You lot can sleep on the floor. You'll find blankets in that chest over there. There's water to wash up."

Skylan had so many questions, he didn't know which to ask first. Before he could ask any, Owl Mother walked off.

She motioned to a sea chest and a pitcher and basin standing on the floor, none of which had been there only moments before. Lying on her back on the bed, she dragged the bedcovers up to her chin, folded her hands over her chest, and closed her eyes.

Skylan and the others stared at her in astonishment.

"How could she say something like that and then just go to sleep!" Skylan demanded, glaring at the slumbering old woman, who had now started to snore.

"Hush!" Aylaen whispered. "She'll hear you."

"I hope she does," Skylan muttered, but he said the words beneath his breath. Aylaen yawned and slumped against him. He smoothed her hair and kissed her. "You are exhausted. You and Farinn get some sleep. I'll keep watch."

"What about you?" Aylaen asked, yawning again.

"I'm not tired," Skylan said. "I need to think."

Farinn and Aylaen took blankets from the chest and spread them on the floor. The blankets had been folded away with sprigs of dried lavender; their fragrance filled the room. They bathed as best they could, what Aylaen termed a "lick and a promise."

Skylan settled himself in a straight-backed wooden chair. Owl Mother's chair by the grate was the most comfortable, but when he tried to sit there, he could feel her watching him, even through closed eyelids.

Farinn sprawled on the floor and was almost immediately asleep. Aylaen was wakeful. She lay on her side, her cheek pillowed on her hand, gazing into the darkness. Her expression was solemn, grave. Skylan wondered what she was seeing, what she was thinking about. She shifted her gaze to him.

"I love you so much," she said softly. "Remember that. Always."

He thought this an unchancy thing to say; almost as if she had spoken bad luck words. He felt chilled and so he made a jest of it.

"I am not likely to forget it," he said. "For you will remind me of it daily."

Aylaen smiled and closed her eyes.

The night was eerily quiet, or would have been but for Owl Mother's snoring. Skylan was restless, uneasy. He tried to make sense of what had happened, but all he could hear, over and over, was:

Gods and men, the threads wrap around us, bind us tight.

30

Skylan woke from a doze with a stiff neck and an aching back. Faint sunlight crept beneath the tapestry. The others were still asleep. He stretched and the wooden chair made a loud creaking sound, causing Aylaen to stir.

Fearing he would wake her, Skylan left the chair and crossed the floor, moving quietly. Going to the archway curtained off by the tapestry, he stepped into the room, letting the tapestry fall behind him.

Dim, soft light filtered through curtains as sheer as if they had been woven by spiders. Bunches of herbs hung from the ceiling and a basket stood on a low window seat. The herbs were dry to the point of crumbling to dust and their fragrance was faint, ghostly, giving him the impression that they had been hanging there a long time.

Skylan walked over to the window seat. The basket contained old, faded rose petals. He drew aside the curtains.

The window itself was a marvel to him, for it was made of myriad small panes of crystal cut in the shape of diamonds, bound together with lead. He looked out on what was presumably Tsa Kerestra, the Kingdom Above, and stared, amazed and confounded.

Dela Eden had claimed the kingdom's beauty stole the breath. She had described lofty silver spires rising out of the storm clouds and he had pictured castles floating among the mist and fog.

What he saw was a forest of ancient trees spreading their boughs protectively over small dwellings with thatched roofs and the same lead-paned windows. Ivy covered the walls, roses climbed to the eaves.

Lilies slept, their heads bowed, waiting for the sun. There were no streets, only rustic paths that led from house to house, worn by friends coming to visit.

"Dela Eden was right," he said to himself. "This land is very beautiful. It reminds me of home, and I don't know why."

The forests and verdant grass and lush flowers of Tsa Kerestra did not in the least resemble the rugged shores of Vindraholm, where waves crashed among the rocks and crops struggled to survive in the stony ground. Perhaps it seemed familiar because he felt a sense of restful ease, as he always felt when he returned home after a long voyage.

Skylan let the curtains fall.

"Tsa Kerestra is beautiful, but it is wrong, all wrong," he muttered.

Something poked him sharply in the back. He had not heard a sound and he whipped around to find Owl Mother standing behind him.

"Don't sneak up on me like that!" Skylan said. He could feel his heart pounding.

Owl Mother chuckled. "Well, what do you two think of the place?" she asked, giving him a shrewd look.

"I was wondering how clouds grow flowers," Skylan replied, meeting her gaze.

Owl Mother pursed her thin lips. "You're not as stupid as you look."

Shoving aside the basket of rose petals, she sat down in the window seat and made Skylan sit down. She snapped her fingers and a peach appeared in her wrinkled hand. Owl Mother split the peach in two and dug the pit out with her gnarled fingers.

"I'm not hungry," said Skylan.

"I didn't tell you to eat it, did I?" she snapped.

She handed one half of the peach to Skylan.

"Realm of Stone," she said. "This half is the Realm of Fire."

She balanced the pit on the palm of her hand. "The pit in the center is Tsa Kerestra."

"A peach pit," said Skylan.

"Think of it this way." Owl Mother opened the curtains a crack, to let in more light, then conjured up a piece of charcoal and used it to draw a circle on the floor.

"This circle is the Realm of Fire."

She drew another circle so that it overlapped with the first, then tapped the new circle. "This is the Realm of Stone."

Using the charcoal, she colored in the area where the two circles overlapped to form an oval.

"This is Tsa Kerestra. Not the Kingdom Above so much as the Kingdom In Between."

The circles and the oval made about as much sense to Skylan as Acronis's squiggly-lined maps.

"The city is on the ground," he said, frowning at the drawing.

"On the ground in our realm, which floats in the clouds in your realm," said Owl Mother.

Skylan looked out at the clear, peaceful sky, just beginning to brighten. "But where is the storm? The silver spires? I saw them."

"You saw what you wanted to see," said Owl Mother. She paused, then said quietly, "The clouds are like a wall around the city, a moat to keep out our foes."

"But why do you hide?" Skylan asked. "With all this magical power . . ."

"You were in our world," said Owl Mother. "You saw the ruins of what was once a beautiful city. But our world was ruled by cruel men who delighted in killing. Our ancestors had to escape or they feared we would perish. Some of the daring followed the dragons through the portal to the Realm of Stone. Our people could have lived there, but it was already populated by savage beings: humans, ogres, and Cyclopes. We foresaw endless trouble, wars and more killing. With the help of the Great Dragon Ilyrion, our people formed their own realm—between the other two. We could live in peace with no one the wiser.

"Then came Torval and his rampaging gods. He killed Ilyrion and claimed the world, and discovered our realm. We made a pact with Vindrash. She promised to keep our secret and we promised to leave the world in peace. She gave us the spiritbone as a show of good faith. Then came the stranger gods and with that an end to our so-called peaceful way of life."

"Life seems peaceful enough here," said Skylan with a glance through the curtains.

"The life of a sparrow in a cage seems peaceful enough! But would you want it?" Owl Mother asked with a snort of disgust.

"We are humans, like you, but because we can boil an egg with our minds we think we are better. We knew Torval and the other gods were neglecting the world, keeping careless watch. That wasn't our concern."

Owl Mother shrugged. "Vindrash hid the power of creation out of fear. The world was dying for the lack, yet still we did nothing."

"Is that why you came to live with us?" Skylan asked.

"There were some of us who wanted to live *in* the world, not above it," said Owl Mother. "We moved out to form a new kingdom, Tsa Terestra. The Kingdom Below. And some of us traveled farther than that."

"Why?" asked Skylan.

"The arrival of Aelon and the Gods of Raj. Torval dropped the hammer on that one. Poor blighter. He never thought some god would do to him what he did to Ilyrion. I needed to speak to Vindrash and to the dragons. The Gods of Raj were not a threat. They had their hands full trying to keep the ogres and the Cyclopes from cutting each other's throats. But Aelon, the Faceless God, was a different kettle of fish. He came poking and prying and snooping about and it wasn't long before he discovered the truth about Tsa Kerestra. He was sweet as honey dripping from the comb when he came to us, asking for 'tribute,' saying it would be a shame if he was forced to destroy our peaceful way of life.

"Aelon was powerful. The so-called wise agreed to pay him. Anything to be left alone. Of course, Aelon lied and sent his spies to discover the secret of the stormholds."

"What are the secrets to the stormholds?" Skylan asked. "What do they do?"

"They are the gates that allow us to travel between realms. Those of us who live in the Kingdom Below come to visit friends and family. All of us must periodically return to our place of origin, the Realm of Fire, to replenish our magic."

"I saw the great stone globe hanging in midair," said Skylan. "How does it work?"

"The seneschal lowers the globe and the gate opens," said Owl Mother. "Oh, it's much more complicated than that, having to do with all manner of magic hoopla and folderol. But that's what it boils down to."

Skylan frowned. "And so Aelon's spies discovered the secret and now Raegar knows how to lower the globe and open the gate."

Owl Mother snorted and began to rub out the drawing of the realms with the toe of her shoe. "Even if he knows the secret, he isn't a wizard. He can't work the magic."

"So what is the problem? If Raegar doesn't know the secret, then the stormhold won't allow him to pass though the gate, and Tsa Kerestra will be safe in the clouds," Skylan said. "Give us the spiritbone and we will leave."

"The damage has been done," said Owl Mother gravely. "The moment the traitor told Aelon that he would hand over the spiritbone, Tsa Kerestra fell."

Skylan didn't understand, but he supposed it had something to do with magic.

"Stop this traitor! Chain him up. Kill him."

"I'd feed him to a chimera, if I could!" Owl Mother said with a vicious snap. "But I can't prove my suspicions. If I accuse Baldev, he will simply deny it. He is well respected in Tsa Kerestra and I am a cranky, rebellious old crone who told my people to go to hell and walked out."

"Then I will steal the spiritbone," said Skylan, jumping to his feet. "We will go now, while everyone is asleep."

Owl Mother eyed him. "And will you be the one to unravel the magical spells that guard it, Skylan Ivorson?"

"You could do that," said Skylan.

"The spells are known only to the three Lords of the Storm, the governing body of the Kingdoms Above and Below. Baldev is one of those lords. He wants to be the sole ruler. I would guess that is the deal he made with Raegar."

"Then my warriors and I will fight Raegar's army and take the spiritbone from him," said Skylan.

"How many warriors do you have?" Owl Mother asked.

"Many hundred," Skylan replied proudly. "Ogres and my friends and Cyclopes. And we have the Dragon Kahg."

Owl Mother rose to her feet. "Come with me."

"Where?" Skylan asked.

"Where I tell you," Owl Mother returned.

She rose to her feet and led him to the door, which opened onto a small garden, now overgrown with weeds and brambles. Apples lay rotting on the ground beneath their trees. Beans had withered on the vine. A ragged hedge, grown to the height of a man, surrounded the garden like a leafy green wall on three sides. The fourth side was guarded by a stone wall like the one that surrounded the ill-fated city in the Realm of Fire.

Owl Mother led Skylan through the withered garden to the wall. She squinted at it intently, almost touching the stone with her nose, and ran her hands over it, poking and prodding.

One of the stones wiggled and, after some work, Owl Mother managed to pry it loose and pull it out of the wall. Sunlight shone through the hole. Owl Mother stood back, indicating with a gesture that Skylan was to look through the gap.

"What will I see?" Skylan asked, hesitating.

"Look and find out," Owl Mother growled.

The gap in the wall was about two hand-spans in length, located at Owl Mother's eye level, which meant Skylan had to stoop to see through it. He gasped and stepped back.

"The ground . . . The ground is far below us! And yet"—he eyed the ground beneath his feet—"we are standing on solid ground."

Owl Mother flourished the peach pit. "What the eye sees is not always what the eye sees. But never mind about the ground and whether it's above or below. You have bigger problems. Look to the west."

Skylan put his eye to the hole again, trying not to think about the ground. Beyond this solid wall of gray stone another wall of gray, this one more insubstantial, the storm clouds that wrapped protectively about Tsa Kerestra. At Owl Mother's words, the clouds parted and he saw the sun shining down on the plateau, sparkling on the sea and gleaming on twin hulls of an immense galley.

The ship bristled with oars like quills on a porcupine as the galley rode at anchor. Soldiers, small as bugs from this distance, jumped from the decks and began wading ashore, carrying their equipment over their heads. Smaller boats ferried even more soldiers and supplies to the beach, where men were busy unloading supplies, assembling siege engines, and pitching row after row of tents.

Skylan stared in blank dismay. He had figured Raegar had about four thousand troops. He could not guess at the number of soldiers, but there had to be twice that number in one galley, and another twin-hulled galley, as big as the first and crowded with even more men, sailed toward the shoreline. Triremes and other ships packed with soldiers and supplies traveled in their wake. All were flying the serpent flag of Oran, Empire of the New Dawn.

To complete his ruin, three dragons flew in lazy, sweeping circles overhead. One was the Dragon Fala, whom Kahg had said had chosen to serve Aelon. The other two Skylan recognized, for they had been among those who had sailed his dragonships to this place from Joabis's isle. These two had apparently liked Raegar's odds of recovering the spiritbone better than his, and decided to switch sides.

Skylan had seen more than enough and he sank back against the stone wall. The breath left his body in a sigh that was like the last breath of the dying. A bitter taste filled his mouth, and his stomach heaved. He had been so proud of his fleet of dragonships, his army of a few hundred ogres and Cyclopes and Vindrasi warriors.

In the past, when all had seemed lost, Skylan had known that his wits and his sword, his faith in Torval and in himself would win the day.

But not this day. Raegar would roll over their shield wall, grind their bones into the sand, and spill their blood into the sea.

Owl Mother's rough, calloused hand rested on his arm.

"Go home, Skylan," she said. "Take Aylaen and the spiritbones with you. You tried to defeat Aelon and you damn near succeeded. No one can fault you. Not even Torval."

Skylan gave a faint smile. "That is because Torval will be dead and so will we. If we flee, we put off the inevitable. We will sail home and death and destruction will follow us. Raegar will destroy the Stormlords and then he will cross the ocean and destroy us."

Owl Mother shook her head. Skylan glared at her.

"You Stormlords could stop Raegar and his army!" he said angrily. He gestured to the storm clouds, to the wall, to Tsa Kerestra, a world between worlds. "You could slay every one of those soldiers with as little effort as I could slay a hill of ants."

"We could," said Owl Mother. "We did. You remember that I told you that the Realm of Fire was occupied by cruel men who found it easy to kill, who took delight in the killing."

"Yes," said Skylan impatiently. "What of it?"

"Those men were us," said Owl Mother.

She sat down beside him, putting her back against the wall.

"You have seen the tapestries. A reminder of what we once were.

We have thrived here, and in all these centuries, we have never killed another human. But the hunger is still inside us. We know what would happen if once we started."

She shrugged. "Oh, we would tell ourselves that we were only defending the innocent and that once the enemy was destroyed, the killing would stop. But it would never stop. For there is always another enemy. In the end, we would turn on you."

Skylan regarded her, troubled.

"Don't worry," she said, resting her wrinkled hand on his shoulder. "We are not a threat to your people or any others in this world. We have made our plans. And if you decide to stay to fight, we will give you what help we can."

She gave Skylan a pat on the shoulder and then stood up and headed back toward the small house.

He looked again at Raegar's army. He sat there for a long time, watching as more and more men poured off the ships. Their officers were starting to form them into ranks and they seemed to stretch to the end of the world.

Skylan touched the amulet. "I will fight, Torval. I will fight until death takes me. But I will not win."

"Skylan . . ."

He looked up to see Aylaen standing in front of him. He wondered how long she had been there, if she had heard him. The sorrowful look in her eyes told him she had.

"I am sorry, Aylaen," said Skylan, rising to his feet. "My pride, my arrogance brought us here."

"Love brought you here," said Aylaen earnestly, clasping his hands. "Love for our gods, for our people. Whatever is done in love will always triumph."

Skylan gave a rueful smile. "Someday I hope to be the man you think I am. Come back to the house. I don't see how we can obtain the spiritbone, but we have to try. Our only chance is to summon the Great Dragon Ilyrion."

"I have been talking things over with Owl Mother and we have a plan," Aylaen said. "You're not going to like it, for it means we must part, for a little while at least."

She spoke with a catch in her voice and he noticed that she kept her eyes averted.

"You are right," he said. "I don't like it."

She raised her eyes to meet his. "Hear the idea first. I will stay here with Owl Mother. She will take me to the spiritbone."

Skylan shook his head. "Owl Mother told me the spiritbone is guarded by powerful magicks. Only the Lords of the Storm can remove them and one of those lords is the traitor."

"So we will let him remove them," said Aylaen. "Owl Mother says that when the magical gate opens, the Stormlords will surrender and Raegar will enter the city in triumph. Baldev will take him to the spiritbone. Once Baldev removes the spells, Owl Mother and I can steal the spiritbone."

"Raegar will come after you," said Skylan.

"Not if his fleet is in peril," said Aylaen.

Skylan thought back to the galleys, riding at anchor in the shallow water, and an idea formed in his mind.

"I can create an immense problem for Raegar, one that will draw him from the city. But you are right. We must part. I must go back to the *Venejekar*," Skylan said. "And you must stay here to save the spiritbones and summon the dragon."

"I am Kai Priestess," said Aylaen. "The responsibility for the spiritbones is mine. And I am the only one who can summon Ilyrion. You are Chief of Chiefs. You must lead the army."

Skylan brushed back the flame-red hair from her face. "When I became Chief of Chiefs and learned I had to marry Draya, a woman I did not love, because she was Kai Priestess, I was fool enough to try to find a way around the law. I went to the Vogogroth, the Law Giver, and asked him to change the law for me."

"What did he say?" Aylaen asked, drawing near to him.

"'The marriage of the Chief of Chiefs and the Kai Priestess is a marriage of two halves of a clan, a nation. It is the marriage of every man and every woman. It is the marriage of the worldly and the godly, the marriage of faith and logic, the marriage of the sword and of the shield,'" Skylan replied.

The words had rankled at the time, opposing his will. Now he understood their wisdom.

"The song isn't about you and me," said Skylan.

"It never has been," said Aylaen.

Skylan and Aylaen went back to the house to explain their plans to Owl Mother. She listened without interruption and, at the end, sat thinking it over.

"You realize how dangerous this is?" she asked abruptly

"We do, Owl Mother," Skylan replied.

Owl Mother snorted. "I doubt it. Neither of you young things have the sense god gave a goose."

She rubbed her head, looking from one to the other.

"But it's a good plan, for all that. I must go talk to the Lords of the Storm."

"Wait a moment," said Skylan, frowning. "Can you trust these lords? You said one was a traitor?"

"I trust two of them," said Owl Mother. "They are my brothers."

Seeing their astonishment, she added with a grin and a wink, "I'm the member of the family they don't talk about. Keep an eye on Wulfe. Don't let him go roaming. I'll knock three times. Don't let anyone else inside."

After Owl Mother had gone, Skylan and Aylaen sat together by the fire, talking in low voices while Farinn and Wulfe still slept. They held each other close, knowing soon that they must part, perhaps forever. They talked of when they were little, when the three of them—Skylan and Aylaen and Garn—had been inseparable.

They remembered the happy times—the mischief, the fun, the laughter. They spoke of the sad times—the mistakes, the misunderstandings, the follies and faults. For a man's wyrd is made of both the strong and the weak twisted together to form a single thread woven into the tapestry of the lives of gods and men.

And then, when they had said all that was in their hearts, they held each other and watched the flickering of the dying embers in silence until they heard Owl Mother's three taps at the door.

"My brothers have agreed," Owl Mother said. "And, now, Skylan, it's time for you to go. You'll have to travel back through the Realm of Fire, but I gave Wulfe a safer route. If you run into any monsters, take to your heels. I don't have time to make the stars fall."

Owl Mother raised a bony finger. "And when we get back home, you owe me a day's work."

"I look forward to it, Owl Mother," said Skylan.

Bending down, he kissed her wrinkled cheek.

Owl Mother shoved him away. "None of your flirting, Skylan Ivorson. You're much too young for me."

Skylan went to wake up Wulfe and Farinn, only to find Wulfe was awake, curled up in a corner, shivering.

"I smell iron. A lot of iron."

"Raegar's army is here," said Skylan. "He has iron enough to fill the ocean. You are coming with me. Aylaen is going to remain here. Farinn, you will stay with Aylaen."

Drawing Farinn to one side, he added in a low voice, "Take care of her."

"I will, Skylan. I promise," said Farinn.

Skylan took Aylaen in his arms. "When this is ended, we will go back to our village and live in my father's house. I will have to add a room for the children."

"Two rooms. Twins, remember," said Aylaen. "A boy and a girl."

Tears shimmered in her eyes. He clasped her tight and his own tears fell, sparkling, in her red hair.

"We may have to be apart for this short time," Aylaen said. "But our wyrds will always be bound together. No matter what happens, Skylan, we will find each other again."

He held on to her, not wanting to let her go. Something deep inside told him that once he did, he would never hold her again.

"Aylaen . . . ," he began, fear clutching at him.

She stopped his words with a kiss, then slipped out of his embrace. "Torval walk with you, my love, my husband."

Skylan walked away from her, not letting himself look back, knowing that if he did, his heart would fail him.

Skylan joined Wulfe, who led him around the house to a different part of the garden, where a thick stand of walnut trees had been overrun by blackberry bushes, some grown to the height of a man.

"There's a door in the wall on the other side of those bushes," said Wulfe.

The canes with their sharp thorns covered the ground and trailed up among the branches of the trees, so thick and tangled that Skylan started to draw his sword, prepared to chop his way through them.

Wulfe saw Skylan's hand on the hilt and hissed at him. "Stop it! No iron!"

"Then how do you propose we reach the door?" Skylan demanded.

"Magic," said Wulfe, grinning, and he began to sing.

> *Wither leaves*
> *And branches crack*
> *I need to find*
> *The right way back.*

The canes began to writhe like snakes and a tunnel opened up, about large enough for a dog.

"You can fit through that," Skylan said. "But what about me?"

"You just have to hunker down," said Wulfe. He turned to wave to Owl Mother, Aylaen, and Farinn, who were watching from the doorway. "Good-bye!"

"Take a bath once in a while," Aylaen called, waving back.

Wulfe started to duck through the blackberry bushes, then he stopped, turned, and dashed back to the dwelling. He flung his arms around Aylaen in a fierce hug, and then ran back.

Skylan looked at Aylaen. A ray of sunlight gilded her hair burnished red-gold. She put her hand to her lips, then waved farewell. He touched the amulet he wore.

"Torval, watch over my beloved wife, keep her safe."

Wulfe dropped onto all fours and crawled through the hole in the bushes. Skylan hunkered down, as ordered, and squeezed through the canes, snapping off branches and scratching his arms on the thorns.

He found the door, which was old and weathered and looked as if a breath could blow it open. Skylan shoved on it and it did not budge, though he could see no sign of a bar or lock. Wulfe stood watching him with a grin on his face.

"More magic?" Skylan asked.

Wulfe nodded and, tapping on the door three times, he began to sing.

> *Realm of Fire*
> *Realm of Stone*
> *Take us back*
> *To our home*

"'Home' and 'stone' don't really rhyme," Wulfe added in a whispered aside to Skylan. "But the magic doesn't know that."

The door started to swing open. Wulfe looked back at Skylan. "Where are we going?"

"*I'm* going to my ship," said Skylan. "You're going back to your mother."

Wulfe thrust out his lower lip. "I'm not. I'm coming with you. You need me."

"Like an arrow in my backside," said Skylan. "Wulfe, there's going to be fighting, blood and swords . . ."

Wulfe cast him a sly glance. "Since Aylaen's gone, who's going to talk to the dragon?"

Skylan glared at him. "You claim the dragon doesn't like you."

"He doesn't," Wulfe conceded. "But I can talk to him and you can't."

"Dela Eden can talk to dragons . . ."

"But do you want her talking to *our* dragon?" Wulfe asked.

Skylan didn't. He had come to like Dela Eden, but he wasn't quite ready to trust her completely. She was a Cyclopes and their ways were not the ways of the Vindrasi.

"I don't think the Dragon Kahg would want to hear you call him 'our' dragon," said Skylan.

"Then I can come?" said Wulfe.

"So long as you'll do what I tell you to do," said Skylan.

Wulfe grinned and, taking hold of Skylan's hand, led the way through the door and onto the deck of the *Venejekar*.

BOOK
3

CHAPTER

32

Raegar had ordered the commander of his flagship, *Aelon's Miracle*, to wait to make landfall until the troops were ready to receive him with the ceremony due to the Emperor of Oran. He needed to put on a show, not only for his soldiers and the priests. The Stormlords would be watching.

Raegar's barge, painted purple and adorned with gold, ferried him to shore, where slaves had spread red carpets so that he would not soil his feet on the sand.

He was wearing new ceremonial armor made of steel adorned with gold and silver serpents, matching shin guards and bracers, a purple cape that hung from golden clasps at his shoulders, and a golden crown fashioned in the form of a serpent biting its tail, with ruby eyes and glittering diamond scales.

He was accompanied by a personal guard in similar armor, though not decked out in gold, wearing helms trimmed with purple plumage. The men had been selected for their height, each standing well over six feet, and they were an impressive sight. His standard-bearers led the procession, followed by Aelon's standards and two priests with sour expressions, angry that Raegar's standards came first.

The two were wearing white robes with golden serpents embroidered on the back and they had their heads together, whispering as they walked. These two had been on board his ship as representatives of the priest-general, who had remained behind to rule Sinaria in the emperor's absence. The priests had always hated him and they did not believe his account of Treia's mysterious disappearance. He knew, because he had caught them questioning his slaves and servants, though, of course, the priests denied it.

Raegar made a mental note to see to it that their names headed the list of those who died in battle.

As he walked across the carpet, basking in the cheers of his soldiers, a winged shadow swept over him. He glanced up with pride to see Fala circling high above him, glaring down at him. Extending her feet, she curled her claws, like a hawk prepared to dive down on a mouse. Raegar hurriedly looked away.

Fala had been furious to hear of Treia's death. The dragon and Treia had formed a bond and when she heard Treia was dead, Fala had threatened to leave Raegar's service and take the other two dragons who had recently arrived with her. Aelon had been forced to intercede with Fala, promising the dragon her pick of the jewels from the rich city of the Stormlords. Fala had allowed herself to be persuaded on one condition—that he summon her using sand gathered from the beach, making her and the other two dragons out of earth, the strongest of the four elements.

Raegar had deemed a fire dragon more useful in fighting the Stormlords, but he dared not argue. Fala and the other two flew above the parade, their scales the brownish color of the mixture of sand and dirt he had slathered on the spiritbones.

Fala was scanning the skies; undoubtedly searching for her mortal foe, the Dragon Kahg. The traitor dragons had told him Skylan and his ragtag army of subhuman ogres and freakish Cyclopes had made landfall on the Spirit Coast. Unfortunately, they had lost track of them since. Fala and the other dragons were searching for Kahg and Raegar had sent out scouting parties to find Skylan.

He made an inspection of the troops and oversaw the preparations for war. This involved walking among the tents with the hot sun beating down on his head, and Raegar began to regret the purple cape and heavy armor. But only a few miles to the north of where he had established camp, thunder clouds boiled, lightning flared, and torrential rains fell on the plateau below.

The Stormlord's city of Tsa Kerestra hides among those clouds, the spies had written. *When the magic of the stormhold is activated, the gate to the city will open.*

"Let them bluster," Raegar remarked as he observed with satisfaction the various types of war machines: ballistae and the stone-throwing onagers, siege towers and battering rams. "Much good a few rain clouds will do them."

Once his inspection was complete, Raegar made a brief speech to his soldiers, then went to the royal pavilion, which had been outfitted with every luxury. Raegar looked around with pleasure. Slaves had spread soft rugs on the floor and carried in chairs and couches and his ornately carved wood-framed bed, so heavy it required ten men to haul it from the ship.

Looking at the bed, Raegar felt a cold qualm creep into his bowels, for he had been accustomed to sharing that bed with Treia. Her smell seemed to linger on the bedclothes, making him gag, and he longed to order the damn thing be hauled off and burned. He dared not do so, however, for that would cause talk and increase the suspicions of the priests.

He scowled, his pleasure in his tent gone and he cursed Treia roundly. Even dead, she continued to plague him. He found some consolation in the cradle they had set up for his son. The baby would remain on board his ship in the care of the wet nurse until the war was over. When Raegar was crowned king of Tsa Kerestra, he would carry his son with him as he rode his chariot through the city in triumph.

The heat in the tent was stifling. Raegar was sweating in his armor and he walked outside into the fresh air to find Eolus speaking to the commander in charge of the search detail.

"Have they located the dragonships of the Vindrasi?" Raegar demanded.

"They saw no sign of them, sir," Eolus reported. "But they did find evidence that there was a battle."

"Blood soaked into the sand, sir," said the commander. "Shields and weapons, broken spears and arrows. The tide had washed much of the evidence away, but we did see some huge footprints that could belong only to ogres among others that were human."

"Battle?" Raegar was puzzled. "Who did they fight?"

If the Stormlords would not fight him, he could not see why they should bother with Skylan.

"Looks to me as if they ended up fighting each other, sir," said the commander. "Likely they had a falling out."

"No bodies?" Raegar asked.

The commander shook his head. "If there had been, they would have been carried out to sea or devoured by wild beasts. Or worse."

"Worse?" Raegar asked.

"Ghouls. We are very near the land of the fae, sir," said Eolus.

"Too damn near," Raegar muttered. "Once Aelon reigns supreme, she will wipe out that scourge."

"They did find evidence that before the battle, the filthy savages paid a visit to the stormhold," Eolus continued. "Perhaps that was what they fought over."

Raegar grunted. Having been born one of those "filthy savages," Raegar wondered if Eolus was aware that he had just insulted his emperor. Raegar had left that part of his life far behind him, but he knew others—especially among the noble classes and the upper echelons of the priesthood—remembered the days when the slave, Raegar, had walked ten paces behind his master.

Eolus returned Raegar's scrutiny with equanimity and Raegar relaxed. His soldiers admired him; perhaps for the very reason that the priests did not. Raegar was a warrior—one of them. Affairs of state either bored him or galled him. He likened the priests to Aelon's serpents; tangled in a writhing knot, each head striking at the others.

Although not a particularly good emperor, Raegar was a good general. His men deemed him strict, but fair. They liked and admired him because he looked out for their welfare. Raegar made certain that his soldiers, sailors, and rowers were well paid *and* well fed. An army marches on its belly, as the saying goes.

"Did they do any damage?" Raegar asked.

"As you commanded, sir, we did not enter the stormhold, but we saw no signs of damage," the commander replied.

"Do you want the men to keep searching, sir?" Eolus asked.

Raegar was Emperor of Oran, commanding twelve thousand troops, the largest army ever assembled in the history of the world. He was about to force powerful wizards to kneel before him. If he continued to expend manpower and resources searching for a few hundred "filthy savages," his soldiers would start to doubt his leadership, if not his sanity.

"So Skylan is out there," Raegar muttered. "So he has four spiritbones. What of it? He won't get the fifth. And even *he* isn't stupid enough to attack an army that is better equipped, more skilled in fighting, and outnumbers him ten to one. It's just . . . I keep killing him and the bastard won't die!"

"What did you say, sir?" Eolus asked.

"I was going over battle plans," Raegar responded. "What did you ask me?"

"If you wanted us to keep searching for the Vindrasi?"

"That won't be necessary," Raegar answered. "As you say, it is obvious they had a falling out. What can you expect of savages?"

Eolus and the other commander both laughed.

Raegar glanced at the sun crawling toward its zenith. Morning was advancing. Time to get started.

"Assemble the troops," he ordered. "And summon the priests. We are going to the stormhold."

Eolus and his guard and the elite troops chosen to accompany the emperor to the stormhold were ready to depart within minutes. Raegar was forced to wait for the priests. He had told them to stay in one location so that they would be ready to leave and while a few had done as he ordered, most of the others had wandered off to gape at the siege machines or investigate and then complain about the fact that they had to sleep in tents.

Raegar was angered, but he feigned nonchalance. If the priests hoped to make him lose his temper in public, they were in for disappointment. He spent his time studying the stormhold on the promontory through a spyglass, commenting on its features and discussing strategy with Eolus and the other commanders, although all he could think about were the pain-twisted faces of the two dead spies. The traitor Baldev had assured him the spies had given him the secret of how to undo magic. But Baldev was a wizard and therefore not to be trusted. Aelon had claimed she had killed the priests, but she could also be lying in order to trick him into thinking he had nothing to fear from the magic. Raegar had not lost faith in Aelon, but he was starting to realize that he should be putting his own interests first.

As for the stormhold, he would sooner take a spear to the gut than have anything to do with wizards or magic, and now he was forced to deal with both.

"The priests are assembled, sir," Eolus reported.

Raegar lowered the spyglass and glanced at the priests wearing their heavy robes in the hot sun, undoubtedly broiling.

"We're in no hurry," he said, and he turned to one of his servants. "Bring me wine and something to eat."

Servants went running. Slaves brought out a chair and a small table. Raegar ate and drank at his leisure while the priests sweated and his soldiers grinned. Finally, Raegar rose to his feet, drank the remainder of the wine, then handed the goblet to a slave and announced loudly that everyone was to join him in prayer.

"Revered Aelon," Raegar bellowed, shouting at the heavens, "we ask that you assist us to remove the magical spells so that we may safely enter the city of Tsa Kerestra." Thinking a little flattery would not be amiss, he added, "We want all the world to fear you, great Aelon."

Dressed in his finest armor, purple cape, and the royal crown, and escorted by his guard, elite troops, and a hundred priests of Aelon, Raegar undertook the long climb up Gray Beak to the stormhold.

The march revived Raegar's spirits. He listened with pleasure to the rhythmic tramping of feet, the familiar jingle and rattle of armor, the flapping of the flags in the wind. He took confidence in the discipline and resolution of his men, and when he saw one of the men glancing askance at the storm clouds roiling above the plateau to the north, Raegar grinned.

"These wizards are impotent old men, shaking their canes at us and mumbling curses through toothless gums," Raegar said loudly, making a rude gesture at the clouds.

The troops cheered and word spread, as Raegar had known it would. His soldiers loved him.

He arrived at the stormhold to find that his troops had cordoned off the building. The soldiers, resplendent in their armor, stood at attention in well-disciplined order. The ancient stone tower with its crumbling walls did not look particularly daunting. Eolus assured him that, as he had ordered, no man had entered. Having heard the rumors about the lethal magicks inside, no one had been tempted.

"The men have seen nothing, heard nothing, sir," said Eolus. "The stormhold appears to be deserted."

"No sign of that traitor Baldev?" Raegar asked in a low voice.

"No, sir," said Eolus.

Raegar grunted. He'd ordered the wizard to be here, but hadn't really expected the arrogant bastard to obey. Damn all wizards to hell anyway.

"If the blasted place is guarded by deadly magicks, the wizards don't need anyone inside," Raegar remarked.

"True, sir," said Eolus. "Should we enter now?"

"We have to wait for the priests. And I've told you before, Commander, that I'm going in alone," Raegar added.

"I wish you would reconsider, sir," said Eolus earnestly.

The priests of Aelon eventually came straggling up the cliff, hot and tired and grumbling after the long hike. They formed a circle around the stormhold, preparing to offer up their prayers to Aelon.

Raegar stood outside the door, trying to will himself to enter.

The spies had left detailed instructions on how to remove the magical spells. He had committed these instructions to memory, reciting them so many times he could say them in his sleep. But he was loath to walk into that silent darkness. Had he been on his own, he would have turned and run back down the trail.

As it was, his men were watching him expectantly, and so were the priests.

"No matter what happens," Raegar told Eolus, "do not enter."

Eolus looked unhappy and shook his head.

"I don't like it, sir."

"All will be well, Commander," Raegar said. "Soon we will have all the wizard gold and silver and jewels we can carry. And we will show their women what real men are like."

"Yes, sir," said Eolus. "Aelon be with you."

Unfortunately the blessing reminded Raegar of the two dead priests. Aelon had been with them, too. He reminded himself that she wanted him to bring these wizards to their knees. He drew in a breath and ducked beneath the archway.

He stopped for a moment to let his eyes adjust to the darkness after the bright sunlight and tried to calm the pounding of his heart. Once he could see, he continued down the short corridor to the central chamber that was open to the air.

Gray light filtered through the clouds. He located the stone globe and cautiously approached the wall that surrounded it, being careful not to touch anything.

The spies had described the globe, but their description did not prepare him for the sight of the immense ball of stone suspended in midair. He stared in awe and was forced to admit that up until now, he had never truly believed in a city built among the clouds. He had supposed it would turn out to be a trick of some sort, like those of rogues on the street who cheated men of their money by making beans disappear beneath walnut shells. He was forced to admit, with a gulp, that this huge hunk of rock was floating in the air like a will-o'-the-wisp. Outside the stormhold, the priests began to chant prayers to Aelon, their voices resounding like thunder.

Raegar felt sick and suddenly, he could not remember a single word of the spy's instructions for removing the magic. He reached into a pouch and took out the notes and tried to read them. The words seemed to crawl around like bugs, and made no sense.

He gazed in silent agony at the globe. He was supposed to step on certain flagstones on the floor, treading on some and avoiding others. Then he was supposed to push in certain stones on the walls until they clicked, but he couldn't remember whether he had to count five over and ten up from the wall or ten over and five up. If he made even one mistake, he would be pummeled by blasts of wind, shaken by concussive thunder, and fried by bolts of lightning. Not to mention what Aelon could do to him.

Raegar cast a longing glance at the exit, only to picture to himself what would happen if he ran out of here in a panic. He would be finished. The people would view him with scorn. The priests would see to it that he was deposed and sent into exile, or they might just forgo the trouble and hire an assassin to avoid the cost of an execution. Aelon would be furious. She would spurn him, cast him out . . .

I'm risking my life for her, Raegar thought angrily. I've been loyal to her. I've brought glory to her name, made her the most powerful god in the world, amassed wealth for her church.

What has she done for me? She claims she lifted me from slave to emperor. Yet, looking back, I see that she did very little. I was the one who did all the work. She has repeatedly lied to me, sided with Treia against me, scolded and humiliated me, lured me on with promises of her favors that have yet to come to pass. She has let her priests mock me and conspire against me.

And where is Aelon now? Raegar glared around the stormhold. I am alone. She could have at least come to support me, shine down her radiance on me, use her godly powers to dismantle the magic. And once *I* open the gate to Tsa Kerestra, Aelon has promised the traitor Baldev he would rule it!

Outside the stormhold, the priests were chanting Aelon's name. Inside the stormhold, Raegar was looking at a gigantic ball of stone suspended in midair by a magic more powerful than he could fathom . . . and all he could see were the faces of the two dead spies.

They had been loyal and faithful to their god and what was their reward? A horrible death.

Grimly, angrily, Raegar decided to take a stand.

"Aelon, if you want these wizards to fear you," he shouted, raising his voice to the cloud-covered heavens, "then do not make me play their silly game! Do not make me dance on tiles and shove stones! Smite this rock! Tear apart their storm clouds! Smash the gates to their city! And make *me* their master!"

Raegar drew his sword. Aelon would either back him in this or she would not. If she didn't, the magic would kill him and that was fine.

"I am emperor of the mightiest nation in the world, Aelon," he said through gritted teeth. "I am no longer a slave and I would rather die than let you treat me like one!"

He grasped his sword in both hands, raised it over his head and struck the stone globe.

Sparks flew; the force of the blow numbed Raegar's arms to the elbow. Nothing happened at first and he drew in a shivering breath. Then he saw a crack in the stone, small at first and then growing and spreading.

Raegar watched, awed, as the stone globe fell from its magical moorings, plummeted into the darkness, and burst asunder.

The ground trembled. The walls shook. Stones cascaded down from above as sections of the walkway gave way. Raegar was cut by shards of rock. A chunk of the wall struck his shoulder and another hit him a glancing blow on the head, knocking off his crown.

Raegar staggered and fell, dazed. He tried to stand, fell again, and then strong hands grabbed hold of him by the shoulders. Shouting for help, Eolus began to drag Raegar toward the door. Two other members of his guard came to assist Eolus and between them, hauled Raegar outside, just as the stormhold broke apart.

The tower crashed to the ground with a horrendous roar. The air was filled with a blinding, choking cloud of dust and debris, and for a moment it seemed to Raegar as if the sky itself were falling down.

And then suddenly bits of debris stopped hitting him and the rumbling ceased and the world grew blessedly quiet.

Raegar spat out rock dust and was amazed that he was still alive. He moved gingerly, trying to feel if anything was broken. His shoulder hurt and he had a splitting headache and grit in his eyes, but that appeared to be the worst of his injuries.

"Are you all right, sir?" Eolus asked in between fits of coughing.

"I am," said Raegar. "Thank you and your men for disobeying me."

"Only doing our duty, sir," said Eolus.

Raegar grunted. He'd make certain Eolus and the others were well rewarded for "only" doing their duty.

Getting to his feet, he looked around, assessing the situation.

It wasn't good.

The stormhold was a pile of smashed and broken rock. In the distance, storm clouds boiled over the plateau, with no magical highway in sight. He had failed Aelon, after first defying her, and he began to wish the building had fallen down on top of him.

He had to find some way of appeasing her. Most of his soldiers were unscathed, only a few suffering from minor injuries. The priests were nowhere in sight.

"Where are those confounded priests?" he asked.

He needed them to intercede with him, to ask Aelon for forgiveness.

"They ran off when the ground started to shake, sir," said Eolus.

"Bastards . . . ," Raegar muttered, then stopped to consider. "Aelon can't blame me. I did my duty, though I nearly died. It was the fault of her priests who stopped praying and ran off at the first sign of trouble."

"What are your orders, sir?" Eolus asked

Raegar sighed. What were his orders? Pack up everything, dismantle the siege engines, return to their ships, and sail back home in shame and ignominy?

He groaned, and Eolus regarded him with sympathy. He was about to say something when he was interrupted by loud cries of "Aelon be praised!" and "All praise to Aelon!" coming from the beach below.

"What the devil's going on down there?" Raegar asked.

Eolus went to investigate and returned to say that priests were assembling on the beach.

"They're having some sort of celebration, sir," Eolus reported. "Dancing and cheering."

"That's why, sir!" cried out some of the soldiers. "Look there, to the north!"

Fierce winds tore apart the storm clouds to reveal silver spires and golden domes shining in the bright light of a fiery sun. As Raegar watched in disbelief, spires, domes, wall, and all descended from the sky. The city fell from the clouds and landed on the plateau beneath.

A voice exploded behind Raegar.

"You thrice-cursed barbarous clod, what have you done?" Baldev snarled.

Emerging from the ruins of the stormhold, the wizard came striding toward him, robes flapping, shaking with fury.

"You destroyed the magic! My city is now in the Realm of Stone!" Baldev yelled. "The other Lords of the Storm suspect me! There is still a chance I can take over the city, but you must follow my instructions—"

His voice sent pain shooting through Raegar's head.

"Kill him," he told Eolus.

Baldev gave a nasty laugh. He drew a piece of paper out of his sleeve and waved it at Raegar. "You blithering idiot! You can't kill me! You need me to recover your precious spiritbone! You will do what I tell you or I'll—"

Raegar looked away from the raving wizard to the shining city squatting ignominiously on the ground.

"I don't need anyone," he said.

He nodded to Eolus, who swiftly and efficiently thrust his sword into Baldev's back.

Baldev gargled and looked in amazement at the sword sticking out of his gut. Eolus yanked the blade free and Baldev fell to his knees, clutching at his stomach as blood spilled over his hands. He made a gurgling noise and pitched forward, falling on his face. The body twitched a couple of times and then lay still.

Raegar bent down and took the piece of paper from the wizard's limp hand. It was some sort of hastily drawn map. He thrust it into his belt, then turned back to look at Tsa Kerestra.

The city was surrounded by a stone wall pierced by a massive gate. Domes and spires, gabled roofs and graceful minarets rose from behind the walls, all seemingly made of precious metals that shone with a blinding light in the sun. He had never seen anything so beautiful or so rich, and it was his.

"I worked this miracle," Raegar murmured. "Not even Aelon can take credit for it, for if she'd had her way, I would have been hopping from flagstone to flagstone like a frog on a hot griddle."

The sky above the city was a clear, deep blue without the wisp of a cloud. The sun was warm and seemed to caress Raegar, easing the pain in his sore shoulders, while a gentle and fragrant breeze soothed, like delicate fingers, the ache in his head.

A man appeared on the battlements of Tsa Kerestra and, unfurling a white flag, began to wave it back and forth.

"They're offering to surrender, sir," said Eolus, grinning.

Raegar turned to see his soldiers regarding him with admiration and now, by god, the priests were chanting *his* name.

"All praise to Raegar, Emperor of the World!"

He walked to the edge of the cliff and raised his arms in salute. The crowd on the beach below cheered him.

This was his proudest moment.

"Send to the ship for my son," Raegar told Eolus. "Once I have the spiritbone, he will see *me* crowned king!"

Skylan stepped onto the deck of the *Venejekar* with Wulfe following close behind. Skylan was startled to see the sun shining brightly
overhead. They had left Tsa Kerestra at dawn and now it was midday
and yet it seemed that almost no time had passed since he and Wulfe
had walked through the gate.

"Where have we been?" Skylan asked Wulfe.

The boy gave him a furtive look. "At least there were no chimeras."

Skylan didn't have time to pursue the matter. He had walked in on
an argument among his friends, who were debating what to do in
the absence of their chief.

"We should have killed those soldiers we saw snooping around,"
Sigurd said.

"That wasn't Skylan's plan," Bjorn retorted.

"The hell with Skylan," Sigurd began. At that very moment,
Erdmun saw Skylan and Wulfe standing on the deck and gave an
alarmed yelp.

Sigurd and Grimuir grabbed their weapons, then saw who it was
and lowered them.

"How did the meeting with the Stormlords go?" Bjorn asked.

"Look at his face," said Sigurd. "There's your answer."

Skylan hesitated, wondering how much to tell his friends. What
with Owl Mother and peach pits and falling stars, his tale was complicated, outlandish, and implausible. Before he could launch into it,
however, Wulfe told it for him.

"Skylan met my mother and she took us to the city in the clouds where he fought a chimera and Aylaen and Farinn stayed with Owl Mother to steal the god bone."

Skylan rounded on him. "Go talk to the Dragon Kahg. Tell him about Raegar's forces and the other three dragons."

"He's not there," said Wulfe, pointing to the prow. "It's just wood."

"Where is he?" Skylan asked, turning to the others.

"The dragon flew off," said Bjorn, shrugging. "We don't know where. So is what Wulfe says true?"

Skylan sighed. "I know you have questions—"

"Damn right! You fought a chimera?" asked Sigurd eagerly.

Bjorn cast him an exasperated glance. "That's not what's important."

"Maybe to you," Sigurd muttered.

"I wish I could tell you what I saw and heard, but the truth is it's mostly magic and I don't understand much of any of it. Owl Mother was waiting for us in the city. She's one of the Stormlords—"

"That figures," Grimuir said. "I never did like that old crone."

"That 'old crone' is going to help Aylaen take back the spiritbone," said Skylan. "The Stormlords never meant to give it to Raegar. One of them is a traitor and he sold them out."

"You left Aylaen there, alone in that city of wizards?" said Erdmun.

"She is Kai Priestess," said Skylan. "The duty to her people is hers by right, and, as Chief of Chiefs, I support her."

Skylan waited in silence for his friends to challenge him, especially Sigurd, who was Aylaen's stepfather.

To his surprise, Sigurd said with gruff pride, "Aylaen would do her duty, no matter what the cost. She's a Vindrasi and my daughter."

The others nodded their agreement. Skylan was relieved. The worst was over. He could proceed on to the next part that, even though the news was dire, was far easier to explain.

"While I was in the city," Skylan continued, "I saw Raegar's fleet make landfall. He has two enormous galleys, each one bigger than our village, and he brought with him as many soldiers as there are grains of sand on the shore."

Sigurd gave a shrug. "So you're saying we're outnumbered."

"And Raegar has three dragons," Skylan said. "Two of them were with us, so he knows *our* numbers and maybe even that we are hiding here."

"If that's true, we might as well have stayed dead," Erdmun remarked glumly. "Save Raegar the time and trouble of killing us all over again."

"Skylan has a plan," Bjorn said.

"It better be a good one," said Grimuir.

"It is," said Skylan. And he was about to explain his plan when the sound of an explosion echoing among the trees caused the birds to rise from the branches, screeching, and brought the conversation to a sudden halt.

"What the hell was that?" Sigurd demanded.

Skylan couldn't see Gray Beak through the thick leaves of the mangroves, but he knew in his heart what had happened.

"The blast came from the direction of the stormhold," he said. "Something's gone wrong. According to Owl Mother, Raegar was supposed to use the stormhold's magic to open the gate, not blow it up."

"Dela Eden and some of her Cyclopes went up to Gray Beak to keep watch," said Bjorn. "They'll tell us."

"I don't think we have to wait for them," said Erdmun, craning his neck.

The Dragon Kahg circled in the air above them. He was hard to see, for his body was the same blue as the sky. As a dragon of air, he could change to gray to blend in with rain or black to meld with the night. Skylan now wondered if the dragon had known all along that the dragons who had sailed with them had been planning to betray him.

Kahg remained in the air a long while, flying just above tree level. Skylan, eager for news, was wondering impatiently what the dragon was doing when Kahg descended and returned to his form on the *Venejekar*.

"Go talk to him," Skylan told Wulfe.

Wulfe hesitated. "You didn't tell me he was real now."

"This is why I let you come," said Skylan. "Go talk to the dragon."

Wulfe went off, dragging his feet, keeping a wary eye on the dragon while Kahg kept a fiery eye on the boy. Wulfe spoke to the dragon, then turned to report.

"Kahg says Raegar and a bunch of soldiers and priests visited to the stormhold," Wulfe reported. "Raegar went inside and blew it up."

"By Torval, maybe our luck has changed!" Skylan said.

"The only time our luck changes is to get worse," Erdmun said.

"It gets worse. The city in the clouds fell," Wulfe said, his eyes wide. "It's not in the clouds. It's on the ground."

Skylan stared at him. "On the ground! Did it crash? Was it destroyed?"

All he could think about was Aylaen and if she was safe. Wulfe asked the dragon, who growled in anger. Wulfe turned to Skylan.

"Kahg says I have it wrong. The city didn't really fall. It just isn't where it used to be. It's in our realm now."

Skylan remembered the peach pit and thought he understood—at least as well as he would ever understand. The magic had gone awry and the city that was once in between realms was now in this one. He breathed easier.

"I take it this wasn't the plan," said Bjorn, who had been watching Skylan's expression.

"No," Skylan admitted. "It wasn't."

"Kahg says to tell you the Stormlords are waving a white flag." Wulfe looked puzzled. "What does that mean?"

Grimuir sneered. "It means the bastards are giving up without a fight."

"I say we fight their battle for them," said Sigurd. "Kill Raegar and his men, storm the city, find Aylaen, and take her home."

"With thousands of soldiers standing in our way, we would never get close enough to even see the city gate," said Skylan.

"We have to do something," said Bjorn. "You know what he and his soldiers will do to those people once they're inside the city walls."

"I know," said Skylan, thinking. "And so do the wizards. Maybe this is part of *their* plan."

He made up his mind.

"No matter what happens, Aylaen will do everything in her power to find the fifth spiritbone and summon the dragon Ilyrion," said Skylan. "She'll be relying on us and we must put our trust in her *and* in the gods. Vindrash will not abandon her priestess and Torval will not abandon us."

"If Torval's still around," Erdmun muttered, but no one paid any attention to him.

"So what is this plan?" Sigurd asked.

"We all know Raegar and the Sinarians," said Skylan. "Remember what they did with us after the Legate took us captive? They marched us into the city in triumph. Everyone came out to gawk at us. This is Raegar's greatest moment. His moment of triumph. What will he do?"

"He'll hold a celebration," said Sigurd, grinning.

"And we're going to ruin the party," said Skylan.

Skylan met with Bear Walker and Dela Eden to explain his plan, which was greeted with enthusiasm. Even the sour-faced shaman, Raven's-foot, expressed his approval with a shake of the gourd.

"We need tow and resin to make the flaming arrows," said Dela Eden. "We don't have those supplies with us, but if we can use one of the dragonships and if your friends will help us row, we can sail back to the Cyclopes village to fetch what we need."

Skylan dispatched Sigurd, Grimuir, Erdmun, and Bjorn to assist the Cyclopes. Skylan had no fears the dragonship would be seen. They were traveling south, away from Tsa Kerestra and the enemy encampment. Lookouts atop Gray Beak would have seen them, but Dela Eden reported that Raegar had declared victory and pulled all his forces off the promontory.

After the dragonship had sailed away, Skylan went in search of Wulfe and found him in the Cyclopes camp, curled up on a pile of fishnet, taking a nap. Wulfe grumbled when Skylan woke him.

"When are we going to eat? I'm hungry."

"Soon," Skylan promised, realizing that he, too, was hungry. He had been so caught up in his preparations for war that he had forgotten about food.

"If we're not going to eat, why did you wake me up?" Wulfe demanded.

"I need to talk to the Dragon Kahg and I need you there to tell me what he says."

"After that we can eat?" Wulfe asked.

"Yes," Skylan promised.

As they went on board the *Venejekar*, Skylan asked Wulfe why he wasn't complaining about being asked to speak to Kahg.

"The dragon still doesn't like me, but he says he's gotten used to me," Wulfe explained. "He says I'm like scale-mites—annoying, but harmless."

Skylan hid his smile, for he had something serious to discuss with the boy. "After we talk to Kahg—"

"You said we would eat," Wulfe reminded him.

"After we eat I want you to go back to stay with your mother. There's going to be fighting. Men with iron. I don't want you to get hurt."

"I don't want to go back to my mother," said Wulfe, making a face. "She makes me take a bath and wear those itchy clothes and fusses with my hair. I heard Dela Eden say the Cyclopes were going to shoot fire and I've never seen anyone do that. And you might get into trouble again and need my magic. I guess I'll come with you."

Skylan was more than a little alarmed. The last thing he needed was Wulfe's magic, which, while occasionally useful, tended to be erratic and unpredictable. He couldn't think how to get rid of him.

"Just stay out of the way," said Skylan. "And don't change into a wolf."

"I'll try," said Wulfe cautiously. "I can't promise. Sometimes I change into the wolf and sometimes the wolf changes into me."

They found the Dragon Kahg in his customary form on board the *Venejekar*, sleeping with his eyes open, at least that was what Wulfe claimed when the dragon didn't immediately respond to Wulfe's shout. When Kahg finally woke, Skylan explained his plan and the dragon's role in it, expressing his hope that the dragon would consent to take part.

"The dragon says your plan is a good one," Wulfe said, speaking for Kahg. "He might even add some touches of his own."

"Tell Kahg I have appreciated all his help and that he will be rewarded with his pick of jewels when we return to our homeland."

Skylan saw Kahg's eyes darken, the flame diminish.

"What's the matter?" Skylan asked. "Did I say something wrong?"

Wulfe listened, then turned to report. "The dragon says you might not have a homeland. Torval's Hall is burning."

Skylan stood in silence, his hand clenched on the hilt of his sword. He had been going to ask Torval for his help, but it seemed the gods were fighting for their lives in heaven. The battle here below was left to him and Aylaen, their small band of warriors, a fae child, and a dragon.

The Cyclopes returned with large quantities of tow—short fibers of carded flax. They also brought with them Kamau and twenty other Cyclopes warriors, who were angered when they heard about the fall of Tsa Kerestra, and wanted to fight.

Dela Eden explained the technique used by Cyclopes to prepare their arrows, showing Skylan how they tied pieces of tow around the shaft beneath the arrowhead, then dipped the tow in the resin.

"After that, all we have to do is light the tow on fire and shoot the arrows," said Dela Eden.

Skylan was impressed and made a mental note to take that technique back to his people.

Leaving the Cyclopes to their work, he went to say good-bye to Bear Walker, and Sigurd and the other Vindrasi. They were setting out early, before nightfall, for they would travel overland to reach Raegar's encampment.

"I will meet you there," Skylan told them. "The Cyclopes and I will set sail after dark. You *must* wait for my signal to attack."

Skylan was adamant on that point. Bear Walker agreed. Skylan wasn't worried about the ogres obeying him. Drawing Keeper aside, he told him to keep watch on Sigurd and Grimuir, who were so eager for battle they might take it into their heads to start killing before it was time.

The Vindrasi wore leather armor that had been given to them by the gods on the isle of Joabis. Made of reindeer hide, the armor was lighter than plate and chain mail and the Vindrasi considered it stronger. Each carried the weapon he liked best, as well as gifts from the gods. Sigurd and Grimuir fought with battle axe and spear. Erdmun carried a war hammer and Bjorn had taken a liking to the Sinarian combination of spear and short sword.

The ogres wore heavy armor and carried massive shields, spears the size of trees, and either swords or axes given to them by the Gods of Raj. They had painted their faces to look particularly fearsome, with black lines across the nose and the rest of their faces a ghostly white.

Raven's-foot wore a black feather cape; he had tied feathers to the gourd and daubed his entire body in white paint.

Dela Eden had chosen thirty of her best archers to accompany her on the *Venejekar*, which was all the dragonships could carry. Those who marched with the ogres wore strange-looking armor woven of bamboo and armed themselves with clubs and knives.

Before they left, the warriors assembled in front of Skylan, who stood on a boulder to speak to them. He knew he should make an inspiring speech. He was sending this small force to face overwhelming odds and it was quite probable that none of them would return. True, they had all died once, but that did not make dying easier. He could think of nothing to say and realized that this moment was too sacred for words.

"Great Gods of Raj," said Skylan. "Mighty Torval and gods of the Vindrasi, we go to battle in your names. Grant us your blessing and victory over our foes!"

The warriors bowed their heads. The ogre shaman solemnly and reverently shook the gourd. Skylan hoped Torval wouldn't be offended that he had included the Gods of Raj in the prayer.

"Give me a spear," said Skylan.

Sigurd handed him a spear. Shouting out Torval's name, Skylan hurled the spear in the direction of the foe, dedicating them to the god. The ogres gave a cheer that shook the ground while the Cyclopes raised their voices in a shrill, eerie wail that raised the hairs on Skylan's neck.

His small force set out. Skylan contrasted these few hundred with the thousands they would soon face.

"We just have to keep Raegar occupied and give Aylaen time to find the spiritbone," he said to himself.

Touching the amulet, Skylan spoke softly. "Torval, we will make you proud."

He only hoped the god was still alive to hear him.

36

The Dragon Kahg had been keeping a watchful eye out for his foes, Fala and the traitor dragons she had persuaded to abandon the Dragon Goddess Vindrash and join Aelon. Fala claimed she didn't revere Aelon; she was serving the god in return for jewels.

There are so many gods tromping about heaven these days I don't know one from the other, Fala had once told him. *I care for no gods, any gods. Why should I? They have no care for us."*

Kahg remembered because he agreed with her. He had discovered the truth about the five spiritbones and had been furious to find out Vindrash had lied to him and the other dragons. Since then, his anger had subsided. Vindrash had paid for her folly. He was aware of the bitter battle the gods were waging against Aelon and his forces. He knew the fate that awaited the gods, no matter what the outcome.

Kahg had to admit Torval and Vindrash and the others had acted nobly, and he would do his part in honor of their sacrifice. He would do all in his power to assist the human Skylan and the Bone Priestess Aylaen to obtain the fifth spiritbone. (The fact that he remembered their names was itself a high honor; the dragon had served so many humans they all tended to blur together.)

He had one concern before he would agree to undertake this mission. He had not expressed that concern to the humans, because he knew they would not understand. While the humans were busy preparing for battle, Kahg left the ship, searching for the Dragon Fala. He found her lazily flying above the two galleys anchored in the water some distance from the shore.

Fala and the two other dragons had taken the form of earth dragons: big, bulky, and slow moving. He wondered if that had been their
choice or the choice of the human who held their spiritbones.

Kahg stopped when he was within hailing distance of the three
dragons, placing himself in a position where he could beat a swift retreat if necessary. In his form as an air dragon, he could easily outfly
and outmaneuver the ponderous earth dragons.

Fala was the first to see him and she paused in her flight, drifting
on the air currents.

"The mighty dragon Kahg," she called out to him. "Are you here
to join the victors?"

"I see no victors, Fala," said Kahg in disparaging tones. "I see three
dim-witted lizards foolish enough to serve humans who have yet to
pay them."

He had no idea if the dragons had been paid or not. He was merely
hoping to nettle Fala, lure her into giving him information. His plan
worked. She gave him information, but certainly not what he had
expected.

"We are not like you, pitiful Kahg. We no longer serve humans.
We serve only ourselves."

This was amazing news, if it was true.

"Big words from a small mind," Kahg returned, his lip curling in
a sneer. "So long as the humans hold your spiritbones, you serve
them."

"They do not hold my spiritbone," Fala returned. "The human
Raegar is a fool who murdered my Bone Priestess and would make a
slave of me. Therefore I took my spiritbone from him. He has no way
of commanding me. I do what I choose."

"So you fight for the god Aelon. You trade one master for another."

Fala was scornful. "I fight for myself. As do my two comrades."
She flew a little closer, and Kahg kept a wary eye on her. "Where are
your humans, mighty Kahg? Did you mislay them?"

"They ended up fighting each other," said Kahg. "I grew disgusted
and left."

"Come join us, Kahg," Fala said and her tone was soft and persua-
sive. "We do not need to work for humans or gods. The city is rich,
filled with jewels. We will force them to give us what we want and
then we will kill them."

Kahg was both saddened and angered to hear such talk. "We left the Realm of Fire to escape a life of such butchery. Go back there if you want to spend your days in killing and slaughter."

"The fire has gone out of your belly, airy Kahg," Fala said scornfully. "You are nothing now but a bag of wind."

She preened, pleased with her jest.

Kahg was weary of this conversation. He had found out what he needed to know, although at this point he wondered why he had bothered.

"May you someday learn better sense, foolish Fala," he told her.

He turned his spiky back on her and flew away, taking his time, not to seem to be fleeing from her.

"May you someday fall from the skies, mighty Kahg!" Fala angrily cried and tried to chase after him. She flew for only a short distance before giving up the pursuit. Kahg gave an inward smile. Even a dim-wit like Fala could see that an earth dragon was no match for a swift-flying dragon of air.

Winging his way back to the *Venejekar*, Kahg reflected on what she had told him. She and the others had taken back their spiritbones. He had been worried that the humans were carrying the spiritbones of the dragons. If he killed the humans, he might well have killed the dragons and he had vowed never to destroy his own kind, no matter how misguided they might be. He had seen too much of that in the Realm of Fire and he had planned to try to find a way to warn her she might be in danger, if he could do so without imperiling Skylan's mission. That was no longer necessary.

Kahg was free to act, to assist with the attack. They would strike by night, when Fala and her dragon friends were either away hunting or sleeping with full bellies. He would do his part to help Aylaen summon the dragon. He let himself dream, briefly, of meeting, perhaps even flying with, the Great Dragon Ilyrion.

He did not let himself dream long, not wanting to have to face the sorrow of disappointment. He did not have much hope for a successful outcome. The humans, Skylan and Aylaen, were well-meaning, but humans were so fragile and their foes were strong and powerful, numbering a god among them. The Vindrasi gods would try to help, but they were having difficulty helping themselves.

The Dragon Kahg knew what he would do if they failed. He would not live in a world ruled by Aelon. He would return to his home in the Realm of Fire and take his chances there.

He went back to the *Venejekar* to tell the human Skylan, whose name he still remembered, that he would undertake the mission. The dragon then said what might be his final prayer to the Dragon Goddess Vindrash.

"I know my anger has cast a shadow between us. I would not have that shadow remain. Wherever the stars guide you, Vindrash, I wish you well."

Aylis the Sun Goddess sank into the west, letting her radiance shine for what might be one last time. Tomorrow Aelon of the New Dawn might rule the world. Skylan and the Cyclopes boarded the *Venejekar* and, guided by the Dragon Kahg, the sleek, fast dragon-ship stole out of the river and sailed into the sea.

Skylan and Dela Eden scanned the darkening sky, watching for the signal from Bear Walker that the ogres were in position and they were cheered to see a single flaming arrow arc through the air, then drop back down.

The sun had disappeared and the afterglow had faded from the sky by the time the *Venejekar* sailed around Gray Beak. The white rock looked ghostly in the night. There was no wind. The waves lapped against the shore. Skylan had prayed to the Sea Goddess for calm waters and he was grateful his prayer had been answered.

The plateau and the fallen city of Tsa Kerestra came into view. The storm clouds that had swirled for centuries above the plateau were gone. The night sky was clear and cloudless and filled with so many stars that they cast their own cold, brittle light. The moon looked strange, round and fat and radiant, almost outshining the sun.

Skylan decided that Aelon must have captured the moon. The god wanted all the universe to see the glorious rout of his foes.

"You will get an eyeful," Skylan promised.

In addition to the white light of stars and moons, a bright orange glow lit the night. At first, Skylan could not figure out what it was. As the *Venejekar* slipped over the waves, drawing nearer to the Sinarian camp, they realized the glow came from enormous bonfires, lighted to celebrate victory.

Only the city of Tsa Kerestra was dark, a black blotch on the horizon. No lights shone anywhere.

Skylan looked back at the bonfires. He could see the silhouettes of people coming and going. Skylan did not like to use the magic glass that made people who were far away seem to jump suddenly at the legate's face, but he needed to see what was going on. He picked up the glass and put it to his eye.

The firelight blazed in front of him, so close it seemed he could touch it.

"What is happening?" asked Dela Eden. "Do they celebrate?"

"Joabis would be proud," Skylan replied wryly.

The soldiers of Oran were good fighters, fearless and well disciplined. Skylan had reason to know, for he had lived among them, fought with them and against them. He also knew the Sinarians drank as hard as they fought.

And why not celebrate? They had good reason. The fabled city of the Stormlords had fallen—literally so—without a blow being struck. They had won the greatest victory the world had ever known and Raegar would see to it that his men drank to his triumph and enjoyed themselves. Many were probably roaring drunk by now, including their officers.

The *Venejekar* glided swiftly over the waves, stealing close to the massive galleys. The captains would leave a few men on board to keep watch. The rowers, who were also trained soldiers, and most of the rest of the crew would be ashore.

The two enormous galleys floated at anchor within hailing distance of one another, but far enough apart so that they wouldn't collide. Lanterns hung from the bows and sterns to signal their positions. The smaller boats and wherries used to ferry men and supplies clustered around the galleys, reminding Skylan of baby ducklings huddled around their mothers.

He could hear loud talking and drunken laughter coming from the decks of the galleys. Apparently those keeping watch had been supplied with food and drink to make up for the fact that they were missing the celebration. A good captain would have seen to it that those on watch drank nothing stronger than watered wine. Judging by the sounds of raucous laughter drifting over the water, Raegar had few good captains.

Skylan stripped off his armor and gave his sword into the care of Dela Eden.

"Keep watch over Wulfe," he told her.

Dela Eden glanced at the boy, who was talking with the oceanids, and shook her head.

"The Gods of Raj go with you," she said.

Skylan slipped over the rail and dropped into the dark water, where he was immediately accosted by the oceanids, all agog with excitement, wanting to know what he was doing.

"Wulfe!" Skylan called irately, spitting out a mouthful of water. "Tell your fish friends to leave me alone!"

"They're not fish," said Wulfe.

Skylan started to say something and swallowed more water.

"They only want to help," Wulfe added.

The beautiful fae women with the sleek silvery bodies and long sea-foam hair eagerly nodded. Catching hold of Skylan, they almost dragged him under in their enthusiasm.

"They can help by keeping out of my way," Skylan said, spitting out more water as he tried to fend off the oceanids. He coughed and motioned to Dela Eden. "Send down that barrel. And stop laughing."

Grinning at him from the rail, Dela Eden used ropes to lower the barrel of resin into the water, taking care not to let it splash, though it was doubtful if anyone celebrating aboard the galleys would have heard.

The barrel landed near Skylan, briefly sank, then popped back up to the surface. They had filled the barrel only half full of resin, so that it would float. Skylan grabbed the barrel, rested his hands on it and propelled himself through the water with powerful kicking. The oceanids swam at his side, darting around him, gliding beneath him.

He swam to the largest of the small boats drifting near the closest galley and stopped in the water to watch and listen. He kept his head down, hiding among the boats that had been lashed together to keep them from drifting away.

The men on duty on the galley were playing a favorite Sinarian gambling game in which one man tossed a handful of stones on the deck while the others placed bets on how many he would throw.

Skylan heard the men shouting out the bets, groans from the losers and cheers from winners.

He raised his head. Judging by the smell, the boat he had chosen had been used to haul the cattle and pigs on which the men were probably now feasting. Skylan lifted the barrel up and over the gunwale and let it fall onto the deck, cringing at the loud thud. He waited a tense moment for someone on the galley to hear it and come investigate. The game continued uninterrupted, and he breathed easier.

He caught hold of the gunwale, and pulled himself on board the livestock boat and dropped onto the deck in a crouch so that he wouldn't be seen in the moonlight. Removing the small axe he had cinched around his waist, he chopped open the barrel and dumped the resin liberally around this boat and others lashed to it, holding his breath to keep from inhaling the fumes.

This done, he risked standing upright in order to wave his arms to let Dela Eden and her archers locate their targets. Then he slipped over the side, swam to a safe distance, treaded water, and waited.

A torch flared on board the *Venejekar*. He could see the light moving from person to person, and the smaller flares of the resin-soaked tow wrapped around the arrows bursting into flame. The archers aimed at the resin-soaked boats and fired. Some arrows fell into the water with a sizzle and others struck the hulls, but several landed in the boats. The resin burst into flame. The fire spread rapidly, and soon four boats were burning.

The Dragon Kahg appeared, sleek and silent, a dark shadow against the moonlight, his silver-gilded scales faintly shining. He circled overhead once, then dove so fast that Skylan barely had time to swim out of the way before the dragon unleashed a blast of air that hit the burning boats. His breath fanned the flames, spreading them from the four boats to others massed around the first galley.

Kahg waited until the boats were all blazing brightly. He glided over the water, drew in his breath, and blew a gust of wind on the burning mass, shoving the flaming wreckage up against the hull of the galley.

By now, the men on board the galley had caught sight of the flames and rushed to the rail to peer over the side, exclaiming in alarm at the sight of the burning boats bumping against the galley's wooden hull. One of them caught sight of Skylan's fair hair shining in the moonlight and, pointing at him, let out a yell.

Skylan grinned and waved, knowing he was safe. The fire had spread to the oarlocks and was running along the benches where the rowers sat. One of the enraged soldiers hurled a spear at Skylan. The spear splashed into the water some distance away, missing him, but reminding him that this night's work had only just begun.

He swam back to the *Venejekar*, surrounded by the excited oceanids, who were jeering at the soldiers. The Cyclopes archers shifted targets, aiming their fiery arrows at the sails and rigging aboard the galley, keeping the crew busy above deck while the fire continued to spread below.

Dela Eden helped haul Skylan back on board.

"Time to sail to shore," said Skylan.

With the dragon gone, the dragonship had to rely on rowers. The Cyclopes laid down their bows and manned the oars. They were accustomed to rowing their fishing vessels and soon the *Venejekar* was speeding over the waves, heading for the shore near the base of Gray Beak.

Handling the tiller, Skylan had his back to the flaming trireme and he had to twist to look over his shoulder to see the Dragon Kahg making another pass. This time, the dragon sucked in a huge breath and blew the galley—now engulfed in flames—toward another group of small boats surrounding the second galley, *Aelon's Miracle*.

The galley's crew was helpless to save their ship. They were few in number. The thousands of rowers needed to move the ship were all ashore, and even if they had been on board, they wouldn't have been able to extricate the ponderous galley from the blazing mass of smaller boats now setting fire to the hull.

Kahg fanned the flames and the blaze spread. The soldiers shot arrows and threw spears at him, but such puny barbs simply bounced off his scales. Sucking in another enormous breath, the dragon blew the entire mass of flaming wreckage, including the two burning galleys, toward the other ships in the fleet.

The conflagration lit the night. The soldiers on board the burning galleys abandoned ship, jumping into the water, while those aboard the ships in the path of the fire were shouting for help that was going to be slow in coming.

The *Venejekar* sailed into shallow water. Sigurd and the others ran out to help pull the ship onto the beach.

Assisted by Sigurd, Skylan hurriedly strapped on his armor. Dela Eden was making use of the magic glass, which she declared to be a marvel.

"What's going on?" he asked.

"Confusion and chaos," Dela Eden reported, grinning.

Skylan touched the amulet in thanks to Torval. The first part of the plan was working. Time to launch the second.

"They won't know what hit them," said Sigurd, handing Skylan his sword.

"They will, soon enough," Skylan said.

He buckled on his sword, his thoughts with Aylaen. The last stanzas of the song belonged to her.

38

Aylaen and Farinn stood together at the window of Owl Mother's dwelling, watching Aylis the Sun Goddess rise high into the sky. The time was almost noon. Aylaen was thinking that Skylan would be back on the *Venejekar*, making plans for tonight's attack.

"Skylan will be looking up at the very same sun," said Aylaen, "and I know what he will be thinking. That he will never live to see another sun rise. Isn't that right?"

She glanced at Farinn, who thought he should make some sort of protest, but in the end he could only nod.

"He knows that he will die this night in battle and he is not afraid, for he will go with Torval no matter where the god will wander, even into exile, cast out of this world. For that is how the song must rightly end."

"The song rightly ends when you and Skylan and the gods are safely home," said Farinn.

"That would be a good ending," said Aylaen. "But sometimes good endings are not meant to be."

"I wish you trusted me enough to tell me what you are going to do," Farinn said, brooding.

"I am going to obtain the fifth spiritbone and summon the Great Dragon Ilyrion," said Aylaen. "You know that."

"I don't think that's all," said Farinn unhappily.

"Perhaps that is all I know," said Aylaen. "Skylan and I both trust you, Farinn, and that is why he wanted you to stay with me. Whatever the future brings, you must make a record of it for our people."

"One god saw the future," said Farinn. "What Sund saw drove drove him mad."

"Sund lost his faith in men," Owl Mother said, coming up to stand behind them.

"But isn't it the other way around, Owl Mother?" Farinn argued. "Isn't mankind supposed to have faith in the gods?"

"Faith is a river that runs both ways—upstream and down," said Owl Mother. "Men have faith in their gods, but the gods must also have faith in men. Sund had too little faith in men and so he was afraid of the future. Torval had too much faith in men and he let the future go to hell. Put that in one of your songs."

"I don't understand," said Farinn.

"Someday, if all goes well, which it generally doesn't, you might," said Owl Mother. "Ah," she added somberly, cocking her head. "There it is."

They had all heard the sound of an explosion.

"What was that?" Aylaen asked, alarmed.

"The sundering of the realms," said Owl Mother and she gave a sigh, then shrugged. "Let's have supper."

She started to head for the kitchen, but she stopped, staggered a little, and put her hand to her eyes.

Aylaen put her arm around Owl Mother's shoulders. "I am sorry."

"I'm not," Owl Mother insisted, dabbing at her eyes. "Don't mind me. I'm just being an old fool. The realms are sundered and there's an end to centuries of disdain and blind conceit. The closing of the portal is something I've long advocated and I should be happy. I *am* happy."

She wiped her nose with her sleeve. "It's just going to take a little getting used to."

"What happens now?" Farinn asked.

"Tsa Kerestra will appear in this realm. The city will look the way Raegar expects it to look—stone wall, gates, silver spires, gold domes— and those of us who chose to stay will act the way Raegar expects us to act. We will negotiate terms of surrender, which, of course, Raegar has no intention of honoring. That should take all afternoon. We will open the gates at sundown."

Aylaen was pensive. "Skylan won't be expecting any of this. I think you should have told him."

"Your Skylan will figure out what to do. He's a good man, Aylaen. Maybe even a great one," said Owl Mother. "And if you tell him I said that, I'll deny it."

Owl Mother and Farinn went to "magic up" supper, as Farinn put it. Aylaen walked out to the garden that now lay in shadow to look through the chink in the wall. Raegar's armies had massed on the beach that was now within walking distance; so many soldiers that their glittering ranks, bristling with spears, seemed numberless. Three dragons flew overhead, circling, menacing. Those handling the negotiations had only to tell the wizards to look over the wall to see their doom and they would effect easy terms of surrender.

Skylan is out there somewhere, revising his plans, Aylaen thought. He has no fear for himself. He's worrying about me. He is a good man, as Owl Mother says. Maybe even a great one.

She felt connected to him, the tugging of the threads. Their wyrds could never be severed. No matter what happened.

39

As twilight came, Aylaen made her preparations. She put on the dragon-scale armor and then, one by one, removed the spirit-bones from the embroidered pouch and laid them out on the floor.

She was already wearing the Vektan Torque around her neck. She took up the second, the spiritbone that Vindrash had given the mad god Sund, and Sund had given to Aelon in the desperate hope of saving himself. She lifted the golden chain over her head. The dragon with its golden wings and emerald eyes came to rest on her breast.

She picked up the third, her wedding gift from the Sea Queen, and slid the golden bracer bedecked with pearls onto her arm. She smiled as she pinned the brooch of Joabis onto the soft leather tunic she wore beneath the armor. Pressing her hand against the Vektan Torque, she moved within her own being, trying to sense the spirit within the bones as she did when she touched the spiritbone of the Dragon Kahg, feeling it stir and quiver, a part of the living dragon. She felt nothing from these spiritbones and she wondered with a pang of fear if they were empty, dead. Perhaps the spirit of the great dragon had long ago fled the world.

Troubled, she touched the brooch of Joabis and saw again the children playing in the garden. She heard their laughter as the girl, Holma, teased her brother and the boy, Skylanson, stood at her side, both of them ready to fight each other or fight *for* each other, whichever fate offered.

Joy spread through her body, tasting like summer, warming her like honey mead, banishing fear and doubt, regret and sorrow. Such joy had been missing from the world for a long, long time. It would be her privilege, her own joy, to bring it back.

Feeling strong, prepared to face down any obstacle in her path, she was buckling on the sword of Vindrash when she heard a low-voiced conversation being carried on in the other room.

"Owl Mother, do you know what Aylaen is going to do, what will happen to her?" Farinn was asking.

"No, child, I don't," said Owl Mother. She paused and then added, "But I can guess."

"Does she know?"

"As much as a mortal can know. She was given the choice when she became Kai Priestess and she made it with her eyes open."

"Then . . . I don't suppose it would be right to try to stop her," Farinn said, dispirited.

"Your part and mine is to stand by her, young Farinn," said Owl Mother. "As if we were standing shoulder to shoulder in the shield wall. The welfare of your people depends on her and on us."

"I was scared to death in the shield wall," Farinn admitted.

Owl Mother snorted. "You'd be a damn fool if you weren't."

Aylaen walked into the room. Farinn saw the spiritbones and his lip trembled, but he managed to give her a smile, working hard to be brave and supportive.

Owl Mother scowled when she saw the shining dragon-scale armor and glittering spiritbones.

"What is wrong?" Aylaen asked, alarmed.

"Your fire burns more brightly than the sun," said Owl Mother. "You can't walk through Tsa Kerestra looking like a star fallen from the heavens. People will notice."

Rooting about in a large wooden sea chest, she dragged out a long, hooded cloak that would cover Aylaen from head to toe. She wrapped the cloak around the priestess and, indeed, the small hut seemed dark and shadowy when the light was extinguished.

"The gates of the city are opening," said Owl Mother, cocking her head, listening to some sound only she could hear. "Raegar and Aelon and the god's priests and soldiers will be entering the city. Time to go."

She put her hand on the door handle, then looked at Aylaen. "You can turn back, child."

"Skylan and my people have put their trust in me," said Aylaen.

She smiled to see Farinn brace himself, very much as if he were standing in the shield wall, taking his place beside her.

Owl Mother opened the front door and walked outside. Aylaen and Farinn started to follow her, then came to a startled halt. The quaint houses and wildflowers flourishing beneath the ancient trees had disappeared, replaced by a wide paved street, silver spires soaring into the sky, and sunlit burnished golden domes.

"This way," said Owl Mother.

She led them past marble facades, columned porticos, ornamental trees, and splashing fountains.

"But what happened to the small houses with the gardens?" Aylaen asked.

"As I said, Raegar needs to see what he expects to see. Otherwise he would grow suspicious. Our way lies up the hill, toward that shrine with the golden dome."

"Which city is real?" Farinn wondered. "And which is the illusion?"

"One could say both," said Owl Mother, looking somber. "What we thought was real turned out not to be."

As they walked up the hill, they were joined by other people, wearing robes of green and brown or blue and silver.

"Are *they* real?" Farinn whispered.

"Of course, they're real," Owl Mother snapped. "Those wearing green are from the Kingdom Below and those in blue are from the Kingdom Above. They walk together now, for both are gone."

Several greeted Owl Mother, though they did not call her that, but spoke to her by another name. She answered them with only a grunt and a snort. Aylaen noticed that although the Stormlords appeared to be aware of her and Farinn, they deliberately took no notice of them.

"Jyoti," said Aylaen to Owl Mother. "Is that your true name?"

"One of them," said Owl Mother.

Night fell fast around them. Silver spires and golden domes vanished in the darkness. They walked in the lambent light of the stars and Aelon's shining, gloating moon that turned the Stormlords into gray shadows, as if Tsa Kerestra were populated by ghosts. Aylaen shivered and reached out to clasp Farinn's hand, needing the warmth of a human touch. They were were about halfway up the hill when the silence was broken by the sound of tramping feet and jingling armor.

"Raegar," said Owl Mother.

Owl Mother took hold of Aylaen and Farinn and guided them into the shadows just as the standard-bearers, who marched first, rounded a corner, and came into view. Flaring torches shone brightly on the flags and standards of Oran, Empire of Light.

A group of priests, looking supercilious and disdainful, walked behind, chanting Aelon's praises in loud voices.

Four soldiers carrying a litter bearing a corpse marched next in line. The lower part of the body was covered with a bloody blanket, leaving the face exposed. A murmur spread among the Stormlords, who up until now had been silent.

"Baldev," said Owl Mother in bitter tones. "Right when he might have been useful in removing the magic spells, he gets himself killed. Well, that's torn the tapestry."

"But even if he's dead, the other Lords of the Storm, your brothers, can remove the magic," said Aylaen.

"They could if they were here," said Owl Mother. "Unfortunately, they're not. They left with the others."

"Left to go where?" Aylaen asked, dismayed.

"To the Realm of Fire," said Owl Mother. "When they sundered the realms, we had to choose: one realm or the other. The portal is closed. Or to be more precise, there's no longer a portal."

"But that means you'll never see your brothers again," Farinn said. "And what about your magic? We were told the Stormlords had to return periodically to the Realm of Fire to replenish it. What will happen?"

In the darkness, Aylaen could see the old woman's eyes faintly glimmer.

"Our magic will fade over time. When it does, we'll have to learn to make do without. Like the rest of you."

"I am sorry, Owl Mother," said Aylaen, clasping the old woman's hand.

"I'm not," said Owl Mother. "My people lived in two realms and did no good in either. Perhaps now that will change. The question is, what do we do about the spiritbone?"

"What we have to," said Aylaen.

Owl Mother quirked an eyebrow and glanced at Aylaen in surprise. Aylaen was herself surprised at her own calm. She had no idea how they were to remove the magical spells guarding the spiritbone, yet that didn't seem to matter. It was as if bright wings folded around her and a voice said, "Have faith."

The soldiers carrying the body marched past them. Owl Mother bowed her head and other wizards did the same.

"He was one of us," said Owl Mother.

Raegar walked last in the place of honor, surrounded by his guard, wearing a purple cloak over his armor, a golden crown, and a wide grin. He waved mockingly to the Stormlords, who watched in silence, with an air of quiet expectation and resolve. When Raegar was gone, the Stormlords continued on their way, walking toward the tower at the top of the hill.

"Is the spiritbone in the tower?" Aylaen asked. "Will all these people be there?"

"No and no," said Owl Mother. "Well, we've seen all we need to see. Best not dawdle any longer."

Taking hold of Aylaen's hand and Farinn's, Owl Mother muttered something beneath her breath and the next moment, they were standing in pitch darkness that smelled of dirt, dampness, wine, and onions.

Owl Mother struck a spark on her finger and dropped it onto a piece of cloth floating in a dish of oil. The spark glowed, the cloth caught fire, and Aylaen was startled to see that they were in what appeared to be an underground cellar.

Walls, floor, and ceiling were dirt. There were no windows and only one entrance—a wooden door, held closed by a loop of rope attached to a hook in the wall. The cellar was packed with barrels, boxes, jars, chests, jugs, and other oddments, all jumbled together.

"Why bring us to to this place?" Farinn asked. "Are we hiding from Raegar?"

"No," said Owl Mother. "In fact, this is his destination."

"A root cellar?" Farinn asked, amazed.

"A shrine," said Aylaen. "For the spiritbone."

Farinn stared at her as though she'd gone mad.

Owl Mother picked up the lamp and led Aylaen and Farinn toward the back of cellar. They had to move slowly, wending their way around wooden chests banded with iron and covered with dust, barrels stained with wine, and sacks that, judging by the smell, contained onions, apples, and various vegetables.

At the very back, Owl Mother stopped to point to what looked like the dragon-head prow of a Vindrasi ship.

"Hiding in plain sight," she said.

Aylaen took the lamp from Owl Mother and drew closer.

The prow, stashed carelessly in a corner, was covered in dirt and dust. Brushing away some of the dirt with her hand, Aylaen saw that the carving of the dragon had been done with loving care. She pictured a craftsman whiling away the lonely hours of the dark, bitter cold winter nights, giving life to a block of wood, turning it into a dragon.

The unknown craftsman had taken the time to carve each individual scale on the graceful neck. The head was a long tapered snout with the lips parted in a roar to reveal wooden fangs. The dragon's crest consisted of five spikes, four on the neck and a single large spike at the forehead. Below the crest, wide wooden eyes gazed blankly at nothing.

Aylaen rested the lamp on a barrel, causing the light to waver. The dragon's eyes flared to life and then shifted to look steadily at her. A flash of gold on the spike glinted in the fluttering flame.

Lured by the intelligence in the eyes, Aylaen looked more closely and realized the spike was made of bone, not wood, and that the crest was not a part of the prow. The crest was a helm, made to fit over the dragon's head.

"The spiritbone," Aylaen murmured and reached out toward it.

"Don't touch it!" Farinn cried, grabbing her and dragging her back. "Remember the magic!"

"Hush!" Owl Mother hissed a warning and blew out the flame.

Outside the door, Aylaen heard priests chanting the name of Aelon, the clashing of arms and the sound of booted feet marching nearer and nearer. A commanding voice called a halt. Booted feet stamped and were silent. The priests now sounded hoarse and had lost much of their enthusiasm. Their chanting straggled to a halt.

"This foul place is dark as death," said a voice. "Eolus, hand me a torch."

"Raegar!" Aylaen said in a smothered voice.

"Hush!" Owl Mother repeated.

A moment's pause, as though he were looking around, and then Raegar bellowed in anger.

"This is no shrine! It's a goddamn root cellar! We must have taken a wrong turn! Eolus, give me Baldev's map."

"You see, sir, we came up the hill to the tower that is clearly marked 'the shrine of the spiritbone.'"

"I know what it's supposed to be!" Raegar snarled. "Why isn't it?"

"Send the men away, Raegar," said a woman's voice, cold and imperious. "Order your soldiers and the priests to wait for you at the end of the street."

Raegar gave the orders and they heard the commander and his troops and the priests marching away.

"You promised me, Revered Aelon, that you would lead me to the shrine with the spiritbone," said Raegar, sounding subdued.

Owl Mother muttered, "Aelon! Damn and blast it. We have to get away from here!"

She grabbed Aylaen's hand.

"No," said Aylaen, snatching her hand away.

"You can do nothing, child!" Owl Mother argued. "We are in danger. At least, the magic will protect the spiritbone from Raegar. We can come back . . ."

"I am where I need to be," said Aylaen. "You should go and take Farinn with you."

"I'm not leaving," Farinn whispered.

"Stubborn Vindrasi fools," Owl Mother muttered.

"Stop whining, Raegar," Aelon was saying, "and trust me. The spiritbone is here. The Stormlords tried to trick you, hoping you would give up and go away."

"If that is true, not one of them will be left alive by the time I'm through with them!" Raegar said angrily. "I'll burn this city to ashes."

He must have kicked the door with his foot, for they heard wood splintering and then torchlight flared, making the room come alive as the shadows flowed across the floor and crawled up the wall.

The sight was alarming, and Raegar sucked in a startled breath. "How do I remove the magic? Baldev said powerful spells guarded the spiritbone."

"Baldev also said the spiritbone would be in a shrine, not a root cellar," Aelon retorted. "Throw down the torch. We will search using my light!"

A harsh burst of radiance filled the cellar. Owl Mother and Farinn ducked down behind a barrel. Aylaen was going to join them. Then, hearing a whisper, she stopped and turned around.

The helm shone in the god's light. The first spike, rising from the top of the helm, was made of a single bone, long and curved and sharply pointed. The other three spikes were gold twined with silver and sparkling with diamonds. The helm itself was bronze, trimmed with silver and gold.

"I know the secret to the magic," said Aylaen softly.

"Do you?" Owl Mother asked, casting Aylaen a shrewd look.

"I do," said Aylaen.

She unbuckled the sword of Vindrash and handed it to Farinn.

"Tell Skylan that our wyrds are forever bound and that no matter where I am, he will know how to find me."

She walked toward the statue of the dragon.

Farinn watched Aylaen approach the dusty dragon-head's prow that to him looked as if it had been discarded and forgotten. He longed to stop her as he had once longed to flee his place in the shield wall.

He had been so scared then that he had thought he might die of the terror before even a spear pierced his body or an axe sliced open his throat. He had stayed for only one reason, the song and the right to sing it. For he knew that if he failed his people, the song would fail him. The music would leave his soul cold and empty and without words.

He had held his place in the wall alongside the other warriors, though (Torval forgive him!) he had closed his eyes when death had thundered straight toward him. By some miracle, the wave of battle had surged around and past him, leaving him untouched, unscathed, shaking, and in wonder.

He watched Aylaen draw nearer and nearer to the old, forgotten prow and he clutched the sword of Vindrash in its sheath that she had given to him and bit his lip till the blood came, fighting the impulse to cry out, "No! Please, don't touch it! Go home and be happy!"

"You are the witness for all people," said Owl Mother softly. "You must be as brave as she is."

Her admonition helped. Farinn drew in a deep breath. Aylaen was very near the dragon.

"I heard voices! Who is there?" Raegar called out.

"It must be Skylan and his priestess!" Aelon said. "They come for the spiritbone."

"I can't see them," said Raegar. "The light is too bright. Can you see where they are?"

"I can see where they are not," Aelon replied, sounding sullen.

"That's a bloody big help!" Raegar raised his voice. "Cousin Skylan! So now I find you skulking in the shadows! I always knew you were a coward. Come fight me like a man or I will kill you and your bitch of a wife!"

Farinn shuddered and Owl Mother dragged him back behind the barrel. Aylaen appeared oblivious to Raegar's threats and the presence of the god. Her dragon-scale armor glowed in shimmering opalescence, her red hair flamed, and Farinn wondered that neither mortal nor immortal eyes could see her, for her radiance seemed to banish night. She was gazing, rapt, at the dragon, paying heed to nothing else. If she knew Raegar and Aelon were there, she did not seem to care.

Raegar waited impatiently for an answer that did not come.

"Skylan would never let such an insult stand, Revered Aelon," he said, sounding nervous. "Are you sure it's them? Maybe it's the wizards."

"Wizards! Bah!" Aelon returned with scorn. "I have pulled the teeth of those vipers. We have no time to waste. The spiritbone is here. Go fetch it."

Farinn heard the rattle and scrape of a sword sliding out of a scabbard as Raegar started moving toward them and he felt the old, sickening fear fill his mouth with gall. He looked at Owl Mother. She seemed very frail in the light, an old woman, dried up and wrinkled. The portal was closed. Perhaps her magic was already gone.

I will have to stop Raegar, Farinn thought, gripping the sword. There is no one else.

Aylaen seemed utterly entranced by the dragon. She did not look at Farinn or Owl Mother. She did not look back at the god or Raegar. Reaching out, she lifted the helm from the dragon's head.

Raegar was hampered in his search by the clutter in the cellar. Farinn heard him kick something out of the way, then there was a clatter, as if he'd bumped into something else, and finally a thud and swearing, as if something had fallen on him.

"You are a god!" Raegar cried, angry and frustrated. "Tell me where to find the damn bone!"

"I told you," said Aelon, through gritted teeth. "I cannot see."

Raegar muttered something and was about to continue when a voice hailed him from outside.

"Emperor! You are needed! The matter is urgent!"

"That's Commander Eolus calling me," said Raegar. "Something's happened."

"Something *will* happen if you don't find that spiritbone," said Aelon.

Raegar drew in a seething breath and went charging, half blind, through the shadowy storage room, heading straight for them. Farinn heard him slamming into objects, stumbling and tripping, yet coming ever closer.

Farinn drew the sword from the sheath, his hand shaking so he almost dropped it. He had no idea how to use a sword and he knew Raegar would likely laugh as he killed him, but he needed to be able to tell Skylan, when they met in the gray ruins of Torval's Hall, that he had tried.

Owl Mother's hand closed over his.

"I said you should be brave. Not foolish."

"We have to do something!" Farinn whispered, agonized.

"Have faith in the gods," said Owl Mother. "They are fighting the last battle."

Farinn scarcely heard her words. All he could hear was Raegar coming closer and closer, hurling aside objects in his impatience to reach Aylaen, who seemed to have no idea of the danger.

She was holding the helm in both hands and, as Farinn watched, diamonds sparkled and dazzled. Gold burned in her hands, setting the gold and silver of the other spiritbones ablaze.

Aelon appeared, drawn by the light.

"Raegar!" she cried, smiling, triumphant. "Come quickly. I have found her!"

The god's eyes went to the spiritbone on the golden helm, then to the others: the torque, the necklace, the bracer, and the brooch. Her gaze lingered on the spiritbones and her smile stiffened; triumph was replaced by fear. She managed to control herself, however.

"You have been deceived, Kai Priestess," said Aelon, soft and wheedling. "Your gods lied to you. The spiritbones are not life. They are death. Give the helm to me and live. . . ."

Aelon drew near, hands outstretched.

The god did not reach her. Vindrash stood in the way.

Turning her eyes to Farinn, Vindrash held out her hand. As he silently gave Vindrash the sword, the blade of which burned with her light, the goddess seemed old and frail. Aelon cast Vindrash a look of scorn and tried to pass. Vindrash raised the blade to Aelon's throat, steadfast, unwavering.

"How can you protect her? She holds your doom! Let me pass!" Aelon cried. "I will stop her, save us both!"

Vindrash shook her head. "We were not very good gods. But unlike you, we meant well. I suggest you take this time to flee, Faceless God, find some new world."

Aylaen raised the helm. Diamonds glittered. Gold gleamed. Silver flashed. Aylaen placed the glittering gold helm on her head.

Aelon, her eyes wild with fear, stumbled back.

Aylaen fell to the floor, her body limp.

Farinn gave a heartbroken cry and started to go to her. Owl Mother held him fast, and try as he might, he could not break the old woman's grip; her fingers dug into him, sharp as wyvern talons.

Vindrash dwindled and disappeared. The golden light started to fade. Aylaen lay still and unmoving. Aelon raised her head to gaze at the body. Her eyes narrowed. She made no move to approach it.

Raegar appeared, rushing into the waning light, his sword in his hand. He was disheveled, bruised, dirty, and angry.

"I have looked everywhere! You said you found her, Revered Aelon. Where is she?"

Aelon pointed to the floor. Raegar looked at the body and gave a startled gasp.

"Aylaen! Is she . . . is she dead?"

"I tried to keep her from putting on the helm," Aelon said. "The magic of the wizards killed her. The spell is broken. You can safely take the spiritbones."

Raegar stared at the corpse and gulped. Sweat rolled down his face.

"You want me to take those bones? I won't touch the evil things. That could be *me* lying there!"

"But it isn't," Aelon returned in sharp tones. "Have faith in me.

Take the helm and the other spiritbones. I assure you, you are perfectly safe."

Raegar eyed her, frowned, and made no move to obey. Instead he half turned to look back at the entrance, where the cries for the emperor were growing louder.

"Something has gone wrong." he said. "I must go find out—"

Aelon caught hold of him.

"Leave Skylan and his warriors to me! Take the spiritbones! Have you faith in me or not?" she demanded.

"Skylan!" Raegar repeated, looking back at her, his expression dark. "What do you know of Skylan? What warriors?"

Torchlight flooded the room, sending the shadows fleeing. A voice shouted.

"Sir!" Eolus shouted. "Where are you? Are you in here?"

"I'm in the back, Commander," Raegar called. "What is so urgent that you disobey my command?"

"The fleet is under attack, sir," the commander said. "The galleys are on fire and so are most of the other boats. A messenger brought the news."

"Attack . . . ," Raegar repeated.

"We do not know who the foe is, sir," Eolus added.

"I do," said Raegar, grinding the words. "Surrender terms be damned. We will butcher every man, woman, and child and put this city to the torch, starting with this foul cellar. Burn it down!"

He stared at Aelon in grim ire, then tore his arm free of her grip. Leaning close, he said to her, "If you want those accursed bones, *you* take them!"

"You will pay for this!" said Aelon.

The god vanished. Raegar grunted, turned away, and stalked out.

The torchlight grew brighter as his soldiers flooded into the cellar, setting fire to whatever they could find, then flinging the torches into the blaze. The air grew hazy with smoke. Flames crackled and the soldiers hurriedly departed.

Coughing in the smoke, Farinn ran to Aylaen. He put his hand on her wrist, beneath the bracer that held the spiritbone. Her skin was cold to the touch, and he could feel no pulse. Tears filled his eyes.

"The gods failed," he said, choked. "They let her die!"

"Do you know the secret?" Owl Mother asked, coming to stand behind him. "The secret Aylaen knew?"

"Who cares?" Farinn cried, looking up at her. "She is dead! The secret is worthless!"

"Love," said Owl Mother.

Farinn heard a sound, a soft sigh. He raised his head and looked into a radiant golden light.

The pain was terrible, but ended quickly.

Aylaen lay in the comforting darkness, feeling the five bones quiver with life. The sparkling drops of dragon blood that had once rained down upon the world combined to form an ocean and came rushing back to her in waves, filling her, nourishing her body.

The five broken bones began to knit together and other bones sprang from these five: rib bones, the thick bones of the enormous legs, the bones of a massive skull, the vertebrae of the spine, the graceful arched neck, the tip of the tail, and the thin, finer bones of the wings.

Muscle and lungs and a heart, so long stilled, now beating. Fang and claws of iron and stone. Scales of gold and silver and flame.

Her heart beat. Her blood flowed. Her wings stirred.

Aylaen opened her eyes and looked forward to the end of time and backward to the beginning.

She saw the world Ilyrion had loved, for which the great dragon had died, a tiny star in the vast forever, teeming with life, burgeoning, blossoming. She saw the world Aylaen had loved, withering, languishing without her. Her love was without end.

In that moment the wyrds of god and mortal joined.

Skylan stood on the shore watching Raegar's fleet go up in flames. The two galleys were ablaze, the fire casting a lurid orange glow over the waves, so that it seemed the ocean was burning.

"Raegar's army will have to walk home," said Bjorn, laughing.

"What's left of them when we get finished," Sigurd added with a grin.

Watching the sailors who had jumped overboard desperately swimming through the flame-streaked water, Skylan nodded agreement. Wulfe's oceanids were doing their part, swamping rescue boats and overturning them or pushing them back toward shore.

Fala and the traitor dragons must have been either still out hunting or sleeping with full bellies, for they were not around to challenge the Dragon Kahg and he was able to continue his attack unimpeded, fanning the flames with his breath and sending burning boats smashing into others that were trying frantically to escape.

Skylan wondered if Raegar was out there somewhere watching victory disappear in smoke. Skylan hoped he might meet Raegar before the end, to let him know who was responsible. But perhaps Raegar already knew. For good or ill, their own wyrds were bound.

Skylan's thoughts had no need to go to Aylaen for they were always with her. He was wondering where she was, if she was safe, if she had found the spiritbone. Sigurd rudely jostled him.

"Are we going to admire the view or do some killing?" he asked impatiently.

Bear Walker growled in agreement, and the rest of the ogre warriors shook their spears in the air or clashed their swords against their shields. Dela Eden and her Cyclopes waited in silence, armed with clubs and knives, ready to do what needed to be done. Skylan observed the confusion in the enemy camp and judged that it was time to put the second part of his plan into action.

"Our goal is to spread as much destruction and chaos as we can in the short amount of time we will have," he reminded his warriors. "We will be facing well trained and disciplined troops and we must stay together, not run wild."

He looked particularly at Sigurd as he said this. "If Raegar's soldiers manage to separate us, split us apart, they will cut us to pieces.

"This means"—Skylan now fixed a stern gaze on Dela Eden and her Cyclopes—"you must listen for my signals and heed my commands. We face an army of thousands. When the time comes, we will stand together and fight."

He almost said "fight our last fight," but caught himself just in time. The others knew as well as he did that this battle would likely end in death, but no need to say the bad luck words.

Dela Eden gathered her Cyclopes around her and spoke to them in a low voice, perhaps saying some sort of prayer to the Gods of Raj, for many of them bowed their heads. Raven's-foot rattled the gourd at Bear Walker and the rest of the ogres. He was about to rattle it at Skylan, who glowered at him. The ogre shaman thought better of it.

Sigurd and Grimuir were making bets on who would kill the most men. Bjorn was talking quietly with Erdmun. As usual before a battle, he was looking sick.

"What do you need me to do?" Wulfe called.

"What are you doing here? I told you to keep away from us," said Skylan irritably. He had lost track of the boy and was annoyed to see him lurking in the tall grass that covered the sand dunes.

"I want to help," said Wulfe.

Skylan felt inclined to point out that it would be difficult for Wulfe to help with the fighting while keeping a safe distance from the warriors and their iron weapons.

"I don't have time to argue, Wulfe," Skylan said, growing impatient.

"I don't want to go back to my mother," said Wulfe. "I already told you that."

"Go wherever you want to go, then! Jump in the sea with your fish friends," Skylan said, exasperated. "Just stay away from the fighting!"

Wulfe scowled, but he left, walking off down the beach, though he was slow about it, his steps dragging. Skylan bid the boy a silent farewell, wondering briefly if the fae child would remember him after he was gone and, if so, for how long.

Skylan shifted his attention to the campfires of their foes, to the rows of tents that stretched on and on in seemingly endless ranks and the hundreds and hundreds of soldiers milling about like angry hornets searching for the foe that had knocked down their nest.

Skylan put his hand to the amulet. "Torval, strengthen my sword arm and embolden my warriors, and, although this might be the end of our song, we will make this a song to be sung for generations."

His last thought was for Aylaen. He pictured her grieving his death, as she had grieved for him once before, knowing this time he would not return. He imagined her walking the sunlit shore, going on with her life, leading her people, keeping him in her heart.

He kissed the amulet and added, "Watch over her and, if it be possible, Torval, let me meet Raegar one last time!"

Skylan drew his sword.

"For Torval!" he cried.

"For Torval!" the Vindrasi yelled.

"For the Gods of Raj!" Raven's-foot howled.

Armed with spear and sword, shield and hammer, axes and clubs and a gourd, Skylan and his warriors ran, thundering like Torval's wrath, headlong toward their foes.

Wulfe didn't like the stench of iron and the thought of the fighting and dying made his stomach shrivel. He didn't want to stay and at the same time he didn't want to go. He resented being told to run off to his mother, as if he were some stupid Ugly child. His mother and her court would be watching the battle from a safe distance, of course, for the fae were always amused by the spectacle of the Uglies killing each other.

Wulfe didn't want to be safe. He wanted to help Skylan. He just needed to think of some way to help that didn't involve coming anywhere near swords and axes and bloody entrails. He flattened himself among the grass-covered sand dunes and slunk on his belly, doglike, as close to Skylan as he dared.

Skylan was talking to his Ugly god.

"And if it be possible, Torval, let me meet Raegar one last time!"

Wulfe pricked his ears. He hated Raegar, who had beaten him and sent soldiers to kill him. The Uglies believed faeries could grant wishes, or so his mother had told him.

Stupid Uglies.

Yet perhaps Wulfe could grant Skylan's.

Wulfe watched Skylan and the other warriors eagerly rush toward death and then he stood up, scratched himself, and looked into the fire-lit water where some of the oceanids, his adoring subjects, were swimming in the shallows, hoping to be of use to their prince.

Wulfe waded into the sea and the oceanids eagerly gathered around him and asked if wanted to join their friends, who were screeching with delight at the fun of capsizing boats and watching the Uglies flounder in the water. Wulfe was tempted, but he declined, holding fast to his resolve.

"I need to find the Big Ugly," he told them. "The one with the purple cape and silly crown."

The oceanids laughed. "A centaur said the one who calls himself emperor went into the city."

Chewing his lip, Wulfe walked toward the gate of the walled city on the plateau. The gate was surrounded by soldiers who were covered head to toe in iron. He had no idea how to find Raegar or what he was going to do to bring Raegar and Skylan together, but Wulfe wasn't worried. The fae never planned ahead. As his grandmother said, the future was the present in one eye blink and the past in another, so why bother?

He was confident he'd think of something when the time came.

43

S kylan could see the light of campfires reflected off shining breast-plates and helms. The soldiers who had been tasked to guard the camp's perimeter had remained at their posts despite the celebrating, although their comrades had seen to it that they had their share of the food and wine. The sight of an unknown foe coming out of the night to attack their ships caused them to drop their flagons and grab their weapons.

The guards were few in number. Beyond them were the first rows of tents, barrels, and wagons filled with supplies and stacks of armaments.

The guards were obviously nervous, their attention divided between watching the flames devour one ship after the next, and peering out into the night. They heard Skylan's force before they saw it and he could imagine their growing fear and uncertainty, as they listened to the howls of the ogres and the uncanny wailing of the Cyclopes, and felt the ground shake with the thudding of many feet.

Moonlight glimmered off swords and shields, and battle lust glittered in the eyes of those who had given themselves into the hands of the gods. His warriors surged through the camp like a tidal wave of blood, smashing and breaking, stabbing and slashing and trampling men underfoot, setting fires as they ran. The guards shouted a warning and then died.

The warning came too late. The soldiers of Oran were overwhelmed by the suddenness and ferocity of the attack. Thinking the war won, they had laid aside their weapons to celebrate and had to scramble to arm themselves. Many had run into the sea to try to save the burning ships, leaving their camps deserted. Some took one look at the rampaging warriors and bolted for the woods. Those brave enough to stand their ground met death instantly, speared, decapitated, or trampled. Skylan and the ogres stopped only long enough to grab torches or snatch blazing branches from the bonfires and hurl them into tents, setting them ablaze, while the Cyclopes smashed water barrels and set fire to wagons, food supplies, and stacks of weapons.

Faces popped up in front of Skylan and were gone in a sword stroke. Beside him, Sigurd was bloodied to the armpits, eerily laughing as he swung his axe, chopping down foes as though cutting through wheat. Grimuir matched Sigurd, though without the unnerving laughter. Bjorn was workmanlike, methodical, while his brother, Erdmun, slashed wildly at anything that moved.

Bear Walker wielded a gigantic sword and carried a shield as big as a house and, like all the ogres, started the battle with a fistful of spears that he hurled with deadly accuracy or drove clean through breastplates. Raven's-foot howled and cast his shamanistic magic, freezing soldiers dead in their tracks with a rattle of the gourd.

Glancing back, Skylan was amazed to see how much ground they had covered and all of them relatively unscathed. Flames crackled, the air was thick with smoke, and soldiers lay dead or groaning. He could also see the lumbering ogres were slowing down, falling behind, and the Cyclopes were scattered all over the beach. He caught up with Sigurd, who was racing ahead with Grimuir, both mad with battle lust.

"Run, you pissants!" Sigurd was shouting at the soldiers. "Run all the way back to Sinaria!"

Skylan gave Sigurd a shove in the back, causing him to stumble. Sigurd turned to glare at him.

"What did you do that for?"

"Slow down!" Skylan commanded. "Wait for the ogres and the Cyclopes. We can't get separated."

Sigurd glowered, but then obeyed. Grimuir came over to join him, all of them gasping for breath. Sigurd and Grimuir were so slathered in blood Skylan couldn't tell if they'd been wounded and he doubted if they could either.

"I think our road has reached its end," Skylan said.

They could all now hear beating drums and see what they had long been expecting to see: officers trying to calm the chaos, attempting to gain some sort of control of their troops. To Skylan's surprise, Sigurd gripped him by both shoulders.

"You have taken us on an amazing journey, Skylan," said the older man. "And this last battle—the best of all. I haven't said it," he added gruffly, "but you have turned out to be a good chief. I am proud to stand in the shield wall with you."

Skylan was taken aback, didn't know what to say. Fortunately by this time, the ogres and the Cyclopes were catching up to them. Sigurd changed his grip on Skylan's shoulders to a punch, then turned to make some undoubtedly crude remark to Grimuir.

Skylan greeted Bear Walker and Dela Eden, pleased to see that both were unhurt. They reported that their people had suffered few casualties thus far. Both knew that couldn't last.

"And do not expect help from your dragon," said Dela Eden.

Skylan glanced overhead to see three shadows wheeling among the stars. Raegar's three dragons had apparently heard the battle and were closing in on Kahg, who was still wreaking havoc among the Sinarian fleet. The dragon had long vowed he would never fight his own kind, but he might not have a choice. Skylan wished the dragon well and turned back to his own problems.

He had been keeping watch for some high ground on which to make a stand and although the ridge of dunes rising between him and the sea wasn't ideal, it would have to do.

"Form the shield wall!" Skylan bellowed out the command and Sigurd and the other Vindrasi passed the word all had been waiting to hear.

Cyclopes archers had shot the last of their flaming arrows into two massive siege engines. Wooden towers mounted on wheels, they blazed into pillars of flame that lit the camp as bright as day.

The ogres, led by Bear Walker, began jostling with one another for places. Dela Eden and her Cyclopes had used up all their arrows and they melted into the night, waiting with club and knife to rush into the melee to strike when least expected.

Skylan took his place at the center of the front row. He put Sigurd on his left and Bjorn on his right, their shields overlapping. Keeper stood behind him, a solid wall, ready with the other ogres in the second row to support the front row and keep them from breaking.

Sigurd was laughing with Grimuir, who was on his left. Bjorn smiled confidently. To his right, his brother, Erdmun, was looking nervous and sick and casting glances over his shoulder as though searching for some place to hide. The immense ogre standing behind him would see to it that he did not try to retreat.

Not that there was anywhere to go if he did, Skylan reflected. Their backs were to the sea.

If Aelon's soldiers had been prepared for battle, they would have easily routed his smaller force. His attack on the ships and now the raid on the camp had taken the Sinarian troops by surprise, thrown them into confusion and turmoil. Surprise was over, replaced by fury.

Soldiers began forming into ragged ranks, armed with whatever weapons they had been able to grab.

Skylan's warriors stood quietly, no one taunting or jeering at the enemy, who would come soon enough. Skylan was under no illusions. The Sinarians were well-trained, disciplined soldiers who would sober up and remember their training and their discipline.

Skylan looked at his men, his heart aching with pride.

"We will meet in Torval's Hall," he cried, raising his sword. "If we have to rebuild the damn thing ourselves!"

His words brought laughter and a cheer and they braced themselves for the end of the song.

W ulfe crouched in the waves that lapped onto a strip of beach not far from the city gates and wondered what he was going to do now. He'd been stranded here in the shallows for some time, his way into the city blocked by enemy soldiers milling about on the beach below the plateau.

He shook his wet hair out of his eyes and studied the situation. The large, flat plateau on which the city was built rose out of the grassy dunes some distance from the beach. The city wall was situated almost on the edge of the plateau, leaving only a very narrow strip of land between. Anyone walking out the gates who took more than ten steps would walk off the rim of the plateau and end up, after a short tumble, on the beach below. The only way into the city was along a narrow road winding up the rise to the top of the plateau.

No iron wielding soldiers were on this stretch of beach. They were massed outside the city gates, most of them drunk and eager to start looting and killing. The fae had gathered here, some distance away, to watch the exciting events in safety and exchange the latest gossip, among them several satyrs who had come to the water's edge to tease the oceanids.

Wulfe was still trying to locate Raegar and he had asked the satyrs if they had seen an Ugly matching his description, saying he was taller and uglier than all the other Uglies, strong and powerfully built and wearing a long, purple mantle. The satyrs remembered him seeing him enter the city or they thought they remembered him or they wanted to remember him, but couldn't quite.

The one good piece of news was that at least no one remembered seeing Raegar leave the city.

Catching sight of a centaur who had strolled over to watch the fighting, Wulfe climbed out of the water, shaking himself like a dog, and went to speak to him. Centaurs were considered prideful by many of the other fae, because their horse bodies were strong and powerful. They were more serious minded, and they feared very little.

The centaur acknowledged Wulfe with a dignified nod of the head, introducing himself as Swiftwind. The two satyrs quit teasing the oceanids and came to join them, while the oceanids swam about in the shallows, keeping a fond eye on Wulfe and a distrustful eye on the satyrs. The centaur held himself aloof from both satyrs and oceanids, though he was gracious to his prince.

Wulfe again described Raegar.

"I saw a fine warhorse carry one of the Uglies to the gate," the centaur offered. "I don't think he was the one you describe, but I heard him tell the other Uglies that he had an urgent message for the emperor and the Uglies let him inside the gate. That's all I know."

"You could always ask the ghouls," one of the satyrs suggested, snickering.

The oceanids were appalled and cried out in anger, "No, our prince cannot talk to ghouls! Get away, get away and stop bothering us!"

And they splashed water on the satyrs until they grew annoyed and sauntered off.

"The satyrs are right," said Swiftwind, keeping his voice low so that the oceanids would not hear him. "The ghouls are hungry and they have been keeping watch on their prey."

Wulfe eyed the loathsome creatures hiding in the shadows near the gate with a shiver.

Ghouls were evil fae who gathered at the site of battles to feed on the bodies of the dead. The fae wouldn't have minded so much if the ghouls ate only dead Uglies, but during the First War between faeries and humans, the ghouls had fed on their own kind.

"I will talk to them," said Wulfe, sending the oceanids into a frenzy.

"Do not go near those fiends, Your Highness!" the oceanids begged him, fluttering in alarm. "Your mother would not like it!"

Their wailings angered the centaur.

"Leave him be, women," Swiftwind said sternly. "Don't make a prattling mama's boy of our prince." He reached out his hand to Wulfe. "I'll take you to the ghouls, Your Highness. Climb on my back."

Swiftwind took hold of Wulfe's hand and pulled him up on his broad horse back that began at the centaur's torso. Swiftwind was a male centaur; his human face was handsome and chiseled, with a long mane of hair that extended down his human back.

"Don't go tattling to my mother," Wulfe ordered the oceanids, who were watching him anxiously from the water.

They promised him they wouldn't, though he had seen several swim off to do that very thing.

"I'm not afraid of the ghouls," Wulfe boasted to the centaur as they galloped along the beach. He hoped that saying the words aloud might make them true.

"Nor should you be, Your Highness," said Swiftwind in disdainful tones. "Ghouls are craven cowards who feast on dead men because they are terrified of the living."

Wulfe could understand why ghouls would not dare come near Swiftwind. Unlike many fae, centaurs were expert in using weapons. Swiftwind carried a bow bigger than Wulfe and a quiver of stone-tipped arrows slung over his shoulder. With the powerful arms of a human and the slashing hooves of a horse, centaurs had no fear of iron and had been known to battle Uglies.

"I don't want the soldiers to see me," Wulfe told the centaur. "Is there a back way to reach the gate?"

Swiftwind investigated and found a wide, deep crevice in the rock that would take them near the top of the plateau. He climbed swiftly and with ease until they reached the shadows of the wall and Wulfe called a halt, fearing the ghouls would catch sight of the centaur and flee in a panic. He slid off the centaur's broad back.

Swiftwind offered to wait to make certain the boy didn't get into trouble. Since getting into trouble was Wulfe's goal, he didn't think the centaur would be much help, so he thanked Swiftwind and said he could manage on his own. The centaur raised his head, said he heard sounds of battle, and, wishing his prince well, galloped off to view the fighting.

Wulfe heard the sounds of battle himself and thought that Skylan was likely in the middle of it, and he had better hurry. He crept along in the shadow of the wall, sneaking up on five ghouls, who had their backs turned, gazing hungrily at the gate and the soldiers guarding it.

Wulfe could see them clearly in the moonlight and they were even more loathsome up close. Always ravenous, with a hunger that could never be sated, ghouls were thin and gaunt with bulbous heads on skinny necks, wide mouths filled with long, sharp teeth and pale skin drawn tight over fleshless bones. Their ragged clothes were stained with the leavings of their feasts and the stench made Wulfe sick to his stomach.

He was very close now, priding himself on his stealth, when one of the ghouls pricked up its ears, hissed a warning, and turned to stare at him with lidless eyes.

Wulfe stared back, hard and unblinking, until one of the ghouls seemed to shrivel and shrink away from him.

"What are you looking at?" a ghoul asked Wulfe, leering.

"He's His Highness," the groveling ghoul warned.

"His Highness should find his own food," another growled, fixing Wulfe with a hungry gaze. "He eats well enough, by the looks of him."

Wulfe repeated to himself that he wasn't afraid, then said, putting on a bold front, "I want to know if you have seen an Ugly wearing a purple cape. He's really big."

"We saw him. Lots of meat on his bones," said one of the ghouls as the others began to gibber and drool.

Wulfe gave himself a moment to appreciate the thought of Raegar being devoured, then returned to business.

"Is he still inside the city? Did you see him come out?"

"He is still inside," said several, licking their bloodless lips.

"He will make a fine, fat corpse," said another.

"Not skinny, like His Highness," said a third, reaching out a blood-stained, filthy finger to poke at Wulfe.

Wulfe bared his teeth and growled, and the ghouls slunk off. Keeping to the shadows, Wulfe drew nearer the gate. The guards were watching the ships burning and saying that the emperor would be angry and he would make whoever was responsible pay with their blood.

Wulfe had been trying to think of how he would bring Raegar and Skylan together and this gave him an idea. Raegar would be furious at any foe who had set fire to his fleet and he'd be out-of-his-mind furious when he knew that person was Skylan.

But here was Raegar in the city at one end of the beach and there was Skylan fighting at the other end. Wulfe needed to bring the two together and suddenly he knew how to do it. The problem was that he had never worked such powerful magic himself. He'd seen it done; other fae used it all the time to play tricks on the Uglies.

He was reciting to himself over and over the spell he was going to cast when he heard the clatter of horse's hooves and Raegar's voice bellowing for the guards to open the gate.

The guards sprang to obey, lifting the heavy bar that kept the gate closed. Wulfe began to sing softly to himself.

> *I can be*
> *Any face I see.*
> *Make you think*
> *I am not me.*

The magic started to work. Wulfe watched his short, scrawny body grow tall and muscular. He added leather armor and long, blond hair and a face he knew better than his own. The guards hauled on the gate and Raegar, mounted on a horse, galloped out onto the road. He took one look at the burning galleys and gnashed his teeth.

"Who did this?" he demanded.

"I did!" Wulfe shouted and he jumped to Raegar's side, put his hand on the horse's bridle, looked at Raegar and said, "Me—Skylan Ivorson! What are you going to do about it?"

Raegar stared at him blankly, then his face contorted, his mouth twisted, his eyes blazed. Roaring in fury, he reached for his sword.

Wulfe made a crude gesture and ran off down the road, heading for the beach.

"Don't just stand there! Stop him! Seize him!" Raegar yelled at the soldiers around him.

No one obeyed him. The soldiers were running headlong for the open gates, pouring into the fallen city to claim the spoils of war. Wulfe heard Raegar swearing at them, and he grinned as he ran.

The beauty of this magic spell was that it worked only on someone who either loved or hated with such passion that he would believe in his heart that the illusion was real, even though his head told him it couldn't possibly be true. For if Raegar had stopped to think, he must have wondered why Skylan was now seven feet tall. Wulfe had been a bit off on his calculations.

Raegar didn't take time to think. He kicked his horse in the flanks and charged after Wulfe, forcing those in his path to leap out of the way or be trampled.

Wulfe ran onto the beach with Raegar galloping behind. All Wulfe had to do now was find Skylan.

The real Skylan.

45

The burning siege engine blazed like a huge torch, shedding a lurid orange glow over the beach, seeming to vie with the bright, cold moon to see who could best illuminate the field of battle. The moonlight glittered on the swords and armor of Aelon's soldiers, rank after rank, stretching far into the night. Flames tipped spears and shone in the eyes of Skylan and his warriors lined up shoulder to shoulder, shields overlapping.

The soldiers of Oran cast grim glances at each other, no one wanting to lead the charge. Skylan grinned in sympathy. He had faced ogres in a shield wall and knew that the first wave crashing against those boulder-size bodies would end up in a foaming, churning mass of blood and bone.

Even as he thought this, he heard a command and the jingling of armor and felt the ground shudder as the soldiers began to march toward them.

Spears leveled, weapons in hand, shields locked, Skylan and his warriors braced for the shock as the front ranks crashed into them. Ogre spears pierced helms and shattered skulls. A Sinarian spear point thudded into Skylan's shield. The spear split in two the next moment when a second spear slammed into it.

Skylan used his shield to block a sword strike aimed at Sigurd, driving God-rage into the Sinarian's throat. He was vaguely aware of Keeper, behind him, reaching over him to jab his spear into the chest of a soldier about to cleave open his head.

After that, all Skylan saw were flashes of bloodied steel and disembodied faces set in fierce grimaces, intent upon killing. He fought and ducked, kicked and stabbed. God-rage shone red in the fire's light.

Men screamed and the faces vanished, only to be replaced by more. His hand was slippery with blood and then the faces were gone. The Sinarians had fallen back to rest and regroup and drag their wounded from the field.

Skylan gasped for breath, grateful for the respite, and looked swiftly up and down the line. Their shield wall had held.

Erdmun had fallen, but one of the ogres in the row behind had stepped up to take his place. Sigurd was grinning and wiping blood and sweat from his face. Grimuir had lost his own helm and replaced it with one from the corpse of a Sinarian. Bjorn was grim and tight-lipped.

"What happened to Erdmun?" Skylan asked.

Bjorn only shook his head.

The Sinarian ranks came again, as more and more soldiers heard the clash of arms and hurried to join the battle. Their blood burning, the soldiers shouted in anger as they ran, heedlessly trampling the bodies of the dead, and smashed into the shield wall.

Three men crashed into Skylan, knocking him off balance. He floundered in the wet sand, desperate to stay on his feet, for if he went down he was finished. The three slashed at him, but they were so tightly bunched together none of them could manage to hit him. Sigurd dispatched one and Bjorn attacked another. Keeper caught hold of Skylan by the scruff of his neck and hauled him upright.

"You're wounded!" the ogre roared.

Skylan felt a vague burning pain somewhere; the blood on his armor did not all belong to his foe. He was still standing, still breathing, still able to wield his sword, however, and he shook his head.

Keeper gave a great heave and shoved Skylan back into the battle just as the front line of the shield wall crumbled. Sinarian soldiers flooded through the gaps and Skylan was fighting Sinarians on both sides. He slashed a soldier's sword arm open to the bone, causing him to drop his weapon, and backhanded another in the face with the sword's hilt, breaking his jaw and sending him reeling. Before Skylan could recover, a soldier darted through the opening left by his fallen comrade to finish Skylan with a vicious slice of his short sword across his neck.

Skylan ducked and the blow meant to cut off his head glanced off his helm and sliced open his cheek. He jabbed his sword into the man's breastplate, hoping to gain time by shoving the soldier off him until he could reestablish his footing. To his astonishment, God-rage pierced through the metal and the flesh and bone beneath and tore into the soldier's vitals. The man screamed as blood flowed down the breastplate. Skylan jerked his sword free and the man slid off the blood-smeared blade and hit the ground.

Skylan looked up to see two more Sinarian soldiers stare in shock at their dead comrade and then glance fearfully at Skylan's sword. The two veered off, seeking easier prey. Skylan touched the amulet and said a prayer of thanks, then looked around for another foe, only to find that the battle had flowed past him.

He paused to catch his breath and that was a mistake, for now he felt the pain of his wounds. Blood oozed out from beneath his breastplate and it hurt to breathe. He gave the pain to Torval and turned back to the battle to see where he was needed.

The front line of the shield wall had vanished and the ogres in the second line wavered. Bear Walker bellowed a command, urging them to press forward. The shield wall gave a great heave and the howling ogres bowled over the Sinarians, trampling them beneath their feet and swinging their axes like scythes.

Skylan cheered hoarsely, though he knew he was watching the last defiant gesture of the doomed. Sinarian soldiers fell before the ogres, but he could see more flooding in behind them, attacking the ogres as well as the Cyclopes, who had been holding the rear.

Skylan was about to join them when he saw, to his amazement, another Skylan standing only a few feet away, shouting and yelling and waving his arms. Even more astonishing, this second Skylan was as tall as a giant, half naked, bare chested, and carrying neither sword nor shield.

Skylan put his hand to his head where the sword had struck him. He had started seeing ghosts of himself, and he shut his eyes to make it go away. He opened his eyes again, only to see himself still standing on the beach and a man mounted on horseback charging at him. Firelight shone on the man's face and Skylan recognized Raegar.

Skylan shouted in triumph, crying out Torval's name.

The ghost Skylan suddenly vanished and in his place stood a wolf.

The beast turned its golden eyes on Skylan, then fled across the sand and into the forest.

Skylan turned back to Raegar, who had been riding recklessly, leaning half out of his saddle, his sword raised, readying to cut down his foe, when his foe changed into a wolf before his eyes. Raegar pulled at the reins with such force that the horse reared up, hooves flailing, unseating its rider. Raegar fell heavily to the sand. Cursing the horse, he picked himself up, unhurt.

Skylan stood over him.

"Well met, Cousin," he said.

Raegar blinked, confused, glancing to the empty place in the sand where Skylan had been standing to where this Skylan now stood—a Skylan covered in blood, wearing dented armor, and carrying a sword that seemed to blaze with fire.

Raegar gave a shrug, as if to shake off the strange occurrence. He was wearing his ceremonial armor and a purple cape that had torn loose from one of the shoulder clasps and dragged on the ground. With an impatient yank, he tore it loose and let it fall.

Looking closely, Skylan saw no sign of a spiritbone, no torque or brooch, and he smiled. His plan had worked. Raegar looked past Skylan to the battle and *he* smiled. Skylan had no need to look. He knew what he would see—his own forces being driven back step by bloody step into the sea.

"We may have lost, but you have not won, Cousin!" Skylan shouted over the din of battle. "You do not have the spiritbone."

"No one has it," Raegar returned, his voice grating. "Aylaen is dead."

The words struck Skylan a mortal blow, driving into his gut, cutting off his breath, draining his life's blood.

"You killed her!" he cried, lunging at Raegar, who managed at the last moment to raise his sword in time to block Skylan's blow. The two closed, grappling.

"I did not kill her, Cousin," Raegar hissed, his breath hot on Skylan's face. "Your own gods killed her. Aylaen found the fifth spiritbone and fell down dead."

"I don't believe you," Skylan said through grit teeth as the two heaved back and forth. "She is not dead!"

"I can prove it!" Raegar snarled. "Where are the Vektia dragons?

If Aylaen was alive, she would have summoned them. Yet all I see is the bright light of Aelon's glory."

"All I see is the bright fire of your defeat!" Skylan roared.

Raegar gave a great heave and shoved Skylan with a force that sent him staggering. His foot turned in the wet sand and he fell heavily onto one knee and did not immediately rise.

Raegar stood nearby, watching him suspiciously, fearing Skylan was merely feigning injury in order to lure him into some deadly trap.

Skylan was not pretending. He knew in his soul Raegar was telling the truth. Aylaen was dead. He was suddenly very tired, with the weariness that comes from loss of blood and, worse, loss of hope. He did not see the light of a grinning moon. He saw only bleak and unending night. His plan had failed. He had led his men to death and defeat for nothing and left his people to the mercies of Aelon.

The spiritbones that were supposed to be their salvation had instead been their doom. Perhaps the gods had lied. Perhaps they had been mistaken. None of that mattered, for they, too, had paid a terrible price. Skylan wanted only to die, to meet Aylaen in the ashes of Torval's Hall, and hold her close throughout eternity.

He had something to do first, however.

Skylan paid no heed to the fighting, to the cries and screams of men bleeding, dying. His battle came down to one man.

By his looks, Raegar had been enjoying the life of an emperor. The muscular arms and shoulders were soft and flabby, his pudgy gut leaked out from beneath his breastplate. His face was puffy from an overindulgence in wine, and shining with sweat and he was breathing hard from even their brief encounter.

Skylan rose slowly, limping, favoring his right knee.

Raegar watched him, shifted the sword to his left hand to flex his fingers and wipe the sweat from his face, then nervously shifted it back. He seemed to have just realized that he was in a dangerous predicament, for he was alone and on foot in the midst of a raging battle, with no guards, no elite troops to protect him. In his mad pursuit of Wulfe, Raegar had left his retinue behind and now he was looking for help.

"You men, there, I need you!" he shouted to a group of soldiers running past to join the fighting.

The men glanced at him in the light of the flames that flared up to illuminate faces, only to plunge them again into shadow. Seen dimly by darkness and fire, Raegar was just another foot soldier. The men kept running.

"I am your emperor!" Raegar angrily shouted after them. His cry was lost in the din.

"You will have to kill me yourself," said Skylan.

Raegar gave a grim smile and took up a fighting stance, planting his feet firmly in the sand. "And this time I *will* kill you, Cousin! No god can save you now."

Raegar may have grown fat and sleek from good living, but Skylan didn't underestimate his cousin. Raegar was a Vindrasi; he'd been raised to battle. He was taller than Skylan, with a longer reach, and he was not using the standard Sinarian short sword. Raegar had his own sword, an enormous weapon, made of steel, finely crafted. And although flabby and out of shape, Raegar was still as strong as an ox.

Skylan had one advantage: Raegar had everything to lose and Skylan had lost everything.

Once before, Skylan had given himself to the madness of Torval, a state of being in which a warrior loses all sense of fear. Time slows so that he is keenly aware of every second, seeing everything around him in minute detail with astonishing clarity. The madness can open a warrior's eyes, give him insight into his foe. The madness leads to glory.

Skylan could feel the warm sticky blood running down his leg; he could feel his life ebbing away. In the heavens, Torval was watching his great Hall burn. Glory for both man and god had turned to blood and ashes and the bitter grief of loss. Skylan did not give himself to Torval's madness. He joined Torval in his despair. He had one last goal to achieve before he joined Torval in death—to avenge his gods, his people, and Aylaen.

Skylan limped until he deemed he was close enough to Raegar to attack, then his limp drastically improved. He sprang at Raegar, hoping to catch him flat-footed, aiming to drive his blade into Raegar's throat. Soft living had not dulled Raegar's reflexes, however. He knocked Skylan's sword aside and kicked Skylan in the shin.

Skylan staggered, almost losing his balance, and Raegar was quick to follow his advantage, lifting the blade to bring it down on Skylan's head, cleave through his helm and split his skull.

Skylan shifted to one side and Raegar's blade whistled past him with such force that his sword stuck in the sand. He yanked his blade free with a curse, but Skylan used the time to try to drive his sword into the gap left between Raegar's breastplate and belt. Raegar twisted around, swinging his sword in an arc, striking Skylan's sword a jarring blow that sent stingers through his arm and numbed it to the elbow.

Skylan had to stumble back, transferring the sword from his useless right hand to his left. As he was wiggling his fingers to try to get some feeling into them, he was assailed by a sudden sickening wave of faintness—the herald of death. Skylan swore and fought to hang on. His head cleared in time to see Raegar charging at him.

Skylan still had no feeling in his right hand and he was forced to clumsily block the blow with his left. He managed to deflect the killing stroke, but the blade stabbed into his midriff. Ribs broke and blood spurted and pain tore at him from somewhere deep inside. Groaning, he sagged to the ground.

He tried to get back up, but he was too weak. He could not stand, but yet he would not fall. Not before Raegar. On his knees, Skylan lifted his sword.

"Why aren't you dead?" Raegar shouted, his face twisted in fury.

He ran at Skylan, who managed with his waning strength to slash the blade across Raegar's legs. God-rage bit deep through the ornate heavy leather boots into muscle and tendons and bone, and Raegar stumbled and fell, clutching his bloody shins and howling in pain.

Skylan sank to the ground and, lying there, felt the world quake and shiver.

At first, Skylan dazedly imagined the tremor was Freilis, the Goddess of the Tally, coming for him. The shaking grew stronger; the ground rolled beneath him. Raegar had quit howling and staggered to his feet, looking about in fear and wonder as the charred remains of the siege tower toppled and crashed to the ground in a shower of sparks.

Soldiers were shouting in alarm and pointing toward the city. Golden domes and silver spires and stone walls shone with a brilliant golden radiance. Tsa Kerestra blazed like a star and suddenly everyone on the beach could hear panicked shouts and terrified cries coming from those soldiers who had rushed inside the city to loot and kill. They cried out in fear and then fell horribly silent.

As the morning mists faded with the dawning of day, Tsa Kerestra disappeared. The pale, brittle light of Aelon's moon shone on an enormous dragon with scales of shining gold flying above an empty, flat, and desolate plateau.

The dragon spread her wings and soared high among the clouds with graceful ease. Golden sparks showered down from her wings; she trailed flame like the tail of a comet. She gave a clarion call of triumph and joy.

"Aylaen!" Skylan breathed, gazing at the dragon. "You didn't die. . . . You summoned the dragon. . . ."

The fighting stopped as friend and foe alike stared in wonder at the vanishing city and the great dragon flying above it, shining in the heavens with a radiance that rivaled the sun.

"Ilyrion!" Dela Eden cried, her single voice rising, breaking the silence. "Ilyrion!"

The Cyclopes gave their eerie wailing calls. The ogres roared and beat their weapons against their shields.

Biting his lips against the agony, Skylan picked up his sword and slowly and painfully rose to his feet. Aylaen was alive and she would find him among the dead with his sword in his hands, victorious.

"Raegar!" Skylan meant to shout, but the word came out a gasp.

Raegar heard him, however, and, limping on his bloody legs, turned to see what he must have thought was a draugr, an apparition, crawled out of the grave.

Skylan pressed his hand against his side, blood welled black from between his fingers. Every breath was blazing fire and he wavered where he stood, but he kept standing.

And then he started walking toward his foe.

Raegar blanched at the ghastly sight and backed up a step. "Why won't you die?" he cried and then, clutching his sword, he rushed at Skylan in a rage. "Why won't you die!"

Raegar swung his sword in wild, savage arcs, without thought or skill, desperate to kill. Skylan had to conserve his waning strength. He watched and waited as his father had taught him and, timing his blow, he struck at Raegar's sword and knocked it from his hand.

Raegar knelt to make a grab for it, only to find the point of Skylan's blade at his throat. Raegar froze, on his knees, his eyes wide with terror. Skylan saw himself reflected in Raegar's fear: pale as death, grim as death, holding death in his hand. He put his foot on Raegar's sword.

"You will not die a warrior."

Raegar shuddered and waited for the end.

Skylan meant to strike the death blow, but his arm wavered, his fingers trembled. He tightened his grip, but Raegar saw his weakness. His eyes went to Skylan's sword and his hand twitched, as though he would grab it. His eyes went to Skylan's eyes and he hesitated.

Skylan heard a shout, someone calling Raegar's name. Sigurd came splashing out of the red-tinged waves, dripping blood and seawater, carrying an axe that was not his own. Grimuir was beside his friend, as always. His helm was gone, his face horribly mangled and covered in blood. He could still see out of one eye, however, and that eye was fixed on Raegar. Bjorn walked with them, slogging through the wet sand, his face grim and dark. His sword blade was notched, but still sharp. Farinn came running up behind them. He carried no weapons, and his face was deathly pale.

Skylan was too weak to ask how the young man came to be here. Perhaps he had been sent to witness the end of the song.

Skylan smiled.

"I do not have the strength to kill you myself," he said to Raegar. "But, if you wait, my friends will be glad to finish you."

Raegar rose slowly to his feet. Blood covered his legs. His face contorted in pain, and tears of anger and frustration cut furrows down his cheeks. He cast Skylan a bitter, hate-filled look.

"Some god loves you." Raegar sneered and spat in the sand at Skylan's feet. "For all the good it has done either of us."

Turning, he hobbled off and vanished in the night.

Skylan's sword slipped from his hand. He sagged and fell onto the blood-wet sand. Strong arms caught him and held him, lowering him gently to the ground.

"Skylan!" Farinn cried. "Skylan, no!"

Skylan gasped and choked, then smiled to see his friends, with their weapons drawn, stand protectively over him, their fallen chief.

Farinn pressed his hand over the worst of the wounds, trying vainly to stop the bleeding. Skylan watched the dragon soar into the sky. Shedding golden sparks, she dove down, flying low to the ground. Men fled in terror at her coming, trampling each other, plunging into the sea.

"Farinn, tell me the truth," Skylan whispered. "Aylaen is alive. . . ."

Farinn hesitated the briefest moment, then said firmly, "Yes, Skylan, she is alive."

The dragon flew nearer, her head turning this way and that until she seemed to find what she sought. Her flight slowed. Her wings barely stirring the air, the dragon hovered over Skylan.

"Tell Aylaen I love her," said Skylan.

He reached out his hand, feeling for his sword, and, finding it, clasped his hand over the hilt. His eyes closed, his head lolled in Farinn's arms.

Farinn looked up at the dragon. A single golden tear fell from the dragon's eye and splashed on Skylan, washing away the blood on his lips and his body.

The dragon gazed down on him a moment, then looked at Farinn and nodded slightly. Lifting her head, with a single flap of her golden wings, she effortlessly soared back into the heavens.

The song was supposed to end with the glorious death of the victorious hero. Farinn held Skylan in his arms and lowered his head and wept.

He wept because he knew it wouldn't.

46

Raegar hated Skylan with a hatred that twisted and roiled inside his belly; his was hatred that suffocated him, made it hard to even breathe. Whatever beautiful object Raegar possessed, Skylan smashed. Whatever victory Raegar won, Skylan snatched from his grasp.

The most feared city had fallen to Raegar's might. Dread wizards had bowed to his will. He had been the most powerful person in the world, his god the most powerful god. He would have ruled a mighty empire. Every human, ogre, and Cyclopes would have been subject to his will, would have meekly offered prayers to his god. But now, Raegar had only to look out to sea to watch his dream sink into the flame-lit water.

Raegar could have sworn he had finally killed Skylan, only to see the corpse stand up and come after him. Raegar had taken one look at Skylan's pale visage, smeared with blood, seen the fell doom in his burning eyes, and known he had been right to run.

Not even a god had been able to kill Skylan Ivorson. A mere mortal like Raegar had not stood a chance. He was alive and that was what counted, especially on this night when death was reaping a bountiful harvest.

Men tried in vain to flee the monstrous, gold-glittering, fire-raining dragon as she flew past, leaving behind a trail of blood.

Raegar cast a fearful glance over his shoulder as he limped across the beach on his wounded legs, watching the dragon swoop down on the panic-stricken troops, scattering flaming cinders like rose petals at a wedding. Her vast wings seemed to brush the stars and knock them loose, sending them cascading down around Raegar. He watched the dragon soar past, and hurried on his way, ignoring pleas for help from the wounded.

The arrival of the dragon had rallied his foes. The ogres and Vindrasi and Cyclopes, who had been standing knee-deep in seawater and their own blood, had gone on the offensive, attacking with such ferocity that his soldiers were running for their lives from them as well as from the dragon.

And where was Aelon? Raegar waited for the god to come defend her people, defend her emperor, take on the mighty dragon. But the smoke of the burning ships rising to the heavens had begun to obscure the moon's light, giving it a blood-tinged hue. No god came.

"Why?" Raegar muttered, even as tears stung his eyes. "I loved you!"

He pushed and shoved and fought his way through the mass of panic-stricken people. He had already made his plan, knew what he was going to do. He and his son would start life anew, some place where no one knew him, far from Sinaria, for once news of this disaster reached Oran, the people would be howling to see his head on a pike.

Reaching the pavilion where he had left his son was not easy, however. The dragon was attacking the soldiers again, raining flame and spewing noxious fumes. Camp followers were shrieking, children wailing. Men threw down their weapons as they tried to flee, some running into the sea, others into the forest. Even in their panic, however, no one ventured near the plateau, where the vanished city had once stood.

Raegar stumbled over a group of priests prostrate on the ground, desperately begging Aelon to come to their aid.

"Fools!" Raegar muttered.

He had a new fear now, for many of the tents were on fire and he imagined his own pavilion in flames. He had left the child in the care of nursemaids, under guard, but he did not trust them. He knocked down any man who got in his way. When he saw his tent still standing, unharmed, he heaved a sobbing sigh of relief.

No one was around; the guards and the nursemaids must have fled. When Raegar heard a baby crying, he almost cried out a blessing to Aelon, then choked it back with a curse. His son was alive in spite of

her, not because of her. By the healthy sound of his screams, the baby
was unhurt.

Raegar dashed inside the pavilion, nearly taking down a post in his
haste, and came to a halt. The interior was dark and smoky. He couldn't
see a thing.

He groped his way among the furniture to his desk and after a few
fumbled tries due to his shaking hands, he managed to light a lantern. The baby was in a frenzy, crying and kicking his legs and flailing with his tiny fists. Raegar stared at him helplessly. He supposed
the baby was hungry, but there wasn't much he could do about that.

"We'll soon be away from this accursed place, my son," Raegar
promised, giving the child an awkward pat. He'd think of a name
for the child later. His son sure as hell wasn't going to be named
after Aelon.

Raegar examined his wounds. The cut across his right leg had struck
clear to the bone and was deep and ugly. His left leg was slashed,
though not as badly. He splashed wine over the wounds to stop them
from putrefying, groaning at the pain, and then bandaged his leg as
best he could.

After that, he stripped off his ceremonial armor. It was valuable, and
he could have melted it down for the gold, but it was also heavy and he
didn't want to lug it about. Somewhere along the way, he'd lost the
crown, which was a pity, for he could have sold the jewels.

In need of clothes, he hastened to the back of the pavilion, where
the head priests had their quarters, and rifled among their things until
he found a robe that came close to fitting his great bulk. The robe
was too short, reaching only to his shins, and he covered it with a cloak
with a hood, then hurried back to his quarters.

Raegar had hidden a bag of silver coins in his sea chest for use in
just such an emergency. He was going to retrieve them when he caught
a glimpse of something golden on his desk, shining in the lantern
light.

He went to look more closely. The object was a massive ring made
of gold with a square-cut ruby surrounded by diamonds.

Raegar picked it up to admire it. The ring was obviously extremely
valuable and quite beautiful and he could think of only one who would
have left it for him.

"Aelon, if you are trying to buy your way into my favor, you are too late," he said aloud, thrusting the ring onto his finger. "Still, I thank you for this gift, which I am certain will fetch a fine price."

The ring pricked his skin, as he put it on. He paid no heed, assuming it was only a flaw in the gold that would need to be smoothed down.

Raegar went to fetch his child, then he stopped, alarmed, feeling the first twinge of pain. That subsided and he took another step, then doubled over in agony, as if he were being stabbed with red-hot sword blades. He couldn't feel his legs and he collapsed onto the desk. Chill sweat rolled down his face; he began to shake and tremble. Remembering the prick he'd felt, he fumbled at the ring and managed to yank it off. On his finger was a spot of blood and he saw the tiny needle that had popped out from the back.

Raegar cried out in pain and rage, his scream ending in a horrible gurgling sound as his body convulsed. Jerking and thrashing, he knocked over the lantern. Flaming oil spilled, setting the rug on fire. Flames licked his flesh. He tried to call for help, but his breath rattled in his throat. The last sight he saw was Aelon, standing over him.

The Norn, cackling, cut the thread.

Aelon cast a dismissive glance at Raegar's corpse, then walked past it to the crib and the screaming child. She lifted the baby and held him close.

"You and I will find another world, little one," said Aelon in soothing tones, rocking the child. "This world is of no more use to us. I will raise you to be a king. A far better king than your dolt of a father."

Pulling the hood low over her face, the god held the baby close, covered him with her cloak, and slipped out of the tent and into the night.

The fire spread, eating up the rug. Hevis emerged from the darkness, where he had been hiding. The god crouched beside the body of Raegar, whose lips were frothed with foam, his eyes frozen in his head. Picking up the ring from the floor, Hevis laid it on the corpse.

"Rest easy, Treia," Hevis said, and fanned the flames with his hand to speed them along.

The Dragon Kahg had been served by humans for much of his three
centuries of life. They ferried him in their ships while he rode at
his leisure, and gifted him with the gemstones that were the progeny
of Ilyrion. He would sort through the gems, finding those that were,
unbeknownst to the humans, baby dragons, far more valuable than
any jewel. In exchange, he would give the humans his spiritbone and
perform tasks for the Bone Priestess. Generally the tasks the humans
gave him were humdrum: kill some ogres, set fire to a village. He
rarely enjoyed his work, as he did this night. He found something
deeply satisfying in burning Aelon's galleys to cinders.

As a dragon of air, Kahg could have blasted the ships with breath
more powerful than any typhoon and completely obliterated them.
He understood the need to create chaos among the troops and he pri-
vately agreed with Skylan that the sight of the emperor's grand fleet
of ships burning on the dark ocean, set ablaze by some unseen foe,
would have a demoralizing effect on his army. They had won a great
battle, but how were they going to get home?

The operation was not as easy as it might have seemed. Once Skylan had set the smaller ships on fire, Kahg was tasked with pushing
the boats across the water so that they bumped up against the hulls
of the galleys, then using his breath to cause the fire to spread.

The first time he blew on a ship, he blew so hard he doused the
flames. The second time he was more successful, blowing gently, puffing the ship across the water. When it nestled against the galley, he
used his breath to fan the flames.

He took additional pleasure in the sight of the sailors looking up to see a dragon, sleek and black, materialize out of the night air right on top of them. Most of the terrified men jumped into the water, where they were at the mercy of the oceanids.

He kept watch for Fala and her cohorts to come challenge him, but he was not particularly surprised when they didn't appear.

Fala had thought herself very clever in taking her spiritbone from the humans, not realizing in her youth and arrogance that by doing so, she had severed all contact with the humans, who could have alerted her to Kahg's attack. As it was, she was probably curled up in a field somewhere, sleeping soundly.

Kahg was not often wrong, but he was that time. He had set the two galleys on fire and was about to start work on the smaller ships when he caught sight of movement: black wings against the stars. He swiveled his head and saw the hulking dragon Fala accompanied by the two traitors.

He had planned to flee if he saw them approach, knowing that with his swifter, sleeker body he could easily outfly them. The three dragons were far too close, however, and Kahg was forced to give Fala grudging credit for having successfully sneaked up on him. And she had caught him at a disadvantage, flying low to the water, which left him little room to maneuver.

Fala was staring in openmouthed fury at the burning ships, which she was supposed to have been guarding. The flames blazed in her bulging eyes. Drool dripping from her gaping jaws, she roared in outrage and dove for him.

Fala expected Kahg to turn tail and run, try to gain sky room. Instead, Kahg flattened his body, spread his wings and glided underneath her belly.

"I do not think your humans will pay you for this night's work, Fala," Kahg told her, as he flew past.

"I will roast you alive, Kahg!" Fala shrieked, giving a great belch and shooting a stream of molten magma at him.

Magma could be a deadly weapon in an earth dragon's arsenal, for it was hot enough to melt through steel armor, kill humans in large numbers and send them fleeing in panic. Magma was not much use as a weapon against another dragon, however, as Fala would have known had she been more experienced. The heavy magma dropped in globs from her mouth.

Kahg was able to easily dodge the fiery lava, which, as luck would have it, fell onto the deck of one of the triremes, causing it to burst into flame. Kahg laughed at this, infuriating Fala to the point of madness. He was aware of the two male dragons circling around him, preparing, along with Fala, to attack him from three directions, but he feigned ignorance.

Kahg was at another disadvantage, though these dragons did not know it. He meant to keep his vow never to kill one of his own kind, no matter that they were intent on killing him. Sucking in a bellyful of air, he blew a blast of wind at Fala that caught her with her wings extended.

The gust hurled her backward and tore a hole in one of the membranes of her wing, almost sending her tumbling into the water. That would have been disastrous, for she would have sunk like a rock slide. Fala managed to remain airborne by wildly flapping her wings and flailing about with her legs and tail.

Kahg rolled and twisted, but not fast enough, and he felt searing pain run down his spine. He glanced over his shoulder to see one of the males had hit him with a stream of fire that was now smoldering on his back. Kahg sucked in a breath and saw the offending dragon fly off hurriedly, to avoid the same fate as Fala.

The third dragon was starting his attack. Fala had recovered and was returning to the fight. Kahg conceded he was beaten and, unlike humans, he cared nothing about honor. He knew when to retreat.

Kahg wondered if Aylaen had found the fifth spiritbone and the courage to use it. He had done everything in his power to aid her and he wished her well, as he wished these three reckless, vainglorious young dragons well. He hoped they lived long lives, long enough to gain some sense.

Kahg soared high into the air, moving with a speed the three heavier dragons could not hope to match and he hovered above them, flying in wide, sweeping circles.

"The Stormlords have sundered the realms," he called down to them. "The portal back to our homeland is starting to close. Leave now and you may yet have a chance to return to the Realm of Fire.

Delay and the portal will slam shut and you will be left in this world. If you want proof, look at Tsa Kerestra, fallen from the clouds. The city fell when the realms were sundered."

The two male dragons looked at each other. They had been around Kahg during the voyage and they had come to know him. Both looked back at the city of the Stormlords that had once floated among the clouds and was now on the ground. Fala saw her friends start to doubt and turned on them in a rage.

"Kahg is trying to scare you off. Are you hatchlings to believe him?"

"I do not lie, Fala," said Kahg. "As those who know me can attest."

He could see that the two males were now truly concerned. The portal used by the dragons to travel between realms was located in the land of the Cyclopes—a difficult journey for these dragons, who had no ships to ferry them. The land of Cyclopes was far away and the dragons would have to stop often to rest and find food.

"My mate and young are in that realm, Fala," said one of the males.

"The city has fallen," said the other. "And where are the Stormlords? They have returned to the Realm of Fire, and so should we."

"You had best make haste," Kahg suggested. "Once the portal starts to close, nothing will stop it."

The two males exchanged alarmed glances, spread their wings and prepared to depart.

"You promised to serve me!" Fala cried.

"We have served you," one of the males said, twisting his head to look back at her. "And we have nothing to show for our pains."

The two flew off. Fala glowered after them, fuming, bits of molten magma drooling from her clenched jaws. Kahg watched her with a certain amount of pity. He did not fear that she would attack him. She was trying to find a way to leave while still maintaining some shred of dignity.

"What will you do, mighty Kahg?" Fala asked, sulky and sullen and grudgingly admiring.

"I haven't made up my mind," Kahg replied with airy nonconcern, as if both realms were his for the asking.

Kahg was in no hurry. He believed the dragon's portal might remain open for some time, longer than he had led the naïve young males to believe. The sundered realms, with nothing to connect them, would drift apart and eventually the dragon's portal would close.

"You should return with me, mighty Kahg," said Fala. "We would make a good team. The Realm of Fire is your homeland."

Kahg considered her words. He had no intention of teaming up with Fala, who was far too young and immature, but he could go back to heal his wounds.

He realized in that moment he didn't want to go back. He had no young in the Realm of Fire. His children had long since grown up and gone out on their own. He detested that world and its brutal savagery, cruel men, and horrific monsters. Perhaps the Stormlords could bring about a change for the better, but if so, their fight would be long and hard and bitter and he wanted no part of it.

Kahg had come to like this Realm of Stone with its humans whose names he could never remember. He enjoyed observing, with a touch of sympathy, their ceaseless struggles to overcome the myriad obstacles the gods threw in their path. He even admired their vain attempts to find meaning in the meaningless until the threads of their wyrds snapped and their fleeting and fragile lives ended.

As he was thinking, pondering, he caught sight of a beam of golden light shining from the darkest part of the fallen city. Kahg stared at the glow in wonder and dawning hope.

The light shone brighter and brighter, so that the radiance burned his eyes and Kahg had to turn away. Suddenly the voices of the soldiers who had rushed inside the city to loot and burn, rape and steal rose in cries of terror and the light flashed and went out. The city was gone, the plateau barren and empty.

Fala gasped in shock. "The city was rich, filled with casks of jewels! Aelon promised them to me! Where did it go? What happened?"

"If it is any comfort, wretched Fala, the jewels were never there, just as the city was never truly there," said Kahg. "It was all illusion. The jewels were no more real than Aelon's promises."

"I hate this world," Fala snarled, gnashing her fangs. "I am going home."

"You might want to hurry," said Kahg softly.

The golden light blazed forth, as bright and hot as the sun.

Reborn, the Great Dragon Ilyrion spread her vast wings, lifted her proud and beautiful head, and sprang up off the earth, causing the ground to tremble. She soared into the sky, showering sparks of golden fire.

Fala turned tail and fled.

The Dragon Kahg stared a moment, enraptured, and then flew slowly toward the magnificent dragon, whose wings seemed to span the heavens. Her gaze turned to him.

She is not afraid, he realized. What has she to fear?

Her gaze was questioning. *What do you want of me?*

"It would be my honor and my joy to join you in flight, Ilyrion," said Kahg reverently. "Just once. Before you leave."

The dragon graciously inclined her head, then dove toward the ground, sending the terror-stricken humans into a frenzy of panic, all except a group of warriors—humans, ogres, and Cyclopes—who were gathered protectively around their fallen chief.

"Please don't hurt them, great Ilyrion," said Kahg, both proud and apologetic. "Those people are mine."

The dragon shifted her head to regard him and he saw tears shining in her eyes.

And they are mine, said Ilyrion.

She glided over the waves and in the proudest moment of his life, the Dragon Kahg joined the Great Dragon Ilyrion in flight.

Skylan Ivorson arrived at Torval's Hall to find that it was gone, burned to the ground. An old man and an old woman stood together among the ashes. The bitter wind of coming winter caught the smoke that rose from the black, smoldering beams and blew it away. Skylan wondered who these two were for a moment and then, with a sorrowful heart, he recognized Torval and Vindrash.

The two had cast aside their armor and put down their weapons, for the long fight had ended. They were dressed in clothes such as wanderers wear, those who are going on a long journey, far from home.

"Ah, Fish Knife," said Torval, catching sight of him. "Come to say good-bye?"

The god's gray hair hung in two thick braids down his chest. He wore a simple leather tunic and a fur-lined cloak, leather trousers and boots, and a warm fur cap. His sword was gone. He carried a worn, gnarled walking stick.

Skylan was dismayed. "Do not leave us, lord! Ilyrion has returned. Aelon has fled!"

"Our time is ended here," said Torval. "The world will be in good hands."

"Better hands than ours," said Vindrash.

Like Torval, she was dressed in a simple leather tunic and trousers with a fur cloak around her shoulders. Her silver-white hair was done in a single braid wrapped around her head.

Skylan looked for his friends. "Where are Garn and my father and Chloe and Acronis? I had hoped to join them."

"They are in the care of others now," said Vindrash. "Their peace and rest will be assured."

Skylan shook his head in denial. "What of your friends, the other gods? What of them?"

"Sund is dead. In his madness, he killed himself. Joabis died, valiantly fighting to defend his souls. Hevis has vanished. We have no idea where he has gone. Skoval and Aylis and the rest wait for us beyond."

"Let me come with you, lord," Skylan begged. "Let me serve you still."

Torval smiled, his blue eyes, almost lost in a web of wrinkles, warmed.

"I have worked long and hard and taken trouble to forge you, Skylan Ivorson," said Torval. "I won't cast you aside."

"The world is going to change for the better, but our people will find the change difficult to bear," Vindrash added. "They will need your wisdom and your guidance."

Torval clapped Skylan on the shoulder. "You were an arrogant, selfish young fool, Fish Knife. Many times I despaired of you, but you came out better than I expected."

"What he means is that you have made us proud," said Vindrash.

Skylan could not talk for his grief, could scarcely see for his tears. And yet joy filled his heart, for he knew that he would live and he would go back to be with Aylaen. They would grow old together, old and toothless.

Torval rested a hand on his shoulder. "Sometimes a hero is not one who gives his life for his people, but one who gives his life *to* his people. Remember that."

"I will remember *you*, Torval," said Skylan. "And I will honor you always. And when the span of our wyrds end, Aylaen and I will find you."

Torval cast a troubled glance at Vindrash, who slightly shook her head. Coming to Skylan, she embraced him and kissed him on the cheek. Torval reached out his hand to her. They looked one last time at the wreckage of their Hall and then, clasping hands, they walked away.

Skylan wondered why they had looked at him so strangely and why Vindrash had kissed him so tenderly, as if she grieved for him. He pondered it as he went to visit the Norn, the three old women who spun and wove and cut the wyrds of men and gods at the foot of the World Tree.

The World Tree remained; it was flourishing. The Norn were nowhere to be found. They had packed up their spindles and their wheel and departed.

Skylan himself was about to leave when he saw something shining amid the roots of the World Tree: a pair of shears, the ends blunted, the blades rusted. A single thread, unbroken, stretched on and on.

Alone.

The Great Dragon Ilyrion stood guard over the world until the Faceless God, Aelon, fled, never to return. Ilyrion bid farewell to Torval and the Vindrasi gods, bearing no grudge, feeling only a sorrowful melancholy for the fall of what once had been mighty. She gave greeting to the Gods of Raj, who watched her from a respectful distance, glad for her help, but eager for her to be gone.

Ilyrion flew over the empty, desolate plateau and the blood-soaked sand.

At the coming of the dragon, the soldiers cast down their weapons and ran. They would have a long trek home, for the Empire of Oran was many hundreds of miles to the north. Their magnificent fleet had been reduced to scraps of charred wood floating sluggishly on the waves. Flames had destroyed their tents and their food supplies and their wagons, leaving the survivors nothing except their lives.

Ilyrion let them go, not bothering to hunt them. With winter coming on, they would suffer enough.

Far below, a knot of priests huddled for shelter from the cold wind behind some rocks, crying out to Aelon to save them. Their prayers would go unanswered, of course. Eventually, cold and hungry, the priests would give up and start walking.

Ilyrion slowed her flight and circled in the air above the victors, a small band of warriors—ogres, Cyclopes, and Vindrasi—tending to their wounded, guarding their dead, and their fallen chief.

Ilyrion gazed down upon Skylan Ivorson with sorrow and fond pride. He had chosen his time to die and he would not understand, at first, why his choice had been denied him. He would come to, eventually, as he would come to understand the choice Aylaen had made.

Ilyrion dipped her wings in salute and then turned her head and left them. Gliding over sea and over land, she flew among the clouds and the rain, the sun and wind, gazing down upon the world she had loved and claimed as her own for so long. At her death, she had let her blood rain down upon the world. In her rebirth, she rained down her joy, with each drop bringing life to a world that had been withering, dying.

Her world restored, Ilyrion shifted her gaze to the heavens, to blazing stars and worlds unnumbered and the vast expanse of boundless, limitless time through which she could fly free for eons upon eons. She lifted her head and spread her wings and soared into the universe.

The Great Dragon Ilyrion was going home.

Skylan was adrift on a burning sea. Flames spread over an oil-covered surface, so that he was forced to dive into the dark water to escape them. His lungs bursting, he swam back to the surface to breathe, only to be burned in the fire.

He battled for days it seemed, tormented by pain and fear, longing to sink below the waves and give up the struggle. Every time he tried to let go, a touch, a voice, would call him back.

And then one day he wearily swam again to the surface to find that the flames had gone out. The night had ended. The sun was shining.

He opened his eyes. He was lying in a bed with a colorful blanket spread over him in an unfamiliar place—a crude wooden hut. Sunlight streamed through a door that was little more than a hole in the wall. The air was warm and smelled of green living things and the sea.

"You have come back to us," said Dela Eden.

She was sitting on the floor beside his bed, which he could now see was low to the ground. Rising to her knees, she placed her arm under his head and lifted him and pressed a cup to his lips.

"Drink this," she said.

He was thirsty and he drank. The liquid had a slightly bitter taste, but it eased his thirst.

Dela Eden gently laid him back on the bed.

"I want to see Aylaen," Skylan said.

He expected to hear his voice and was startled when the words came out in a hoarse whisper.

"She is resting," said Dela Eden.

"Is she all right? She is not hurt," Skylan pressed.

Dela Eden smiled. "Drink some more. You have nearly burnt up with the fever."

He obeyed, sipping the liquid and looking around at his strange surroundings. "Where am I?"

"You are in a hut in the Cyclopes village," said Dela Eden. "We found you dead on the battlefield. The great dragon healed your wounds and we brought you here to tend to you. Now you must sleep."

He was weary, but he could not rest, not until he knew what had happened.

"The battle . . . ," said Skylan. "My men . . ."

"Ilyrion struck terror into the hearts of the Sinarians and they fled. Their ships all burned. They will have to walk home. A very long walk," Dela Eden said drily.

"What of the tally of the dead?" Skylan asked.

"Erdmun was killed, as well as the ogre shaman, Raven's-foot, and many others, though not so many as you might think. We built a pyre on the beach below the ruins of the stormhold and sent their souls to the Gods of Raj."

"The Gods of Raj . . . ," Skylan murmured. He remembered his talk with Torval. *The world is in good hands . . . better hands . . .*

"Go to sleep," said Dela Eden. "Your fever is gone. Your sleep will be easeful, not troubled."

"One question more. What became of Raegar?"

"He is dead."

"How did he die?"

"That is a mystery. After the Sinarians fled, Sigurd and Grimuir searched the battlefield, recovering objects that might be of use."

"You mean they looted the camp," said Skylan, faintly smiling.

Dela Eden shrugged. "They found the charred remains of the royal pavilion with Raegar's body inside. The tent had burned down around him, but the body was untouched by the flames. Sigurd checked to make certain he was dead. When he touched the body, it disintegrated. Knowing Raegar was cursed, Sigurd and Grimuir both fled. And now you must sleep."

Skylan slept and this time, as Dela Eden had promised, he dreamed no dreams.

He woke feeling hungry. The sunlight was waning; the air was cooler with the coming of evening. He could see shadows of people walking past, outside the hut. Hearing someone moving inside, he turned his head.

"Aylaen . . . ," he said joyfully.

"It is Farinn," said the young man. He closed the leather flap that covered the door, then came back to sit beside the bed.

Skylan saw the sorrowful expression on Farinn's face and fear gripped him.

"Where is Aylaen?" he demanded.

Farinn lowered his gaze and murmured, "I am sorry, Skylan. So very sorry."

"She is dead? I don't believe you!" Skylan cried. "How could she have died? She summoned the dragon!"

Farinn moistened dry lips. "I don't know how to tell you, because I fear you won't believe me."

"I must go find her," said Skylan. He tried to stand up and collapsed.

Farinn caught him and eased him back down. Skylan lay there, cursing his weakness, while Farinn fetched cool water.

Skylan saw again the unbroken thread of his wyrd, lying beneath the World Tree, alone.

"Tell me what happened," he said.

"Owl Mother took us to what looked like a cellar," said Farinn. "Aylaen found the spiritbone in a helm on the statue of a dragon that stood, forgotten, in a corner. She was drawn to it, as though it spoke to her.

"Then Raegar entered the cellar with his god, Aelon, who told him Aylaen was there. Raegar threatened to kill her. Aylaen paid no heed. She walked over to the statue, to the spiritbone. She said she knew the secret of the magic."

Farinn fell silent. Skylan gripped his hand tightly. "Go on."

"Aelon came after her. I picked up Aylaen's sword. I was going to fight, but Owl Mother wouldn't let me," Farinn said in shame.

"You would have fought a god?" Skylan said. "That was foolish. And brave."

Farinn sighed. "That is what Owl Mother told me. Vindrash took up the blessed sword from me and refused to let Aelon pass. Aylaen picked up the helm and put it on her head. She fell down, dead. Or so it seemed."

Skylan watched him with quiet intensity.

"Raegar found us then," Farinn continued in a low voice. "When he saw Aylaen he thought she was dead, and so did Aelon. The god told him to take the helm and the spiritbone. But Raegar didn't want to touch it; he was afraid. Aelon threatened him and he was about to pick it up when one of his men shouted that the fleet was on fire. Raegar knew you were responsible. He called upon Aelon to kill you, but he couldn't find her. The god had fled in fear.

"A golden light spread through the cellar and Aylaen rose to her feet, laughing with joy. She was beautiful, Skylan, and radiant and proud." Farinn's voice grew hushed, reverent. "The jewels on the spiritbones blazed and became her blood, the bones of the dragon became her bones. Then I don't know what happened. The light grew so bright it burned my eyes and the ground shook. Owl Mother cried out that we had to run. I didn't want to leave Aylaen, but Owl Mother said Aylaen had made her choice and I must honor her."

Skylan lay still and quiet. He pictured Aylaen, happy and proud and joyful, and thought perhaps she might have looked as she had looked on the day of their wedding.

"If I had known, I would have stopped her," he said.

"She knew," Farinn said. "That is why she didn't tell you."

"Did she know what would happen when she summoned the dragon?" Skylan asked.

"She did," said Farinn steadily. "She willingly made the choice."

"She made the choice to leave me," said Skylan in bitter, anguished tones.

He was angry with her even as he knew his anger was not fair. She had made the same choice he had made when he took his place in the shield wall—to sacrifice himself for their people. Only she had died and he had survived.

Farinn looked stricken, not knowing what to say.

Skylan sighed. "The city vanished. What happened?"

"Owl Mother and I escaped through a secret door that was in her garden. By this time, Raegar's troops were inside the city, running through the streets, setting fires and looting. They looked for the people, crying that they would slaughter them. But the city was empty. The Stormlords had disappeared.

"We were standing outside the wall when the Great Dragon Ilyrion rose up into the air and spread her wings that seemed to fill heaven. The soldiers saw her and screamed in fear and there was a flash of light and the soldiers were gone. And so was the city of Tsa Kerestra. Owl Mother and I stood alone on an empty plateau. Owl Mother said the Stormlords took the city and the soldiers inside to the Realm of Fire. 'A cruel land for cruel men.'

"She sent me to find you, but everything on the beach was chaos. Men were running and shouting and cursing. Someone knocked me down and almost trampled me and then Wulfe found me. He told me where you were."

"I remember," said Skylan, adding tonelessly, "You said Aylaen was alive."

"She is, Skylan," said Farinn.

Skylan turned his head away.

"I know she is," Farinn persisted. "When Ilyrion was flying over the battlefield, she saw you lying there and a tear fell from her eye. The tear splashed down on you and washed away the blood, and you shuddered and drew a breath. She brought you back to life."

"She did me no favors," said Skylan. "I made my choice as she made hers. She should have let me die."

"Our people need you, Skylan," said Farinn. "Now more than ever. Our lives will change. Aylaen knew that."

And so did Torval.

The sun had set. The moon rose, round and warm, what the Vindrasi called a harvest moon, for its light shone so brightly that they could work in the fields. The interior of the hut was dark. Farinn offered to light a candle, but Skylan preferred the darkness.

He could hear people laughing and talking, and smell the scents of wood smoke and cooking pots. Parents were calling their children to come home. Farinn sat by his bed in uncomfortable silence.

"Leave me," said Skylan.

Farinn hesitated a moment, then stood up and made his way through the dark hut to the door. He drew aside the flap and had started to go out when Skylan stopped him.

"Make a song for her," he said.

Farinn nodded and left and Skylan lay alone and awake, staring into the darkness.

51

Many days later, Sigurd, Grimuir, and Bjorn shared a meal of fresh-caught fish and rice and some sort of strange fruit, and discussed making the attempt to sail home.

All of them had been wounded. Sigurd was limping from an ugly gash on his leg that had opened his thigh. He had various other injuries, but he was proud to say that the wound on his leg was the worst.

Grimuir's face had been slashed by a sword. Part of his nose was chopped off and the sight in one eye was destroyed. He shrugged off the hideous scars it would leave, saying he had never been that handsome to begin with.

Bjorn had suffered a blow to the head that had cracked his skull and knocked him out cold. He had fallen into the sea and would have drowned if Bear Walker had not seen him fall and pulled him out.

They had said farewell to Bear Walker and Keeper and the rest of the ogres, who had been eager to return to their homeland now that they could brag to their families that they had driven away Aelon. Sigurd had given the ogres three dragonships, which they would have to sail themselves, for there were no dragons.

"I hope their ogre gods are watching over them," Sigurd remarked. "The lumbering oafs overturned one of the ships, and that was just when they were boarding it. They should be thankful one of the Cyclopes offered to go with them to navigate. Without Kamau to guide them, the lubbers would probably sail off the edge of the world."

"That takes care of the ogres," said Grimuir. "What do we do?"

"I think we remain here during the winter," said Bjorn. "We are all recovering from our wounds. None of us is up to the task of sailing all the way back to Vindraholm. The seas will be rough with the coming of winter."

At this, Sigurd and Grimuir grinned and nudged each other.

Bjorn was offended. "What is the matter? Every word I said was true."

"Right after the battle, you were eager to leave for home," said Grimuir. "You said the seas would be calm with fair winds. Now you talk of gales and driving rain and snow and say that the voyage would be too dangerous and we should remain here with the Cyclopes."

"With one Cyclopes," said Sigurd, winking at Grimuir.

Bjorn flushed. "I have been helping Dela Eden tend to Skylan . . ."

"Helping? Is that what you call it?" Sigurd leered. "I'll be glad to help Dela Eden in that way myself."

"You're a pig, Sigurd," said Bjorn, throwing a fish head at his friend.

"I know," said Sigurd, picking up the fish head and tossing it back. "But relax. It so happens that I agree with you about staying here through the winter months. Without the dragon, the journey would be dangerous, even if we were fit to make it. And we're not. We will sail in the spring."

The words came out sounding more somber than he had intended. Each man realized how much he missed his homeland. For a moment no one spoke. Sigurd sat with his head down, toying with a piece of mango.

"We should ask Skylan," said Grimuir at last. "And Farinn," he added as an afterthought.

"I asked Skylan," said Bjorn. "He doesn't care. He says we should stay or go as we please."

"That doesn't sound like Skylan," said Grimuir. "He is the Chief of Chiefs. He's never shrunk from making decisions before."

"Aylaen is dead and Skylan has buried himself in her grave," said Sigurd. "Women die. Men die. Skylan needs to go on with his life."

"Is she dead? We don't know what really happened to her," said Grimuir in a low voice.

"Farinn said she died summoning the dragon," Bjorn returned sharply. "Such magic is dangerous. She is not the first Kai Priestess to die while attempting to use the spiritbones."

"Farinn is a poet who will say whatever suits his rhyme," Sigurd added, shrugging. "I say that we spend the winter here with the Cyclopes, since they have invited us. Are we agreed?"

"Yes," said Bjorn. "What about Farinn? Should we ask him?"

"He stayed to guard Skylan's body," said Sigurd. "He has proved himself a warrior. We should ask him."

Skylan had no interest in whether they sailed for home now or months from now. He took no interest in anything. As the days went by, he did little but lie in the sun, gazing into the clear blue and cloudless skies, searching for a golden dragon he knew would never return.

Dela Eden tried to talk to Skylan about Aylaen, but whenever she spoke her name, he would stand up and walk off, and eventually she stopped. Skylan knew Farinn was making a song for her, but he did not want to hear it. Farinn had to sing it softly, to himself.

A month passed in this manner. The others settled into life with the Cyclopes. Grimuir and Sigurd both soon found women who were glad to make the Vindrasi warriors feel welcome. Bjorn did not seem to want companionship, or so Skylan thought at first.

He said something to Sigurd about Bjorn being lonely.

Sigurd chuckled. "Where are your eyes? You can't see what has been happening right under your nose. Bjorn is in love with Dela Eden."

"What? Those two?" Skylan was amazed.

"He talks of nothing but her. How could you not know?"

"I guess I wasn't listening," said Skylan.

Sigurd gave him a look of disgust. "Make up your mind to either live or die, Skylan. You can't do both."

Skylan did not often pay heed to what Sigurd said. In this instance, however, he found himself pondering the older man's words. In spite of himself, his body was mending, gaining strength. Food had started to taste good again. Now when he lay in the sun, he found himself growing restless.

One day, he was idly watching some of the Cyclopes children playing at their version of King of the Mountain on one of the sand dunes.

"You're doing it all wrong," Skylan said. He jumped to his feet. Joining the dune's defenders, he showed them how to form a shield wall, laughing with them as he fended off the attack of some six-year-olds.

"It is good to hear you laugh again," said Dela Eden.

He looked up to see her smiling at him. He stopped laughing and left the game, stalking off toward his hut. Dela Eden ran after him.

"You are angry with her," said Dela Eden. "And you feel guilty for being angry."

Skylan kept walking.

"You are angry that she left you," Dela Eden continued, walking at his side. "I know what you are feeling. I was angry at my first husband when he died. He drowned trying to save a sheep that had fallen into the river. Silly man, giving his life for a sheep. But he could not bear to see any animal suffer."

Dela Eden sighed. "I loved him very much and yet I was so mad at him I could have choked him with own my hands. Later I understood that he died being the man I loved. If he had not been that man, I would not have loved him and his death would not have caused me such pain."

Skylan slowed his step, turned to look at her. "You are right. I am angry."

"Aylaen told me that when she chose to go on this voyage, everyone tried to stop her," Dela Eden said. "Her mother begged her to stay at home. Her stepfather berated and insulted her and the other people in the tribe laughed at her. All except you. You were the one who said she was strong enough and brave enough to come.

"Aylaen stood at your side in the battle against giants. She fought with you in the gladiator games and swam with you beneath the sea. She sailed to the Isle of the Dead to find you. She carried the sword of a goddess and braved the wrath of a god. In the end, she was strong enough and brave enough and loved you enough to give her life to save her people. Was that the woman you loved? Was that why you loved her?"

"Yes," said Skylan.

"Keep her here, in your heart," said Dela Eden, resting her hand on his chest. "And let her go. You will meet again."

"I do not think so," said Skylan. "For I do not know where she has gone. But thank you, Dela Eden. You are wise. When we sail in the spring, I hope you will sail with us."

"I would like that," she said. "Though I do not know if I will like the cold."

"I think perhaps Bjorn will keep you warm," said Skylan, smiling. He found it good to smile again.

That day was a turning point for him. He and the other Vindrasi spent the winter fishing and hunting with the Cyclopes, learning how to make and use the Cyclopes bows. At night they shared stories around the fire, listening to Farinn sing the old songs of their people and to the Cyclopes tell tales of their own. They also learned about the Gods of Raj.

When spring came, they celebrated the wedding of Dela Eden and Bjorn. Skylan sniffed the air and observed the moon and said that it was time to set sail for home.

When they had first arrived at the Cyclopes village after the battle, they had carried the *Venejekar* to a safe, secluded place inland, hiding it among the trees and covering it with branches. When the winds grew warm and the days grew longer and the flocks of birds flew north, they brought their dragonship out of the forest to the shore. Their thoughts turned to home and friends and family, and even Sigurd shed a tear, though he claimed it was only because he got sand in his eyes. They worked to make the dragonship ready for the long ocean voyage and gave the dragon-head prow a fresh coat of paint to honor Kahg.

No one had seen the dragon since he had taken them from the field of battle to the Cyclopes village. His spiritbone had vanished from the nail where it had always hung. The dragons were gone, or so Dela Eden said. They had returned to the Realm of Fire through the portal before it closed forever.

And Skylan had not seen Wulfe since the night of the battle. Skylan guessed he had gone home to his mother. He hoped the boy was all right.

The night before they were going to sail, Skylan walked alone on the beach, gazing out to sea. He would miss this land and these people. They talked of meeting again. He and the others had promised to sail back to these shores, but Skylan knew they wouldn't. Life would change for the Vindrasi. The days of the dragonships had come to an end, along with so much else. He touched the amulet he wore around his neck, the small hammer dedicated to Torval.

Only a few days ago, Bjorn had asked him why he still wore it, since Torval and the gods were gone.

"It is all I have left," said Skylan.

He sat down on the beach, enjoying the solitude. The night was clear, the sea was calm; the waves made a whispering sound as they glided onto the shore. He could hear distant laughter coming from the village, where a farewell celebration was brightening the night. He was thinking he would go join them, when he was startled by a voice.

"You were going to leave without telling me."

Skylan turned to see Wulfe plop down in the sand beside him.

"How could I tell you when I didn't know where you were?" Skylan asked. "We've been here six months and you never came to visit."

"I've been busy," said Wulfe, shrugging.

Skylan didn't ask how Wulfe knew they were planning to leave. The oceanids, who watched them every day with avid interest, would have kept their prince informed.

"Are you going to sail with us?" Skylan asked. "We are returning to our homeland. You would be welcome."

Wulfe shook his head. "I'm going to stay here."

He paused, then added with a smile that was both shy and proud, "After the battle, my mother took me to see my grandmother, the queen, the one who cursed me and sent me away and told me never to come back. My mother told Grandmama that I helped defeat the Faceless God who killed so many of our people. My grandmother said maybe she had made a mistake about me. I wasn't so bad after all. She kissed me and said I was to sit beside her. I didn't want to, because she is very fierce, but my mother said I had to be polite."

"I'm glad," said Skylan. "You and your family should be together."

"We are going to live with my grandmother in her kingdom, which is very beautiful. My grandmother is going to teach me the proper way to use my magic. She says the way I use magic is a disgrace." Wulfe heaved a sigh at the thought.

"I think you are right to stay with your people. You are their prince. Someday you will grow up to be their king."

"I don't know about that," said Wulfe, squirming uncomfortably. "I don't think I want to be king. You have to wear clothes that itch. I came back to tell you good-bye and to give you this."

He pressed something into Skylan's hand. Skylan held it to the light of the stars shining off the sea.

"Is this . . . this is Kahg's spiritbone!" Skylan was amazed. "How did you get this? Dela Eden says the dragons left to go back to their own realm."

"Most are gone," Wulfe replied. "Some stayed behind. Kahg is one of them. The dragon said he would take you home in honor of Aylaen, but after that, you are on your own."

Wulfe peered at Skylan from beneath his shaggy hair. "My mother says the great dragon took Aylaen away. Is that true?"

Skylan closed his hand over the spiritbone until he felt the sharp edges dig into his flesh. He gazed out into the sea and far beyond, into the stars.

"That is true," he said.

"I'll miss her," said Wulfe. "She was nice to me most of the time. Except when she made me take a bath."

Wulfe stood up and shook himself like a dog. "I have to go now. The centaurs brought me here and they're waiting to take me back home."

Skylan rose to his feet. "Farewell, Wulfe. I will miss you."

Wulfe grinned and waved, then ran off down the beach. He had only gone a short distance before he suddenly turned around and ran back and flung his arms around Skylan, who hugged the boy close and gave him a father's kiss.

"I will miss you, too," said Wulfe. "You're my favorite Ugly."

With a final hug, he let go and ran off down the beach.

"And Aylaen was right. Take a bath sometimes!" Skylan yelled after him.

Wulfe laughed and kept running. Skylan watched until the boy had vanished among the sand dunes, then he climbed over the hull of the *Venejekar* that was beached in the sand. Tomorrow, at high tide, he and Sigurd, Bjorn and Dela Eden, Grimuir and Farinn would haul the dragonship into the water to start the long journey back home. But there was something he had to do tonight.

On the deck, he made his way among the sea chests and the oars that were neatly piled in the center, along with the furled sail, until he came to the prow. He could not see the nail in the starlit darkness, but he knew approximately where it was and he found it by touch, running his hand along the neck of the dragon until he felt the nail beneath his fingers.

He hung the spiritbone on the nail by its leather thong.

"Thank you, Kahg," said Skylan.

Looking up at the fierce, proud head, he saw the dragon's eyes glow red.

Skylan and his friends were glad to have the Dragon Kahg guiding the *Venejekar*, for they would have soon been lost at sea, or so Sigurd claimed. Acronis had left behind his maps and charts and one of his strange navigational instruments, but no one except Farinn could read the maps or use the tools. As they sailed toward Vindraholme, he took readings every day and insisted he knew where they were, even showing them their location on the map, but few believed him.

"You can't make the world into squiggly lines," said Sigurd.

The voyage was peaceful, but they thought it would never end. The longing for their home grew with each passing day.

"We have been away a year. Our people will have forgotten us," said Bjorn. "Or think we are dead."

"They will have a new Chief of Chiefs," said Sigurd, eyeing Skylan. "You might have to fight the Vutmana to regain it, if the new chief won't give it up."

"I won't fight," said Skylan. "I don't want to be chief."

He didn't add that he had never felt he truly deserved the honor of being chief of the Vindrasi, since he had not slain Horg in a fair battle. Skylan had kept Draya's terrible secret that she had poisoned her husband this long and he would keep it to the grave. She had paid with her life and he would not betray her memory.

They had been voyaging for two months when Sigurd recognized a landmark near their home—One Tree Rock, that denoted the border of Vindrasi lands. Their excitement grew, as each familiar bit of shoreline or group of boulders brought back the memory of a raid or a hunt. Then came the day that the *Venejekar* rounded an outcropping of rock and they watched with tears in their eyes to see the Chief's Hall of the Torgun come into view.

"We are home," said Skylan, touching the amulet. "Thank you, Torval," he said softly, even though he knew the words would be lost in the freshening wind.

The Dragon Kahg proudly steered the *Venejekar* toward the shore. Before they had reached it, Skylan and Sigurd, Bjorn and Grimuir and Farinn had all jumped out, wading knee deep in the water, guiding the boat onto the beach.

Several Torgun fishermen stopped to stare at the amazing sight, then dropped their nets and abandoned their catch to run back toward the village.

"Hey, Jorge, it's me!" Sigurd yelled, recognizing one of them.

The men kept running, without even a backward glance.

"They have no idea who were are," said Bjorn.

"Perhaps they think we're here to attack them," Skylan said.

"Numbskulls," Sigurd muttered.

They went back to the *Venejekar* and helped haul it up onto the beach. Skylan went to the prow with Dela Eden to thank the dragon, but Kahg had already departed; the red glow was gone from the eyes.

"I wonder where he went," said Skylan. "He told you the portal between the realms had closed."

"So he said after the battle," Dela Eden confirmed. "Perhaps he found his own way home."

Bjorn called to her and she went to join him. He was eager to show her where they would live. Skylan lingered near the dragon-head prow. Resting his hand on the carved scales, he silently wished the dragon well and then he noticed that the spiritbone was still hanging from the nail.

Skylan regarded it thoughtfully for a moment, then he removed the spiritbone and placed it inside his sea chest. No one thought to ask what had become of the dragon and Skylan did not tell them.

He and his men unloaded their sea chests and began to clean the ship, neatly stacking the oars in the center and scrubbing the deck. As they worked, they talked about what they would tell people, how they would explain what had happened to them, where they had been.

No one came from the village, not even the usual group of curious children. They were starting to grow uneasy.

"If Erdmun were here, he would say that our people think we are ghosts and they are arming themselves to send us back to hell where we belong," said Bjorn.

He meant it as a jest, but after the words were spoken, they didn't seem that funny.

"For all his gloom, Erdmun was right more often that he was wrong," Grimuir remarked in an ominous tone.

Their unease increased when they heard a low murmuring sound that grew in volume as it drew nearer; voices raised, an indistinct babble of fear, excitement . . . No one could tell.

"We could always put out to sea again," said Farinn nervously.

"And go where?" Skylan asked. "This is our home."

They left the ship and stood on the shore and waited. He was proud to see none of his men even think of taking up a weapon.

A crowd of people appeared, walking over the sand dunes, heading for the beach.

"At least they're not carrying spears," Sigurd remarked.

Skylan walked forward to meet them, thinking to say something reassuring. Before he could speak, an elder, a friend of his father's, came up to him.

"Chief of Chiefs, we have long awaited the day of your return," he said. "We know of your battle, Skylan, son of Norgaard. You have made the people of the Torgun proud."

Men and women cheered and ran to embrace them and laugh and share the news of the momentous events that had happened while they had been gone. The little children hung back, staring at them with wide eyes, awed and overcome.

"How did you know about us?" Skylan asked the elder.

"Your friend, the ogre, told us."

Keeper had recently paid a visit to their village, sailing in one of the dragonships, and he had told them tales of all of their adventures, starting with how they had been captured and made slaves in Sinaria to the final battle with Raegar and the return of the Great Dragon Ilyrion.

"We saw the great dragon," said Holma, Aylaen's mother, who

folded Skylan in her arms. "The emperor's fleet had anchored offshore and the soldiers were starting to disembark, while strange and terrible serpents flew overhead. The great dragon flew down from the skies. She sank her claws into the serpents and flung their corpses into the sea. Seeing that, the soldiers in the ships sailed away as fast as the wind would carry them."

"Aylaen died Kai Priestess, battling Aelon," Skylan said. "She died a hero."

He could speak the words with pride now, not with anger.

"So Keeper told me," said Holma, wiping away her tears. "Aylaen's name will be long remembered."

Skylan noticed Holma didn't ask about her other daughter, Treia. Just as well. Skylan had not been able to find out what had become of her. He guessed her end had not been a good one.

Holma left him to greet Dela Eden, whom Bjorn had proudly introduced as his wife. The other women crowded around, to make her welcome in her new home. With much laughter and celebration the Torgun led them back to the village.

Almost a year had passed since they had left. Skylan could not see the familiar streets through his tears. He put his hand to the amulet, but he did not speak.

Wherever Torval was, he would understand.

A month after his return, a delegation of chiefs from all parts of Vindraholm came to meet with Skylan. They pledged their loyalty to him and assured him he would hold the rank of Chief of Chiefs for as long as he lived. They would not listen to any argument he might make against it.

Skylan could have made a great many arguments, but he kept silent. He had given the matter a lot of thought and talked it over with his friends. They all agreed that he should be chief, even Sigurd.

"You led us to the greatest victory in the history of the Vindrasi," said Sigurd. "I guess you've earned it." He added with a wink, "Not but what I could have done it better."

And so Skylan agreed, on one condition, that he be allowed to remain with the Torgun. He did not want to live in the grand dwelling of the Chief of Chiefs. He moved into his father's house, where he had been born.

Life resumed for Skylan and the others, almost as if they had never left. Sigurd went back to Aylaen's mother, sharing his time between her and his mistress and his sons. Grimuir took over the duties of the blacksmith, who had recently died. Skylan fulfilled his promise to find Farinn a wife, a duty that fell to him as chief, since Farinn had no family.

He had feared this might be difficult, given that Farinn was a poet and had learned to read and write. What women would want such a strange young man? As it happened, however, he was approached by the father of a young woman who had shyly told him of her interest in the bard.

The father apologized for his daughter, saying she was often berated by her mother for spending her time daydreaming instead of doing her household chores. He added that he would give his daughter a large dowry, to make up for the fact.

The young woman was winsomely lovely. Farinn was enchanted and Skylan agreed to the match, reflecting that these two dreamers would get on well, though they would likely never have a decent meal or a clean house.

Bjorn and Dela Eden were happy together. Skylan presented Bjorn with some land as a wedding gift. Bjorn was content to become a farmer, while Dela Eden told stories about the Gods of Raj. The Torgun listened politely at first, and then grew more interested, especially when Dela Eden prayed for rain for their newly planted crops and the rains came.

The months passed, but Skylan scarcely counted them. He was occupied with the duties of the Chief of Chiefs, for the business of Vindraholm had been put off until his return. When he wasn't meeting with his people or settling disputes, he was out hunting or working in the fields. He always went alone and worked until he had worn himself out.

His friends observed him with concern. Skylan rarely smiled these days and never laughed. He could not sleep and was often seen roaming the beach at night. As Bjorn told Dela Eden, Skylan did not wake up in the morning looking forward to a new day. He woke up grimly determined to get through it.

Going out hunting one early morning, Skylan encountered Bjorn, who had come looking for him.

"I have news," said Bjorn. "Owl Mother is back."

"Is she? That is interesting," said Skylan in a tone that indicated little interest.

"She says you owe her a day's work," Bjorn told him.

"Thank you for the message," Skylan said, pushing past his friend. "I'll tend to it."

"Skylan—" Bjorn began.

Skylan pretended not to hear, and kept walking. He knew his friends were worried about him, but he didn't care. He didn't care about anything. The house of his soul was empty and abandoned. Cold, biting wind whistled through the cracks in the broken windows. The frame was strong and would remain standing, perhaps for many long years, but with no warmth inside.

Skylan came to a place in the trail where it branched off in different directions. One path, little used, would take him to Owl Mother's. Skylan paused, remembering with a pang the last night he and Aylaen had spent together in her house. He didn't think he could bear the pain, then he remembered that he had made a promise. He could not go back on his word.

Memory stalked him on the trail. He had walked this path with Aylaen when she had taken him to Owl Mother's to be healed after he'd been gored by a wild boar. And he had taken this path after those nightmarish games of dragonbone with the draugr of his dead wife, only a year ago. A very long year to him now.

He was so lost in the past that he tripped over a tree branch hidden beneath a pile of dead leaves and went sprawling. He lay facedown in the leaves and the muck and wondered if he had the will to stand.

"This is what happens when you walk ahead while looking behind," Owl Mother said with a snort.

Skylan looked up to see the old woman looking down.

"How are you, Owl Mother?" he asked politely, picking himself up.

"I've been worse." Owl Mother said shortly. "You look like something the cat dragged in."

"I owe you a day's work," said Skylan. "What do you need me to do?"

"Follow me," said Owl Mother.

She led the way through the forest to her dwelling. Skylan kept a wary eye out for the wolf that once had guarded her door. The wolf was not there, however—only a few forest creatures that scampered about unafraid and a donkey tied to a tree, munching on apples. A donkey cart stood nearby, the traces lying on the ground.

"I'm closing up the house," said Owl Mother in answer to Skylan's questioning glance. "Setting out on my own."

"Where are you going?" Skylan asked.

"Wherever I want, Skylan Ivorson, and no concern of yours," Owl Mother returned. "I need you to help me put up the shutters and load the cart. First, though, there's something I have to give you."

She pushed open the door and walked inside. Skylan followed more slowly. He remembered the table and the chair in which he'd sat while Owl Mother worked her magic and the tapestry with the men in strange armor.

"Sit," said Owl Mother, pointing to the chair.

Skylan sat down, but stood up again in alarm when Owl Mother reached to pull aside the tapestry.

"Is the wyvern back there?" he asked.

"No," said Owl Mother. She paused a moment, her hand on the tapestry. "My magic isn't what it used to be these days. The wyvern left me."

She walked beneath the tapestry and let it fall behind her.

Skylan waited in uneasy silence, wondering what was going to emerge. He could hear noises coming from behind the tapestry, shuffling footfalls.

Time passed and Skylan grew restless. He stood up and began to pace about the room. Then the tapestry moved and Owl Mother came through it, carrying a large basket. She brought the basket over to Skylan and set it gently on the table.

"For you," said Owl Mother. "From Aylaen."

Skylan looked into the basket and then looked back up at Owl Mother.

"I don't understand," he said, bewildered.

"They're babies, Skylan," said Owl Mother. "You've seen babies before, I take it. Twins. A boy and a girl."

"I know that, but—" Skylan began.

"The boy's name is Skylanson," Owl Mother went on. "The girl is Holma."

Skylan felt his legs start to give way and braced himself against the table.

"Mine," he said softly. "My children."

Owl Mother smiled, her wrinkled face seeming to crack. Her eyes grew dim. "A gift from Aylaen and Ilyrion. Aylaen feared you would be lonely."

"Skylanson and Holma," Skylan murmured. "She told me about them . . ."

Drawing a quivering breath, he gazed down at the two babies swaddled in blankets. He saw two little faces, both beautiful like their mother's, and a sheen of red-gold hair on each small head. One had managed to start sucking on a tiny, perfect fist. Skylan very gently brushed his hand over the petal-soft cheek.

Then he began to sob and he sank down in the chair, buried his head in his hands and wept. Owl Mother said nothing, but gently patted his shoulder until his tears were gone.

The babies began to kick and stir. One opened a pink mouth in a squeaking cry and the other frowned and lashed out with the tiny fist.

"My son," said Skylan proudly.

"Your daughter," said Owl Mother drily. "She's like her mother. Just warning you."

Skylan laughed, a shaky laugh that still held traces of tears. He touched the fist and the baby grabbed at his finger.

"You have a lot of work ahead of you, Skylan," said Owl Mother. "The babies are hungry and you'll need to find a woman to nurse them and help you care for them. You're going to have to add another room onto that house of yours, as well."

"Owl Mother, I still don't understand," said Skylan, unable to take his eyes from the babies. "How is such a miracle possible?"

Owl Mother touched the amulet he wore around his neck and gave it a tap. "Some god loves you."

Skylan Ivorson smiled and gathered his children in his arms and took them home.

EPILOGUE

Skylan Ivorson sat in the large, ornately carved chair that stood at the north end of the longhouse, the Chief's House of the Torgun, listening to the music and the laughter with a sense of deep contentment. The decision he had made was the right one and this night confirmed it.

The Torgun were celebrating the fiftieth anniversary of the historic voyage of the *Venejekar*, the last of the great dragonships, and the defeat of the evil god, Aelon. They honored the Torgun who had sailed with Skylan that fateful day, though only two were yet alive: Skylan and the Talgogroth Farinn.

Sigurd had died five years ago, laughing and talking one moment and dead the next. Grimuir had been taken by a virulent fever and Bjorn had slipped away quietly in his sleep.

Skylan was now the oldest man in the clan, having seen sixty-eight summers. He had listened to Farinn's song of the voyage many, many times over the years and had once chided Farinn about the song, complaining his poetry gilded the truth. Farinn had rightly reminded him that people needed heroes more than they needed the truth. They lived with the truth every day.

Skylan's fond gaze went to Skylanson and his twin sister, Holma. They were standing together, talking and laughing with their friends. He had carried them home from Owl Mother's forty-nine years ago. Both had gray in their hair and were important members of the Vindrasi people, but to their father they would always be his little children, running and playing around his house, bringing joy back to his life.

His son, Skylanson, was now Chief of the Torgun, and he would have been Chief of Chiefs of the Vindrasi, but that title would end with Skylan. His son had suggested the idea of a governing body, a Council of Chiefs, which would give each clan fair and equal say. Skylan considered the idea a good one and he was proud of his son for suggesting it, but it was yet another change.

Skylanson had married one of the daughters of Bjorn and Dela Eden, a dark-haired, dark-eyed, dark-skinned woman. A priestess of the Gods of Raj, she and his son had given Skylan so many grandchildren that he couldn't keep track of them all.

His daughter, Holma, had not married. She had not lacked for suitors for, like her mother, she was beautiful. She had refused all offers of marriage. A warrior, skilled with a sword—Skylan had taught her himself—she had formed a band of female warriors, women who wanted to serve their people and prove themselves in battle. Holma was now War Chief of the Torgun.

As a people, the Vindrasi no longer sailed the seas terrorizing and raiding their neighbors. They were a peaceful people, trading with their neighbors instead of stealing, negotiating instead of fighting. They were driven to fight only on occasion.

The Oran Empire had collapsed, plunging into civil war as rival factions sought to gain control of the empire's great wealth. The chaos spawned evil, masterless men who roamed the world, preying on the defenseless, butchering and plundering. After a few bloody battles with the Vindrasi, however, the thieves tended to make a wide berth around their shores.

His daughter saw that Skylan was watching her and she came over to him. Leaning down, she put her arms around him and kissed his cheek.

"You look unusually happy tonight, Father," Holma said. "I see you are even wearing your sword, God-rage. You must be pleased with the celebration."

"I am, Daughter," said Skylan. "But it is not the celebration that pleases me so much as my children, you and your brother. I am proud of both of you."

His voice softened. "Your mother would be proud, too. I wish you had known her."

Holma knelt by his side and clasped her hands around his. She looked into his eyes, still blue, still clear-sighted even in his advanced years.

"But I did know my mother," she said.

Skylan looked at her, puzzled.

"I never told you this," she continued, slightly flushing, "but I have a very vivid memory of her. My brother and I were about eight years old. We were in a garden playing with wooden swords when we saw a beautiful woman walk out of a shrine. She was wearing dragon-scale armor that glittered like jewels in the sunlight and she showed us a sword that she said a goddess had given to her. She spoke to us and asked our names. She looked at us with so much love . . ."

Holma smiled at the memory, then she shrugged. "A dream, I suppose. But it seemed very real. Especially the love in her eyes. And what is even odder is that Skylanson had the very same dream."

"You never told me," said Skylan.

"We saw that talking about our mother made you sad," said Holma. "And then, growing up, I forgot about it. I just remembered it tonight."

Skylan thought he knew why she had remembered the dream this night. He brought her close and gave her a kiss on her forehead.

"You have my blessing," he said to her. "And your mother's."

Holma was taken aback. She observed him, troubled. "Is something wrong, Father?"

Skylan shook his head and smiled. "Perhaps, for the first time in my life, everything is right. You should go. Your friends are calling for you."

Holma kissed him and then, laughing, went off to join them. Skylan's gaze went to his son. Skylanson was engaged in an animated discussion with some of the other Vindrasi chiefs who had traveled to the Torgun village, which was now one of the most prosperous in Vindraholm.

In the old days, Skylan thought, they would have been talking of war and their glorious deeds in battle. His son and the others were talking of cattle and crops and better ways of marking boundaries on land so that there would be fewer disputes.

All changes for the better. Skylan would not have said so when he was young, but he had grown in wisdom since then.

His son saw him and he smiled and winked and very slightly rolled his eyes. One of the chiefs was arguing over something about which he knew nothing. Skylanson was a diplomat; he knew how to handle men, persuade them to his way of thinking. A good man, Skylanson made a good leader of men. Skylan was proud of him.

Silently, he gave his son a father's blessing, then got up out of the chair with only a slight grimace as one of his knees creaked. His hair was iron gray now, but he was fit and strong and could keep up with any man in the hunt. He could still teach the young ones how to handle a sword and how to stand in the shield wall.

Skylan signaled to Farinn, who was sitting at a table with his own son. Farinn looked unhappy, but he rose to his feet and came to join Skylan. Leaving the warmth and the laughter of the longhouse behind, the two men walked out beneath the stars.

The night was clear. The moon was full and bright. The air was chill from the snow in the mountains, but a warm breeze ruffled Skylan's hair, promising spring.

"You are determined to do this," said Farinn.

"I am," said Skylan.

Farinn sighed deeply.

The two walked down to the shore. The seas were calm, shining silver, rippling black. They crossed the beach, passing the fishing boats drawn up on the sand and climbed among the rocks until they came to a small, tree-lined inlet.

Skylan jumped down off the rocks onto the narrow strip of shore. Farinn followed more slowly.

"How is your history of our people coming?" Skylan asked, starting to burrow through a pile of what appeared to be refuse left behind by a flood: driftwood, broken branches, brush.

"Very well," said Farinn, cheering at the thought.

He had undertaken to write down all the old songs and stories of the Vindrasi so that they would not be forgotten. He also was writing a true account of their adventures during their quest for the spiritbones, an account that was not "gilded by poetry."

Farinn had asked Skylan if he wanted him to read it to him. Skylan had refused. He could not quite get over his belief that reducing a story to lines and setting it down on paper sucked the life out of it.

Farinn helped him remove the pile of branches and brush and, slowly, they uncovered the old *Venejekar*, lying on its side on the beach. Skylan grabbed hold of the dragonhead prow and Farinn took the stern and between them they tilted the dragonship upright. They were about to carry it into the shallow water when a pile of fishnet on the shore began to move.

"Skylan!" Farinn hissed in alarm. "Someone is hiding in there."

Skylan, looking grim, walked over to the pile of net and gave it a kick.

"Come out," he ordered.

A boy of about eleven stood up and threw off the netting and yawned. The boy was dressed in ragged clothes that were too big for him. His hair fell over his face and he glared through the tangle at Skylan.

"Where have you been? I thought you were never coming!"

"Is that . . . Wulfe?" Farinn asked, astonished.

"Is that . . . Farinn?" said Wulfe, mimicking him. He frowned. "You're like Skylan. You got old."

"Happens to all of us," said Skylan. He eyed Wulfe. "Well, at least most of us."

"I tried being old once," said Wulfe, adding with a shrug, "I didn't like it."

He scampered on board the dragonship and, leaning over the hull, began to talk to several oceanids and a couple of dryads who had wandered out of the forest to see what was going on.

Skylan boarded the *Venejekar* and began inspecting it, regarding his work with pride. The dragonship looked very much as it looked fifty years ago. He had spent a long time repairing the old ship, making it like new again.

"What is Wulfe doing here?" Farinn asked in a low voice as he helped Skylan haul his sea chest on board.

"He is sailing with me," said Skylan.

He opened the sea chest and took out the spiritbone of the Dragon Kahg. Walking over to the prow, Skylan hung the the bone, still in its leather thong, on the nail.

"How did the boy know you were leaving?" Farinn asked, trailing after Skylan.

"The fae," said Skylan. "You know what gossips they are. The oceanids have been watching me work on the ship."

Skylan rested his hand on the spiritbone. Memories came alive at his touch, causing him to look up at the head of the Dragon Kahg. The eyes glowed fierce, fiery red.

"The dragon . . ." Farinn stared, awed.

"He left his spiritbone with me," said Skylan. "He knew one day I would make this voyage and that he would come with me."

"Kahg says he's ready to leave," Wulfe announced.

Skylan turned to Farinn. "You should go now, my friend. I need to set sail before they miss me."

"What do I tell your children?" Farinn asked unhappily. "Your people?"

"They must not grieve for me. My song has not ended. It has just begun."

Skylan stood at the prow, his hands gripping the rail, his legs braced. The seawater broke over him, cooled him. He tasted the salt on his lips. He touched the amulet.

"Torval, let Aylaen know I am coming to her. Wherever she is, I will find her."

Farinn waded back to the shore alone and stood watching as the *Venejekar* glided out of the shadows of the alcove and sailed onto the bright, silver-gilded sea.

The final voyage of Skylan Ivorson, the last and greatest Chief of Chiefs.

ACKNOWLEDGMENTS

The description of Raegar's war galley is taken from an actual ship known as *The Forty*, built for Ptolemy IV in the third century. *The Forty* is described by Plutarch in his *Life of Demetrios*:

> Ptolemy Philopator built [a ship] of forty banks of oars, which had a length of two hundred and eighty cubits, and a height, to the top of her stern, of forty-eight; she was manned by four hundred sailors, who did no rowing, and by four thousand rowers, and besides these she had room, on her gangways and decks, for nearly three thousand men-at-arms.

Lionel Casson, in his book *Ships and Seamanship in the Ancient World* (Princeton University Press, 1971), theorizes that *The Forty* was a giant catamaran, consisting of two galleys connected by a level platform on which catapults could be mounted.

—M.W.

ABOUT THE AUTHORS

Margaret Weis and Tracy Hickman have been the all-time bestselling fantasy collaborators for more than thirty years. Coauthors of dozens of novels, games, and other fantasy media, they first gained fame in 1984 with the first novel in the Dragonlance Chronicles trilogy, *Dragons of Autumn Twilight*. Their books have sold tens of millions of copies worldwide. *Doom of the Dragon* is the fourth and final book in the Dragonships of Vindras series. Margaret Weis lives in Wisconsin; Tracy Hickman lives in Utah.